Andrew Vachss
DOWN HERE

Andrew Vachss has been a federal investigator in sexually transmitted diseases, a social services caseworker, and a labor organizer, and has directed a maximum-security prison for youthful offenders. Now a lawyer in private practice, he represents children and youths exclusively. He is the author of numerous novels, including the Burke series, two collections of short stories, and a wide variety of other material including song lyrics, graphic novels, and a "children's book for adults." His books have been translated into twenty languages and his work has appeared in *Parade*, *Antaeus*, *Esquire*, *Playboy*, *The New York Times*, and numerous other forums. A native New Yorker, he now divides his time between the city of his birth and the Pacific Northwest.

The dedicated Web site for Vachss and his work is
www.vachss.com.

DOWN HERE

Andrew Vachss

DOWN HERE

VINTAGE CRIME/BLACK LIZARD
Vintage Books
A Division of Random House, Inc.
New York

FIRST VINTAGE CRIME / BLACK LIZARD EDITION, APRIL 2005

The Library of Congress has cataloged the Knopf edition as follows:
Vachss, Andrew H.
Down here / Andrew Vachss. —1st American ed.
p. cm.
1. Burke (Fictitious character)—Fiction. 2. Private investigators—
New York (State)—New York—Fiction. 3. Rapists—Crime against—
Fiction. 4. Public prosecutors—Fiction. 5. New York (N.Y.)—Fiction.
6. Women lawyers—Fiction. I. Title.
PS3572.A33D68 2004
813'.54—dc22 2003058860

Vintage ISBN: 1-4000-7611-0

Book design by Virginia Tan

www.vintagebooks.com

Printed in the United States of America
10 9 8 7 6 5 4 3 2 1

for . . .
Michael E. Kotler
who rules,
finally.

DOWN HERE

"**S**omebody down here, boss. Asking for you." Gateman's voice, prison-whispering to me up the intercom, all the way to the top floor of a decrepit flophouse.

This dump has been scheduled for a foundation-up rehab for years. In the meantime, the housing inspectors turn a money-blinded eye, and any derelict with a five-dollar bill can buy himself twenty-four hours off the streets.

But not on the top floor. That one is permanently closed. Unfit for Human Occupancy.

That's where I live—unregistered and invisible. The only name anyone ever had for me was last seen attached to a body part in the morgue, before the City did whatever it does with unclaimed remains.

"Somebody" was Gateman's way of saying that whoever was downstairs had come alone . . . and he'd seen them before. If it had been a stranger, he would have reached under the raw wood plank that holds a register nobody ever signs. A concealed button would set off the flashers behind the dinner-plate-sized red plastic disks I have on the walls in every room of my place. That's only one of its custom features. Another is a private exit.

Anytime someone comes looking for me, it's Gateman's call. Even confined to his wheelchair, he's got options. Instead of the button, he could reach for the handgun he always keeps right next to his colostomy bag.

"You get a name?" I asked.

"Pepper, right?" I heard him say to the visitor.

"Short girl, pretty, dark hair, kilowatt smile?" I asked.

"All but the last, boss," Gateman said. "And she's got company."

"What's he—?"

"It's a dog, boss. Big-ass Rottweiler."

That's when I knew the wheels had come off.

Negotiating the narrow flights up to where I live is no job for anyone with an anxiety disorder. You have to make your way past crumbling walls covered with signs screaming DANGER! ASBESTOS REMOVAL IN PROGRESS, dangling exposed wires, and puddles of bio-filth on the unlit stairwells.

It's a nasty trip, but Pepper made it in record time. She quickstepped across the threshold, dragged forward by a barrel-chested Rottweiler she was barely restraining on a short, heavy lead.

The beast recognized me at once, treated me to his "Back the fuck *up*!" growl as he thrust his way into the room.

"Bruiser!" Pepper said, sharply. "Behave!"

The beast gave her a "Yeah, right!" look, but allowed her to walk him over to the futon couch.

She sat down, gave me a searching look.

I didn't say anything, waiting like I always do. Usually, Pepper dresses like a sunburst, to match a personality that could cheer up an AIDS ward. But this time, it was a plain dark-blue business suit over a white blouse with a red string tie, and her famous smile was buried deeper than Jimmy Hoffa.

"Wolfe's been arrested," she said, no preamble.

"What?"

"Last night. They picked her up at her house, in Queens. She's supposed to be arraigned—"

"Arrested for what?"

"Attempted murder, assault, criminal possession of—"

"Slow down," I told her, breathing shallow through my nose to drop my heart rate. "Start at the beginning."

Wolfe had been a career sex-crimes prosecutor, a veteran of

no-holds-barred combat with the bottom-dwellers in the crime chain—rapists, child molesters, wife beaters. And, sometimes, with certain judges—the ones she called "collaborators" to their faces. A few years ago, she had gotten fired for refusing to soft-hand a "sensitive" case.

Wolfe wouldn't cross the street and represent the same freaks she used to put away. So she'd gone outlaw, and now she runs the best info-trafficking cell in the City.

I had wanted Wolfe for my own since the first time I saw her in battle. I'd had—I thought I'd had—a chance with her once. But I had done some things. . . .

"You and me, it's not going to be," she told me then. And I believed her.

All that changed was what I did, not how I felt. My love for Wolfe was a dead star. Lightless, invisible in the night sky. But always, always there.

Pepper's big dark eyes told me she knew some of that. Enough to count on, anyway.

That's the way it is down here. If you can't be counted *on,* you can't be counted *in.*

"Here's all she could tell me on the phone," Pepper said. "Some man was shot, more than once. He's in a coma, and they don't expect him to live."

"So what connects Wolfe—?"

"He named her," Pepper interrupted. "He told the police she was the one who shot him."

"When was this supposed to have gone down?"

"I don't know. I don't know anything more about it, not even the man's name. All I know is they're holding her at the precinct, and they expect to arraign her tonight."

"She's got an alibi," I said, holding Pepper's eyes.

"She's got *plenty* of those," Pepper snapped back, telling me I was standing at the end of a long line. And those ahead of me would come across a lot better in court than a two-time felony loser who had been declared dead years ago. "That's not what she needs, right this minute. She needs to—"

"You got a lawyer for her yet?"

"No. I thought you might—"

"Did she *tell* you to come to me, Pepper?"

As if to answer my stupid question, the Rottweiler made a gear-grinding noise deep in his chest.

"No! All she said was to pick up Bruiser and make sure he was all right until they set bail."

"And you can make—?"

"I . . . guess so," Pepper said. "But I don't know a bondsman, either, except for that crook we used the time Mick was—"

"Never mind," I told her. "Do you know where the arraignment's going to be?"

"At 100 Centre. She said the . . . whatever the cops say happened, it happened in Manhattan, so . . ."

"Yeah." I glanced at my watch. Three thirty-seven. With the usual backlog from the Tombs and the tour bus from Rikers, they probably wouldn't get to Wolfe until the lobster shift, but I didn't want to chance it. "Give me a minute," I told Pepper.

I went into one of the back rooms and pulled a cloned-code cell phone out of its charging unit. I punched in the private number I have for the only criminal lawyer in the City I trust.

"What?" Davidson answered.

"You recognize my voice?" I asked. I hadn't spoken to him in years. Not since NYPD found a severed skeletal hand in a Dumpster, right next to a pistol with my thumbprint on the stock.

"I believe so." He spoke in the pompous voice he uses to distance himself from potential danger in conversations. "Help me out a little bit."

"It's not my ghost," I said. "I've done some jobs for you, and you've done some for me."

"Do you have some, uh, distinguishing characteristic I might recognize?"

"Yeah. I always pay. And that cigar I just heard you light, it's probably from the batch I brought you, a few years back."

"Very good," he said, chuckling. "You should have been a detective."

"I need a lawyer. Not for me. For a friend. Being arraigned tonight. Can you handle it?"

"Can I . . . ? Ah, you mean, *will* I? Are we talking just for tonight, or . . . ?"

"To the end of the road," I said. "First-round TKO, or a decision on points. Any way it plays."

"Would I know this 'friend' of yours?"

"Yeah. Her name is Wolfe."

"Wolfe from City-Wide? Are you—?"

"I'm cancer-serious," I said. "I'm also short on facts. It's either an attempt murder or, by now, a homicide."

"Wolfe? Are they floridly insane?" he said. "Unless you're talking a DV?"

"Domestic violence? Wolfe? Come on, pal. Sure, she's not the kind of woman who'd take a beating from a boyfriend. But with that dog of hers, what kind of psycho would even *try*? No, the vic was a stranger. But he supposedly made a statement."

"Named her?"

"What I'm told."

"Do they have forensics?"

"You know all I know."

"And we both know *she* didn't make a statement."

"Right. Can you get right over there? I don't know when they're going to arraign her, and—"

"I'll make some calls, see if I can find out," Davidson said. "But don't worry; I'll be there when they bring her over. I should be able to speak to her in the pens before they—"

"Listen. She doesn't know about this. Me hiring you, I mean. Just tell her Pepper set it up," I said, looking over at Pepper, catching her nod of agreement, "okay?"

"Done. My fee will be—"

"Paid," I said, cutting the connection.

"Do you know if they tossed her place?" I asked Pepper.

"They didn't have a no-knock warrant," she said. "When they pounded on the door, Bruiser went ballistic. She told them she had to lock the dog up before she could let them in—that kept them out of there for a few more minutes."

"How do you know?"

"That's how *I* found out about it. She dialed the office, and left the connection open while she talked to the police. And when she finally let them in, she kept the phone going. I have the whole thing on tape, what they said to her, everything."

"Did she sound—?"

"She sounded strong," Pepper said. "One of the cops, he didn't want to cuff her. Another one said it was procedure. Wolfe told him—the cop who wanted to cuff her—if they tried to perp-walk her she'd make someone pay for it."

That was Wolfe. "She drinks blood for breakfast," the *Daily News* once said of her, in an article about New York prosecutors.

"The cops were scared of Bruiser; but he wasn't even barking, once she told him to stop. The one who wanted to cuff her said if Bruiser made a move he was going to blow him away. Wolfe told them if they wanted to arrest her she was ready to go. And if they didn't, *she* was leaving, so they better shut up about shooting her dog.

"I heard the door close. Then I heard Bruiser making little noises, like he was . . . in mourning. But he stayed, right where she told him. So I ran over there and got him."

"You did the right thing, Pepper. They'll be back to vacuum her place. If you hadn't gotten him out of there, it would have been a bloodbath."

"Yes. She called me later, from the lockup. That's when she told me about the man who—"

"But not his name, right?"

"No."

"Okay, don't worry. We'll get that tonight, at the arraignment."

"Burke . . ."

"Go back to the office, Pepper. Put your crew on alert. I'm sure Mick is—"

"Mick is *crazy* from this," she said. "I've never seen him be so . . . I don't know what."

"Keep him close, then. If Wolfe wanted you to get anything out of her place, she would have found a way to tell you, right?"

"Sure. We have a code for—"

"Okay. I'm going to be carrying a cell phone twenty-four/seven until we know what's going on. Write down the number. . . ."

Pepper gave me a withering look. Held it until I lamely recited the number. She nodded her head sharply, letting me know she had it . . . and it wouldn't ever be on a piece of paper.

"Don't show up at arraignment tonight," I told her. "Mick, either. You two, you're her hole card now."

As soon as Pepper and the Rottweiler left, I started working the phones. First stop was Hauser, a reporter I went way back with. All the way back to my old pal Morelli, the dean of organized-crime reporting in New York. A hardcore reporter from the old school, he had been covering the Mob for so long they probably asked *him* for advice.

Morelli was off the set now. He'd finally hit it big. After years of threatening to do it, he wrote a book, and it blossomed out sweet. He's been on the Holy Coast for a while now, tending the harvest.

But a pro like Morelli doesn't move on until he's trained new recruits. J. P. Hauser had been his choice.

"I ask the kid, go over and see this guy, supposed to be an informant, staying in some rat-trap over in Times Square," Morelli had told me, years ago. "This guy, his story is that he's got a bad ticker. So he wants to make his peace with God, give me all the inside dope on a muscle operation that Ciapietro's crew is running out at the airport. So I tell J.P., get me everything, all right?"

Morelli smiled, taking a sip of his drink. When we were coming up, he lived on Cutty Sark and Lucky Strikes. By then, he was down to red wine and off tobacco. "Okay, so, a few hours later, I get this frantic call from the informant. He's screaming blue murder. Said J.P. rips his place up worse than any parole officer ever did, takes the serial number from this guy's clock radio, looks at the labels in his coat, checks his shoe size.

"And then he whips out one of those little blood-pressure cuffs—you know, the kind you slip over your finger? Wants to see if this guy's *really* got a bad heart. You ever hear anything like that?

"J.P., he's a fucking vacuum cleaner, you understand? He's going to pull the dirt out until they pull his plug. I fucking *love* this kid."

Hauser wasn't a kid anymore. And he hasn't freelanced in years; he's got a regular gig with the *National Law Journal* now, mostly covering major tort litigation. I didn't have a direct line for him, but the switchboard put me through quick enough.

"Hauser!" he barked into the receiver.

"It's me," I said.

He went quiet for a second. Then said, "Not . . . ?"

"Yeah."

"I'd *heard* you were . . . back, I guess is the word. But I haven't worked the streets for a long time, so there wasn't any way I could know for sure."

"You don't need to be on the street for what I need now," I said. "Can you make a couple of calls for me?"

"I . . . suppose. Depends on what you want me to—"

"Nothing like that," I assured him. "You know Wolfe's been busted?"

"Wolfe? Get out of—"

"It's righteous," I said. "I wish it wasn't. All I want is to find out if the cops are planning to splash it. She'll be arraigned tonight. I need to know if there's going to be coverage."

"Something like that, it'll certainly make the—"

"I don't care about TV, or even the radio. I just want to know if there're going to be reporters *in* the courtroom. Especially veterans."

"Ones who might recognize you?"

"*You* wouldn't recognize me," I promised him. "I just need to know who's going to be watching, you understand?"

"There's a story in this," Hauser said, an apostle reciting the creed.

"Thought you didn't do crime anymore," I said.

"I spend all my time covering lawyers," he laughed. "How far away do you think *that* takes me?"

"The story is, Wolfe's being set up. I don't know anything else about it. Not yet, anyway."

"But when you find out?"

"It's all yours, pal."

"Call back in twenty minutes," Hauser said.

"*E*verybody's on it," Hauser said when I called back. "But the DA isn't making any statements . . . yet."

"So there'll be reporters on the set?"

"Guaranteed," he said. "Come on by and say hello."

I took a quick shower, shaved extra-carefully, and put on a slouchy black Armani suit over a midnight-blue silk shirt, buttoned to the throat. I added a pair of natural alligator shoes, a two-carat solitaire ring set in white gold, and an all-black Rado watch. There wasn't enough time to get the right haircut, but a gel-and-mousse combination got me close enough to the look I wanted.

The emergency surgery that brought me back from what was supposed to be a *coup de grâce* bullet had changed my face forever. Once, I could have passed for a lawyer, with the right clothes and props. And I had done it, plenty of times. Now the best I could hope for was to be taken for a higher class of defendant.

I walked downstairs carefully, a Mini Mag lighting the way. Gateman was where he always is.

"Thanks, partner," I said, palming a fifty in my handshake.

"We expecting more company, boss?"

"Could be. But not the blue boys," I said, telling him what he needed to know. Gateman's on parole. New York City parole, which means all he has to do is call in every few months, so they know he's alive. But a visit from the cops would be a real problem for him. Gateman doesn't like surprises. And he's a shooter.

It was only a few blocks to my car. I keep it behind a ratty old two-pump gas station that scratches out a living from used tires, dented hubcaps, and tired batteries. They also sell some specialized parts for cab drivers . . . like recalibrated meters that tick off a mile for every four-fifths they run. Word is you can buy other things there too, but I never asked.

My '69 Plymouth Roadrunner sat outdoors in a chain-link enclosure, under a roof made of woven concertina wire, protected by a combination lock thick enough to sneer at two-handed bolt cutters.

The setup had been built for the owner's prize pit bull, a vicious old warrior who had been retired to stud a few years ago. The owner kept a couple of bitches, too, so his champion wouldn't get bored and maybe chomp his way through the chain link. I'd talked the owner into letting me park the Plymouth inside the cage. It cost me three bills a month, and a few weeks' daily investment in getting the pits to accept me enough to let me inside whenever I showed up, but it was worth it. The back of the gas station was always in darkness or shadow, and the dogs made sure nobody got too close a look at the anonymous junker stashed back there.

One of the bitches strolled over to the fence as I walked up. She snarled softly, just warming up.

"It's me, stupid," I said.

I didn't know any of their names. But they knew me, and they knew I never came empty-handed. The big rooster trotted over, chesty and confident, knowing he was going to get first dibs.

I took a slab of porterhouse out of the plastic bag I'd been carrying and unwrapped it. Then I slipped it between the sections of metal tubing that framed the doors.

The pits went to work on their prize as I dialed the lock. I walked past them, leaving the doors open behind me. They never try to leave—the fence is just to keep people out.

I unlocked the Plymouth and climbed inside. I pulled out the ashtray, toggling the off-on switch so that the ignition key would work. When I fired up the engine, it was like pulling a heavy layer of dusty burlap off a marble statue—the torque-monster Mopar crackled into life, hungry for asphalt.

I let it warm up for a minute, checking the oil-pressure gauge, while I got the steak smell off my hands with a few scented tow-elettes I took from the glove compartment. Then I eased the Ply-mouth through the opening in the fence, jumped out, and relocked the gate. The two bitch pits sat on their haunches, watching. The old stud was already lying down, sleeping off his lion's share of the booty I'd brought.

I wheeled the Plymouth up Canal, then worked my way over to Mama's restaurant. I parked under the pristine white square with Max the Silent's chop painted in its center. The calligraphy sensei who created it comes by and renews his masterpiece every so often, so it always looks new.

Even without all the security devices and the fact that it didn't look worth stealing, I wouldn't have been worried about anyone making a move on the Plymouth. In this part of the City, every-body knows Max's sign.

A thug in a white kitchen apron let me in the back door. I'd seen him plenty of times before, but I didn't know his name, and he didn't care about mine.

I walked over to the bank of pay phones along the wall that sep-arates the kitchen from the restaurant seating area. Mama still keeps a Mason jar there, filled to the brim with quarters. More than enough for a half-hour call to Taiwan, but AT&T won't let you do that anymore—they want everyone to use one of their pre-paid phone cards. Once a monopoly . . .

I picked out a coin, slotted it through, and punched in a 718 number.

"Yes?"

"It's me," I said. "Can you and your father please meet me at the spot?"

"My father is not here now, mahn. But he will call soon. Shall I come by my—?"

"I need you both," I told him.

"I understand, mahn. Do we need to bring—?"

"It's not like that," I said. "Not yet, anyway."

"Sure," Clarence said, hanging up.

I was reaching for more quarters when Mama appeared. Her round, ageless face was impassive under her perfectly coiffed hair. Her ceramic-black eyes were expressionless.

"Not visit?" she said, making a gesture with her jeweled hand to show me she wasn't insulted that I hadn't greeted her formally when I'd first come in.

"The Prof and Clarence are on their way over, Mama," I said. "I have to reach out for Michelle now."

"So—you want Max, yes?"

"Please," I told her.

She nodded her head a fraction short of bowing, then turned and walked past me, heading toward the basement.

"If you don't know what to do, and when to do it, you've already left *your* message," the hard-honey voice on Michelle's answering tape said.

"It's me," I said, after the beep. "It's . . . six-oh-five in the afternoon. I'm going to be here in the church for a little while, but I can't stay long. I need to see you. If I'm not here when you call, leave a way for me to get in touch with you, probably past midnight."

I reached for more coins . . . then stopped. I walked around the wall, through the beaded curtain, and into the restaurant.

My booth, the one against the back wall, was empty, as always. So was the rest of the place. Occasionally, some tourists would ignore the filthy, fly-specked front window and wander inside. If the service didn't send them packing, the food they were served would guarantee they'd never come back.

I sat down, glanced at my watch. Not like me to do that—patience is the one card I always keep in my deck.

Mama came through the kitchen, carrying a heavy white tureen on a tray with three matching bowls, slightly larger than cups. She placed the tray on the table, uncovered the tureen, and ladled out a bowl for me. Hot-and-sour soup—Mama's personal creation. I bowed my thanks, took a sip. "Perfect," I said.

At that, Mama sat down across from me, and helped herself to a bowl.

"Not work, right?" she asked me. To Mama, "work" could mean anything, from stealing to scamming to smuggling. What all of us did, one way or another. Our family doesn't care about crap like genetics, but it's got no room for citizens.

"Not work, Mama," I said. "Trouble."

"Trouble for you?"

"Not for me. Not for any of us. It's Wolfe. She just got arrested."

"Police girl?" Mama said, raising a sculpted eyebrow.

"Yeah. I don't have any real facts yet. She's supposed to have shot some guy."

"Not kill?"

"Not . . . yet, anyway. He's in a coma; they don't know if he's going to make it."

"So how talk?"

"Supposedly, he talked *before* he went out, Mama. And he named Wolfe as the shooter."

"You say not work."

"*Not* work, right. Nobody hired me. There's no money in this."

"You and police girl . . . ?"

"It's not that, either, Mama. Look, there's no money in this," I repeated. "Probably end up *costing* money, okay? Only, I'm doing it. And it doesn't matter why."

"Not to me, matter," she said, shrugging to add emphasis to her lie. "You have more soup, okay?"

"I've got to split," I told Mama a short while later. "Over to the courthouse. When Max—"

"Max wait here for you?"

"No," I said. Then I told her what I wanted him to do.

"Okay, sure," she said. "Come when you . . . ?"

"When I light a cigarette. Now, listen, Mama. The Prof and Clarence will be here, too. I'm not sure when. They don't have to actually stick around, just leave numbers with you where I can reach them later tonight, okay?"

"*Sure* okay. What you think?"

"Sorry, Mama. I'm just . . . edgy. See you later."

Night Court never changes. Years ago, when I was trying to make a living as an off-the-books investigator, I sometimes worked the corridors. I was a hovering hawk, searching for marks to steer over to one of the lawyers I had a fee-splitting arrangement with.

First I'd convince the wife or the mother or the girlfriend—90 percent of the crowd was always women—that the guy being arraigned would fare much better with a "private" lawyer than Legal Aid. Not a hard sell. Then I'd find out how much cash they were carrying—none of the lawyers I shilled for would touch a check—and make the connection.

Whatever lawyer I was working with that night would stand up on the case, make a bail argument or a quick deal, then move on. None of that breed ever actually tried cases. Most of them didn't even have an office, just a business card and a mail drop.

Anytime you have a steady stream of people being arraigned, you'll find lawyers like that . . . and men like me trolling for prospects. In the Bronx, some of the fishermen speak Spanish. I heard, over in Queens, there's one who's fluent in Korean, and Brooklyn even has a guy who does it in Russian. All working for two-bit grifters with law licenses.

Those "arraignment only" lawyers take some of the caseload off Legal Aid's back. And the judges like them fine too, because they never make trouble. Even most of the people who hire them go home happy, convinced they did the right thing by their loved ones. Another piece of the "system" you'll never see on *Law and Order.*

I moved through the crowd, looking for Davidson. Most of the people milling around had the dull, slightly anxious faces of cattle being herded down a chute, toward the sound of evenly spaced gunshots.

Davidson wasn't in the hall. I pushed open the doors and walked into the courtroom. It was about half full; people sat distanced from one another, like they do in porno theaters. I didn't recognize the judge on the bench, a dark-brown man with close-cropped gray hair.

I moved down the left side of the courtroom, looking for an aisle seat so I could scan without calling attention to myself.

A clot of gangbangers sat down front, eye-fucking everyone who looked their way. A young court officer, his short-sleeved white shirt tailored to show off impressive biceps, deliberately strolled by their area, playing his role.

A pair of whore lawyers were just over to my right. Those permanent-retainer lackeys spent every night pleading working girls to time served—usually two, three days—and paying their fines. They did volume business, representing the interests of a few pimps with good-sized stables of street girls. Higher-class hookers didn't often get pinched. And when they did, whoever was running them would put real legal talent into the game.

A Spanish woman who looked like she'd just gotten off work—*hard* work—fingered a rosary. Waiting for them to bring her son out, I figured. A skinny, pasty-faced girl with barbell studs piercing her nose, eyebrow, and the top of one ear stared straight ahead, her face as bleak as her prospects.

A woman with a prominent black eye and swollen lip sat with her hands in her lap. Waiting to post bail for the guy who had beaten her up, my best guess.

A fat, sleekly dressed Chinese man was bracketed by two marble-eyed young guns, their leather fingertip jackets marking them as clearly as the tattoos under them.

A heavyset, weary-looking black woman held a sleeping baby on her lap.

A pair of guys in their thirties, dressed costly-casual, sprawled back in their seats, still glazed. I figured the one they were waiting for had been the driver.

I spotted a few press guys, sitting together. Way too many for a typical night arraignment. I was looking around for Hauser when Davidson came from the back, where the pens are, and headed for the door. I slipped out behind him.

Davidson moved through the crowd outside the courtroom with the assurance of an all-pro halfback in an open field. I thought he might be heading for the pay phones, but he passed them by and went out the door.

By the time I spotted him, he was leaning against one of the railings, firing up a cigar.

I walked over, moving deliberately slow.

"Thanks for coming," I said.

He took a long, deep puff on his cigar, gave me a professional appraiser's look, not trying to hide what he was doing.

"Say a few more words," he said, finally.

"You've got two little girls. Born the exact same day, only three years apart. The big one's about twelve now. Natural leader, smarter than you ever imagined. Loves to read, an ace at archery. The little one's going to be a gymnast. Or a sky-diver—she was still making up her mind the last time we talked. In your office. Where you have their pictures on your desk at an angle, so everyone who sits down has to see how beautiful they are."

"Say more," he said, not changing expression.

"A few years ago, a coalition of gay activists hired you to do some very specialized work. You brought me in to help with the investigative end of it," I told him, not mentioning a significant fee that the IRS never heard about.

"The voice is the exact same," he said. "But I never would have recognized you. Word is that you were—"

"I wasn't. And I'm showing you a lot of trust, saying that, right?"

"If anyone's looking for you, you are."

"Someone's always looking for me," I said.

"Fair enough," Davidson said, holding out his hand for me to shake. "But I've got a problem."

"Which is . . . ?"

"You sound exactly like a . . . man I used to know. And somebody *did* call me about this case, or I wouldn't be here tonight. But when I mentioned your name to my client, back in the pens, my client expressed some, shall we say, *concern* about your involvement."

"Meaning . . . ?"

"Meaning, *she* didn't tell anyone to bring you into this. So she wants an explanation. *And* some proof that you're . . . who you say you are."

"The explanation is easy. Just repeat that Pepper came to see me. With Bruiser—she'll know what that means. Pepper didn't know what else to do, and Wolfe didn't give her anything to work with. I think she was going to just *pro se* it when they called her name tonight."

"That'd be like her," Davidson said, nodding. "But after we talked, she agreed that having me do the talking is a better play."

"Good."

"Now, about that proof? What else can you—?"

"Give me a minute," I said, reaching into my jacket. I extracted a single cigarette, said, "Got a light?"

By the time I took my second puff, Max the Silent was at my side. An old army jacket covered a gray sweatshirt; stain-blotched corduroy pants and an abandoned pair of once-white sneakers were topped off by a black watch cap. But even dressed in a vagrant's costume, there was no mistaking the Mongol warrior. Not once he got close enough for you to see his hands.

Max's eyes were as flat and hard as the slate bed of a tournament pool table. And as true. Even with all the assorted humans standing around outside the courthouse, his *ki* was a palpable force, creating a circle of empty air around the three of us.

"Oh!" was all Davidson said. Neither of us had seen him coming—people don't call him Max the Silent because he can't speak.

"Good enough?" I asked Davidson, snapping my cigarette away.

"Absolutely," he assured me. "Let me get back inside. I want to talk to her before the fun starts. I'll meet you right back here, soon as I can, all right?"

"Thanks," I said. "You need any—?"

"Later," he said, walking off.

I gestured to Max that I had to go back inside. Shrugged my shoulders to say that I didn't have a clue what we were going to have to do when I came out. I knew Mama would have already told him why I was there.

I took my cell phone out of its shoulder holster, held it up for Max to see. Then I pulled out its mate—a new one, never used. I held it against my chest, patted my heart.

Max nodded. When I needed him, I'd call. The phone I gave him would throb soundlessly against his chest, the vibrations telling him it was time to move.

I tilted my head in a "come with me" gesture. We walked all the way around to the back of the courthouse. There's never a place to park there, but it's custom-made for lurking. I pointed to the spot I wanted, handed Max the keys to my Plymouth.

With Max, this was a high-risk move. He could tap an enemy's carotid with surgical precision, but he drove like a man who reads the daily papers in Braille. Still, if I wanted a getaway car waiting for me when I called, Max was the only choice—if the Prof and Clarence had already shown up at Mama's, they would have contacted me.

I touched the face of the watch, shrugged again.

Max put his hand on my shoulder for a split second, squeezed just enough to let me know he'd be there, no matter when. Then he was gone.

As I entered the courtroom, I saw Davidson's broad pinstriped back, looming over a young guy seated at the DA's table. It didn't look like the conversation was going well.

Davidson stalked off, in the direction of the pens. I found the same seat I'd had before, settled in.

The parade went on. Most of the cases were disposed of on the spot. Conditional discharges, ACDs—Adjournments in Contemplation of Dismissal, a six-month "behave yourself" deal—misdemeanor probations, time-served walk-offs . . . bargain-basement justice. They even worked out a few bullets—Legal Aid's term for a year on the Rock. Even one day more makes it felony time, and a trip Upstate.

Occasionally, some brief argument would break out, but you could see it was only the lawyer putting on a show for his client. Never affected the outcome.

Prostitution, lightweight drug possession, simple assault, trespass, violation of a restraining order, shoplifting, DUI, car-stripping—anything that could be pleaded down to misdemeanor weight, it was all fair game. The felony cases that didn't plead out all ended in the Kabuki dance of bail arguments.

Davidson came out a little before midnight. Walked over and sat next to me.

"They'll be bringing her up soon," he said. "They weren't jerking her around on the paperwork. Just volume. If they held women in the Tombs, it'd be faster to get them before the—"

"It doesn't matter," I cut him off, not interested in criminal-justice reform.

"I don't have everything I'll get out of the DA's office with my motions," Davidson said, "but Wolfe's still got plenty of friends on the job, and I made some calls, picked up a few things."

"Such as?"

"The name John Anson Wychek mean anything to you?"

"No."

"That's the alleged vic's name. That much I got from the court papers. What they *don't* mention is that Wychek was a serial rapist. That, I got from Wolfe. He worked the whole metro area for almost three years before they caught him. Suspect in at least a dozen, plus a couple of attempts, but they only bagged him for the one. Wolfe tried the case, over in Queens. Convicted on all counts—rape, sodomy, abduction, use of a weapon—enough to max him, easy. And that's what the judge did. Couple of years later, he appeals. He had an 18-B at trial, but for the appeal he had Greuchel."

"Huh! That's big bucks."

"Right. But it wasn't a drug case, so Greuchel never got asked where his fee came from. Anyway, he raises all the usual: ineffective assistance, bad search—even though they never actually *used* anything they took from the place where Wychek was living—'cross contamination' at the crime scene, yadayadayada. Just blowing smoke, getting paid by the page.

"But then he throws in that the Queens cops used information they got from a Family Court case against the same defendant, out in Nassau County. Wychek had been charged with sexual abuse of his live-in girlfriend's kid. It never went to trial. Wychek consented to a finding of neglect, agreed to move out of the house, have no contact with the victim, and that was it."

"What's that got to do with anything?"

"Supposedly, the CPS caseworker testified at some preliminary hearing. About a ski mask that the little girl said Wychek always put on when he was . . . molesting her. And the caseworker found the ski mask; it was still at the home of the live-in girlfriend."

"But you said they never used—"

"They didn't," Davidson said. "The ski mask never came in, even though he wore one during the rape he was on trial for. Anyway, this wasn't a search issue. Wychek was already out of the little girl's home by then, and it was her mother who gave permission. But Greuchel claimed the whole case hinged on information the cops got from the Family Court case, and those records aren't public. They're confidential."

"To protect the *victim,* not the—"

"Maybe that's the *intent* of the law," Davidson said, "but it's not the *application.* You should know that."

"You're not telling me that he walked with that lame pitch?"

"He probably wouldn't have. Greuchel never even raised the issue in the Appellate Division—they affirmed in a one-pager. But then, get this, Greuchel brings a federal habe, claiming that 'newly discovered evidence' showed that the caseworker had told the cops about the Family Court proceedings, so the entire investigation was fatally tainted. Fruit of the poisonous—"

"Yeah. So?"

"So the Queens DA comes into federal court and makes a 'confession of error.' At that time, there was all this media publicity about innocent men going to prison—you know, all that DNA-exoneration stuff—and the DA made this big speech about how his job was to prosecute the guilty, not incarcerate the innocent."

"You're saying they just tanked it?"

"I'm saying the DA's Office did not oppose the federal appeal," Davidson said, picking his words carefully. "And Wychek walked out of Attica a free man. Happened only a few weeks ago."

"Pretty scummy, all right. But where does Wolfe come in? All she did was prosecute him. And she doesn't work for the DA's Office anymore."

"No. But she got a letter there. From Wychek. After he got out."

"And . . . ?"

"I haven't seen a copy, but it pretty much laughed at her. 'You stupid fucking cunt' was one of his favorite phrases. He walked the line pretty good. Said someone 'should' fuck her to death for how she prosecuted an innocent man, but he didn't say *he* was going to do it. And he danced around a lot, hinting that he had done a *lot* of women, and could do more. Nothing you could prosecute him on, but real scary stuff."

"And the cops say Wolfe gunned him down for writing that letter? Hell, if she shot every freak who wrote her a letter like that, she'd make Charles Manson look like a jaywalker."

"The timing *is* bad," Davidson said. "But, by itself, it's nothing, you're right. Only thing is, whoever shot him didn't do a good enough job. The EMTs got him going, but then they lost him again, into a coma. Supposedly, before he lapsed out, he said it was Wolfe who shot him. *That's* their case."

I'm taking a guess," a man said, behind us.

Both Davidson and I turned around.

Hauser. Dressed in a blue chalk-striped suit, with a white shirt and a wine-colored tie. His beard was gone, but I'd have known him anywhere.

"What's up?" Davidson asked, reaching over to shake hands. He and Hauser went way back. Not close, but friendly.

"I was supposed to meet someone here tonight," Hauser said. "Figured I might find him where I found you."

"You did," I told him. "Come on over."

Hauser got up, walked around, and sat down next to me.

"You got something?" I asked him.

"I—"

"They're bringing her out!" Davidson hard-whispered, getting to his feet.

A tall, lanky court officer walked Wolfe over to the counsel table like he was escorting a prom date. Her long dark hair glistened as if she'd just stepped out of a salon, trademark white wings flowing back from her high forehead. She was wearing a white silk sheath, adorned only with a single black spiral stripe, weaving around her body like a protective snake.

Wolfe always wore black-and-white outfits when she summed up before a jury. Combat clothes, hammering home her message: No "shades of gray" here, people. Bruiser's performance must have bought her enough time to change.

"Christ, look at her!" Hauser said admiringly. "It's like it's *her* courtroom."

The ADA who had been at the counsel table all night was suddenly replaced by a much older man, all spiffed out. They read out the charges: attempted murder, assault one, and a bunch of other tacked-on crap nobody paid any attention to.

"That's Russ Lansing," Hauser whispered to me. "Been with the DA's Office a hundred years. He's no trial man, but he won't make any mistakes with the press, I promise you that."

"You know the judge?" I asked him.

"As a matter of fact, I do," Hauser said. "But only because I covered a trial he presided over. Leonard Hutto."

"You covered a case in criminal court?"

"Brooklyn Supreme," Hauser said. "A celebrity divorce. Hutto's a cut above the usual politico that ends up with a bench seat as a reward for loyalty. A good law man. Probably just here tonight on rotation."

"I'll hear from the People on bail," the judge said.

"Given the extraordinary circumstances of this case, the People ask for the defendant to be remanded, Your Honor," the spiffy man intoned.

"What's extraordinary is that Ms. Wolfe has even been *arrested,*" Davidson bellowed. "These charges are absurd on their face. In addition, Ms. Wolfe has *significant* roots in the community. She is a homeowner, a taxpayer, a woman with a long record of public service and no criminal history of *any* kind. Remand, judge? This nonsense should be ROR'ed."

"What is the basis of the People's application?" the judge asked, the soul of judicialness, playing to the press.

"The victim was shot *three* times!" the spiffy old ADA said. "Clearly, the intent was to kill him. But the basis of our application for remand is that this may well become a homicide, even as we stand here before this court. The victim lapsed into a coma, from which he may not recover. And if he does not, the charge will be murder in the second degree, for which remand is mandatory."

"That's a speech," Davidson said. "Not evidence."

"The *evidence* . . ." the ADA said, pausing for effect, "is that, just before the victim lost consciousness, he specifically identified the defendant as the shooter."

"How do we know that?" Davidson demanded. "The People don't have the victim's statement, Your Honor. They've got some *cop's* statement, saying what the victim *allegedly* said. And even if such a statement was *actually* made," he went on, his voice so heavy with sarcasm that it would have taken a team of Clydesdales to pull it, "it's garbage on its face."

The ADA jumped from his seat. "A dying declaration—"

"—has to be made by someone who's *dead*," Davidson finished for him. "I haven't been given a *scrap* of discovery, judge. I thought the DA's Office had this new policy. You know, the one they did all the press releases about? They were going to front-end everything, try and get all the pleas *pre*-indictment. I guess they don't bother when they know they don't have a case."

"Your Honor!"

"Yes, Mr. Lansing? It seems counsel for the defendant has a point, don't you agree? Has it not been the policy of your office to offer at least *basic* discovery at arraignments, for the purpose of expediting the process?"

"It . . . it has, Your Honor. But because things happened so quickly in this matter—"

Davidson fired back, "So quick you don't know where or when the so-called victim was shot? Judge," he said, spreading his arms wide, as if to encompass the entire courthouse, "if we even knew *when* this supposed assault took place, we could probably walk out of here tonight, and the police could go back to looking for the *actual* assailant. For example, if the assault took place this past

Thursday, Ms. Wolfe was delivering the keynote address at the national VAWA Conference in Washington, D.C."

"What's this 'VAWA'?" the ADA said.

"Fucking moron," Hauser muttered under his breath.

"That would be the Violence Against Women Act, counselor," Davidson sneered at him. "You know, the federal legislation?" He turned back to the bench. "But that isn't the point, Your Honor. What we are saying is that Ms. Wolfe may well have the kind of alibi that would convince even *this* office to concentrate its efforts elsewhere, but the DA's deliberate withholding of basic discovery while simultaneously asking for a *remand* is a joke. A *dirty* joke."

"Mr. Lansing?" the judge said, in a voice that told you he was raising his eyebrows as he spoke.

"We . . . we don't know the exact time of the shooting, Your Honor. The victim was . . . discovered by a visitor, lying in a comatose state."

"So *that's* why you didn't put my client in a lineup, huh?" Davidson half shouted. "Because there isn't one single eyewitness to *any* of this. You're asking to lock up my client with no bail, and you've got *nothing*."

"Judge," Lansing squawked, "I don't have to—"

"How about forensics?" Davidson boomed, on full boil now. "Got any of *that*? You got a weapon? Fingerprints? Fibers? Blood spatter? What? Come on! If you've got it, bring it! Give this court one lousy piece of evidence besides what some scumbag *supposedly* said to some *unnamed* cop, I'll drop my bail application right now, how's that?"

"Oh, this is perfect," Hauser said, scribbling and chuckling at the same time. "Lansing's trying to do push-ups in quicksand, and Davidson keeps stepping on his head."

"Your Honor! I must protest. Counsel's description of a gunshot victim as a 'scumbag' is well beyond the bounds of—"

"Tell this court that this 'victim' of yours *isn't* a convicted rapist, and I'll apologize," Davidson said. "You think just because you conveniently forget to mention it we couldn't find out on our own?"

"Good one!" Hauser said, absently, intent on his writing.

"He's a *serial* rapist, judge," Davidson said, passionately. "With victims scattered all over the city. If you're looking for someone with a good motive to shoot Wychek, you don't have to look past—"

Wolfe stood up quickly, tugged sharply at Davidson's sleeve, shutting off the lava flow. She pulled at his lapel, whispered something in his ear.

"Judge," the DA said, "there's the statement. . . ."

"*What* damn statement?" Davidson shot back. "There's nothing in writing. All the People have is a word he spoke. *Supposedly* spoke. One word. 'Wolf.' That could mean anything, Your Honor. 'Wolf' can be a *first* name, too. There's probably a couple of thousand of them in the Manhattan phone book alone. And it's a common street name, too."

"That's ridic—" the DA said.

"I'll tell you what's ridiculous," Davidson stepped in. "Charging a citizen on crap that's not even going to get past the Grand Jury. For all we know, the victim was saying he sold one too many 'wolf' tickets, and someone popped him for it."

"Your Honor!" the DA protested.

Davidson rolled on, undeterred, spreading his arms wide in a "look how reasonable I'm being" gesture. "Judge, the purpose of bail is to ensure the defendant's presence at trial. The People aren't even going to *pretend* they believe my client is going to flee the jurisdiction. The so-called victim could be in a coma for months, for all we know. When he recovers, or when the DA's Office finally kicks loose enough information for us to prove Ms. Wolfe couldn't *possibly* have done this, who is going to compensate my client for all that time out of her life then?"

"Do you have an updated medical report?" the judge asked the DA.

"As of . . ." Lansing replied, glancing at his watch, "two hours ago, the victim's condition was unchanged."

The judge eye-swept the front rows, picking out the press like a pigeon pecking edible morsels off an alley floor. "In view of all the competing considerations placed before this court, bail is set . . ." He paused for effect. ". . . in the amount of five hundred thousand dollars."

"Judge . . ." Davidson began.

"That's all, counsel," the judge said, banging his gavel lightly.

"Very cute," Hauser said, in disgust. "He knows any remand would get overturned by the Appellate Division, but he doesn't want anyone saying he gave special consideration to a former prosecutor. So he sets bail, but makes it a monster. How is Wolfe going to raise—?"

"Your Honor," Wolfe said, on her feet, "may I be heard?"

"Is the defendant discharging her counsel and going *pro se?*" Lansing asked snidely, playing to the gallery.

"Ms. Wolfe is my *co*-counsel, judge," Davidson shot back. "As such, she is—"

"I will hear you, Ms. Wolfe," Hutto said. *"Briefly."*

"Thank you, Your Honor," Wolfe said, her courtroom-honed voice knifing through the buzz and hum from the back benches. "I understand you've already made your ruling concerning bail. And though I anticipate, with all respect, that your decision will not withstand appeal, my purpose in addressing this court concerns my conditions of confinement while awaiting release."

"Do you wish to be held in protective custody?" Hutto asked.

"No, judge. That doesn't concern me. I have every confidence that the Department of Corrections will see to my safety."

Wolfe deliberately turned sideways, making it clear she wasn't speaking only to the judge. "What I wish to place on the record is that I am *not* going to discuss this so-called case with anyone other than my own attorney. I am not going to be having *any* private conversations with inmates, correctional officers, or *anyone* else while I am confined."

Wolfe shifted her body some more, virtually turning her back on the judge. "So, if the DA's Office trots out some jailhouse snitch who claims I 'confessed' to them, everyone will know that such a statement is pure perjury."

"Christ, she's beautiful!" Hauser whispered to me.

"Judge, that is an *outrage,*" Lansing yelled. "The defendant has just accused our office of—"

"—trying to rescue your garbage cases with testimony from jail-house informants?" Wolfe sneered at him. "You've got that right."

"Ms. Wolfe," the judge said, mildly, "you have placed your statement on the record. And now, if there are no further—"

"The People demand an apology!" Lansing shouted.

"You going to give *me* one, when the truth comes out?" Wolfe shouted back.

"You mean, when they *let* it out!" Davidson out-volumed her.

"Take the defendant," the judge told the court officer.

"Talk to you later," I told Hauser, pulling out my cell phone and hitting the speed-dial number.

My Plymouth was waiting out back. When I saw Clarence behind the wheel, I knew Mama had passed the word.

I climbed in next to him. The Prof and Max were in the back-seat.

"Did she get to go, bro?" the Prof asked me.

"No," I said, shaking my head so Max would pick up on it, too. "They set her bail at a half-million." For Max, I held up both hands, fingers spread, to indicate "ten." Then I pointed toward the sky, for "power," and held up one hand plus one thumb. "Ten to the sixth" means a million to anyone raised on street-shorthand. I sliced my hand down, signifying "half." Max nodded.

"Mama's holding enough of mine for the points," I told them. "But I don't know how long it would take for her to put her hands on the green. And we'll still need a bondsman who'll write the paper for a number that high."

"Big Nate?" the Prof said.

"He's the only one I know I could lean on that hard," I agreed.

"You *who*?" the Prof said. "Big Nate won't get on the case if he don't know your face, Schoolboy. Burke be dead, remember?"

"That's what they say about Wesley, too, Prof," I said, very soft. "What *some* say?"

"You going to be the ghost with the most, huh? All right, son. Let's ride."

That night, Wesley was riding with us. He had once been the most feared assassin in the city. An artist of death. His reputation went all the way back, and not a word of it was a lie. Wesley was the ultimate contract man. The only way he ever interacted with the human race was to remove some of it.

Wesley didn't make statements. He just made people dead. And he only did it for money. Nobody ever saw him; nobody ever wanted to. Everything was done over phones and dead-drops.

I'd known Wesley since we were little kids. Both State-raised, without parents we ever knew. Back then, I was always scared. I was incubated in terror, and it took only a glance, a gesture, or even a smell to open the floodgates inside me.

But nothing scared Wesley. Fear is a feeling. "I'm not a man," he told me once. "I'm a bomb."

When I was a young man, he was everything I ever wanted to be. Ice-cold, remorseless, never-miss efficient. You could kill Wesley—at least, that's what *some* people thought—but you could never hurt him.

I finally found my family. The one I chose; the one that chose me. Wesley never looked for kin. Only for targets. No friends, no family, no home. And, finally, no reason to be here anymore.

The end kicked off when a Mafia don named Torenelli didn't pay Wesley for some work. Bodies started dropping all over the city, all family men. Torenelli went into hiding. Wesley kept killing, sending the message. When that didn't make the Mob give him up, Wesley decapitated Torenelli's daughter, right in her own upscale co-op. Telling them he didn't play by their Hollywood "code." Rules and roles didn't matter to a man who believed the difference between a priest and a pimp wasn't what they sold, only what they charged.

Then Torenelli played his last card. An old viper named Julio I'd known since prison. Years before, Julio had hired me to do something about a freak who was sex-stalking his niece. That was a straightforward job, and I got it done easy enough. Julio said he had hired me, instead of using one of his own men, because he was Old School—you never mixed private business with family business. It had sounded right when he said it.

But when Julio hired me to meet Wesley, offer him whatever money the assassin wanted to call off the hit on Torenelli, I knew I was being middled. Just carrying the offer would be enough to convince Wesley I had gone over.

It didn't happen like that. Julio thought Wesley and I were stalking each other, but what we were doing was making a trade.

After a while, they all got dead.

That should have ended it. But by then, Wesley's hell-bound train had finally jumped the tracks. A decade before Columbine became an American nightmare, Wesley walked into a suburban high school with enough ordnance to take out every living creature in the place. After lobbing some grenades, then gunning down dozens of random victims, he released a deadly gas from the truck he had driven to the scene.

While the cops thought they were still negotiating with the maniac they had trapped inside, Wesley climbed to the roof of the high school. Before the police helicopters could even get off a shot, he held a bunch of dynamite sticks taped together over his head, like a psycho version of the Statue of Liberty, and blew himself into atoms.

We watched him go. Live on TV. It was on every channel, just like when they cover a war.

The package arrived a couple of weeks later: a nine-by-twelve flat envelope, thick with paper. His dark thumbprint was at the bottom of the last page.

That part of the package found its way to the cops. My inheritance from Wesley, a "Get Out of Jail Free" card, taking the weight for some of the things I'd done.

But there was another part to it, one the cops had never seen. A pocket-sized notebook, filled with Wesley's precise printing. His accounts book.

Our kind don't make out wills. But we do leave legacies.

We went over the plan as Clarence drove. At that hour, even the FDR wasn't crowded; we were over the Willis Avenue Bridge and into the South Bronx badlands in minutes. The Plymouth blended right in.

My cell phone buzzed.

"What?" I answered.

"You tell me, sweetheart." Michelle.

"Honey, have we got anybody out on the Rock, in the Women's House?"

"I can find out. What's up?"

"Wolfe's been arrested. Just got arraigned. Judge put a half-million bail on her. She may be there for a while. I don't want anything to—"

"Wolfe? They'll probably build a throne for her, as many wife beaters as she's put away."

"Still . . ."

"I'm on it, baby."

Michelle rang off just as we found what we were looking for. Big Nate's place was a freestanding cinder-block building with cross-barred windows—it looked like a small-town jailhouse sitting on a prairie. A faint dirty-yellow glow came through the glass. Red neon promised bail bonds in several languages.

We gave it one slow circuit before Clarence docked the Plymouth, backing it into getaway position.

"Everybody set?" I asked.

"You going heeled, mahn?" Clarence asked, patting his chest to the left of his heart, where his nine-millimeter always rested.

"No," I said. "We'll do it the way I laid it out." I had a never-registered .357 Mag in a hidden compartment next to the Plymouth's fuel cell, but I didn't want to chance a pat-down at the door.

The Prof held up a small bundle, wrapped in an old army blanket. He didn't have to say any more. When I first met him, he was on his last prison stretch, and part of his rep was as a master of the twelve-gauge sawed-off.

"All right," I said. "One more time. Me and Max go in. I'm the front man for a sweatshop that just got raided. I'm looking for someone to write a lot of little bonds—get the workers out and gone before they say something stupid and put INS on alert. Max is with me, covering the tong's end of the deal . . . if they even ask.

"If we come piling out the door, you know what to do. Keep it high, Prof. Soon as they hear your scattergun, they'll probably get back inside. And, around here, nobody's calling 911."

"You drop the name, you gotta carry the game, son," the Prof warned. He unwrapped the sawed-off and laid it on the seat next to him.

I rang the bell. Waited for whoever was running the security camera to buzz us in.

The place hadn't changed. A pair of low-grade industrial desks, a wall of khaki file cabinets. A splattering of hand-lettered signs, all warnings of one kind or another.

There was a man at each desk. One was in a cheap brown suit jacket, sitting behind some kind of ledger. The other was in a black nylon windbreaker, feet on the desk, a copy of *Soldier of Fortune* open in front of him. I figured the suit for the money man, the windbreaker for a bounty hunter.

The bounty hunter looked barroom-tough. The money man looked weasel-dangerous.

Max moved so he was standing against the left-hand wall. I walked over to the money man.

"I want to see Nate," I told him.

"There's no Nate here, friend," he said. "You want a bond, you came to the right place. Otherwise . . ."

"He's here," I said, letting my eyes drift over to the door against the back wall. The one that said "Men" on it, with a "Closed for Repairs" sign plastered across its face. "He doesn't let anyone else drive his Rolls," letting him know I'd seen the immaculate old Silver Cloud sitting out back.

"Give me a name," the money man said, not blinking.

"Nate wouldn't like that," I said. "And he wouldn't like *you* looking at me that close," I said, turning to face the bounty hunter.

The bounty hunter gave it about a second's thought, then he dropped his eyes.

"Just tell him someone's out here asking for him," I said, keeping my voice a monotone. "Don't be thinking crazy, because I'm not. Everyone knows you don't keep cash around here."

"I can't do that," the money man said.

I stepped close to the money man's desk. "Then tell him this," I said, very softly. "Tell him, if I wanted to do him, I wouldn't let people see me, like I'm letting you, right now. I'd just turn this place into a barbecue pit, and pick him off when it got too hot for him inside."

The money man looked everyplace but my eyes.

"Don't worry," I said. "You tell Nate what I said, it won't make him nervous: it'll calm him down. He'll know who I am then. We're old pals. Tell the tough guy over there to go ahead and pull his piece, keep me covered, if it'll make you feel better, okay?"

The money man slitted his eyes. I counted to six in my head. "Step back," he said. "Just a few feet, all right? I need some privacy. This is a long-distance call."

I did what he wanted. He picked up the receiver, covered the mouthpiece with his hand. I looked over at the bounty hunter. He was a real professional: too busy playing stare-down with me to notice Max closing the gap between them.

"Go on back," the money man said.

I turned to Max, barked something in quasi-Chinese. Even after all those years at Mama's, I didn't understand one word of the Cantonese and Mandarin she spoke interchangeably, but I could imitate the sounds enough to fool anyone who didn't speak either one. It helped that Max nodded, like he was acknowledging what I said.

"I told him to wait out here for me," I said to the money man. "He doesn't speak English."

The money man didn't say anything. Max slid along the wall, just a few inches, to improve his angle of attack if the bounty hunter decided to role-play.

I walked over to the men's room, tapped lightly. Heard a seriously solid deadbolt snap open. Turned the knob, and walked inside.

Big Nate was behind a flimsy little wood desk . . . and a transparent wall of Lexan thick enough to bounce a bullet, even at that close range.

"Come closer," he said, speaking into a microphone he held in one tiny hand. "Talk into the speaker."

I moved forward slowly, sat down on a chrome barstool with a cracked red leather top. That brought my mouth level with the speaking grid.

Nate was looking down at me. Behind his desk was a raised platform. It compensated for his four-and-a-half-foot height, the same way the specially built-up pedals on his Rolls let him drive.

"I need a bond," I said. "A big one."

"Never mind that," he said, his frail voice amplified into resonant strength by the microphone he was holding. "You said something outside, to my man. Can you back it up?"

"Lucien Lagrande," I said, pulling the name from my ghost brother's accounts book. "You want more?"

The silence between us was thicker than the Lexan. But, from the moment I'd said that name, Big Nate knew he was done. Wesley had started his walk.

"You're not saying you're . . . ?"

"I'm his brother," I said. The blood-truth.

Even as I said those words, I remembered the "home" they'd sent me to when I was an orphaned kid. What they did to me there. And what Wesley had whispered to me one night when we were together in the institution: "They're easier when they're sleeping," the baby monster told me. "Fire works."

It was all down in Wesley's accounts book. Big Nate had been a visionary. Between the Jakes running ganja, the DRs moving powder, bikers cranking crystal, college kids selling Q, and everyone else slinging rock, money was stacking all over the city. The Italians had a hundred different laundries, but even if they had been willing to take in outsiders, nobody trusted a "family" that didn't trust its own relatives.

That had become Nate's real business, setting up custom-tailored laundries. Had them everywhere, and kept all the records in his head. His stock in trade was honesty. You gave Nate a hundred K cash, you got back whatever percentage he promised . . . and a string of receipts that would give a CPA an orgasm.

One night, a man named Lucien Lagrande came to visit Big Nate. Lagrande told him he knew the bail bonds weren't the little man's real business.

"You sitting on gold with this bail-bond front," Lagrande had told him. "But that all finished now. You being . . . encompassed."

Big Nate had laughed at him. Which Lagrande expected. Then he dropped the hammer. Big Nate had a piece of a Vegas casino. A little piece, but in his own name. If that came to light, Big Nate would lose *both* licenses—it's illegal for a bondsman to have a piece of a casino, in either direction.

Big Nate felt his heart stop. "Actually fucking *stop,*" is what he told people, later.

"You got a week," Lagrande told him. "Then you turn it over, or I turn *you* over. That simple, my man. Don't worry, now. You get a taste. You keep *on* getting a taste. Once you *encompassed,* you part of my operation. A partner, even.

"You don't play, you lose it all. Everyone scramble for pieces, I get some, but not all, I know that. This way, you go with me, I get the pie, sure, but you get to keep a nice fat slice."

Lagrande lived in a three-story frame house in Brooklyn. It stood alone on a large vacant lot, the last in a row of condemned-then-razed derelict buildings. Word was, the whole thing was slated to become what the Mayor called an "oasis of greenery."

The place was a fortress, surrounded by iron fencing, patrolled by dogs, lit by klieg lights at night, and occupied by no less than a dozen of Lagrande's heavily armed crew. Nobody could get within a hundred yards without being spotted.

It was broad daylight when the house exploded into flames. Lagrande didn't even make it to the fence before a sniper picked him off.

The police later figured that the shots must have come from a certain rooftop, more than a quarter-mile from the scene. Seven shots. Three into Lagrande, the other four into the men who had run out the front door with him.

"We know this much," the press conference cop told his audience. "The recovered slugs were all fired from the same weapon. It's as if whoever was shooting put one into each of them to bring them down, then scanned the field to make sure which one was Lagrande, before he finished him off with those head shots. As impossible as that sounds . . ." he finished, lamely.

That was a lot of years ago. But crime time runs different than citizen time. For permanent outsiders like us, time only matters when you're doing it.

"I'm not a blackmailer," I said to Big Nate. "And I didn't come here to make threats. That name I said, it was just to prove in, okay? So you know where I've been, and what I know."

And what I can do, I said in my mind, vibrating the unspoken words out to him.

The little man looked at the ceiling, as if he was considering a proposal. Then he picked up the microphone and whispered what everyone is too terrified to ask out loud. "Is Wesl—? Is he really . . . ?"

"Nobody knows," I told him. A face-down hole card. The whisper-stream had it that Wesley was a falcon on my glove. Nobody knew for sure, and nobody liked the odds.

I watched his eyes. Stayed gentle inside myself, showing him respect by acting like I believed he was actually considering calling my bet.

"How big a number I need to write?" he finally said, tossing in his hand.

"That's a huge-ass bond," the Prof said on the drive back. "Sure hope that fucking dwarf don't think he too big to drop the vig." The Prof was a couple of inches taller than Big Nate, on a good day.

"I ran it all down for him," I said. "He knows Wolfe's not going to jump. And she's got a nice house, out in Forest Hills Gardens; cover him for more than the nut, it came to that."

"So we don't have to put up the fifty large?"

"Not a dime."

"Honeyboy, listen to me for a minute. You wearing a murder face now. Not like you mad, like you . . . the way Wesley looked *all* the time. Got those straight-line lips and glass-cutter eyes, you hear what I'm saying?"

"I don't care—"

"Right. Know you don't. Know you won't. Only thing is, you *know* how people get when you scare them deep enough. They'll tell you anything you want to hear."

"Meaning, you don't think Nate's actually going to write the bond?"

"He's either going to write it, or he's going to run, son. Get down, go to ground, not be around. Not until this one's all done."

"If he—"

"Yo! Ice up, youngblood! What's wrong with you? The little midget pulls a burn, he gets to learn. But that's down the line, another time. What *we're* here for is to get your girl the door. Say I'm on time with all that rhyme."

"You're right, Prof," I assured him.

I didn't want to take a chance on calling Davidson at his home. I had the number, but it was almost five in the morning by then, and I didn't want to spook his kids—that kind of move could cost me some ground. Figured he wouldn't have his cell turned on, either, so I called his office number and spoke into the tape.

"Go spring her; it's covered. Surety is Korlok Bonding Company, in the Bronx." I gave him the rest of the particulars, including the phone number and who to ask for.

"What's next, mahn?" Clarence asked as I got back into the Plymouth.

"We have to wait a few hours," I told him, signing the same message to Max. "Make sure Wolfe gets bailed, first. I have to find out some stuff. Figure, another twenty-four hours, we know exactly what we have to do. I'll leave word at—"

Max tapped my chest. Shook his head "no" at me. Made the sign of a man eating with chopsticks.

"All right," I told them all. "Mama's at five this afternoon. Tell Michelle, too, okay?"

"**S**he came back, boss," Gateman greeted me as I walked in the door of the flophouse.

"How long ago?"

"Around midnight. Had the Rottweiler with her again, too. Plus a guy. He's been up before, last year. I remember him. Big guy. Looks like a farm boy, but he's no Hoosier, I could tell."

Mick, I thought. Good. If he was with Pepper, he wasn't prowling the city, looking for someone to hurt.

"What did you tell them?"

"Boss, I told them you wasn't in. The girl, she gave me two choices. I mean, she didn't *say* the choices, but that's what they was. I could either let them go on up and wait for you, or I could shoot them all."

I nodded my head, telling Gateman he'd done the right thing. "Which one would you have gone for first?" I asked him.

"Got to be the Rottie," Gateman said, professionally. "I could have cleared leather before any of them could move. That usually stuns them for a second, gives you some options. And they weren't standing that close. But that only works with people, not dogs. And that fucking Rottie was *ready,* if you get my drift."

Bruiser *was* ready. I heard his warning snarl as I came up the last flight of stairs.

"It's me," I said.

The beast didn't recognize my voice. Or, more likely, he did. I heard Pepper say, "Bruiser, down!"

She was sitting on the futon, Bruiser at her feet. Mick was standing off to one side, so he could see if there was anyone coming up behind me.

"We didn't want to risk a cell call," Pepper said. "And we only have—"

"I already got the bail secured," I cut her off. "She'll be out later on today."

"That's great!" Pepper said, clapping her hands. The Rottweiler jumped to his feet. "No!" she said, jerking the dog's short lead. "It's all right, Bruiser."

"You're *sure*?" Mick asked me, his voice thick with threat.

"I'm not walking in there with a half-mil in cash," I said. "It'll be a bondsman. I went to see him myself. Just got back. And I don't think there's much doubt."

Mick made a noise in his throat. Bruiser looked up at him like a kindred spirit.

"Listen, listen!" Pepper said, excitedly. "This is what I couldn't say on the phone. There's a detective, Sands. He was working Special Victims when Wolfe was head of City-Wide. Do you know him?"

"Never heard his name," I said, truthfully.

"He called us. At the office number. He wants someone to meet him. At seven in the morning. *This* morning. A bar called the Four-Leaf. Do you know it?"

"If he means the one around here, I know where it is," I said. And I did. If you went westbound on Chambers Street, past the little park and all the way across the West Side Highway, you could find it, tucked into a corner, right near the river. "But I've never been there."

"He says he has some things for us. Things that could help Wolfe."

"Probably working for the DA. Hoping you'd be dumb enough to have a landline in the office, so they could find out where to serve the search warrant," I said. Wolfe's operation didn't have a street address. She met with her clients the same way I did—anyplace else. "Or maybe he just wants to pump you. The cops have to know that Wolfe has a network, and that you're with her."

"No, no," Pepper said. "He's not with them. He's for Wolfe. For real."

"And you would know that exactly . . . how?"

"Because . . . All right, I *don't* know it. Not for sure."

"You ask Wolfe?"

"How could I? I haven't talked to her since . . . since this happened."

"So?"

"So that's why I'm . . . why *we're* here. Why we waited. Detective Sands said he wanted to meet—"

"You told me that."

"Here's what I didn't tell you," she said, lips tight with self-control. "He didn't ask for me. What he said was, 'Send anyone you want. Ask whatever questions you want. Or don't say a word—I'll do all the talking. You understand? I could be wired like a radio station, it wouldn't do the other side any good.' Now what does that sound like to you?"

"Like he's for Wolfe. Or he's smarter than the average cop."

"Or *both,* right?" Pepper said, eagerly.

"We *have* to go," Mick cut through it, his voice no-dispute hard. "If he's got anything that could—"

"Pepper's right," I said to him, getting it for the first time. "If he's working for the other side, even getting a *look* at you or Pepper would be another round in their cylinder. Especially if you're going to be her alibi, down the road. But my face won't mean anything. . . ."

"You'll go, right?" Pepper asked, big dark eyes pressuring and pleading at the same time.

"Seven? You mean, in less than two hours, then?"

"Yes. That's why we waited here. It's pretty close by. If you hadn't shown up, we would have had to—"

"I'll do it," I said. "But I don't know when Davidson's going to call and—"

They were already on their way out, the Rottweiler leading the way.

Less than two hours before the meet. A half-hour walk from my place, max.

I don't drink coffee. And stims scare me, the way they throw off my pulse rate.

So I took a long hot shower, followed by a fifteen-second blast of only-cold spray. A quick, careful shave. A glass of grape juice and some rye toast, to settle my stomach. I threw down the motley assortment of vitamins and minerals and Devil-knows-what-else I swallow every morning, a habit I'd gotten into when I was holed up in the Pacific Northwest, after the ambush that was supposed to have totaled me. I wasn't running from the shooters; I was staying down to make sure there weren't any of them left. Besides the ones I'd already found.

I let the whisper-stream declare me dead and gone, and just . . . waited.

I was home only a short time before I got involved in a case. A case for real, like I used to have when I first was trying to make it as something other than what I am—a criminal in my heart. Wolfe helped me on that one. Oh, she got paid. Said that was why she did it, for the money.

But I never believed her, not completely. That case was a lot of things for me, but, for me and Wolfe, I thought it was a test. The prize I was playing for wasn't as big as a promise, just something to let me know I could get back in the game.

And I brought it home. Got it done. Found out who had killed the teenage daughter who was a gangster's darkest secret. I did it all the right way. Investigated, interrogated, interviewed. Came up with a plan. Put together a team. And spooked the truth out of the shadows.

Along the way, some people got dead.

They didn't die for justice, and they didn't die for money. I'm no vigilante, and I'm not a hit man—although the whisper-stream has made me out to be both over the years.

Wolfe knew about some of it. Figured it out for herself. But I never got the chance to tell her the ending.

An hour later, I was walking down Hudson toward Chambers. Dressed in a worn leather jacket over a dark-blue hooded sweatshirt, jeans, scuffed ankle-high boots on my feet, a pair of canvas gloves in my back pocket. A man going to work.

I couldn't do anything about my face. Once, I was so generic-looking that I could get past almost anyone who wasn't raised where I was. But now I had two different-color eyes, which no longer tracked exactly parallel. One bullet had made a keloid beauty mark on my right cheek; another had neatly sliced off the top of the opposite ear. Now I had a face people would remember.

Worse, they could see me coming.

Burke had never had a tattoo. Most guys who start to jail early end up covered with ink by the time they're on their second or third bit, but that depends on who schools you—gang kids or pros.

With kids, it's all about *owning* something. Something they can't take away, even when they beat you for the fun of it, and toss you in a tiny dark room with only the stink of sorrow for company. Some kids know who "they" are from birth—only the faces change.

There's other reasons to ink up. Jailhouse tattoos aren't painless. And a tattooed tear for each time you've been down marks you as a veteran.

When you're done with the juvie joints, when they put you Inside for real, sometimes you have to take a mark just to stay alive. The White Night crews make you fly their flag on your body, and the Latins are even harder about it. Some of their bosses are so heavily inked, it takes over their skin, makes them into some different race.

But the Prof had pulled my coat early. "You ain't got but one trick for when you hit the bricks," the little man had counseled me. "You're going to do crime, all the time. That stuff you see mother-fuckers put on themselves? That's 'cause they going to *stay* here, understand? But you, you're still a young boy. The gate's in your fate. You know what you going to do, so do it true," he said. "Body art ain't smart, Schoolboy. It's like using vanity plates on a get-away car."

But the man walking down Hudson that morning had a tattoo. A tiny blue heart, between the last two knuckles of his right hand. A hollow heart.

That was for Pansy, my partner. A Neopolitan mastiff I'd raised from a tiny pup. She had taken some of the bullets meant for me when I walked into that ambush. Taken one of the enemy with her, too, before she went over.

"You're still the same," my people kept telling me.

Maybe I was.

I wasn't worried about recognizing this supposed cop. A lot of waterfront bars open early, to catch the crowd who hadn't been picked in the morning shape-up. But this joint wasn't close enough to any of the working piers, and the crews prepping the Twin Tow-ers site for new construction would already be on the job by seven.

The caller had told Pepper whoever she sent would recognize him by his white hair . . . and he'd be sitting in the corner booth farthest from the door. I checked my watch: 6:58. Close enough.

As soon as I walked in the place, I understood why the cop had picked it. To my right was a flat wall, broken only by the clearly marked doors to the toilets. Dead ahead, a long, straight bar with a murky mirror behind it. Only four of the stools were occupied. To my left, running almost the full length of the window, a row of booths—all wood, no padding anywhere in sight.

The second booth and the last were the only ones with people in them. A guy nursing a beer while studying the *Racing Form* was closest to me. All the way in the back was a man in a dark-tweed sports jacket. He had a thick mop of white hair, and eyes I could feel even at that distance.

I walked over to where he was sitting. Noticed the last booth was just beyond the length of the window. A nice precaution, even though it would have taken a radiologist to read anything through that grimy glass.

I sat down, uninvited, my back to the door. No point being cute—if it was a trap, it was already sprung.

"What do you have?" I said.

"I've got mine," he said, holding up a double shot glass of something amber.

"Not what *will* you have," I said. "What *do* you have."

He nodded, as if I'd given him some secret code word.

"How do I know you're from—?"

"That wasn't the deal," I said. "I don't have any questions. You said you wouldn't have any, either. All I had to do was listen. That's what I'm doing."

The cop tossed down his drink, rapped his glass on the table. "You want . . . ?" he asked.

I just shook my head.

A man in what looked like a butcher's apron came over. He took away the cop's shot glass and replaced it with another. Neither of us said anything until the barkeep had gone back to his post.

"My name's Sands," the cop said. "Molton James Sands, Jr. My friends call me Molly."

I didn't call him anything.

"I worked with Wolfe," he continued. "For years. Best prosecutor I ever knew. She was one of us. In Sex Crimes, I mean. One of the squad. She's getting railroaded by that candyass DA. Not the Manhattan guy—the head of City-Wide. The same faggot who fired her."

I hadn't come there for an editorial, especially from a lush. "Tell me something we can use," I said.

His blue eyes darkened as he narrowed in on me. The veins in his slightly spread nose got redder. "*Here's* fucking something," he said. "That mutt who got shot, he's no more in a coma than I am."

"Wychek?"

"Wychek. Oh, he *was* unconscious all right. But as of a few hours ago, he's come around. Whoever's representing Wolfe . . ."

"Davidson."

"Good! That's a *man*. Now, listen. This should get her bail dropped all the way down to—"

"Her bail's covered," I said, cutting him off. "This Wychek, he's conscious now, right? You telling me he changed his statement?"

"I don't know about that," the cop said, leaning closer to me. "But I do know this. He doesn't want to be discharged."

"The wounds—"

"—are bullshit," he finished for me. "He got hit three times. Front of the right thigh, upper left arm, and right shoulder."

"That could still be—"

"—with a fucking twenty-five," he said. "What does *that* tell you?"

"Nothing by itself."

"You don't want to say, a twenty-five, that's a woman's gun, right? Well, it's also a punk's gun. Little piece-of-shit nothing, make a Saturday Night Special look like a Glock. Street Crimes probably confiscates more Raven twenty-fives a year than all the other pieces put together. Anyway, they got the bullets out like pulling a bad tooth, big deal. Cocksucker won't even be walking with a limp."

"The coma was a fake?"

"I . . . I don't know," the cop said, a flicker of uncertainty in his eyes. "I don't think so, from what I heard. But this part is gospel— Wychek's scared. *Big* scared. Demanding a police guard, the whole works."

"Scared Wolfe's going over the wall at Rikers, swim to the

Bronx, steal a car, pick up a *real* gun this time, and hunt him down at the hospital?" I said, not a trace of sarcasm in my voice.

"Don't be fucking stupid," he said, showing me his street roller's stare. "Look, I don't have a lot of time; I'm supposed to be on a case in the Jamaica courthouse at nine—not that the fucking pussy ADA is ever on time himself—so listen up. For right now, the DA's going along with it. You understand what I'm telling you? Full police guard. Why? Because the official story is that Wolfe's put out a contract on him."

"Yeah, that'd be smart," I said. "Believe me, if there's one person in this city who wants that scumbag alive, it's Wolfe. Davidson's going to dice and slice him so bad on the stand, the case will never get to the jury."

"I'm not arguing," the cop said. "Something else is going on. I just don't know what. But him not being in a coma anymore, that's worth something, right?"

"How much?" I said, slipping my hand inside my jacket.

Sands' eyes snapped into violence. One of his big fists clenched. When he spoke, his voice was tightly constricted, like an overwound spring.

"Listen, pal. You don't know me. And I don't know you. So I'm going to be real fucking patient. This once. I meant, worth something to *Wolfe*. You think I don't go way back with her? You think I don't know what a filthy little maggot this Wychek is? How many rapes he got away with because, in this whole stinking town, only Wolfe had the stones to take the case to trial, even when it wasn't a slam-dunk?"

I nodded, not affirming his connection to Wolfe, just the truth he spoke about her. When Wolfe was running City-Wide, if there had been any damn way to bring the other victims in, she would have done it.

"I know something else, too," he said, leaning even closer. "That 'Ha ha!' letter he sent Wolfe? He must have sent other ones, too. 'Cause that's the kind of fucking degenerate filth he is. You want to know who *really* tried to kill him, *that's* where you start."

"Where would I get—"

"Been nice meeting you," the cop said, holding out his hand for me to shake. "Maybe I'll see you around sometime. You ever go out to Platinum Pussycats? The strip joint, out by JFK?"

"No," I said, arranging my face into a mute question, as I palmed the piece of paper he had slipped to me.

"Ah, you can't miss it," he said. "It's behind that giant storage-unit place they have out there."

"Yeah, okay," I said, in a dismissive voice. "Anything you want me to tell—?"

"Anything I want to tell her, she already knows," the cop said.

As I was walking back over to my place, the cell phone in my pocket rang.

"What?" I answered.

"Got your message." Davidson's voice. "Nice work. I'll have her out by—"

"There's new stuff," I said. "Call me as soon as you get her sprung, so we can meet."

I was starting to feel the fatigue knocking at all my doors by then, but I had to pick up whatever the cop had in that storage locker, and do it fast. If he was being straight, if he really was with Wolfe, I couldn't leave him hanging out there, exposed. And if it was a trap, if they had a camera on the unit so they could get a look at the members of Wolfe's crew, I couldn't turn the job over to Pepper.

The Prof and Clarence were probably back in their crib, over in East New York. Which was kind of on the way to the airport, if I took Atlantic Avenue all the way through Brooklyn into Queens. But with the key in my hand, I didn't need the Prof for the locks. And this had to be a no-guns deal, which meant Clarence wasn't coming.

The Mole was all the way up in the South Bronx. But even if he'd lived close by, he wouldn't be the man for this job—his idea of personal protection is heavy explosives. And I still wasn't sure where Michelle was.

But Max's place was off Division Street, and I knew everybody in his house would be awake.

I liberated my Plymouth, drove over to the warehouse where Max has his dojo on one floor and his family home on the next. I probed until I found the hidden switch that raised the metal doors to the loading bay, drove inside, and closed it behind me.

By then, I knew Max was watching, from somewhere. As I got out, a dark shape vaulted over the second-floor railing, dropping next to me as lightly as a Kleenex on velour.

Max. Not showing off, showing up.

I started to gesture out what we had to do, but he held one finger in the air for silence, then used it to point upstairs before he flowed his hands together in a prayerful gesture. I took a quick glance at my watch, to tell him we didn't have a *lot* of time, and then I followed him upstairs.

"Burke!" the teenage girl shouted, as she ran to me. Flower, the only child of Max and his wife, Immaculata.

The girl slammed into me like a linebacker making a goal-line stop, knocking me back a few feet as I held on to her. "Hey, kiddo," I said. "Easy!"

She stood on her toes, gave me a messy kiss on the cheek. "I'm sorry," she said. "I'm so used to Daddy."

"Daddy?"

"That is what she *persists* in calling her father lately," Immaculata said, her voice mock-severe. "Flower's manners have suffered greatly, now that she is *so* grown up."

"Mom!"

"You see?" Immaculata smiled at me. She turned to her beautiful, glowing daughter. "Have you invited your uncle Burke to come into our home, child? To sit down? To share our breakfast with us?"

"Aaaargh!" the girl said, rolling her eyes. She stepped back a couple of paces, bowed formally, said, "Uncle, please come into our home and share our meal with us. We would be honored."

"It would be *my* honor," I said, bowing back.

Max regarded his wife and daughter with his standard mixture of stunned amazement and fierce love.

Immaculata was in a plum-colored robe heavily brocaded with silver. Her hair was tied in a chignon. Her daughter was wearing pink jeans and a black sweatshirt that came almost to her knees. Her hair was pulled into three pigtails, with two on the right.

We all sat around the teak table with rosewood inlays that the family used for all its meals. I don't know what was in the eggs Immaculata served, but they tasted wonderful.

"Drink," she said, putting a glass of some ginger-colored stuff she had just mixed up in front of me. "For energy."

"Thank you," I said, not remotely surprised that she could tell I needed it.

Max disappeared. Came back in a few seconds with a framed document of some kind.

"Oh my *god*!" Flower exclaimed, dramatically.

I took the document from Max, read through the glass. Flower's PSAT scores. Verbal: 80. Math: 78. Writing: 80. Spending all that time with teenagers last year had schooled me enough to understand that those scores, coupled with Flower's school activities, made her a mortal lock for a National Merit Scholarship.

"Congratulations!" I said to her.

"Oh, this is so *embarrassing*," the girl said. "I mean, it isn't a Nobel Prize, for goodness' sake!"

"When you win one of those, will you still throw a fit if your father wants to show it off?" I asked her.

"Burke! You're supposed to be on *my* side."

"Honey, it's not like Max is making a window display out of it."

"Well, he *wanted* to, I think. And when he showed it to Grandmother, *she* wanted to build a *shrine* to it. I'm *serious*!"

"'Grandmother,' huh?" I teased her. "You don't call her 'Granny,' then?"

"She wouldn't *dare*," Immaculata laughed. "This child has always been able to bully her poor father, but Mama . . ."

"Yeah," I said. "Mama's like me. She doesn't put up with any guff from the younger generation."

"You are so tough," Flower said, getting up from the table. She bent forward to give me a kiss, slipping her hand into the side pocket of my jacket, as I had taught her to do when she was just a little girl. Back then, she always found candy. Later, it was the kind of junk jewelry preteens love . . . or pretend to, anyway. Now it's a fifty-dollar bill. "I must get ready for school now," she announced.

"Hold on a damn minute," I said. "I want to tell you something. Something important. You're old enough to hear it now."

Flower's eyes were rapt. There was nothing she treasured more than vindication of her status as a mature young woman.

"I've known your father for a *long* time," I said. "He is my brother. I love him. You know the amazing skills your father has. But I was never jealous of him. Not until now. Do you understand?"

"Oh, Burke," she said. She gave me another quick kiss, then fled to her room, tears flowing.

Even though we were heading away from Manhattan, the inbound HOV lane cut down our options. That, plus the reverse-commuters and airport traffic, clogged the artery enough to keep us below the speed limit for pretty much the entire trip.

The highways that crisscross the city during rush hour carry a United Nations of passengers. Perfect for the kind of traveling I like to do—nothing stands out. Besides, the average commuter is either talking on a cell phone, eating his breakfast, or staring blankly through the windshield like an overtranq'd mental patient. A zebra-striped stretch limo with a palm tree growing out of its sunroof wouldn't get more than a passing glance, never mind my purposely anonymous Plymouth.

We took the long right-hand sweeper exiting the BQE for the

LIE connector to the Grand Central. Behind us, some congenital defective, in a white Mustang with blue racing stripes, decided we weren't moving quick enough. He jumped into the service lane, shot past us, then whipped back to his left to cut us off. A gentle tap on the four-piston brakes, concealed behind the dog-dish hub-caps on the Plymouth's modest sixteen-inch steel wheels, was enough to keep us out of his trunk.

Max gave me a "Should we?" look. I shrugged, not expecting we'd get a chance.

But the Mustang was going the same way we were, so we stayed right with him until the highway forked—left for Long Island, right for JFK.

The Mustang went right. Max looked upward, then nodded in agreement. It was true—I usually don't like to call attention to myself when I'm driving, but fate *had* made the decision for us.

The Mustang cut across two rows, looking for the outside lane. As he made his move, I dropped the Plymouth down a gear and nailed it. The Roadrunner exploded past his left quarter panel like a train past a tree. By the time the full-on roar of the Plymouth's stump-puller motor registered in his ears, the Mustang was behind us, stunned.

I glanced in the mirror, caught the driver looking frantically to his right, trying to figure out what had happened. The ancient bucket of bolts he'd cut off so easily *couldn't* have just blasted past him like that, but . . .

Past JFK, traffic lightened up considerably. The Mustang tail-gated relentlessly, flashing his brights, making it clear he wanted that left lane for himself. I glanced at the tach—3200 rpm, about 70 miles an hour. Nothing ahead for quite a distance. Even Miss Cleo could figure out what would happen as soon as the lane next to us cleared.

I watched the mirrors. When the Mustang swung out and made his move to pass on my right, I let him get a half-length on me before I gave it the gun, keeping him pinned in the middle lane.

At 105, the Mustang was still coming, but he was a man trying to scale a Teflon wall with greasy hands—the Plymouth had enough left to run away and hide anytime I asked.

A fat SUV in the middle lane finished it. The screech of the Mustang's brakes was ugly—I guessed the chump hadn't seen the need for big brakes to go along with his giant chrome rims.

I shot past the SUV, sliced across the highway, and disappeared into the next exit ramp.

We circled back toward the storage facility. Once we had it spotted, I pulled over. We took out a pair of bogus Jersey plates—backed with Velcro bands so they could snap on and off in seconds—and put them in place, just in case there was some sort of surveillance cam working.

The facility was a huge grid formed by lines of connected units, like windowless row houses. I'd been in smaller towns.

There was no fence, just a billboard-sized warning sign at the entrance. All I caught with a quick glance was: NO LIVING OR SLEEPING IN THE UNITS.

We motored through slowly, navigating by the alphanumeric on the piece of paper Sands had given me. A brown Chevy sedan with white doors rolled past us. The quasi–police shield decal on the doors didn't exactly give me the tremors. All those patrols ever did was watch for people prying open the units that management sealed up when the rent hadn't been paid.

Some of the units were bigger than apartments people paid a fortune for in Manhattan. Even the smallest ones would hold anything you could stuff in a pickup.

People keep everything in places like this, from toys to treasures. If you were evicted, you could stash your furniture while you slept in your car and tried to put together enough money for a new crib. If your collection of vintage paperback books was too much for your apartment—or your wife—one of these units could be the solution.

For that matter, all you needed was a chainsaw and an ice chest and you could keep a body in one of them for long enough to be in another country by the time it was discovered.

Sands' unit was near the end of a long row. I backed the Plymouth up to the door, and Max and I got out.

The lock yielded to the three-number sequence that was on the piece of paper Sands had slipped me. I'd brought a flashlight with me, but I didn't need it: a switch on the wall lit the place nicely.

The inside of the storage unit looked like the loser's share of a divorce settlement. An old La-Z-Boy recliner, upholstered in seasick-green Naugahyde. A swaybacked couch the husband had probably spent most of his nights on before the breakup. A fold-up workbench. A set of black iron free weights. Two bowling-ball bags that looked full. A pair of metal file cabinets someone had once painted white, with a brush. A decent assortment of power tools—looked in good condition. Stacks of magazines. A nineteen-inch TV. A mid-range stereo receiver, with matching speakers.

And seven large file boxes of heavy cardboard, designed for transport. They were in two stacks, ready to go.

I grabbed the top one. It was full—had to weigh a good thirty, thirty-five pounds. Inside, nothing but paper. Case files; every single page a photocopy. I leafed through them quickly. As soon as I saw the name "Wychek" a dozen times in thirty seconds, I knew we were home.

Even with the fuel cell and the relocated battery hogging part of the space, there was still enough room in the Plymouth's cavernous trunk for all seven cartons. I kept watch while Max did the loading, the best use of both our skills.

Before I turned off the light to the storage unit, I took a quick glance around. Removing the boxes didn't create a visually empty space—it looked like everything else had been there for a while. I wondered where Sands lived.

I dropped Max and the cartons in front of my building. By the time I'd stashed the Plymouth and walked on back, a quick jerk of Gateman's head told me the Mongol had already gotten them all upstairs.

As I walked in the door to my place, the cell phone chirped in its holster.

"What?"

"They're . . . 'producing' her, is what the lawyer said." Pepper, sounding more like her usual upbeat self.

"When?"

"Today, for sure. Probably not until late afternoon, or even tonight. But it might be quicker. It depends—"

"—on the bus, I know. Look, I'm not going to be there this time. And you shouldn't be, either. *None* of you, understand?"

"Yes."

"As for going out to her house, you—"

"I *got* it," Pepper said, voice edged with annoyance. "We didn't start doing this yesterday, okay? I didn't call for advice; I called to give you some information. Like I said. *I* got it. Now *you* got it."

Max had laid the cartons out on the floor, waiting for me to decide what we were going to do with all the paper inside.

There were a hundred things I wanted to do. But I had this overwhelming feeling of stumbling blind, trying to disarm a bomb in the dark. I knew what my system was telling me. I put my palms together, held them to one side, and laid my cheek against them. Telling Max I needed sleep.

I pointed to my watch, gestured that I wasn't going to be able to make the meet at Mama's. There wasn't enough to tell anyone yet, anyway.

Max scanned my face, a cartographer reading a map. He nodded agreement, signed that Mama would know where to find him, I should leave word when I wanted us all to get together.

I went into the back room, took off my jacket, and . . .

The phone buzzed, somewhere close. I reached out, flipped it open.

"What?"

"It took a bit longer than I anticipated." Davidson's voice. "Longer than it should have. The whole thing . . . Never mind. My client's been released."

"Is she with you?"

"I have no idea where she is. But I thought you and I might profit from a meeting."

"Say where and when."

"My office. ASAP."

"One hour, no more," I promised.

Where I live, most of the light is artificial. Oh, there are windows, but they haven't been cleaned for generations. Even the skylights are encrusted, and the surrounding buildings block off direct sunlight, anyway. I knew it was late, but seeing my watch read 10:44 knocked me back a bit. I'd been out for a long time.

A quick shower and change of clothes and I was on my way. I'd promised an hour, so the car was out of the question. I walked over to the subway on Varick, swiped my Metrocard through the turnstile, and grabbed an uptown 1-9 train. Davidson's building was on Lex, just off Forty-second. The 1-9 is a stone local, but even with the crosstown walk when I got out, I beat the deadline with ten minutes to spare.

All the dull-eyed "security guard" at the front desk in Davidson's office building wanted was for me to sign the register, so he could go back to his mini-TV.

Davidson's office is on the twenty-eighth floor. I took the elevator to nineteen and walked up the rest of the way, on the off-chance that not everyone in the lobby was watching television.

The door to the suite was open. The receptionist's cage was deserted. I walked on back, past where Davidson's own secretary would normally be working. His door was open. So was one of the windows, but the air was still thick with cigar smoke.

"This case is dirt," he greeted me.

"I know it is," I said, taking a seat. "I just don't know how deep it goes."

"Me first," Davidson said. "Once I verified the bond was in place, I was all set to spring her. Then, out of the blue, I get a call from Lansing at the DA's Office. The little fuck tells me they're bringing her down tonight, so I can make an application for bail reduction."

He leaned back, took a deep drag, face dark with anger.

"Then he says, here's the deal: Just make the same application I made before. Ask for something reasonable, like fifty, and his office will *consent* to it."

"Maybe the judge thought it over, had his law secretary make a few discreet calls," I said.

"It's possible, but I think this was their own play. Question is, why?"

"Because they know she didn't do it," I said. "And they're afraid she's going to find out who did."

"Why would they give a damn if . . . ? Wait! You're saying they already know Wolfe wasn't the shooter? Not that they *suspect* it, they *know*?"

"Do I think the skell admitted it wasn't Wolfe who shot him?" I said. "I don't know. But here's what I *do* know. Never mind Wolfe, it's their so-called victim who doesn't want out."

"What the hell are you talking about? How could he admit *anything,* much less ask to stay in the hospital?" Davidson said. "He's in a coma, right?"

"Not anymore, he's not," I said.

Davidson shook his head, like a fighter who had just taken a hard shot but wouldn't go down. "How could you possibly—?"

I told him what Sands had told me, word for word. I can do that. Always could, even when I was a little kid. I would have made a perfect witness against the people who did those things to me. Only, back then, they didn't bring stuff like that into court.

"Christ on a crutch, Burke!" Davidson said, when I was finished. "That's more questions than answers."

"Yeah."

"Those fucking cocksuckers. They didn't say word one about this guy being out of his coma. They just consented to my application for a bail reduction."

"What did you get?"

"Since I knew it was wired, I repeated the ROR app. Bail money's just for showtime now—no reason they couldn't just release her on her own recognizance and be done with it. But instead of just going along quiet, they weasel back with the fifty K.

"The judge looks over at me like somebody should let him in on the joke. So I figured, fuck Lansing and his deals. I say to the judge, If something isn't *real* wrong with the case, how come the DA's Office itself had just dropped their bail demand so radically?

"By now, Hutto's looking at Lansing very strange. Then Lansing goes into a whole speech about needing time to develop their case in full, and since Ms. Wolfe isn't considered a flight risk . . .

"So I immediately start stomping on him like a fucking grape. It was pitiful. Anyway, bottom line, Hutto's off the hook now, so he sets it at the fifty the DA asked for."

"Beautiful."

"And we don't need that bondsman of yours," Davidson said. "That amount, Wolfe put it up herself. In cash, from nice clean assets. That's what took so long: getting the damn paperwork done."

"You've still got your discovery coming," I told him. "And I've got some of my own to do. But so far, everything this Sands has told me has been gospel."

"You want me to run his name past Wolfe?"

"I'd rather ask her myself."

"I don't know if she—"

"Ask her," I said.

The next day I called Big Nate on one of my cells.

"You heard?" I asked him.

"I heard," his amplified voice said. "But—"

"You and me, we're both the same," I said, very softly. "Sometimes, there's things you don't want to do, but you do them, because all the other choices are worse. You were ready to do what you had to do. So was I."

"Yeah. So—we're quits?"

"You'll never see me again," I said, cutting the connection.

I was in my booth when Michelle came in, dressed in that princess/slut style only she can bring off.

She sashayed over and took a seat. Mama was only a few steps behind her, clapping her hands for more soup.

"I took care of it," Michelle said. "Turns out I was right. Anyone tried to hurt Wolfe out there, it would have been a major mistake. I got *that* just off the first phone call.

"Then I found that they'd brought Hortense down from Bedford Hills to testify in some other case. As *if.* So I went out and visited her myself. No problems after that, guaranteed.

"On my way out, I left money on the books for 'Tense. I didn't do the same for Wolfe, just in case anyone was . . ."

"Thanks, honey. You're perfect."

"This is true."

"And Wolfe's already sprung."

"Yes! They dropped that bogus—?"

"No. Not even close. But Wolfe's got friends on the other side, too."

"Sure, friends?" Mama asked.

"Looks like, so far, anyway," I told them. Then I filled them in on what I'd gotten from Sands, and what happened when Davidson went back to court.

"Have you looked through all that paperwork yet, honey?" Michelle asked.

"Just a quick glance. That cop must have spent all night at the photocopier. Took some big-time risks."

"If the stuff's real, he did."

"Wolfe's out," I reminded her. "Soon enough, we'll get a straight answer. And—I had an idea. Remember when we had all that paper, on that girl who got killed out on—?"

"Yes," Michelle interrupted. "You want Terry to scan it all into a computer for you again?"

"That, and maybe do some sorting programs. . . ."

"Well, let's go get him," she said, flashing her gorgeous smile.

"Michelle, he's all grown up now, remember? He drives his own car. We don't need to go all the way up to the Bronx. Why can't he just—?"

"You know why," she said, winking at me.

I'd been out to the Mole's place so many times, my eyes didn't even register the burnt-out buildings, or the burnt-out humans who staggered between them, pipe-dreaming.

They say real estate in the city is so precious that every square inch of it is going to be gentrified someday. If that ever happens in Hunts Point, I'll believe it.

Michelle's cat's-eye makeup didn't mask her excitement. She was going to people she loved.

Terry was her son. I had street-snatched him from a kiddie pimp years ago, and Michelle had adopted him in that same minute. Back then, she was still pre-op, and still working car tricks, fire-walking with freaks every night. Michelle came from the same litter I did. Our hate made us kin.

Michelle had claimed Terry for her own. But it was the Mole— a for-real mad scientist, living in an underground bunker beneath the junkyard he owned—who really raised the kid.

For years, Michelle and the Mole orbited around each other, never touching.

Finally, she had the operation. She had been talking about getting it done for as long as I'd known her, but it wasn't until the Mole became Terry's father that Michelle became his wife. I remember, a long time ago, when she asked the Mole if he could ever understand how it felt, to be a woman trapped in a man's body.

"I understand trapped," is all the Mole said. It was enough.

The surgery didn't change Michelle to any of us. She was always my sister, from the beginning. Always Terry's mother. But maybe it meant something between her and the Mole. I don't know.

The Mole doesn't like to leave his work, and his work isn't portable. Michelle didn't even like *visiting* the junkyard.

None of that mattered.

I pulled up to the entrance, a wall of razor wire, growing like killer ivy through the chain link. The pack of feral dogs that inhabit the place assembled quickly, but I knew the Mole's sensors would have announced us way before I brought the Plymouth to a stop.

The dogs watched, too self-confident to bark, except for a few of the younger ones, who were still learning.

"Looks like Terry's not here, honey," I said. "He would have been out to pick us up in the shuttle by now."

"Then Mole will just have to come himself," she said. "The exercise certainly won't kill him."

Not being clinically insane, I didn't say anything.

Eventually, we spotted the Mole's stubby figure, making his way toward us. He was wearing his usual dirt-colored jumpsuit, Coke-bottle lenses on his glasses catching the late-afternoon sun. He shambled over to the sally port, threw open the first gate, then moved aside to let us through.

I drove the Plymouth in, extra-slow. The Mole locked up behind us.

He came around to my side of the car, standing in the river of killer dogs like a kid in a wading pool.

"Mole!" I said.

He answered me the way he usually does—a few rapid blinks behind his glasses, waiting for me to get to the point.

"We're looking for Terry," I said. I could feel the cold heat from Michelle's ice-pick eyes at the back of my neck, but I knew they weren't aimed at me. Mole had gone to the wrong window, and the poor bastard would have to pay that toll by himself.

"Not here," he said.

"Right. But I've got Michelle with me—"

"Oh," he said.

"—and I thought we could hang out a bit, while we wait for Terry to show."

"Where is that . . . *Jeep* thing you use?" Michelle demanded, over my right shoulder.

"Back at the—"

"Well, go *get* it," she said, tartly. "I'm not going to—"

"I can drive this one back there," I told her, trying to pinch off the burning fuse before it reached the dynamite. "Mole, you want to—?"

But he was already moving. Away from the firing line.

I drove gingerly around the obstacle course of mortar-sized craters and rusted chunks of metal. The Plymouth was no off-roader, but its Viper-donated independent rear suspension and gas shocks handled the trip easily enough. Even the occasional *thunk* didn't upset the rollbar-anchored chassis with its heavy subframe connectors.

I pulled up to the Mole's lanai—a set of cut-down oil drums with haphazard cushions and a sisal mat big enough to play shuffleboard on.

The Mole was waiting for us, sitting down. He was awkwardly smacking a scarred old beast on top of its triangular head, in what the two of them had mutually decided constituted "patting the dog."

"Simba!" I said.

The dog's ears perked, a lot more trustworthy than his ancient eyes. A bull mastiff–shepherd cross, Simba was still the reigning king of the pack, despite being somewhere around twenty years old. "Hound's so bad, probably even scares off Father Time's ass," the Prof said once.

Michelle pranced over on her four-inch ankle-strapped burnt-orange stilettos. She bent to give the Mole a kiss on his cheek, which turned him the same approximate color, and said, "Well?"

The Mole looked at her the way he always does—stunned and strangle-tongued.

"Mole! Aren't you glad to see me?"

"Yes," he said. "I am always—"

"You like my new shoes," Michelle said, torturing him unmercifully, making him pay. Asking the Mole if he liked a pair of shoes was like asking a cat if it liked algebra.

"They are . . . very nice," he tried.

"Nice? *Nice!* They are absolutely *gorgeous,* you dunce! They are stunning. Magnificent. *Perfect.* Yes?"

"Yes. I—"

"Oh, never *mind.*" Michelle probed in her purse, handed the Mole her cell phone. "Call my boy, please," she said. "Tell him we need to see him."

The Mole didn't move.

"You *do* know where he is, don't you?"

"He has a cell phone, too," the Mole said, defensively.

"Well, then?"

"He is still at school. Is this—?"

"Yeah, it kind of is, Mole," I assured him.

While he was dialing, Michelle took out one of her extra-long, ultra-thin cigarettes. Pink was the color of the day, apparently. I lit it for her.

"He's coming," the Mole announced, handing back Michelle's phone.

"What are you working on now?" she asked him.

"A new polymer," the Mole said. "It is—"

"Well, I can't understand all that," Michelle cut him off. "While we're waiting for Terry, you'll just have to *show* me. Come on."

The Mole followed obediently, his face flaming.

I sat down with Simba, and we told each other lies about when we'd been young.

It took Terry over an hour to show up. I took a tenth of that to tell him what I wanted.

"Sure!" he said. "I can do it, easy. The scanning's pretty much mechanical. Take some time, though, even with the setup I've got. But you might want something better than a simple-sort."

"Go slow, kid," I cautioned him. "Remember who you're talking to here."

"I can *write* a program, but you'd have to spell out for me what fields—never mind, just the kind of things you want to *connect*, okay?"

"I'm not sure I'm . . ."

"Look," he said, enthusiastically, "it would be nothing to sort by, say, time of day, or if he used a weapon, like that, see? But if you wanted to make an ANOVA . . . Never mind. If you wanted to know the extent to which different factors impacted on the model . . ."

"*Terry* . . ."

"Okay, wait. I got it. Look, let's say the 'standard' attack was between four and six in the afternoon, and the guy used a knife, all right?

"But in *some* of the attacks he was, I don't know, dressed all in black. Does him dressing in black affect the time of day or the weapon? See? The more . . . factors I have, the more I can help you find the pattern."

"Could you superimpose?" I asked him.

"Now you've got *me* confused," he said, grinning.

"If you had all the addresses where the rapes occurred, could you put a map of the metro area *over* it, somehow?"

"Sure. But what would you want that for?"

"The rapes went down in a lot of different counties. But no one was ever actually arrested, so the different offices probably didn't share information. In fact, I can't figure out where . . . Wolfe's friend got them all. Anyway, maybe there's some main highway that gets him in and out of *all* the areas, so, if you look at where he hits, you might get an idea where he's striking *from,* where his home base is."

"No problem," the kid assured me. "If it's in the data you've got, I'll write a program that will tell you a lot more than what's already on paper, I promise."

"Isn't he a genius?" Michelle said, beaming.

"Pop taught me all of it," Terry quickly disclaimed.

"Well, you certainly didn't get your fashion sense from him," Michelle snapped back. "Or those good looks, either."

"All from you, Mom," Terry said, putting his arm around her. "And a ton more."

The kid was a scientist in his soul. He understood that if a lab ran his DNA, they'd know he hadn't come from the Mole and Michelle. But he knew something else, too. Something we all know down here—some of the truest truths never make the text-books.

On the return trip—Michelle still glowing, humming to herself like a happy little girl—my cell phone buzzed.

"What?"

"She wants to talk to you." Pepper, no-nonsense voice.

"Wherever she—"

"Do you remember the last place you met with her?"

"Yes."

"There."

"When?"

"Soon as you can make it. She's waiting."

As if it had been eavesdropping, the Plymouth's engine answered.

The office building was on lower Broadway, a few blocks north of what outsiders keep calling "ground zero." Since 9/11, you don't want to be bringing a car into that area after dark. Too many eyes.

Last time I'd been there, Mick had been working the lobby desk. Wolfe's crew had some kind of deal with the people who ran the building: they rented out little pieces of it for a few hours at a time.

I tried the front door. Locked. I buzzed for the night man. Not surprised to see Mick, wearing a pair of dark-green pants and matching Eisenhower jacket, with some company's name stitched in gold on the front.

He let me in, relocked the door.

"Same place?" I asked him.

He turned his back on me without answering, walking toward the freight elevator. I followed, got in the car. Mick threw a lever, and the car dropped, slow and noisy.

He let me out in the basement. I heard the door close behind me, so I walked around the corner to where Wolfe had been the last time.

And there she was, sitting on a double-height set of lateral file cabinets. She was dressed in denim overalls and a red pullover, her long, dark hair tied behind her, no makeup.

"Behave!" she said to the Rottweiler, before he could even threaten me.

"You okay?" I asked her.

"You mean the lockup?" she said. "Sure. It's been years since I was putting people away, and *those* ones wouldn't be on Rikers, anyway."

"Yeah," I agreed. Rikers Island was a jail, not a prison. People were sent there to await trial, or to serve misdemeanor sentences. Wolfe hadn't won all her bouts as a prosecutor, but when she landed her Sunday punch, the opponent always went down for the count.

"It doesn't need to be personal," I said. "It's a bad joint. Things happen."

"Something *did* happen," she said, the faintest trace of a smile

on her lips. "A very large woman came up to me while I was waiting on the chow line. In fact, she bulled her way in, right in front
of me.

"I just ignored it—I wasn't going to fight over a place in line.
Then she turned around and spoke to me. Not shouting, exactly,
but loud enough for everyone nearby to hear. 'Honey,' she said,
'don't say a word to me. Not one word. I know you're not about
talking. Just wanted you to know you got friends here. So, if anyone gets stupid with you, all you got to do is point them out. Not
even with your finger. Just nod your head, and it'll be taken care
of.' Wasn't that nice of her?"

"Hortense is a righteous woman," I said. "Always has been."

"I appreciate what you . . . I appreciate what *she* did," Wolfe
said. "But it wasn't me who told Pepper to—"

"Pepper did the right thing, and you know it," I said. "And
Davidson's the right man for the job."

"The *job,*" she repeated, bitterly.

"Look, I know you didn't—"

"Didn't what? Didn't shoot that maggot? *How* do you know?"

"It's not you."

"*What's* not me?" she challenged. "Maybe I read that letter he
sent me, and went over to his house to tell him to step off. Maybe
he got aggressive, and I panicked. Pulled out a gun and shot him.
And then ran."

"Right. As if you'd go to meet a freak like him without backup."

"What if my backup helped me get away?"

"He was shot with a twenty-five."

"Isn't that a woman's gun?" she said, unknowingly echoing
Sands. "And three shots—*sounds* like panic, doesn't it?"

"You don't carry," I said. "And if you did, it wouldn't be a toy
like that one."

"You're so sure?"

"Oh, I'm a lot surer than that," I said. "A person can change
their habits, but not their personality."

"What is that supposed to mean?"

"You don't walk around packing, although I suppose you *could,*
if you thought you had to. But one thing I know you'd never do."

"Shoot?"

"No. Panic."

"Ah," she said, smiling for real now.

"Besides, there's one other thing that seals the deal," I said, pointing at the Rottweiler. "Him. Maybe those little bullets didn't have enough to get the job done, but no way Bruiser didn't."

"You're right," Wolfe said. "*If* I had sent him."

"A situation like that, I don't think he'd give a damn whether you sent him or not," I told her. "He's a dog, not a robot."

"He's also a big bully, aren't you, Bruisey?" Wolfe said, scratching behind the dog's ears. "He gained ten pounds in the few days Pepper had him."

"Pepper probably stuffed him because she felt bad for him," I said. "Besides, she's an actress, so she appreciates a good performance, and he probably went around pretending he was starving."

"Maybe . . ."

"I need to ask you some questions," I said.

"And I need to ask you some," she shot back.

"Go," I told her.

"Why are you in this? *Still* in this, I mean. I know Pepper . . ."

"You want me to tell you a story about my religious conversion? How I'm going to devote the rest of my life to protecting the innocent? You know why. You've always known.

"If you *had* drilled the miserable little fuck, you think that would matter to me? If you didn't have a dozen better ones, I'd be your alibi. And if I had known about him threatening you, this never would have happened at all."

"You're not my protector," she said, eyes narrowed. "Self-appointed or otherwise."

"I'm not anything to you," I told her. "You think I don't know that? But what I do, I'm good at, and you know that, too. Tell me you want me off this thing, and I'll walk out of here right now, never say another word about it."

Wolfe tapped a cigarette from her pack, lit it with a long-flamed butane lighter.

I just stood there, watching her.

The Rottweiler watched me.

Wolfe took a deep drag, blew a jet of smoke at the ceiling. "You're lying," she said.

"Sands, he's for real?" I asked her, finally breaking the silence.

"Molly? He's a piece of gold. When he first made detective, he was assigned to my squad. He *loved* the job. Loved making cases against the dirtbags that my bureau specialized in putting away.

"He didn't come with any bullshit cop prejudices. Or, if he did, he left them at the door. He *got* it, right from the start. In my shop, we didn't play the 'good victim, bad victim' game. If a hooker got raped, if a retarded girl got molested—same as if it were a nun, or a Mensa member. He was a real man on the DV stuff, too. And cold death on child molesters."

Wolfe took a hit off her cigarette, gray gunfighter's eyes watching me through the smoke. When I kept quiet, she picked up her own thread.

"Molly *worked* his cases. Double- and triple-checked everything. Turned over every rock. He never played TV detective on the stand, never tried to out-cute the defense. But there wasn't one jury that didn't *believe* him.

"And then the job broke his heart," Wolfe said, her voice thick with sadness. "When they fired me, everything changed. All they wanted was stats.

"You know what that means. Some of the 'shaky' cases don't get pursued, so you never get the chance to make them solid. The last thing they needed was a cop like Molly. He went from thinking he was a soldier in a holy war to feeling like a report-writing fake."

"That's when he started the heavy drinking?" I asked.

"When he went back to it, yeah," she said, her eyes daring me to make judgments.

"You know he had copies of every single one of Wychek's cases. *Possible* cases, I mean. Every case in which Wychek was a suspect."

"I'm not surprised."

"I can't even figure out where he *got* all that stuff from. There never was a 'task force' thing, right?"

"Right," Wolfe said, disgustedly. "Wychek was a classic pattern-rapist, but he stayed so far off the screen that he never even got himself a press nickname. You know, a 'Night Stalker' kind of thing. No media pressure, no task force; simple as that. But we were working him, preparing for trial, and we grabbed every scrap we could get our hands on. After the trial, the whole package must have gone into dead storage."

"Still, if they ever found out he was making copies—"

"They won't," she said, flatly.

"He got other stuff, too," I said. "The most important thing of all, in fact. Davidson told you—?"

"That Wychek's not in a coma anymore? And that he doesn't want to leave the hospital? Yes."

"So the DA *knows* it wasn't you, no matter what bullshit 'statement' Wychek supposedly made, am I right?"

"How does that compute?"

"Come *on*. Wychek believes you've got a hit squad out looking for him? No way the DA buys that. There has to be another reason for them playing along. You got anything on them?"

"On City-Wide? Sure, there's stuff they wouldn't want to get out. Sexual harassment—not pressure to have sex; trading sex for promotion—stuff like that."

"That's not sexual harassment," I said. "That's a whore and a trick."

"Not alw— Never mind, it's not important. Not right now. Anything else I know—politicians' kids getting guaranteed jobs over better-qualified applicants, special treatment for celebrity defendants, ADAs being pushed to work in re-election campaigns, how a judge gets 'made' in this town—everybody else knows, too.

"Sure, I've made them look like the clowns they are a few times over the years. But if they went after everyone who's done *that,* they'd have to frame more people than they've got cells."

"So, if the answer isn't you, there's only one other thing it could be," I said.

"What?"

"Wychek," I told her. "It's not you they want. It's him."

In the next hour, we held everything we knew up to the brightest light we could find—a pair of diamond-cutters, looking for the perfect place to start our work.

But all we found were flaws.

"What in hell could a lowlife piece of garbage like Wychek do for the DA's Office?" I asked the empty air.

"Maybe they *do* believe him?" Wolfe said, dubiously.

"What if they did?" I put it to her. "What if they actually fucking believed you put a few rounds into that freak? They reserve the kind of protection they're giving him for witnesses who can take down a mob boss or the head of a drug cartel. You *sure* you haven't been working anything that could blow up all over them if it came out?"

"Nothing," Wolfe said, with an undertone of regret. "I haven't worked a real investigation in years. You know the kind of stuff I do now."

"Yeah," I agreed. "But you deal in information. . . ."

"You think I didn't go over that in my mind a thousand times since they grabbed me?" she said. "And, trust me, that was *hard* work. Lockup's supposed to be good for deep thinking, but the noise level is ungodly. And it never stops. You'd need the concentration of a yoga master just to read a newspaper in there."

"You think your friend would do you another favor?"

"Molly? He'd do anything," she said, confidently.

"Could he find out where they're keeping Wychek?"

"Forget it, Burke," she snapped out at me. "What are you going to do, put on a white coat and go visit him in the hospital?"

"I wouldn't do anything like that," I said, meaning it. I'd never been past the ninth grade, on paper, but I was always a great reader. And I had a working felon's functional knowledge of the law. Slipping a little good-bye juice into that freak's IV drip would bother me about as much as an Osama bin Laden heart attack, but it would only make Wolfe a bigger suspect.

"Never mind," she told me. "I don't need any help. Sooner or later, the prosecution is going to have to answer the discovery motions. We get a TPO, that's the end of their case."

"We already know the place. So you're telling me, even if the time of occurrence turns out to be four in the morning, you're covered, no matter what night it was."

"At that hour, I'd be asleep," she said, gray eyes level.

"That's not an iron-clad—"

"Not alone," she said.

"**S**omeone down here, boss. Asking for you. By name."

"Good-looking young guy, light-brown hair, brown eyes, says he's Terry?"

"Bull's-eye."

"Let him pass, okay? Thanks, Gateman."

"**D**amn, boy! What they feeding you at that fancy college? You must have growed half a foot since I last saw you!" the Prof greeted Terry as the kid stepped into my place.

"Hey, Prof!" the kid said, giving the little man a hug. He shook hands with Clarence almost formally, then turned to me. "Can I get a hand with some of my stuff? Pop dropped me off, but I couldn't carry it all up myself. The guy downstairs, the one in the wheelchair, he said it would be safe down there with him. . . ."

"Oh, Gateman's clue is true," the Prof assured him. "Man can't stand, but he can stand *up,* you with me?"

"Sure, but . . ."

"Plus, he can outdraw Billy the fucking Kid, he has to. That's not trash, that's cash. You underestimate the Gateman, you gonna choke on the joke, boy."

"I will come with you, mahn," Clarence told Terry, realizing the Prof would maintain the debate about the absolute security of Gateman's domain for hours rather than spend ten minutes lugging heavy equipment up the stairs.

Terry took over one of the back rooms, and instantly drafted Clarence into assisting him. When they started talking a language the Prof and I didn't understand, we strolled into the front room.

"Have a smoke with me, son?"

This was a real role reversal for the Prof. Ever since I was a kid, his idea of smoking was to smoke one of mine. The little man had hands faster than a cobra on crystal meth—he could usually get to my own shirt pocket before I could, even though he always gave me the first move.

But ever since I was shot, I haven't really smoked. It's not religious, and it's not about health. Cigarettes just don't taste like they used to. A lot of things don't.

I still always carry a pack or two, and I'll have one once in a while. Sometimes, it's to remind people that it's really me. The Burke they knew always smoked, and, with the new face, I'd had to work hard at convincing some people when I'd first come back. Sometimes, it's misdirection. Like the way I drink. I order a shot of vodka with ice water on the side, and swallow the water, leaving just the ice cubes. Then I dump the vodka into the water glass, and let it melt out. When the bartender brings me a refill, the money I let ride on the counter automatically brings me fresh water, too.

Now, sometimes when I'm with an old friend, it just feels . . . companionable to share a smoke. A cigarette tastes pretty good then.

I took the Prof's pack of Kools, still the favorite behind the Walls, and nodded approvingly at the lack of a New York tax stamp. I fired one up, handed him the still-burning wooden match so he could light his own.

As if the Kool brought back old memories, the Prof leaned way back in his wooden chair, balancing on its two rear legs, and said, "You know, back in the day, it never would have gotten this far. Skinner like that one, somebody would have shanked him on the yard, just for the practice."

"Maybe he did it all in PC."

"Punk City's the right place for a fucking freak like him. But, you know, somebody wanted him bad enough, they could do him in there. Remember when Wesley—"

"Yeah."

"Unless he was a *real* badass, maybe?" the Prof mused. "Big enough to run a wing by himself."

"Wolfe says he's about five-eight, a hundred and forty pounds, and flabby at that. 'A chinless, beady-eyed little weasel-faced punk,' I think she called him."

"My girl probably nailed how he look, but that don't say nothing about how he cook," the Prof said, solemnly. "She don't know the show, Schoolboy. Not like we do. We both done time with guys, look like they couldn't break glass, but bad enough to make a gorilla kiss their ass, right?"

I nodded. It was true. There are some men who can turn your spine to water with a look. But I had seen those same men drop their eyes whenever Wesley came down the corridor.

"You gave me an idea, though, Prof. A place to get started. Be right back."

Terry and Clarence were meshing like Formula One gears, paper flying from the stacked cartons to a long table. A giant scanner rested on its surface, cable-linked to a laptop computer with all kinds of wires running out of its back.

"You guys run across anything about Wychek's prison record?" I asked.

"We have his . . . Where is that . . . *Yeah!*" Terry said. "Is this what you mean?"

"No. That'll show he was committed, but not where he landed. We know he went Upstate somewhere, but not which institution. That's what we're looking for."

"If it is in here, we will find it, mahn," Clarence promised.

"There's an easier way," Terry said. "New York State's got a Web site for it. 'Inmate Lookup Service,' or something like that. All we need is a guy's name and we can get his prison record."

"You mean his whole rap sheet?" I asked.

"No, no, I mean, his . . . 'institutional status,' I think they call it. Where he's being kept, what his sentence is, when he sees the parole board . . ."

"But Wychek's out," I reminded him.

"Sure. They'll show him as 'discharged.' But they'll still have the place he was discharged *from,* see?"

"Damn."

"Sure. We just need a phone line. A landline," he said, quickly, before I could offer him one of my cells.

"Not up here, kid."

"What about the man downstairs?"

"Gateman? Sure, he's wired up. But won't you need—?"

"This is enough," Terry said, holding up a laptop and some cords. "I'll tell him you said it was okay, right?"

"Right."

"Come on," Terry said to Clarence. The two of them took off, Wally and the Beaver, on an adventure.

"It was just like Terry said, mahn," Clarence exclaimed, deeply impressed. "Only took maybe fifteen minutes and we got all the—"

"It would have taken a lot less than that if your friend downstairs had anything but a molasses dial-up," Terry cut in. "I'm not nuts about the DSL they've got around here, but—"

"Yeah," I said. "Well, when I'm ready for stuff like that, you'll be the first to know."

"*I* am ready, mahn," Clarence announced. "There is so much . . . value in it. Tell Burke and my father how you knew there was this place to find information about prisoners," he said to Terry.

"It's not such a . . ."

"Come on with it," the Prof urged him. "If my son says it's fun, I got to know how it's done."

"Well," Terry said, sitting down, "there was this girl. At school." He saw me exchanging looks with the Prof, said, "Not *my* girl. I wasn't . . . interested in her like that. She was . . . my friend. Anyway, Tatrine's very socially active. Mostly green stuff, but she never saw a cause she didn't like.

"She met this guy at a teach-in she went to. It was all about prison conditions. This guy, he told her that he was an ex-con, right up front. Tatrine, she treated it like it was a credential. . . ."

Terry caught himself, turning red as he realized who he was talking to. And where his mother had spent some of her youth. "I didn't mean it . . . I didn't mean it was a . . . bad thing, all by itself. Just . . . what you always say, Prof."

"Only thing that's true is what you do," the Prof acknowledged. "The Walls don't make the calls."

"Right. So, anyway, Tatrine was getting all caught up in this guy. I mean, *quoting* him, like he was an oracle or something. It made me nervous. So I asked her, just casual one day, what had he done time for.

"Tatrine said it had been an armed robbery. This guy—her boyfriend by then, I guess—said he had done it when he was, you ready for this, 'pre–socially conscious.' He had some half-baked idea that the merchant was ripping off the community, so he figured he'd do a little justice by stealing from him.

"He told her he came to realize later that the merchant was part of a system, pre-programmed to act a certain way, and robbing him wasn't the right thing to do. Tatrine told me this guy, he was a 'change-agent' now."

"You didn't buy his riff, so you thought you'd take a sniff?" the Prof said, nodding.

"It . . . I don't know how to explain this, exactly. Mom says, sometimes, when people talk, you just *know* they're wrong. Not about the facts—I mean they're wrong *people*. I never heard him talk myself, but, even secondhand from Tatrine, I was . . .

"So I poked around until I found the Web site. And I put in his name. There were actually four guys with the same name in their system, but one was still incarcerated, and the other two were white, so they couldn't be him. His date of birth sounded about right, from the way Tatrine described him, too.

"But it wasn't any armed robbery he'd been sent away for. It was sodomy in the second degree. I looked that one up, too. The only way he could have been convicted of that is if the victim couldn't consent because they were drunk, or drugged, or . . ."

"Or a kid," I finished for him.

"Yeah," he said, teeth clenched.

"You showed this all to Tatrine?"

"Yeah."

"And she didn't believe you?"

"Not . . . not at first. After a while, she did, I know."

"How?"

"Because she came over to where I was sitting, in the library, and asked me to come outside. She told me I had been right. About her . . . about him, I mean. He admitted it. He told her the whole thing had been a pack of lies, cooked up by his little step-sister, because she resented her mother's new husband. That was his father—they were all living together.

"He told Tatrine he had pleaded guilty—he must have thought she knew more than she really did—because they promised him only a four-year max. And he couldn't take a chance on a jury believing the little liar; then they might have put him away forever.

"He said he never told people about it because they wouldn't understand. He wasn't ashamed of being in prison, but he knew nobody would ever give him a chance to tell his side of the story."

"But Tatrine did, huh?" I said, reading his face.

"Yeah."

And you wanted to tell her a few things yourself, didn't you, kid? I thought, into the silence.

"How did it end up?" Clarence asked. Obviously, he had only heard the beginning of the story.

"I don't know," Terry said, not hearing the desolation in his own voice. "I see Tatrine around campus once in a while. But she never comes anywhere near me. And the number I had for her— it's no good anymore."

Three nights later. The trackdown I was working on was taking a lot longer than I had expected. I knew that the woman I was looking for had to be somewhere in New York State. And that she owned a house, most likely in a rural area.

But what I really needed was a phone number. When I have to approach people who knew my old face, voice contact is the smartest first move.

Any other time, I would have gone to Wolfe's network. But I figured they wouldn't be operational, not with all this hanging over her.

I couldn't see the DA's Office investing in full-time surveillance, and I didn't think anyone they had was good enough to shadow Wolfe without her picking it up, anyway. But I wanted to be sure I was the first one to see whatever got turned up.

The phone made its noise.

"What?" I said.

"Hi, chief!" Pepper, almost back to full bounce. "Got time to meet with an old friend?"

"If it's a good enough friend, I've always got the time."

"Great! She's a very good friend, but not an old one. In fact, you just met her recently."

"Is there going to be anyone else there?"

"Oh, *no*," Pepper said. "You know how third wheels always spoil dates."

"Right. Same place?"

"No. She'll be at the message center—say, eleven?"

"Do you really think that's an appropriate spot?"

"Why not?" Pepper said, a faint giggle under her voice. "It's a nice, intimate little place. And you can decide where you want to go from there."

"Eleven," I promised.

"Okey-dokey," she said.

I admired Pepper's professionalism. Even if there *was* a wire-tap order—which was way past unlikely—and even if they some-how knew which phone Pepper was using that night, nothing in our conversation would tell a listener that my date for the night was named Molly.

I started to make myself some soup, and sat down to think things through.

A few years back, Max and I were sitting in my booth at Mama's. It was late afternoon, and we had already spent hours handicapping the night's races at Yonkers. Mama had finally lost her patience. If we had been playing cards, she would have been fine with it. Mama loves gambling, but betting on horses always struck her as downright degenerate.

"No work today, right?" she demanded.

"We're waiting, Mama," I explained, for the fourth time. "We can't go to work until tonight."

"Work for making money. What you do, you lose money. Big circle, no end."

Max hotly defended our two-man gambling syndicate, pulling out his notebook, with our fully documented record for the year to date. We had wagered a total of six thousand four hundred and twenty dollars, and had a solid sixty-five hundred in the kitty.

"So?" Mama sneered, profoundly unimpressed. "You not *lose* money, not lose money *yet* anyway. What is that? Just—how you say it?—big . . . hobby. Men always have hobby. Woman's hobby is work."

"We *are* working, Mama. It's just not time yet to—"

"Sure, sure. Okay for you, Burke. You have no wife," she said, adding a new accusation to her endless list. "And no baby. But *you,*" she said, pointing a gun-barrel finger at Max, "no excuse."

When Immaculata first came into Max's life, Mama dismissed her as a "bar girl," a wide-ranging insult that could mean just about anything. But a nanosecond after Max announced he was going to be a father, Immaculata went from no-status to goddess in Mama's eyes. And ever since, Mama had been pounding Max's blessed fortune in finding such a perfect woman into his head.

Max spread his hands, put a "What the hell did *I* do?" expression on his face.

"You know how cook? Make food?" Mama asked, miming the question as she spoke.

Max made a stirring motion with his fist.

"What you make?" Mama demanded.

Max sipped from an imaginary spoon.

"Soup? You make soup?"

Max grinned, gesturing a man opening a can, pouring into a pot, turning on a stove, stirring.

"That not *make* soup. In kitchen, here, *make* soup. Where you get soup?"

Max gestured his way into a grocery store.

"So! You not *make* soup, you *buy* soup, right?"

Max nodded, glumly.

"What you get soup with? *Money*. How you get money? *Work*. Not play games, work. Okay?"

Max and I decided we'd start a little early that evening.

Now I waited for the soup to warm up on my hotplate. It had come from a container I keep in the refrigerator. Mama's soup, sure. But at least it wasn't from a can.

The "message center" is a basement poolroom, in a building no reputation could be low enough to live up to. Inside, it's like the Fifties never went away. They've got a few top-shelf tables—all heavy, carved wood, with green felt and leather pockets. Lights suspended from the ceiling on long chains hang over the tables; overhead wires are strung with beads, for scorekeeping. It's no Julian's, but not even Julian's is, anymore.

The guy who runs the joint has been an old man since I was a kid. Rumor has it that he was a pro once, but nobody's ever seen him pick up a stick. He keeps the tables beautifully maintained—

tight, grippy cloth, fresh rails, and dead level. But that's strictly a labor of love; people who come to his basement mostly don't give a damn.

The old man is a human telegraph machine. You drop your money in the slot, you send a message. Someone wants to reach out for you, they do the same.

There are other services, too. I have my own cue, a custom job. It was built back before they used special breaking cues for nine-ball. Weighed in at a svelte thirty-two ounces even before I wrapped the butt end in several layers of friction tape. Like all of the good ones, it unscrews in the middle.

But mine has another feature, a little compartment in the fat end. If you know which cue is mine, you come in and ask the old man to rent number thirteen, and he hands it to you . . . after you put up a thousand-dollar deposit.

When you're done playing with my cue, you bring it back. The old man gives you nine hundred and fifty bucks, and removes your message. And whenever I drift down to the basement, I can read whatever you paid the half-century to write down for me . . . after I pay the old man the storage fee that's always past due.

The system is no good for emergencies, and everyone knows it. Even telling the old man direct is only going to work if I call in. He won't *make* calls, not for any kind of money. Not to *anybody,* which is why he's been in business so long.

The poolroom may have regulars—I don't go there enough to know—but it's not Cheers. Greeting anyone coming in by name would be a mistake, one the old man never makes.

I got there around ten, ransomed my cue, and pointed at one of the two tables that are set at opposite ends of the basement, each in a separate corner. I walked over, took the triangular RESERVED sign off the felt, and started knocking the balls around, getting the feel.

If I'd taken any table but one of the two corner ones, sooner or later someone would have drifted over, asked me if I wanted to play something for something. But everyone knew what the corner tables were for. You rent those, too.

It only took a few minutes for me to realize that it wasn't just a case of me being rusty—I wasn't the same, and I never would be. My eyes aren't just two different colors now—they don't work as a team anymore. When you lose binocular vision, you lose depth perception, too. Not such a big deal driving a car—which is why they'll give a one-eyed man a license—but you'll never get work threading needles.

I tell myself that I'm a man who doesn't mourn his losses, just cherishes his memories. Sometimes, that's the truth. And sometimes, when I think of Pansy, or of Belle, it's a lie.

If you believe only a crazy man would miss a dog and a woman with equal pain, you don't know what love-driven loyalty means to our tribe. Or what we'll do for it. Do to *you,* if you get in its way.

I couldn't ever hope to find the cops who shot Belle. Anyway, that hadn't been personal. She had drawn their fire on purpose, to keep them off me, out-driving the whole pack of them, heading for the junkyard. She won that race, but it was her last one. I found her, riddled, hanging on until I could get there and tell her I loved her. The only time I ever did.

Belle's mother was her sister. She had sent Belle running when her father put Belle next on his list. Belle was still running when I met her. A pro getaway driver, as good behind the wheel as any I had ever known. When she put her heart in my hands, she put her trust in me, too.

After she left me, what I had to do was written as clear and clean as her love had been. I found her father, and I killed him.

Years later, people who'd been paid to cancel my ticket set up an ambush. They sprung their trap on me, never expecting a hell-hound to come charging out of the trunk of my car. By the time Pansy had ripped out the throat of one of them, they were shooting in self-defense.

As soon as I escaped from the hospital, I went looking for them. That took a lot longer, because I didn't know who they were. But I found them. When I did, the pain didn't stop. But it changed.

I'll never truly know if I'd done all that for them, or for me. Not for sure. What I did know is, they wouldn't have cared.

You're here now, I said in my mind. *Get what you came for.*

I didn't concentrate on pocketing balls, only worked the white one, focusing on my stroke. I was just starting to feel okay about my draw when Molly Sands came downstairs.

It only took a second for his cop's eyes to pick me out. It took less than that for everyone else there to make him for what he was.

"A little nine-ball?" I asked him.

"Eight-ball's my game," he said. "And I'm used to smaller tables."

Bar tables, I thought, keeping it off my face. "Sure," I said. "I'll rack them, you break."

Sands was an appalling player. He managed to pocket a solid, then muffed an easy shot on the three ball.

"What's new?" I asked him, as I chalked up.

"The techs got a good look at the slugs."

"And?"

"They can't tell for sure, without a barrel to match them to, but the guy they have in charge says he'd bet a year's pay it didn't come from any cheap piece. He says you can always tell the work-manship, and whatever the shooter was using was quality."

"Doesn't mean much," I said, pocketing the ten in the corner, then deliberately blowing a shot on the fifteen.

"Well, a gangbanger might use a cheap-ass twenty-five—in some neighborhoods, they sell them like hot dogs. But a baby cal-iber in a *good* gun, that's something a pro might use."

"A twenty-two, sure," I agreed. "They hit hard enough, if you place them perfect. But a twenty-five? Never heard of it."

"I did," Sands said. "After I checked around, I heard of some-thing even smaller, too. Beretta used to make a twenty-two *short.* Smaller than a twenty-five. The whole piece, I mean, not just the bullet. Fucking *tiny.* The gun guy I spoke with even said it was called an 'assassin's special.' Mossad used to use it, all the time."

"Mossad? Yeah, I'm so fucking sure. Every gun nut around has got a Mossad story, but you're grasping at straws with this one, pal."

"Is that right?" he demanded, face flushing in the overhead lights. "How can you be so positive? You take subsonic ammo, put a silencer on the piece, you could probably do someone in church, nobody'd even look up from praying. And, remember, the shooter picked up his brass; that's a pro touch."

"You're riding the wrong bus," I said. "A pro wouldn't use a bullet like that anywhere but a head shot. Never mind fucking Mossad, okay? Caliber like that, *those* guys would have gone for a triple-tap. Unless you're saying the ammo was tipped?"

"No, it was all hardball."

"No hollowpoints, no cyanide for a make-sure, and no head shots. Plus, whoever tried to do him didn't stay around long enough to finish the job. Yeah, you're right—a professional assassin would be my first guess, too."

"They could have heard someone coming," he said, lamely.

"Not from the way you laid it out the first time. Anyway, we both know, someone walks into the middle of a pro hit, there would have been one more body."

Despite my best efforts, I won the first two racks.

"You want a beer?" I asked him.

"You know a place?"

"I can get you one here. The old man at the desk will part with a bottle or two. No hard stuff, though."

"Yeah," he said. "A beer would go good."

I left him at the table, scored two icy bottles of Rogue Ale from the old man—it's the only brand he carries, so I figure it's what he drinks himself.

"Here you go," I said, handing him a brown glass twenty-two-ouncer and a church key. I put the other, unopened, on a stool.

"Thanks," he said. Then, "They moved him."

"To where?"

He gave me a cop look, said, "I don't think so."

"But not a hospital?"

"Right. Not a hospital."

"And not in a lockup?"

"He's the victim," Sands said, face set in rigid lines.

"You came a long way if this is all you want to tell me," I said, pocketing the thirteen and drawing into position on the eight. "Across the side."

I banked it in.

"Nice shot," Sands said. "I'll rack."

"Make sure you get it tight," I said, coming over to where he was standing.

"He's added a lot of details," Sands said. His voice was pitched so low I had to lean close to pick it up. "Nothing that you could prove wrong. He had plenty of chances to eyeball her during the trial."

"What details, then?"

"What she's supposed to have said, like that."

"So he's staying with his story, that's what you came to tell me?"

"It's a good story," Sands said. "Got to be. Where they're keeping him, how they're doing it, they're spending real money."

"A story about . . . her?"

"That's the part I don't know," he said. "Not yet."

We kept playing. I could see he was deciding whether he could part with another card he was holding. That gun stuff he'd told me was no big deal. We'd get it ourselves—from the discovery motions—sooner or later. All that "Mossad" bilge was a Hail Mary, and he knew it.

I don't know what Wolfe had told him about me, or what he had picked out of the whisper-stream himself. Either way, he wasn't about to tell me where the only living witness who could connect Wolfe to a crime was holed up.

Maybe it was him finally winning a game; maybe it was him knowing that the second beer was also the last. As I racked the balls, he stood very close to me, whispered, "He's got a sister."

"You think she might have—?"

"No," he said. "She was the one who found him."

"That doesn't mean—"

"It wasn't her," Sands said. Since he was ready to blame mythical Israeli assassins based on nothing more than gun-show gossip, I figured he had truly spectacular reasons for excluding the sister, but I didn't press it.

"She'll surface, sooner or later," I said.

"Not till trial, if it goes that far."

"She's a witness. The DA has to—"

"Maybe. Maybe not."

"Let me guess. She's married, doesn't have the same name as him."

"Bingo."

"That's the kind of thing a good PI could dig up on his own," I said, reassuringly.

"You think I'm worried about—?"

"I think you *should* be," I said. "Sometimes, it's a good precaution to change the combination on your lock, just in case the wrong person might have picked up on it."

He regarded me for a long few seconds. Not trying to stare me down, or even read me. My face was just something for him to focus on while he made up his mind.

"Laura W. Reinhardt," he said, very softly, then dropped his voice even more as he spelled her name and delivered her address.

AYW Enterprises," Mick answered the phone.

"I know it's late," I said. "But can you and your partner drop over for a few minutes?"

Was it worthwhile, chief?" Pepper asked, an hour later.

"He had a lot," I told her. "But a piece of it has to be *worked*, okay? I don't want to ask Wolfe, but I don't want to farm it out, either."

"I don't know. . . ."

"Look, Pepper, here's the deal. Sands found out the witness's name. It's Wychek's sister."

"Oh!"

"Yeah. And that's all I got: her name, and an address. I figure I only get one shot at her, and I don't want to go in blind."

"So you want our . . . you want us to do a background for you, but you don't want *her* to know?"

"Right," I said. We both knew the "her" Pepper was talking about wasn't Wychek's sister.

"What difference would it make if we told—?"

"I know how Davidson works," I said, catching Mick looking at me out of the corner of my eye. His face was its usual stone slab. "If he gets the right ADA—not a PR guy like Lansing, whoever's going to get stuck actually trying this turkey of a case—he'll walk Wolfe in there and offer to let them polygraph her."

"Why?" Mick demanded.

"Because, one, he knows she'll pass. Two, he'd have a deal in hand—she passes, they drop the case and start looking for the real shooter. A good ADA would turn around and ask Wychek if *he* wants to try the lie box. See?"

"So what does having us do the background on the sister have to do with that?"

"They're not going to let Wolfe pick her own polygrapher. I'm not saying their guy would be dishonest, but he might not be top drawer. If Wolfe knows about the sister's ID before she's supposed to, that's too much 'guilty knowledge.' She might bounce the needles over to 'inconclusive.' No good."

"Why would knowing that make her feel guilty?" Mick asked.

"Not about herself," I said. "About Sands."

They exchanged a quick look.

"Give us what you have," Pepper said.

Two days later, I was ready to make a move. I picked mid-morning for the call, when someone was most likely to be awake and alert. And not easily spooked.

"It's me, Helene," I said. "Do you recognize my voice?"

"I . . . think so."

"It's been a long time since I visited," I said. "When you had that little apartment over in Ridgewood."

"It's coming back to me, maybe," she said, cautiously.

"That was when you were looking for financing, to buy your house. I'm an old friend of your husband's, and he had asked me to look into one of the possibilities."

"Uh-huh."

"Anyway, I'm going to be in the neighborhood, and I thought I'd drop in to see your husband."

"I'm sure he'd like that."

"Only thing, I know his company runs a tight ship, and I want to make sure I can get past security. My name wouldn't be on the approved list."

"I see. Well, as a matter of fact, I have to run over to his office later today, and I'll ask him to take care of that. But, you know, his company does a rather extensive background check, Mr. : . ."

"Haywood," I told her. "Robert Lee Haywood."

"Oh, of *course!*" she said. "How *are* you?"

"Terrific," I assured her. "Still living in Yonkers. Still working as a paralegal, self-employed."

"I know I have that address around here somewhere. . . ."

"Oh, don't trouble yourself," I said. "Let me give you all the info, so you can update your Rolodex."

Helene's husband was a man called Silver. Him and me went back. Far and deep. The Prof had sent me to him a long time ago, when we were all Inside.

"Listen and learn, Schoolboy," he said. "Silver knows the play, the old way, see? He's a quality thief. Good gunfighter, too, way I heard it."

"A hit man?"

"No, fool. I said gunfighter, not gunman."

"What's the difference?"

"A gunfighter, the other guy's shooting back."

We were talking quietly on the yard, Silver telling me a secret in his hard-sad voice. "I don't mess with the sissies in here. They're like bitches on the street, get you into a knife fight in a minute. My wife's picture's in my house—I jack off to it every night, looking at her. These other guys, they do it to girls in the skin magazines. Those ain't real people—they don't know those girls. Me, I'm making love to my wife. To Helene. Those other guys, they're just playing with themselves."

Silver did his time, counting the days. Never made trouble for anyone.

One bleak day, someone went in his cell and stole his wife's picture. Anyone could have done it; prison's like that. If the thief hadn't turned out to be a black guy, Silver might have turned out different himself.

The Prof tried to ease it down. Told Silver it was just a picture—his wife would send him another one. Told the thief, a rapist named Horace, that he was risking a shank in the back for nothing. Even volunteered to handle the transfer himself. Horace had a better way, he thought. Got himself an African name, joined some crew.

A few weeks later, I filled out a pass for Horace to report to the psychiatrist—he thought he was going to score some meds. Silver was waiting for him in the corridor.

Silver got cut. Horace got dead.

Their blood on the institutional-green concrete walls dried to an abstract even the guards could interpret. Every con in the place knew what was coming next.

When Horace's crew moved on Silver, he went the only place he could. And he'd been with the Brotherhood ever since.

That was another reason I'd never turned over the search for Helene's number to Wolfe's crew—her address wasn't information I wanted them to have. It all went back to when Wolfe was still a prosecutor. We were both hunters then—Wolfe for justice, me for cash—and our paths would cross every once in a while.

One of those times, it was because a baby had disappeared. Rats dug up his body. When Wolfe announced the name of the man they were looking for, the whole city cheered her on. But when Wolfe said she wasn't going to let the baby's mother—and the killer's girlfriend—play Hedda Nussbaum, some of the domestic-violence "support" groups had turned on her, working themselves into a knee-jerk "You're blaming the victim!" froth.

The smart money was that Wolfe had overplayed her hand, especially because the girlfriend was all she had—the killer wasn't in custody, whereabouts unknown.

I ended up in that one. So deep that I came away with a debt of my own.

The killer's name was Emerson. They finally grabbed him, hanging around outside a Welfare center. He was waiting for another woman to come out and turn over the check that was supposed to feed her children. The judge remanded him, and they shipped him to Rikers.

Silver had a stash, one he couldn't get to. Money Helene needed to buy a house, be near him to the end. I got that done.

The day that Silver said he owed me forever for that, I was visiting him on the Rock, dressed up in a lawyer suit. I showed Silver a mug shot. Whispered Emerson's name, as I slid my thumbnail across the throat of the baby-killer's picture.

Silver moved his head a couple of inches.

Emerson never went to trial.

I hadn't seen Silver since.

When I called Helene back, she was friendly but brisk.

"My husband would love to see you again," she said. "I know he had retained a new attorney to work on his appeal, but I had no idea you'd end up being on the case, too, Robert."

"Well, this way, you know he'll get the best possible effort," I said.

"He deserves it," Helene said, sadly.

"Robert Lee Haywood?" Davidson said. "Sounds like you should be from Mississippi, not Manhattan."

"That's where my daddy's from," I told him, straight-faced.

"I see. And how long will I have to be 'representing' this Silver guy?"

"Long as you want. I only need to see him the one time."

"And you do not want me to mention this to my client, for some reason?"

"A good reason," I said. "Trust me."

Davidson gave me a look, but he signed the papers.

The next morning, I drove out to the Delta parking lot at La Guardia, walked through the terminal, and then grabbed the shuttle to Hertz.

Robert Lee Haywood's Visa card didn't draw a second glance from the energetic young woman at the counter. She was too busy telling me that they had this wonderful plan where I could have reserved a car in advance, so it would have been waiting for me.

"Yeah," I said. "I remember those O. J. Simpson commercials."

She gave me a look way too blank to be hostile, then went right back into her spiel, pitching me more options than a high-class whorehouse. We finally settled on a Cadillac, once she checked her computer and told me that they had a dark-blue STS model on the lot.

I took the Whitestone Bridge to the Bronx, grabbed I-95, and headed north.

I always drive on a risk-gain system. If I'm not in a hurry, I don't speed. And if I speed, I don't play around. So I set the cruise control to 70, let the radio's station-finder take me to a moron-hosted talk show, and zoned out.

Terry and Clarence hadn't finished scanning every scrap of paper Sands had photocopied into their computer. But they'd had no trouble pulling out all the institutional stops Wychek had made. As soon as they told me he had done some of his time in Dannemora—they call it "Clinton" now—I had started looking for Helene.

Blacks hate doing time out in the boonies. Not just because it's such a long trip for their families to visit, but because the guard population is all local—which means pretty much all-white. For a man with Silver's brand, it was a better joint than one of the downstate gladiator schools. Quieter, easier to do long time in.

And Helene's house was close enough for her to come every visiting day.

I could tell Silver had stamped his personality on the place by the way the guards dealt with me. Davidson had called them in advance—"Never hurts to be courteous," he'd said—and they knew who I was coming to see. They couldn't have been more polite, even during the obligatory run through the metal detector and cursory search of my attaché case. I returned the favor.

They brought Silver down to the conference room, and left us alone. We did a simultaneous double-take.

I had forgotten how some guys don't age in prison. You'd think the environment would turn them all into old men, real quick. But for some of them, it's a goddamned tonic. Regular exercise, the right food—which means the right connections—and that slow-speed life-style you fall into there. Guys who wouldn't take a shower but once a month on the outside would spend hours on daily personal grooming. Men who never glanced past the sports pages on the bricks would read a newspaper cover to cover. The longer it took to do *anything*, the faster time passed. Once you understood that, you were a convict.

Silver didn't look a day older than when I'd last seen him. And, for the face I was wearing now, there hadn't *been* a last time for Silver.

"I was expecting another guy," he said, across from me.

"You were expecting the guy Helene spoke to on the phone," I told him, keeping my voice down. And, I hoped, familiar.

"Huh!" he said, pulling his head back a little.

"The Prof sends his respect," I said.

"Never lost mine," Silver said. Hard words for someone who hadn't spoken to any black man, except to make threats, in years. But Silver was hard enough to say them.

"You need more?" I asked.

"Not to listen," he said, still guarded.

"To shake my hand?"

"For that, yeah."

"Okay. Before I went into legal work, I apprenticed to an architect," I said, paying the toll. "I can look at a place from the outside, pretty much tell you what it looks like from the inside. I don't care if it's an apartment in Ridgewood or a semi-attached in Gerrit—"

"Sometimes," Silver cut me off, "the way things go down, a guy knows something. He tells another guy. Then this other guy, it seems like he knew it from the beginning. You understand what I'm saying?"

"Yeah," I said, not offended. "So how do you tell, then?"

"Sometimes, you don't," Silver said. "Then all you can do, until you're sure, is keep listening."

"John Anson Wychek," I said, getting right to it. "He did time here. I'm working on something—"

"For him?"

"Against him. He got himself shot a little while back. Didn't die. He named a friend of mine as the shooter."

"So?"

"So he did about six years in Siberia, when you were still up there. I'm trying to get a picture of him. I don't know if he was the bull of his block, or spent the whole time in PC, or anything in between."

"If you know where he did time, you have to know what for, too," Silver said. "He was a skinner. A fucking little tree-jumper."

"That doesn't tell me anything. Remember Mestron?"

Silver nodded, eyes narrowing in on me. Only someone who'd done time with Mestron would know how that heinous freak loved saying that little kids were the best to fuck—you could just grab their legs and split them like wishboning a chicken, slide in on their blood.

If you believed the movies, you'd think a scumbag like Mestron wouldn't be safe on the yard. All convicts hate baby-rapers, don't they? But if you had ever seen men step aside when Mestron came along, you'd know the truth. He was a baby-raper, all right. A baby-raper who carried, and a baby-raper who killed.

Short, hyper-muscled, and viper-quick, Mestron was never without a shank of some kind. You might get away with avoiding him, but you couldn't insult him unless you were ready to risk your life for it. Nobody claimed Mestron. Not the Muslims, not the Mau Maus, not the wannabe Crips and Bloods. But nobody tried to stop him when he moved in on some fresh new kid, either.

"He's not with us anymore," Silver said, his lips barely tracing a smile.

"Whoever took him out should get a pardon for public service."

"He didn't go that way," Silver said. "Motherfucker died of AIDS."

"Oh, Christ. All those kids . . ."

"Nah. He got it right in here. The slimeball wolfed in on a new fish. Everybody in the joint knew the kid was sick, but he killed his mother and father, so he was coming Inside no matter *how* sick he was. But they must have forgotten to tell fucking Mestron. Word is, the kid didn't even put up a fight. Must have wanted to make sure he could kill one more before he checked out."

"Good," I said, wondering why a young man with AIDS would kill his parents. And then not wondering at all.

"The hacks won't come in here," Silver said. "You mind taking off your shirt?"

"So you can see if I'm wired?"

"No. To see if there's anything I recognize."

Then I remembered. The puncture scar below the deltoid on my right side. A few inches lower, and the shank would have found the home it was looking for. That was back when we were both Inside, during race-war time. Silver had come to see me in the infirmary right after it happened.

I stood up, took off my jacket, unbuttoned my shirt. "There's a lot of new ones. From when they had to work on me. That's when my face got changed."

I turned around, pulled up my shirt and T-shirt together, exposing my back and locking my arms at the same time. Voluntarily helpless.

I felt Silver moving in behind me. I stood very still.

"Big Herk sure saved your ass *that* day, brother," he said, softly.

I pulled down both shirts, buttoned up, readjusted my tie, put on my jacket. And shook hands with Silver.

"**W**ychek was no Mestron," Silver said. "He was maybe five-nine. A skinny little guy, a buck-fifty max, and all of that flab. Punk wouldn't have the stones to stab his own meatloaf."

"So he locked down for his whole stay?"

"No," Silver said, eyes tight on mine. "He had protection."

"Wychek? Don't tell me he was a family man?"

"We had him covered," Silver said. "The Brotherhood."

"He proved in?"

"He was a weasel," Silver said. "And I'm not talking about his size. He wouldn't have had the heart to *talk* to us, never mind pass a blood test. Covering him was a contract job."

"So he never inked up?" I asked, looking at the parallel pair of lightning bolts tattooed on the side of Silver's corded neck.

"That wasn't the deal. We didn't have to pretend he was one of us, just get the word out that he was under our protection."

"Like bodyguards?"

"You know how it is in here," he said. "That's *exactly* what it was like."

"I left the max on the books for you," I told Silver. "Still fifty bucks a drop, huh?"

"For visitors, yeah. But there's no limit on what you can hold in your account, if it's mailed in."

"Anything I can do for you in that department?" I asked.

"No. We're square. We've been through all that."

"Done, and done," I agreed. "Same book, but this is a new chapter, right?"

"Not to me, brother," he said.

I let myself go quiet for a minute, working out the odds.

"Contract like that, long-term, must have been expensive," I probed, gently.

"We've done more for less," Silver said.

"It's not against the law, to protect a guy. Not a crime to get paid for doing it."

Silver met my eyes, didn't take the bait.

"People come in here, it's a terrifying place," I said. "If they don't have friends around, if they don't ride with a crew, they have to make choices, quick. Some of them get shaken down. Maybe for their commissary, maybe for whatever they can get out of their families, but it's usually not that much," I went on, leaving out the other ways a man could buy his safety. "Some guys come in here, they got no friends, but they got a lot of money. Or a lot of clout. Or maybe they've got skills," I said, thinking of a fraud-sentenced lawyer I knew who opened an appellate practice in his cell and lived pretty good. "But, the way I see this, Wychek didn't have any of that."

Silver watched me, neutral and waiting.

"So he bought protection. Only it wasn't him paying."

Still nothing from Silver.

"So I'm guessing it didn't go through him at all. The protection was in place before he even arrived."

Silver nodded his head, just a fraction.

"So whoever paid, he'd have to know how to reach someone high in the organization. Someone on the outside, with a pipeline to all the units behind the Walls."

Silver's eyes narrowed.

"And none of that's my business," I said. "But if I could find out who hired the Brotherhood, I'd know something that might help my friend."

Silver shook his head. "Some questions, you ask them, it starts people guessing. I don't want those kind of guesses about me. There was this guy. High up, proved in, even celled with a leader, okay? When he got short, everyone Inside—all over, not just this joint—everyone was watching, because, soon as he made the door, he was supposed to be kicking it off. RAHOWA?"

I nodded, both to confirm for Silver I knew he meant the "racial holy war" the White Night underground has been wet-dreaming about ever since George Lincoln Rockwell, and to keep him talking.

"But he ends up getting busted before it even starts. Some penny-ante bank job that went wrong, or something, I'm not sure. Took a few guys with him when he went down, too. And then comes the bombshell. Turns out the guy's no Aryan. In fact, he's half mud. You see what I'm saying? Nobody gets all-the-way trusted anymore. I can't play myself out of position."

"I understand," I told him.

"This . . . friend of yours. That's legit, right? Not someone you're working for, someone you . . . ?"

"Yeah," I said, tapping my heart twice.

Silver leaned in close. I did the same.

"I could *never* find out who hired us, brother. Can't be done. I couldn't even ask. I'm not the shot-caller in here. Something like that, it would . . . start things, things I can't handle. I promised Helene."

"That's okay. I—"

"I don't know if this will help you. But when you were talking about ink, I flashed on it. Wychek, he had to take shower time with us a lot—you know why. He's got a tattoo. On his forearm. Just a letter and some numbers."

"But he's way too young to have been—"

"—one of those old Jews? Right. Wouldn't be that, anyway. He knew more about Nazi stuff than most of the guys in the organization. Hated kikes himself. Knew all about Nietzsche. Read him in the original German," Silver said. "*Mein Kampf,* too. He was a real smart guy." The undertone of contempt in his voice was so faint I couldn't be sure I was hearing it at all.

"You think maybe the tattoo was just a way of mocking the whole thing?" I asked. "Like the people who say the whole concentration-camp thing was a myth?"

"The Holohoax?" Silver said, one corner of his mouth twisting a little. "No, it wasn't that. I asked him about it once. He told me it was a message, written in the code of Nietzsche. I figured he was one of those guys, tunes into his own private station, you know what I'm talking about."

"Sure."

"But maybe he *was* in a crew, and that was their mark."

"And that would be who paid . . . ?"

"Could be."

"Do you remember what it—?"

"This isn't the kind of place where you keep a diary," Silver said. "But I watch, real close. And I always remember. It was just the letter 'V,' then the number seven, a one, a period, a zero, and another one."

"This?" I asked, showing him what I had written on my legal pad: v-71.01.

"The 'V' was bigger," he said. "Like the first letter of a word. And there was no dash or nothing. Not even a space."

V71.01, I showed him.

He nodded. "That's it."

"Was it facing away from him, or toward him?"

"Away. I could read it right side up."

"He never said anything more about it?"

"No. It wasn't like I ever talked to him that much. Look, it probably doesn't mean nothing. He's a fucking psycho. Who knows what's in their minds?"

"It's more than I had when I came up here, brother," I said.

"Like I said—"

"Yeah. They let you smoke in here?"

"Not supposed to. But the guys who brought me down, they won't care. Go ahead."

"Thanks," I said. I shook a cigarette out of the pack in my briefcase, put it in my mouth. I held the pack out to Silver. He shook his head. I reached down, ripped the page where I had written down the tattoo from the legal pad. Added a few sheets from underneath it, even though I'd used a soft-tip marker. I tore the paper carefully, so the writing was all on one thin strip, a few pages deep. Then I struck a wooden match, held it to the paper until it started burning.

I brought the burning paper to the end of my cigarette, got the tobacco working. I held the paper in my hand until it was flamed down to only a couple of inches, the tattoo writing long since consumed. I dropped the last of the burning paper on the desk between us, let it char the surface with its last flickers.

Finally, I ground the little bit of blackened paper left between my fingers, blew the ash into the air.

"Pretty slick scam, this one," Silver said. "Me having a lawyer for another appeal. I told Helene not to waste any more money on shysters. Even if I could beat one of the cases . . ."

"It's no scam," I said, handing him one of Davidson's business cards. "Ask Helene to send copies of all your paperwork to this guy."

"I just told you—"

"And I heard every word, brother. Besides," I said, winking at him, "everyone knows Jews make the best lawyers, right?"

"It is all ready, mahn," Clarence said, as excited as Terry was. "Come on!"

He showed me how to use what Terry called a "find, match, and assemble" two-key combo. Then he pointed to a huge flat-screen monitor that hadn't been there when I'd last taken a look. "Here is our working grid, Burke," the West Indian said, knowing he was showing off, proud to be doing it.

The screen was paper-white, the letters against it sharp-edged black. "That TFT technique is so sweet on an LCD," Terry said to Clarence, "but it's really wasted on just words and numbers—you should see what it does for graphics."

Clarence nodded gravely. He hit some keys, and the screen filled.

EVENT # _____
Match to Event # _____   # of Fields Matched _____

T / P / O

Location	Macro	Borough		Neighborhood		Transit	
	Micro	House		Apt.		Car	
		Outdoors		Other			
	Address						
	Geographic Profiling	Distance(s) from Prior(s)					
		Distance(s) from Future(s)					
Time	Occurred	Minute/Hour					
		Day/Wk/Mth/Year					
		Lunar Phase					
		Sunspot Activity					
		Holiday/ Major Event Date					
	Reported	Minute/Hour					
		Day/Wk/Mth/Year					

EVENT CHARACTERISTICS

Crime +?	Robbery	Yes/No		Property Taken			
	Burglary	Yes/No		Point of Access			
		Security Present?		Dog	Alarm	Personnel	
	Other						
Sex Crimes	Penetration?	Penile		Digital		Instrument/Object	
	Vaginal						
	Oral						
	Anal						
	Other						

Words Spoken	By Perp(s)		
	By Victim		
Injuries	To Victim	Facilitative	
		Gratuitous	
	To Perpetrator	Known	
		Assumed	
Weapon	Perp's Own	Gun	
		Knife	
		Ligature	
		Bludgeon	
		Other	
	From Vic's Premises or Person	(specify)	
Stylized Aspects	Performance Demanded	Physical	
		Verbal	
	Progression of Assault Event		
	Length of Assault Event		
	Destruction of Property		
	Use of Condom		
	Trophy-Taking		
	Use of Restraints		
	Urination		
	Defecation		
	Threats		
	Apologies		
	Messages		
	Symbols		
	Camera	Still	
		Video	

EVIDENCE							
Forensic	DNA						
	Serology	Semen		Saliva		Blood	
		Urine		Mucus		Fecal Matter	
	Spatter						
	Trace Evidence						
	Fingerprints						
	Objects						
	Tools						
Eyewitness and Earwitness	Primary Victim			Willing to Prosecute?			
	Secondary Victim			Relationship to Victim?			
	Incidental			Connection to Crime?			

PERPETRATOR						
Description Narrative	By Victim					
	By Witnesses					
CJS stats	Height		Weight		Age	
	Race	W__ B__ A__ H__ NA__ O_____ Mixed__				
Speech Mannerisms						
Odors						
Dress						
Tattoos/ Scars/Marks						
Vehicle?						
Mult. Perp?						
Other						

DOWN HERE

VICTIM							
CJS stats	Height			Weight		Age	
	Race			W__ B__ A__ H__ NA__ O_____, Mixed__		Apparent from Appearance?	
Occupation				IRS Confirm?			
At Risk Stalking?	Famous/Controversial						
	History (specify) Stalked						
	Other						
History DV?							
Prior Complaints							
Education							
Siblings							
Prior Convictions							
Conact Info			Change Since Incident?				
OUTCOMES							
Arrest	Crimes Charged						
	Statements?						
	Jailed			Dates		Location	
						PC?	
Prosecuted							
Convicted	Plea						
	Trial						
Sentence							
Imprisoned	Location					Dates	
	PC?						
Released							

"We couldn't get it all on one screen," Terry said, pushing a key so that the list continued to scroll, "not without going to a micro-font, and what would be the point?"

"It's amazing," I said. "You have all this stuff on *each* case?"

"That's just . . . Well, it *is* hard work, but it's just vacuuming, really," the kid said. "Anyone could do it, if they were diligent enough. It's the algorithm that's going to make the difference."

"What would that—?"

"You'll be able to see if he was . . . escalating. Or changing his pattern. Or if he could leave some . . . things out sometimes, but if there were some things he *had* to have in there, every time."

"Yeah . . ." I said, slowly.

"Mahn, explain something to me," Clarence said. "This freak, he *did* all these rapes, yes?"

"That's what we think. For now, anyway. None of the cases have been cleared."

"So what good would it do . . . how would it help your . . . how would it help Miss Wolfe if you could *prove* that he did?"

"We don't have to prove he did any of them," I said. "What we have to figure out is which of the victims was *sure* it was him. Because that's where we'll find our shooter. Maybe."

"What's up with the doubt, son?" the Prof asked. "I thought that was our way to play."

"That's half of it," I said. "We all know what the other half is. We put together enough to nail this freak on one of the rapes he never got arrested for, we trade him that for him dropping this crap about Wolfe shooting him."

"But that means he gets away with—?" Terry said, dampened by reality.

"We have to get cold to make him fold, so fucking what?" the Prof cut him off. The little man's voice was as hard as the choice we might have to make. And as certain.

"It might not come to that," I said. "There's something else now."

I was still laying out what I'd gotten from Silver when the intercom sounded.

"There's a girl down here, boss. Asking for you."

"She new to you?"

"Never saw her before, boss. And, believe me, this isn't a woman any man would ever forget."

"Did she say a name?"

"Nah. What she said was, you send someone down to escort her up; she's not going up those stairs by herself."

I didn't need a closer description—who else plays countess in a flophouse? "Her name's Michelle," I told Gateman. "She's with us, so you'll know next time. Tell her an escort's on the way, would you?"

We were still waiting on Michelle when the intercom went off again.

"Boss, sorry to bother you. And if this is none of my business, just say so, okay?"

"What?"

"That girl—she's on her way up—the kid you sent down for her, that's really her son?"

"Yep."

"No way! She must have had him when she was . . . Uh, boss, is she hooked up?"

"For life, Gateman," I said. "Sorry."

"Not as sorry as me, boss," the wheelchair-bound gunman said. "That woman could raise the dead. And make 'em glad they came back."

"It's Mom!" Terry announced, as Michelle made her entrance. She was dressed in a chrome-colored sheath under a black bolero top, wearing a lipstick-red pillbox hat with matching spike heels.

"Mama said you all were over here." She sat down lightly in the chair Clarence had pulled out for her, flashing him a dazzling smile as thanks.

"I didn't want you to have to deal with those stairs until it was time for your skills," I told her, sidestepping the ever-present possibility that, somehow, I'd hurt her feelings.

"I've got *lots* of skills," she said, honey-voice just this side of sharp.

"We're going to catch him, Mom!" Terry said, conveniently forgetting Plan B. "You should see what we—"

"I'd *like* to see," Michelle said, eyes on me.

"We were just going to start, honey," I said. "Terry's put a *lot* of stuff into that computer. But until we—"

"I already ran a rough sorting code through it," the kid interrupted. "I'm not done with the algorithm yet, but I could print out the first batch now, if you want."

"Please," I said, catching the Prof's slight shrug of resignation.

It was going to be an hour and a half, minimum, Terry told us. Clarence volunteered to go out and get some food, but I could see his heart wasn't in it. What he really wanted was to do whatever Terry was doing, learn some more.

"I'll make the run, son," the Prof assured him.

The little man had barely started down the staircase when Michelle turned to me.

"All this, just to . . . ?"

". . . prove Wolfe didn't shoot him, that's right."

"And you still think one of the . . . one of the women he raped did it?"

"Or her brother or her father or—"

"—her big sister."

"Yeah. Something like that. He *was* a suspect, so at least some of the investigators—cops, DAs, who knows?—could have given one of the victims his name. And maybe they put him in lineups, so he could have been ID'ed, too."

"But if anyone *had* ID'ed him, wouldn't the police have—?"

"I don't mean it that way, girl. Look, here's a scenario, okay? A woman's raped. All she gets is a flash look at the guy who did it. Maybe it's dark, maybe he's got his face covered, maybe he came at her from behind. . . . But there's other things that could finger him. Maybe he always uses a certain kind of knife, maybe he always tells the victims they're whores, maybe he wears a certain kind of jacket. . . . Something tips the cops that he's the same guy who did some others. And—maybe—they've got enough to make an arrest, but not enough to make it stick.

"When it gets down to a lineup, the victim knows *one* of them is the man who raped her. She doesn't actually recognize any of them, but she catches a hint from one of the cops.

"So maybe she didn't know what he looked like before, but *now* she knows, see? From there, it's not that hard to put a name to the face."

"And, anyway, when Wolfe finally nailed him for *one* of them . . ." Michelle said.

"Right. That made the press. Probably TV, too. The other victims, they'd have to assume their turn to testify is coming up. Only that never happens. But, still, he's in prison, with a twenty-five-year top. So they might have figured that'd hold him. And—"

"—then he gets *out*. And the papers play it up, big."

"Exactly. There's more, too. Don't forget, he sent that letter to Wolfe at her—" I stopped short, cutting myself off.

"What, baby?" Michelle said, anxiously.

"Terry!" I yelled.

The kid came on the run. "What's up? Mom, are you—?"

"I'm fine, sweetheart," Michelle said. "As for whatever Burke needed that was so urgent he forgot even a *semblance* of manners, you'll have to—"

"The files, they all have addresses in them. For each victim, right?"

"Sure," the kid said, puzzled.

"The address where the rape occurred, and the address where the victim lived. Sometimes they'll be the same, sometimes not."

"That is right, mahn," Clarence said. "We noticed—"

"Wolfe got that 'Ha ha!' note, remember," I interrupted. "It's part of the prosecution's case against her. They're saying that's what set her off, to go find him and gun him down."

"The database is from the victims," Terry said. "We wouldn't have anything on—"

"Just *listen,* okay?" I said. "The freak didn't have Wolfe's address. He sent it to the DA's Office, and they forwarded it to her."

"I thought she went outlaw a long time ago," Michelle said. "How could they even know where to—?"

"She never gave up her law license," I said. "And OCA—Office of Court Administration—makes every lawyer list a street address. No PO boxes, got to be a real one. Wolfe uses the address of a therapist's office—Lily, remember her?" I said to Michelle, who nodded, paying attention now.

"You think that letter Wolfe got, it wasn't the only one?" Michelle said.

"Could be. Maybe not the same exact letter, but something like it. Wolfe dropped him, what, six years ago? I'll bet the statute of limitations has run on all the rapes. He's home free."

"That means we can't—" Terry said, remembering the backup plan he had hated even *hearing* about.

"Listen," I said. "I've known freaks who get off big-time on 'reminding' their victims. This fuck, in his mind, he probably thinks when he beat that case he raped Wolfe, too, see?"

"So if he sent other letters . . ." Michelle said, face upturned, her antenna fully extended.

"Let's say you'd been raped," I said, to them all. "They never caught the guy who did it, but, later, you heard he went down for a different one. Then he gets out, with the case reversed, after it's too late for anyone to do anything about *yours.* And then you get a letter in the mail. From the same freak who raped you, laughing at you. . . ."

"I would *have* to kill him," Clarence said. "Or that pain would kill me."

Terry didn't say anything.

"Having your face rubbed in it like that . . ." Michelle said, softly.

Terry nodded, slowly.

"Yeah," I said, letting it sink in. "I did time once with a guy who killed a girl. A teenager, is all I remember about it. What he did was, every year, when the girl's birthday came around, he would send her a birthday card, to her parents' address."

"Jesus," Terry said.

"He wasn't worried about it hurting him with the Parole Board," I said. "They were never going to cut him loose, anyway, and he knew it. The administration binged him—threw him in solitary—the second time he did it. Every liberal on the planet got involved. I mean, he was a prisoner, okay, but he still had his First Amendment rights, you know?"

"What happened?" Michelle asked.

"It never got settled," I said. "In court, I mean. They let him out of the bing—because of the lawsuit—but he died before it could ever come to court."

"How did he—?" Terry said, before he caught a warning look from his mother and clamped his jaw.

"Now *this* freak, Wychek, he's not Inside anymore. He's not even on parole or probation. No supervision at all. I don't know which of the victims would have *public* information about themselves available—phone book, driver's license, own a home, like that. I don't know what kind of skills Wychek would have at getting that, anyway. But I'm sure of this much: he'll know every single address where he did a rape. Have them memorized."

"We already have—" Terry started to say.

"Right," I said. "But what we don't have—yet—is which of those women still live at the same address where it happened."

"I can do a public-records search on each name," Terry said. "I should be able to tell you in a few hours, maybe a day."

"I will help you, mahn," Clarence said. "You will show me how to do it, yes?"

"Absolutely," the kid said. "That way, it'll go faster."

"And for the ones you can't find, that's where I come in," Michelle said, both sad and proud to have her son so deep in our work.

"If that is what happened . . . if he sent a letter to one of these women, and she went to shoot him," Clarence said, "I could not trade her in, mahn. Not even for—"

"That plan's dead now," I said.

Lying.

When the Prof showed, he wasn't alone.

"Mama laid so much chow on me, I had to bring the Max man along for the heavy lifting," he said.

Max, despite what looked like a stainless-steel garbage can in each hand, managed a bow to Michelle.

"Let me have that," she said, with a gesture. "No, wait. Bring it here."

Max followed her obediently.

"How did you lug all that back here?" I asked the little man.

"Used Clarence's ride," he said.

I raised my eyebrows. The Prof was only a marginally better driver than Max. My Plymouth had been built to near-NASCAR specs, and it would shrug off just about anything other than a high-speed dance with a stone wall. But Clarence's '67 Rover 2000TC was a fragile, immaculately restored piece of machinery, one he treasured deeply.

"That's right," the Prof said, catching my look. "That boy's my joy. And his trust don't rust."

I heard Michelle in the room I used for a kitchen. She was ordering everyone around while simultaneously complaining about my pitiful lack of decent dishes or tableware.

"Got you covered, little girl," the Prof yelled back to her. "Mama sent some of that junk over; got it right here with me."

In a little while, we all sat around the big table, like a thieves' Thanksgiving.

"Let us pray," the Prof said.

Nobody laughed. "Prof" was short for "Professor" or "Prophet," depending on how you knew him. "I never fall, because I see it all," he'd said when I first met him, half a lifetime ago.

"May jackals refuse your bones," the little man said.

"Amen," Michelle answered. She knew what we all did—when the Prof says grace, he addresses our enemies, past, present, and future.

"Nice of Mama to send all this stuff," I said, gesturing to the food spread out before us.

Max held his hand to his head, scrunched up his eyes to show a person in pain.

"Bitched about it every second, right?" I said.

Max nodded, gestured that Mama didn't understand why, if we wanted food, we didn't come to her place.

"I told her to come along," the Prof said, "but you know Mama don't sing that song."

"It's delicious," Terry said, expertly wielding his chopsticks. Mama had thrown in a fork for me, underscoring her message that I shouldn't try this at home. "Mom, do you know what this is?"

"Oh, it's a combination of dishes, sweetheart," Michelle said, airily. Meaning, she didn't have a clue, and wasn't going to try a bluff, in case someone else did.

I looked around the table. *My table*, I thought. *In my own place. With my own people. It's so* . . . I reached my hand down, to scratch behind Pansy's ears, like I always did, telling her to be patient, she'd get her share of the score in a little while. Felt the dull gray blanket drop over my spirit.

I *shoved* it away. *Walled* it off.

"This is perfect," I said.

"**M**otherfucker didn't like black girls," the Prof said. "Most of them white, a few Latins, couple of Asians. Probably would have done a Cherokee, if he could have found one. But not a one of them black."

"That doesn't tell us anything," I said. "Not yet, anyway."

"Didn't Silver tell you the punk was a master-race freak?" the little man demanded.

"Sure. But so what? Some of the victims were Jewish—at least, that's what you'd think from their names—and they couldn't have been high on his list, either, right?"

"Maybe he was afraid?" Clarence said. "A man like him, he would stand out in a black neighborhood. People might remember."

"Or hassle him, sure," I said. "From the way Silver described him, he was the kind of guy who'd draw that kind of fire. But there's plenty of mixed neighborhoods in the city."

"Rich don't count," the Prof said, sourly. "Money don't know color. But look at the places where he hit. You won't find no doorman fronting any of those joints, true?"

"True," I agreed. "But that doesn't take us where we need to go, Prof. We're not trying to put together some lame 'profile' here. We know *him*. It's the victims we're trying to figure out."

"And this can't be all of them," Michelle said, flatly.

"What do you mean, Mom?" Terry asked, a worried expression on his face.

"Oh, I'm not talking about *your* work, sweetheart," she assured him. "But what are the odds that *every* rape he did even got reported?"

"Zero," I answered.

"On *that* wheel, *double* zero," the Prof said.

"So—it could be that it *was* one of the victims who shot him, but not one of the ones in our database," Clarence said, proudly slipping that last phrase in.

"It's possible," I said. "But not real likely. Lots of ways it could happen, a victim doesn't go to the police. But what we're dealing with here, whoever popped him had to know who he was. And the only place they could get that info would be *from* the cops."

"It is hard to know where to even start," Clarence said.

"We'll start with the ones who are still at the same address where it originally happened," I told them. "Because they're the ones most likely to have gotten a letter like Wolfe did."

"Tomorrow, for sure," Terry promised. "With Clarence helping me, I can have all—"

"I could help, too," Michelle said.

"I need you to help *me*," I said, catching Clarence's quick glance of gratitude. "We'll need a couple of phones, and a bounce from Davidson's office. Business cards, a new set of ID . . ."

"Why don't you just ask—?" Michelle said.

"Wolfe's not in this," I told her. I looked around the table, making sure everyone was tuned to my frequency. "All right?" I said, to all of them, making sure.

"**S**o you want what, exactly?" Davidson said.

"To put another line in your office. Set on permanent forward to a different number. Come on, we did this before; you know how it works."

"That's fine for a business card," he said. "But anyone with half a brain would look me up in the Yellow Pages, and make the inquiry to *that* number."

"Sure. And all you have to say is that I'm working on the case—Wolfe's case—for you, as an investigator."

"You being Robert Lee Haywood?"

"No," I said. "Haywood was a paralegal. On Silver's case. Me, I'm a new man, one you just hired for this case."

"And your name would be . . . ?"

"I'll let you know," I said.

"I don't know you," the skinny guy in the chartreuse silk tank top said.

"But you know *me,* bitch," Michelle said, her slashy smile not blunting the edge on her words. "And *I'm* vouching for him. What's your problem?"

"Oh, stop marking your territory, Gavin," an older man told the skinny guy. He was resplendent in a maroon blazer over a white shirt with a button-down collar and a blue-and-black-striped tie. He patted back his three-figure haircut and ambled over to where Michelle and I were standing at the counter. "Come on in the back," he said. "We'll fix you right up."

"Scott Baker?" Michelle said, looking at the New York driver's license I was holding in my hand. "There must be a million men with that name."

"And your point is?"

"Yes, yes. But if I had the chance to keep picking different names for myself, I would want to select something with a little more . . . panache."

"That's 'cause you're you," I said. "This, this is me."

"That letter he sent you, did you ever—?"

"A *copy* of that letter is all I ever saw," Wolfe said. "So, if you're going to ask me about forensics . . ."

"No. What's the point? We know who sent it."

"So what about the letter?"

"*You* went over it, right? Not for prints, but for . . . whatever it could tell you. Like if it was done on a typewriter, or pasted words out of a—"

"It was a pure generic," Wolfe said. "Type O blood. Even without the original, I could tell you it was typed in Courier, ten-pitch or twelve-point, depending on whether it was a typewriter or a computer font—no way to tell from a copy. Ragged right margins, double-spaced, one-inch border. No misspellings. Nothing bolded, or in italics, or anything like that."

"You look for convict-code?" I asked her. Meaning, messages formed by the first letter of each word.

"Sure," she said, dispiritedly. "The whole thing was a zero."

"Return address? Postmark?"

"The DA's Office didn't see fit to send me a copy of the envelope," she said, cold-voiced.

"Then how would you know how to—?"

"What? Find him? Are you serious?"

"I know *you* could find him. That's what . . . that's one of the things you do. And the DA's Office would know that, too, sure. But Wychek himself wouldn't."

"Is it really that important?"

"It . . . could be. Can you find out if there was a return address on the envelope? And if it was the same one as where he got shot?"

"I hate to ask. . . ."

"Sands? He'll be glad you did," I said, feeling that same truth inside myself.

There's no such thing as a standard victim. Even if you could manage to duplicate a trauma exactly, you could never be sure that any two people would react to it the same way.

Two women. Each of them, her husband beats her all the time, cuts her off from the outside world, threatens worse if she ever tries to leave. Then he brings in the big guns, chopping at her sense of herself, words like scalpels, until she starts worshiping her own worthlessness.

Both husbands beat the kids, too. For their own good. When they don't show him the proper respect. To teach them a lesson.

One of the women takes her place in the food chain, tells the kids they should learn to make Daddy happy so he won't get so stressed out. Because you know what happens when he does. . . .

The other woman takes a long look into her kids' eyes one night. Then she goes searching for her husband's heart. With a kitchen knife.

I've known rape victims who wouldn't get on an elevator if the only other passenger was a man. And others who would look forward to that exact same opportunity, their purses handgun-heavy, and always open at the top.

Therapists say there are stages to recovery from sexual assault, like stages in the grieving process. I don't know about any of that. No matter what kind of painkillers you take, from prescription to perversion, they all have the same thing missing—they don't hurt the one who hurt you.

I had to hold my approach until Terry and Clarence finished running all their programs. No point asking them for progress reports. They were already bilingual in a language I didn't know existed, throwing around terms like "five-nines" as if I had the dimmest chance of following along.

I figured on getting only one shot at each victim. Reading through the files, I couldn't even make a guess as to how any of the women would react to my cover story. That's why I had it set up for Michelle to contact them all first—she could put enough estrogen-empathy into her voice to calm down a kitten in a dog pound.

And I had even better reasons for saving the freak's sister for last.

I was waiting again. That never bothers me—it's one of the things I do best. I learned when I was just a little kid. There were times when it was all I had. Now it's part of me.

I filled the time by making a grid out of the addresses where Wychek had struck. It wasn't just timelines and access points I was looking for. I know some things that aren't in anyone's database.

Years ago, a psychotic in a mental hospital developed this belief that aliens would come to Earth if they saw proof that they were welcome. What the aliens needed was a blood sign. It had to be in the shape of an "X," with the top half much smaller than the bottom, standing on its side, so it looked like a fish sliced straight through the middle of its body. The lunatic never shared his secret knowledge with anyone, not even his medication-dispensers.

One night, he escaped.

The cops caught him before he finished drawing the signal. Which was why the aliens never came.

They decided prison was a better place for the lunatic. I still remember him explaining it all to me.

I put a yellow dot on a metro-area map, one for each rape. But they didn't form anything I could recognize, much less the swastika I had been hoping for.

I wondered if Wychek had produced an alibi for any of the rapes. If he had, talking to *that* person would go on my list. But the files said Wychek had only been questioned a couple of times.

Well, not questioned, exactly. Brought in for questioning. Each time, he said he wanted a lawyer. That always got him cut loose, until Wolfe dealt herself in. That time, they weren't bringing him in to talk. And he didn't get to go.

There was something about handling the actual photocopies of each case that made me feel closer to a trail than any computer analysis would. I felt . . . something. But I wasn't locked in yet.

I bulldogged it, willing myself to penetrate. But I kept shooting more blanks than a man with a vasectomy on Viagra.

"Ready to be charming?" Michelle's voice, on the cell phone.

"Aren't I always?"

"This is Little Sister you're talking to," she reminded me. "Now, listen. I've got the first one lined up. Her name is Jessica Davenport. She still lives in the same place, but she doesn't want you going to her home, or her job, either. So it's going to be a public-place luncheon. There's a very nice little café just around the corner from where she works. I told her you'd meet her at twelve-thirty."

"Am I supposed to wear a carnation in my lapel?"

"No, Cary Grant," she snapped, just a hint of impatience under her brisk business-girl voice. "She's going to ask for Mr. Baker. You'll be there already, waiting for her. Corner table for two, all the way in the back."

"Who do I have to take care of?"

"The girl who works the front. Roni, her name is. Probably short for 'Veronica.' The table isn't primo—it's right near the kitchen—and they really don't do a lot of lunch traffic anyway, so it won't be a problem."

"Okay."

"Don't go all Vegas on her, Burke. Roni, I mean. Like the Prof always says, 'A dime is always fine, but twenty is plenty.'"

"Got you."

"She called, by the way."

"She who?"

"Jessica Davenport!" Michelle said, the impatience light glowing a little brighter on her console. "She called Davidson's office, to check that this was for real."

"Smart girl."

"Careful, anyway," Michelle said, approvingly.

"You got a physical description?"

"No more than you do. White female, age thirty-one—that's thirty-one *now,* understand? The . . . rape was back in '95, so she would have been—"

"All right, honey," I said. "I'll be there."

"Burke, a suit, please."

"Cary Grant *always* wore a suit."

"Idiot!" Michelle said, but I heard a tiny chuckle under her voice.

▌was getting dressed the next morning, idly listening to the TV broadcast news as I moved around the place. I heard someone say "torture," in an approving tone. I stopped what I was doing, went over, and sat down in front of the set.

The moderator was talking to two different men, one in the studio, one in some remote location. The scroll at the bottom of the screen read: "Is the use of torture ever justified to get information from terrorists?"

I wasn't surprised to hear the guy at the remote location go on and on about how the Constitution is what defines America, and if we violate it, we lose the moral high ground.

The other one was just as predictable, saying, "In certain cases of imminent danger to American lives, under strictly controlled conditions, extreme interrogation is a tool that cannot be ruled out."

The moderator was a good-looking guy with glasses and an earnest attitude, who came across as a real journalist. On that network, he had to be a token.

"What if your child was held hostage and about to be executed, and you had a person in custody who knew the location but refused to talk?" the studio guest said to the man in the remote location. "Where would *you* draw the line?"

"That's a purely hypothetical—"

"It's not so 'hypothetical' for plenty of people, all around the world," the studio guest interrupted. "What if we had one of the terrorists in on the Nine/Eleven plot in our hands a couple of days before it happened? Shouldn't this nation be permitted, in its own defense, to use whatever means necessary to protect itself?"

"In the long run, such methods do not 'protect' us at all," the remote guest responded. "They *endanger* us, because they tear at the very foundations on which this country was built."

"When we turn a captive over to a country where we have every reason to believe that torture will be used to extract information, aren't we, in fact, participants?" the moderator asked the studio guest.

"We don't tell our allies how to handle their internal affairs," the studio guy said, self-righteously ducking the question.

"Sure we do," the moderator confronted him. "We do it all the time. Foreign aid isn't unconditional."

"That is correct," the guy at the remote location said. "When we look the other way, we condone—"

"But when the French refused to extradite a convicted murderer and send him back to us, simply because the French oppose the death penalty, you came on this very program and applauded their 'exercise of national sovereignty,' isn't that true?" the moderator challenged.

"It's not the same—"

"Let's hear what *you* think," the moderator said, turning to face the camera head on. "Here's the question: 'Do you believe the use of torture is justified when national security is believed to be at stake?' To vote, just call the number on your screen, and press one for 'yes,' or two for 'no.' Or you can vote online, at . . ."

By the time I was dressed and ready to leave, the screen was showing the vote in progress.

Yes 88%
No 12%

Some polls don't have a margin of error.

Roni turned out to be a tall, model-thin girl with long, frosted-tipped hair and a professional smile. I thanked her for holding a table for my "conference," slipped her a bill, and found my own way.

On some field interrogations, you do things to the immediate site to establish control. All it takes is some pads and pens, maybe an ashtray, a calculator, tape recorder, a cell phone—anything to move the scene from neutral over to your side.

That wouldn't fly here. I had nothing to offer the woman, and no hammer to threaten her with. I had to treat her like a butterfly. Not one I wanted to net, one I wanted to have land on my hand.

I spotted Roni walking over toward my table, leading a much shorter woman—all I could make out was her improbable rose-colored hair done in a pixie cut.

"Mr. Baker?"

"Yes, Ms. Davenport," I said, getting to my feet. "Thank you for coming. And thank *you,* Roni," I said to the tall girl, who had just taken some of the anxiety out of the meeting. The Prof was right, as always—twenty *had* been plenty.

I moved to hold the woman's chair for her, but she waved me away with a tight smile, and seated herself.

Up close, her features were not so much pretty as finely formed. She was wearing a beige business suit over an ice-blue silk blouse, makeup flawlessly applied. A Movado watch on her wrist. Heart-shaped diamond engagement ring.

She picked out a complicated salad and a glass of white wine. I went for the seared tuna on toast points and some ridiculous-priced water.

"I don't know how much time you have . . . ?" I began.

"Well, essentially, what I have is my lunch hour," she said. "Which is why I wanted to do it this way."

"Right. Well, Ms. Davenport, I'm sure the office told you why I wanted to talk with you . . . ?"

"You're representing the woman who shot that—"

"The woman who's been *charged* with shooting him."

"It doesn't make any difference to me," she said, calmly. "I only have two regrets about it—that she got caught, and that he didn't die. That's what it said in the papers, he's in a coma; is that true?"

"That's what they said," I answered, offering my indifference to whether Wychek lived or died as a bond between us, if she wanted it.

"What is it you think I could do?" the woman said. "When it . . . happened, the police, or maybe it was the DA—I don't know, I talked to *so* many damn people then—said there wasn't enough evidence to arrest him."

"You never saw his face?"

"Never once," she said. "I was living . . . where I live now. With two roommates. We all worked. But I was on a split sched-ule—work and school—and I always had Tuesday afternoons off. I really treasured those Tuesdays. It was the only time I had the place all to myself. It's a two-bedroom, one-bath apartment. You can just imagine, three girls. . . .

"Anyway, he was . . . he was waiting for me when I came in. He was already there. I don't know for how long. When I walked in, he grabbed me from behind. I started to fight, then he put a straight razor right next to my nose. He said if I even *moved* he'd take my nose off. I could . . . *feel* he'd do it. Really do it. His voice was so full of hate. Then he—"

"Did you ever get a look at him, anytime during the . . . ?"

"He was wearing one of those ski-mask things. A black one. He had black gloves on, too. All black. He put duct tape—"

"I don't want to take you through it, Ms. Davenport," I said. "I'm sure they took samples of—"

"He wore a condom," she said, flatly. "He didn't have to put it on; it was already . . . in place. He must have been . . . he must have been . . . aroused just waiting for me."

"You think he was waiting for you, then?"

"I just said—"

"I mean, not a burglar you surprised in the act, or anything like that."

"No," she said, grimly. "He was only there for . . . me."

"I'm sorry if this is . . . painful for you," I said, gently. "And I'm sure the police thought of this, but I still have to ask. Who knew your schedule?"

"My schedule?"

"Your Tuesday time-for-yourself afternoons? Who knew about that?"

"I . . . I don't know. Maybe my roommates did, but I couldn't say for sure. We never talked about it, specifically. And they weren't the type to notice much outside their own lives."

"But you *always* came home on Tuesday afternoons?"

"Yes."

"For how long were you doing that?"

"Ever since the semester . . . I guess about . . ." She looked at the ceiling, concentrating. "Eleven, twelve weeks."

"And—"

"Wait a minute! What you said, before."

"What?"

"About the police asking me. They didn't."

"Didn't ask about your schedule?"

"They didn't ask about it; I told them. They asked, what was I doing home at two in the afternoon, and that's when I explained about the schedule. But they never asked me what you just did."

"You mean, who knew?"

"Yes," she said, quietly. "Who knew."

"Your boyfriend . . ."

"I didn't have one then. Nothing steady. I mean, I dated, but there was no one you could call a—"

"Ms. Davenport . . ."

"Jessica."

"Jessica," I said, bowing slightly to thank her for the privilege of using her first name, "was there a *former* boyfriend? One you had broken up with recently?"

"Well . . . yes, I guess so. But it had never been anything all that intense."

"Not to you, anyway."

"I don't understand where you're going, Mr.—"

"Scott."

"Scott," she smiled. "What difference would it make if I had a boyfriend, or if I just broke up with one?"

"A boyfriend would know your schedule. And an ex-boyfriend who knew your schedule and was angry over the breakup could have . . ."

"What? *Raped* me for revenge?"

"It's happened," I said.

"God! That seems even . . . I don't know, uglier. If possible. But I would have recognized . . . my ex-boyfriend. Even with the mask and all."

"By the voice?"

"No. The police *did* ask me about that. The . . . the person who did it had a guard-thing in his mouth."

"A 'guard-thing'? Like a retainer?"

"No. Like boxers wear? So you don't see their teeth when they open their mouths?"

"A mouthpiece, right. What color was it, black?"

"No. It was white. Bright white. Brighter than teeth, I remember. I can't say what . . . specific thing I would have noticed if he *had* been anyone I knew, but I would have noticed *something*, I'm sure of it."

"I don't have any doubt it was Wychek," I said. "I was just interested in the investigation itself. Sometimes, things get overlooked."

"I don't know," she said, glancing quickly at her watch.

"Just a couple more questions," I said. "Have you received any letters in the past three months that seemed strange or odd to you?"

"I did get one," she said, tilting her head slightly, trying to find my eyes. "But it was a postcard, not a letter. I remember it because it was blank—the front of the card—like a white piece of paper."

"Was there a message on the other side? Next to where it was addressed to you?"

"Nothing," she said. "Just one of those stick-on labels, with my name and address. I figured it was some promotional stunt, and the next one would have more information on it. But no other one ever came."

"Did you—?"

"Sorry," she said. "I threw it out. Do you think it . . . ? Oh my God, do you think it was from him?"

"No," I lied. "But it wouldn't hurt to take some basic precautions."

"I take a lot more than *basic* precautions now," she said. "And I *do* have a boyfriend. Instead of two roommates."

"Good. On behalf of Ms. Wolfe's entire defense team, I want to thank you for—"

"There *was* something else," she said, suddenly. "I didn't even find out about it for a couple of weeks afterward. He stole my high-school yearbook."

"You're sure?"

"It *had* to be him. I kept it in my underwear drawer, buried under all my . . . stuff. My roommates would never have gone in there. Anyway, I asked them, and they didn't even know the book had been there. It didn't have any . . . I mean, it was just a sentimental thing. I wasn't like Most Popular or Most Likely to Succeed, or anything like that. I don't even know why I kept it buried in there. For privacy, I guess."

"Did you ever tell the police about that?"

"No. No, I guess I didn't. It didn't seem to matter. I mean, what's a high-school yearbook compared to . . ."

"I know," I said. And something in my voice must have convinced her I did. Her eyes got wet.

"He's going down," I said to her, almost in a whisper. "It's a sure thing."

Hﾞow many of the other victims reported he took something with him?" I asked Clarence.

"I will find it for you, mahn," he said, proud of what he had been learning. I left him to the task.

"An all-white postcard," I said to the Prof. "After what Silver told me . . ."

"If there's more than one, it's him pointing the gun," the little man agreed.

I picked up the phone, dialed a number.

"Mr. Davidson's office, Investigations Division," Michelle answered.

"You got another one lined up?" I asked her.

"Three, actually," she said. "And as soon as you tell me how it went with Jessica Davenport, I'll give them to you."

Dﾞo I remember that trial?" Wolfe said. "I remember *all* of them. Each and every one."

"I don't mean, do you *recall* it. Anyway, we could always re-view the transcript. I was talking about things that didn't get into the record."

"Like what?" she said, eyes narrowing. Not suspicious—work-ing. Homing in.

"I'm not sure yet. But here's one, anyway. Did the perp take anything from the victim's place?"

"You mean, like a—?"

"Anything," I said. "Anything at all."

"A cedar block," Wolfe said, no expression on her face.

"A what?"

"A cedar block," she said, barely keeping the annoyance out of her voice. "You know. It's just a piece of cedarwood, about the size of a bar of soap. People keep them in their dresser drawers. So everything stays fresh, and to keep the moths out. Like having a cedar closet for clothes."

"Oh. I never heard of—"

"Sure," she said, not surprised. "They sell them everywhere. Some of them are pretty fancy, some are plain. But all of them do the same thing."

"You wouldn't keep these things out, just lying around?"

"What would be the point? Unless they're inside an enclosure, they really don't have any effect."

"And the victim, she knew right away . . . ?"

"No. The investigating officers asked her if any of her under-clothing was missing. It's quite common for certain kinds of rapists to . . . you know. Anyway, when she was released from the hospi-tal, she pulled out all her bureau drawers, to check. That's when we found out. The way she was sure is that she had bought a set of six blocks, but she could only find five of them."

"What was she keeping in that drawer?" I asked.

"Sweaters," Wolfe said.

"Nothing else?"

"Just sweaters."

"Nothing else taken, I mean."

"Not as far as we ever knew."

"You make anything of it?"

"We cross-checked it against all the other cases we had at the time. Several reported objects missing, a number of others didn't."

"The missing objects . . . ?"

"I remember two, off the top of my head. A necklace. Costume jewelry, really. Something the victim got as a gift years ago. She never wore it. And a pen. An expensive one. A graduation gift, still in the original box."

"Both kept in—?"

"Bureaus, right," Wolfe said. "Damn!"

"It's probably nothing . . ."

"What are you trying to do, spare my feelings?" Wolfe snapped. "I dropped him on the one case *I* had. This isn't about me, it's about—"

"It *is* about you," I cut her off. "You're the one who's on trial, not him."

"I'm not on trial yet," Wolfe said, grimly. "And there's no way the government thinks it's protecting him from *me.*"

"You're saying the DA already knows his statement was bogus?"

"I don't know. But if they're protecting him, it's not because of *that* story; it's because of another one."

"The case you prosecuted, did he testify?"

"Hah!" Wolfe snorted. "He's an incredibly arrogant person, but he's not suicidal. He *was* going to testify. Had his story all ready. But once I waved *Molineux* in their faces, they went from consent to SODDI in a heartbeat."

"Where could he have pulled a consent from?" I asked her. "He didn't know the woman, right?" SODDI—Some Other Dude Did It—had been the only defense I'd ever heard about.

"She was a bad victim," Wolfe said.

"A hooker?"

"How about a porno actress? How about the star of *The Conquest of Cassandra*? Can you figure out the plot?"

"There's a lot of variations on that theme," I said, hedging.

"Cassandra is a successful businesswoman," Wolfe said, her tone as flat and detached as a pathologist dictating autopsy findings. "Very in control. Dominating. A real bitch. One night, as she's getting undressed for bed, a man breaks into her home. She resists, but he easily overpowers her. Various forms of rape follow. At some point, Cassandra discovers herself aroused by the rape, and switches from victim to participant. At the conclusion of the tape, Cassandra begs the rapist to please come again soon. That last bit was irony," she said, almost snarling the sarcasm.

"So he was going to say he was a fan who believed the video was real? That there was this woman who *wanted* to be raped?"

"I don't know what he was going to say. There's no proof that he knew of the existence of the tape before he . . . The defense did a *thorough* investigation of the victim—I'm guessing that's where it turned up."

"Christ, if the jury ever saw that—"

"I don't think they ever would have," Wolfe said. "Besides the rape shield law, there's the question of relevance. If he wanted to try to slip it past, it would have to be through some form of insanity defense—a delusional disorder, blurring the line between video and reality. There's some judges I *know* would have let it in, on that pretext. But he never filed notice of an insanity defense. Because once I hit them with *Molineux*—"

"What is this *Molineux* thing?"

"That's the name of a case. A very old case, but it's still good law," Wolfe said, switching to a less detached but still academic tone. "Essentially, you can't bring in other bad acts of the defendant to prove he did the ones he's charged with now, or to show his *propensity* to commit them. Just because a man robbed banks a dozen times before isn't proof he robbed this one *particular* bank, okay? But if you can show them that what you're charging him with at trial is part of a *pattern,* you can bring in other acts, as proof of MO. Not that most judges have the courage to let pattern evidence in, unless there's a neon sign over every act.

"Now, with Wychek, we had eleven rapes. All by a perp wearing a ski mask and a mouthpiece. In every case, the rapist entered a dwelling. In every case, he . . . restrained the victim, using duct tape, plus a blindfold. In fact, that's one of the things that nailed him, that one time, with our case."

"The blindfold?"

"The victim had a great deal of . . . experience with blindfolds. Apparently, they're something of a staple in her business. Wychek used a sleep mask. Put it on from behind, then wrapped tape around it. But by tilting her head back, the victim was able to see a thin slice of what was going on around her."

"He took off the mask?"

"No," Wolfe said. "She couldn't see that high, anyway. But he had on a distinctive pair of boots. They were almost to the knee, but he wore them under his pants. From the cuffs down, they would look like a pair of plain black shoes. But these had silver inlays all along the sides. Some kind of design, not what you could buy in a store. The victim got a good look at the boots a few times while he was prowling around her place."

"It doesn't sound like—"

"The victim described the design perfectly," Wolfe said. "She had an eye like a camera. But even without that, we had the cedarwood block."

"If it was just a piece of wood, then his fingerprints . . ."

"*His* fingerprints weren't on it," she said, grim-faced. "But *hers* were."

"Did you find anything else when you . . . ? Wait a minute. On what she told you, how could you even get a search warrant?"

"Oh, it wasn't a search warrant," Wolfe said, smiling. Her voice shifted to that phony "professional" tone cops use when telling a jury that the suspect's rights had been scrupulously observed. "An anonymous phone call was received, indicating in-progress domestic violence at Wychek's residence," she recited. "When the officers arrived to investigate, Wychek answered the door. He made a motion as if reaching for a weapon. The officers were forced to restrain him for their own safety. While doing so, one of the officers noticed the distinctive silver design on the boots the subject was wearing. Recalling a very recent notice concerning a rapist-at-large whose victim had described such a unique object of clothing, the officers, believing they had probable cause for arrest, secured the suspect," she said, straight-faced.

"While doing so, a noise was heard from one of the back rooms," Wolfe went on, her tone unchanged. "Believing a victim of domestic violence might need assistance, one of the officers went back to investigate. No other person was found—possibly the officer had heard a neighbor's TV set. But the cedarwood block, which had also been described in the circular about the wanted rapist, was in plain view."

"But they all look alike, right? Those cedarwood blocks, I mean. And something like that wouldn't hold a print."

"Not the fingerprints you're thinking of," Wolfe said. "The block yielded a very clear sample of the victim's DNA."

"How could she have gotten—?"

"It seems the victim used the blocks as . . . props, in one of her video appearances. And the wood is quite absorbent."

"I'll bet the jury loved that."

"Juries don't have to love the victim," Wolfe said, her eyes the color of dry ice. "They just have to hate the perpetrator. That's my job. The victim was quite candid about what she did for a living, and I voir-dired on that *intensely*."

I nodded, afraid if I tried to use words to express my respect I'd screw it up. That happens a lot to me when I'm around Wolfe.

She took a cigarette from her pack, offered me one. I accepted, and lit us both up.

"DV call, huh?" I said, keeping my voice as neutral as hers had been.

"Yes," she said. "The actual caller was never located."

"The defense never subpoenaed the tape of the call?"

"They certainly did," Wolfe said, her mouth a thin line. "All that could be determined was that the caller was a woman, in obvious distress. The caller said she feared someone was getting killed, and provided the specific apartment number. At the time, it was assumed the call came from a neighbor. However, 911 records indicated the call was made from a pay phone on the corner of the building where the suspect resided. It just so happened that there was a radio car in the immediate vicinity."

"Bad luck for Wychek," I said.

"He deserved some. And, yeah," she said, watching my face, "after we arrested him, we *did* get a search warrant. But none of his other trophies were there. He had another place—*had* to have—but we never found it."

"Yeah. Well, what else did you have, to make that pattern you were talking about?"

"In each case, the perpetrator remained on the scene for some time after the rape was . . . accomplished. Always wore a condom. And gloves. A long list. And we had victims ready to testify. They couldn't ID him, specifically, but they sure could ID the *pattern*.

"It was too great a risk for him to take. If we got the pattern in, there was always the chance some other pieces would fall into place. And I think he was confident—*very* confident—about beating the case, anyway, even without that 'consent' defense."

"Was that in the appeal?"

"What?"

"The ski mask. Did he claim he *would* have used the 'delusional' defense you talked about, except that you would have brought in the little girl? The one from Nassau County? Not for the . . . not for what he did to her, but because she would have talked about how he always used a ski mask when he . . . ?"

"Never mentioned it," Wolfe said, emotionless.

"Davidson said the DA's Office didn't even fight Wychek's appeal."

"Oh, my former office has a special reputation for justice and equity. They do what's right, even if it's not popular. After all," she said, her voice venomous with contempt, "they're 'prosecutors, not politicians.' "

"And that makes them different from any of the others . . . how?"

"It's a matter of degree," she said. "Remember, a little while back, that judge who stabbed his wife a few times, collapsed her lung?"

"Yeah. He got off on insanity."

"He got off all right," Wolfe said. "But there never was a trial. He *pleaded* to insanity."

"How can you——?"

"You can if the DA consents. The poor judge is getting counseling."

"Jesus H. Christ."

"I can't tell you why my former office does any one specific thing. Like with Wychek's appeal. But I know how they work."

Maybe that's why they want you so bad, I thought.

"I'm going back in." Davidson, on the phone. "With a new bail application."

"What for?" I asked. "She already walked."

"It's just an excuse," he said. "So long as there's *any* bail, I can keep making applications for reduction. What I really want to do is get in front of a Supreme Court judge and turn up the heat. I want that goddamned discovery, and the DA's Office is stringing it out as long as they can."

"You need me there?"

"That reporter? The one you're pals with?"

"Yeah."

"The press has gone pretty dry since the arrest. With Wolfe sprung, and the fucking weasel out of his coma, it's not a story anymore."

"Got you," I said. "Just let me know when."

"I was married when it . . . happened," the woman in the floral-print dress said. We were seated in the breakfast nook of a well-maintained brick cottage in the North Bronx. "I'm not now. This," she said, waving her hand to indicate the house and furnishings, "is what I got to keep."

Soft interrogation techniques are all rooted in the same ground. The sequence is critical. Empathy is your trump card. You can't play it too soon, or too heavy. It's not hard to get some people to talk; it's listening that takes real skill. You can't shift to recorder mode until you confirm the channel is open and the signal is strong.

Whenever they volunteer something, they have a reason. Sometimes, it's misdirection they're after. Sometimes, they just need to tell you something important to *them* before they tell you anything important to *you,* like uncorking the wine and letting it breathe before you have a taste. So, instead of expressing any sympathy for a bad divorce, I asked, "You don't have children?"

"Because of the house, you mean? Well, you're right. That's why we bought it. So our kids could have their own room. And a yard. Even a dog. In the City, those things, they cost so much. Ted—my ex-husband—he said this would be a better place to raise kids, even with the longer commute. Besides, we're both from around here. The Bronx, I mean, not right here exactly."

"High-school sweethearts?"

"We were," she said, nodding as if I'd confirmed some long-held suspicion.

I gave her a ten-count in my head, then said, "It just didn't work out?"

"It was working out *perfect,*" she said. "Until it happened."

"I'm not sure I understand. . . ."

"After I was raped," she said, looking in my eyes for the first time since she had let me into her home. "After I was raped, Ted was never the same. Oh, he *said* he didn't blame me for it. How could he? It wasn't like I'd picked up some guy in a bar. Or even if I had been walking around in some bad neighborhood in the middle of the night. It happened right . . . it happened in this house. This same house."

"He couldn't be . . . supportive?"

"Maybe that's the word for it," she agreed. "I think he tried. Ted's an intelligent man. He knew what he was *supposed* to do— we went to counseling together for a couple of months. I think, I *know* he tried. But it . . . it wasn't the same. He couldn't stop *asking* me about it. Over and over."

"Trying to figure out what you *could* have done?"

"Yes! That's what I thought he was doing. He denied it, but it always felt like that. To me, anyway."

"I . . . read the reports, Ms. Stansik," I said. "There was nothing *anyone* could have done."

She made a brushing-away gesture, as if dismissing my lame assurances. "After it . . . after it happened, I read all kinds of things about 'What to do if . . .' You know the kind of stuff I mean?"

"Sure. And none of it fits every situation."

"Some of the things I read said that it's always better to resist. To fight. A lot of time, if you put up enough of a struggle, the . . . the rapist will run."

"Or kill you. And this one, he had a gun, right?"

"Yes. I can still see it. Chrome. The bullets in the round thing on the side. Brass tips. Pointed at my face."

"You did the only thing you could have done," I said.

"You know about this . . . about this kind of thing, Mr. Baker?"

"Yes, ma'am. I do. My work has brought me into contact with it many times."

"With victims?"

"And with perpetrators."

"You mean you worked for—?"

"No," I said, smoothly sliding into the truth on the slope of all my lies. "I never worked for a perpetrator. But I had to interview them in certain cases."

"Why would you?"

"In one," I said, "the victim was suing the apartment building where she lived. She had complained over and over about the broken lock on the front door, but it had never been fixed. I had to interview the perpetrator, because I needed his statement about how he'd gotten into the building."

"Oh. You don't mean you were the one who caught him?"

"No, ma'am. He was already in prison when I spoke to him," I said, back to the truth.

"Why would he tell *you* anything?" she asked.

"Oh, a lot of them *like* to talk," I told her. "And this one, he was very easy."

"What do *you* think?" she said, eyes hard on mine.

"About whether a sexual-assault victim should resist? I think it's exactly what I told you before: it depends on the circumstances."

"I know what you said. It's my fault. I was being too . . . general. Let me . . . All right, will you answer me this? Is there *ever* a time when a man points a gun at you that you *shouldn't* do what he says?"

"Yes."

"Oh!" she said, taken aback. "When?"

"If you're on the street, and a car pulls up, and someone points a gun at you and tells you to get in, that's when."

"What could you—?"

"Run," I said. "Run in the direction that would make him have to reach way out and turn around to get a shot at you. Run and scream."

"But wouldn't he just shoot if you did that?"

"He might. But you'd be dealing with a rapist, not a professional assassin. Odds are, he'd miss. But if you got in that car, he wouldn't."

"Oh. Do you think, maybe, if I had—"

"I read all the reports, ma'am. If you had resisted, he might have killed you. He *certainly* would have done more. . . . I mean, he would have hurt you in ways other than . . ."

"I know what you're trying to say. But that isn't what I want to know. I want to know if—"

"Yeah," I told her. "He would have raped you no matter what. Even if he had shot you first, he would have gone ahead."

"I wish my husb— I wish Ted believed that."

"You're sure he didn't?"

"I don't know what I'm sure of. Not now. I was sure of Ted. 'For better or for worse.' I believed that."

"There's some 'worsts' nobody ever thinks about."

"I can't stop . . . blaming myself. Those kids . . . we never had them. Ted could never . . ."

"Ms. Stansik, I want to tell you something. If I'm out of line, just stop me, all right?"

She looked at me expectantly, a dullness to her eyes that came from a place past fear.

"What if your husband had gone to prison?"

"Ted? Why would he—?"

"Let's say, for something he didn't do. A mistake. But while he was in there, he got raped."

"By another . . . ?"

"Yeah. By a man. It happens."

"I know, but . . ."

"Just say it happened," I pressed her. "And, afterwards, they find out Ted was really innocent. So they let him go. And he comes home. But he can't . . . he can't make love to you. Because he thinks, after what happened to him, that he's not a man anymore."

"That's . . . that's crazy."

"Crazy things happen," I said. "What would you do?"

"Do? I'd tell him it wasn't his fault. And I'd . . . I'd *show* him he was still a man. I'd *prove* it to him."

"See?" I said.

After she stopped crying, she told me everything, as if the details were payment of a debt. Wychek had planned his attack for her husband's bowling night—Ted always went straight from work, didn't get home until eleven, at the earliest.

Ski mask, gloves, mouthpiece, condom, blindfold . . . all the same. Only the pistol was different.

It was almost midnight when Ted had come home. His wife was still strapped to a corner of the bed, still blindfolded and gagged. Drawers had been ransacked, as if the rapist had been looking for something, but all that was missing was a five-by-seven color snapshot Claudia Stansik had kept tucked into a corner of her bedroom mirror. "We went to Niagara Falls on our honeymoon," she told me. "It was so beautiful. . . ."

Yes, she had gotten a strange postcard a few weeks ago. Just a plain shiny white one. Addressed on a machine. And, yes, she had thrown it away.

"Thank you," she said, as I stood up to go.

"I'm the one who should be—"

"You know what I mean," she said.

I put my hands together and bowed my head slightly. "Could I make one suggestion?" I asked.

"Of course."

"Get a dog. You've got a perfect place here."

"You mean, a guard dog?"

"Any dog will guard you, if you raise it right. Some do a better job than others, that's all."

"Do you know a lot about dogs?"

"Yes, ma'am. I do."

"What kind of dog do you think I should—?"

"I know a dog that has a litter of puppies," I said, thinking of the white pit bull who lived in the Mole's junkyard. Satan knows what she had mated with, but her kids would be guaranteed manstoppers. "They're just about weaned now, and they're looking for homes. Would you be willing to adopt one of them?"

"I . . . I really don't know anything about them. But I could learn. I'm good at . . . I could learn. Sure!"

"I'll have the owner's son drop the pup off, ma'am. And I'll call you before he's ready to bring it over, okay?"

"That would be great."

On the way back, I kept thinking about loyalty. And how Ted had walked away from what most men spend all their lives looking for.

Wolfe sat silently at the counsel table, wearing a wedding-white dress.

"If it please the court . . ." Davidson, on his feet, facing the bench. I didn't recognize the ADA seated across from him.

"I don't know him, either," Hauser told me, seeing where I was looking. "Some kid they threw up there for cannon fodder. The judge I know. Name's Griffith. Nothing special about him. Party hack. Been an 'acting' Supreme since forever, not going anywhere. Certainly not up to the AD."

"Counsel," the judge interrupted. "This is a bail application?"

"Yes, Your Honor."

"Your client, I understand, is already out on bond?"

"*Cash* bond, Your Honor. And when the People finally get around to dropping these bogus charges, they're not going to pay interest on the money."

"Your Honor." The ADA stood up. "Bail is *already* well below the minimum for a crime of this—"

"What 'crime'?" Davidson said. "A convicted rapist was shot—"

"That conviction has been set aside—" the ADA cut in.

"Your Honor, the District Attorney has these proceedings confused with *Judge Judy.* May I be allowed to finish my argument without further interruption?"

"Just setting the record straight," the ADA muttered.

"As I was saying, Your Honor," Davidson resumed. "A convicted rapist was shot. True, his conviction was overturned. On a technicality I can only describe as grotesque, but this isn't the forum to argue that. My point is, the appellate court didn't find him 'innocent.' And it's no secret that this same individual is the suspect in *several* other rapes, rapes for which no arrest has yet been made.

"Motive *abounds,* judge. The DA's Office has, quite deliberately, *not* furnished the defense with such simple facts as the time and place of the alleged events. They have *represented* to the court—not this court, Your Honor; at arraignment—that they have a statement from the 'victim,' a statement which allegedly names my client as the shooter. We have never seen a copy of this supposed statement, judge. We don't know for a fact that it exists. What we *do* know is that my client, Eva Wolfe, is the same prosecuting attorney who sent him to prison—"

"And who got a letter from the victim just before he—" the kid DA interrupted.

"Judge?" Davidson said, his voice heavy with weariness.

"Sit down, counsel," the judge told the ADA. "You'll get your turn."

"As the court knows, Ms. Wolfe was once an Assistant District Attorney. In fact, a Bureau Chief. She personally prosecuted John Anson Wychek, the alleged victim in this case. When Wychek's case was reversed, and he was let out, he, apparently, sent a letter which could be construed as threatening to Ms. Wolfe, at the DA's Office. We say 'apparently' because only the DA's Office, conveniently enough, has the original document.

"In any event, the DA's Office maintains that letter represents some 'motive' for Ms. Wolfe to track down and shoot Wychek. But, in reality, that letter proves only one thing—animus running from Wychek to Ms. Wolfe. And, thus, a clear motive for him to concoct a story—something the DA's Office has not seemed to even *consider* in its 'investigation' of this matter."

Davidson waved some paper in one hand, as if it contained proof of what he was saying. "While Ms. Wolfe herself is no longer being detained, her money certainly is. So long as the DA's Office maintains this farce of an accusation, my client's use of her own money is unfairly restricted."

"So take a bail assignment," the ADA sneered.

"Below the belt," Hauser muttered.

"You see the overt hostility being displayed here, judge?" Davidson went on, face flushed but still calm-voiced. "The People would have you believe that the purpose of my application is to free up Ms. Wolfe's funds so that I can be paid for my services. Is *that* what you're trying to say?" Davidson suddenly snarled, whirling on the ADA. "Come on. Get up and put it on the record. If you've got the guts."

"Your Honor," the ADA said, getting to his feet, "the People are not saying—"

"I didn't *think* so," Davidson chopped him off. "Judge, I don't know if the DA's Office are a pack of hapless buffoons, or if something more sinister is going on here. But it's *clear* that the People have been deliberately and maliciously stalling. When the appropriate time has lapsed, the defense will get sufficient discovery to have this pathetic nonsense dismissed. Because, judge, I am saying, right here and right on the record, that the DA's Office is *never* going to put John Anson Wychek into the Grand Jury, unless they're looking to prosecute *him*. For perjury."

" 'Hapless buffoons' or 'something more sinister,' " Hauser said, scribbling madly. "I fucking love it."

"Mr. Warren?" the judge said, turning to the ADA.

"It's only fifty thousand, judge," the clown said, weakly.

"Anything else?"

"No, Your Honor."

"Fine. Bail is reduced to one thousand dollars. That will be all."

"It's good for one more round," Hauser told us on the courthouse steps. "But the story's got no legs."

"That's okay," Davidson said. "A little more heat means a little more light."

"You understand why none of this has come out under my byline?" Hauser asked.

"Not really," Davidson said. "But I see the *Post*—"

"Don't say anything more," Hauser warned him. "My paper is more concerned with the, shall we say, 'business' aspects of lawyering. So, at this stage, I'm covering the story for a . . . colleague."

"Good by me," I said, not wanting Davidson to ask a wrong question.

"Do you have anything to say, Ms. Wolfe?" Hauser asked, turning to her.

"On the record?"

"Yes."

"No."

"Off?"

"Sure," she said, her lipsticked mouth twisting in what no one would have mistaken for a smile, even with the flash of white teeth behind it. "I didn't shoot Wychek. And whoever did, they did it at least ten years too late."

"**W**hen I woke up, he was on top of me," the blonde woman said. She was very pale-complected, the expanse of her broad, doughy face broken only by a half-moon scar that started from the lower corner of her right eye and hooked back toward her nose. "He had his hand over my mouth. I bit him. *Hard*. But there was something in the gloves he was wearing. Like, metal. It felt like I was biting on chains. Then he sprayed me in the face with something, and I saw a knife. . . ."

Everything else she said tallied exactly with the police reports, including the "no sign of forced entry."

"I don't know *how* he ever got in here," she said. "The cops, they didn't say I was stupid, or anything like that. But they asked me how come I could be living in this city and not have a dead-bolt."

"Well, you lived a long time without—"

"My mother used to live here with me," she said. "After she passed, I kept the place. It's rent-controlled. . . ."

"I wouldn't let something like that go, either," I assured her.

"When Mom was alive, I wasn't afraid of anything. *She* wasn't afraid of anything, and that's how I was raised. It was just her and me. My dad was killed in Vietnam—I was only four years old then."

"It must have been hard."

"On my mother, I guess it was. I didn't really know him. I was only a baby when he left. It was just before the end of his last tour when . . . when it happened."

"So you've always lived here? In this same place?"

"Yes. But it wasn't always like this," she said, glancing involuntarily at the bars over the windows. "I used to be a happy person. I worked hard. I had a good education. Mom was always after me to meet men, but . . ."

I sat quietly, to see if she would pick it up on her own. Most people with anxiety disorders have on-off switches for conversation. Either their speech is pressured, almost impossible to interrupt, or you can hardly get them to respond.

"After Mom passed, I went right on. It wasn't sudden. The doctors were very good, very caring. She wanted to die right here, not in a hospital, and everyone worked to make sure she could.

"When it was all done, I went back to work. I had activities, too. And friends. I had friends.

"But after . . . but after I was attacked," she said, touching the half-moon scar, "everything changed. I don't go to work anymore. I don't . . . I don't go out. I can't. I tried.

"At first, I was just scared of, I don't know, different television programs and things I would read in the newspapers. But then people started to make me nervous. I knew something was going to happen. Something horrible. I couldn't explain it, but I knew. It got harder and harder.

"Now I just stay here. I'm on Disability. It's not Welfare," she said, with a sudden spark in her expression. "I worked. I worked all my life, even in high school. I paid into Social Security, like it was an insurance policy; there's no difference. In fact, did you know that the amount of disability you receive is based on how much you paid into the system before . . . before you couldn't work anymore?"

"I didn't know that," I said.

"It's true," she said, the spark fading as quickly as it had appeared. "I don't go out at all now. Except to see the doctor. And that's so hard, I don't know if I can even keep that up."

"You have a lot of courage," I told her.

"Me? I used to be a brave girl. That's what my mother always called me when I was little. Her brave girl. Now I'm afraid of my own shadow."

"That's understandable."

"No, it isn't. Not to me. Other women have been raped, and they go on with their lives. I'm . . . ashamed."

"Your mother died of cancer?" I guessed.

"Yes. It started out as a—"

"Was she ashamed of it?"

"Of having cancer? Of course not. Would anyone . . . ? Oh! You're saying, why should *I* be? But it's different! Just because they have a medical term for what's wrong with me doesn't mean I'm not responsible for it. I'm just too weak."

"Illness isn't weakness."

"How do you know? You're not ill. Or weak."

"How do *you* know?" I came back at her.

"Well, you don't *look*—"

"Neither do you."

"You sound like my doctor. He keeps trying to get me to take medication."

"You're not?"

"No. I'm . . . scared of it."

"What does he want to try you on? Paxil?"

"That's right. How did you . . . ? I . . . I think, if you start taking medication, you can get addicted to it. And then you're *really* trapped."

"A diabetic isn't 'addicted' to insulin," I said, gently.

"Are you a diabetic?"

"No. But I had bypass surgery a few years ago," I lied. "And I have to take my medication. Every day. Or else I wouldn't be able to go out and do my work. I don't feel like an addict; I feel grateful that science has an answer."

"I'm not sick in my body; I'm sick in my—"

"You've got a trauma-induced chemical imbalance," I said. "That *is* your body."

"You don't understand," she said. "You're like a . . . professional tough guy, right? A private eye? You don't know what it's like to be scared all the time."

I reached out my hand. She gave me a look that was half terror, half prayer. Then she reached hers out, too.

"Look at me," I said. "You don't know me. You're never going to see me again. There's no reason for me to lie to you. I don't want anything from you. Understand?"

She nodded.

"I'm going to tell you a secret," I said. "I want you to watch my face. Watch my eyes. So you know I'm telling you the truth. Okay?"

She nodded again.

"I know what it's like to be scared. To be scared *all* the time. So scared I thought my heart would stop from it."

"When you were sick—?"

"No. When I was a kid."

"I don't . . ."

"It's the same," I said, very softly. "*We're* the same, you and me. People hurt us, once. Different people, different hurts, even. But the freaks who do it, *they're* the same, too. All alike. You know why they hurt us? Because they like to. Because they like the way it feels. How it makes *them* feel. And if we let them *keep* on hurting us, they win, understand? Your mother wouldn't want that."

"No," she said, crying. But she didn't let go of my hand.

"Try the medication, Kristin," I said. "*Keep* trying until you get one that helps. Otherwise, the wrong person is in prison, okay?"

She wouldn't say the word, but I took her nod as a promise.

It wasn't until hours later that I realized I'd never asked her about what the freak had taken. What *more* he had taken. Or about a white postcard, either.

"Can you get in touch with our source?" I asked, over the phone.

"Sure, chief," Pepper said. "But it's not a direct-dial, okay? Could take a while."

"That's okay. Will you do it?"

"Okey-dokey."

"Uh, Pepper, one more thing."

"Speak."

"You don't need to tell her about this, am I right?"

"This one time, you are," she said.

"That other thing you were looking into for me?"

"We still are," Pepper said, her voice chilly. "And not for you."

Walking back to my car, I wondered if Pepper thought she was telling me anything Wolfe hadn't said herself.

"His favorite time is between mid-afternoon and ten at night," Terry said. "A six-and-a-half-hour block. When we ran the

ANOVA—never mind," he said, intercepting my look, "we didn't see any significant departure keyed to the other factors . . . not even location."

"So he's got some centralized strike base, takes him about the same amount of time to do his work, and get back home?"

"It . . . looks like that," Terry said dubiously. "But Clarence says . . . You tell him," he said, turning to the West Indian.

"You believe that apartment building in Queens, the one where he was arrested in Ms. Wolfe's case, that would *not* be his home base, yes, mahn?"

"I don't see how it could," I told them both. "I mean, sure, he was *living* there. But he had to have another place, where he kept his tools and his trophies. The cops Hoovered the holy hell out of his apartment, and they couldn't find a trace of anything to connect him to the other crimes."

"But Queens," Clarence said, "it really is in the center of the grid we made. If you lived, say, near one of the major connectors—the Grand Central, the Van Wyck, the BQE, the LIE, the . . . You see where I am going, mahn? From such a spot, it would not take more than ninety minutes to get to *any* of the places where he struck. If he knew the roads," the West Indian continued, "getting to Westchester or the Island or into the City, all pretty easy."

"It makes sense," I said. "But the place where he was shot, that was in Manhattan. That would make using a car a lot less likely."

"But we don't have those records," Clarence said, in the annoyed voice of a scientist denied data. "We cannot know what they found in *that* place, mahn."

"I'm working on it," I promised them.

I was in Mama's, asking her if she could get me someone who spoke fluent Thai, just in case I got double-lucky with Sands, when my pay phone rang in the back. We used to forward the number

from a Chinese laundry in Brooklyn, but when the city broke up
into extra area codes, we had to bring the bounce closer to home,
to keep the 212 mask in place. Now the chain starts in the back of
an antique dealer's in SoHo.

"What?" I answered.

"Okay if he comes there?"

"Okay with me," I told Pepper.

I was in my booth when Sands came in the front door of the
restaurant. As he walked past Mama's register toward my booth,
she left her post to rearrange the dragon tapestry that's always on
display in the front window. Three dragons, all identical. Red,
white, and blue.

Our country has its own brand of patriotism. Mama would
replace the white tapestry with the blue—a warning to any members of our crew that the law was inside.

Sands sat down across from me. Didn't offer to shake hands.

"You want something?" I asked him, waving my hand to indicate I meant something from the restaurant.

"Food good here?" he said. "I haven't eaten since breakfast,
and that was one of those Mc-somethings."

"Very good," I promised him, watching Mama approach.

"Could we have the house special, please?" I asked her,
politely.

"Uh!" is all Mama said, before she went back into the kitchen.

"Have you ever been to the crime scene?" I asked Sands.

"Me? No. It's not my case."

"Just thought you might have been curious about it."

He didn't say anything.

"Sooner or later, the DA has to kick loose the address," I said.
"It's not really a secret."

He opened his mouth to say something, but just then Mama
came back to the table, carrying a tray in both hands. She

offloaded the single heavy white tureen and a pair of bowls, blue-glazed and very deep. Not saying a word, she filled each of our bowls, re-covered the tureen, and bowed.

"Thank you," I said.

"House special," she said. "Good with cold beer. You want?"

"What kind do you—?" Sands started to say.

"Very good beer," Mama interrupted him. "You see."

"Try the food," I advised him. "You'll see, she's always right."

"What is it?" Sands said, peering into the bowl. Between the dim lighting and the dark glaze, it was all guesswork.

"It's never the same," I told him, using my fork to scoop out a piece. I chewed it, reflectively. "Beef in oyster sauce, I think," I told him.

"What the hell," Sands said, digging in.

Mama came back, carrying two dark-amber bottles without labels and two sparkling pilsner glasses.

"This is delicious!" Sands told her.

"Today only," Mama said. And walked off.

"The crime scene . . ." I began, watching Sands pour himself a glass of dark, grainy-looking brew.

"Yeah. You said."

"I'm kind of curious myself."

"They've been over it," Sands said. He took a sip of his beer, nodded approval, and went for a longer hit. "They've been *all* over it, believe me."

"Looking for proof she was there."

"Not the techs. They just take what's there. What*ever's* there. The detectives, they'd be the ones looking for that."

"Sure," I said. "We already know they didn't find so much as a goddamned hair follicle, or they would have been asking her for samples."

"I don't know *what* they found," he said. "Past cases, that's one thing. But an active case, outside my precinct, there's no way to—"

"I don't want to see the report," I said. "I want to see the scene."

"It'll be taped, and—"

"Anyone can buy a roll of that stuff," I said. "You're not telling me they have a man on the door?"

"I'm not telling you they *don't.*"

"But you know where it is."

"All I know, it was a building on West Forty-ninth. Over by the river. I don't even know which apartment."

"I'll just look for the yellow tape," I said. "Okay?"

He took another long drink, put down the empty glass. I nodded in the direction of the other bottle.

"You don't want it?"

"I'm not a beer man," I said.

He poured himself another. Held the glass up to the light, appreciatively.

"You ever follow a car?" he asked me. "It's not as easy as the movies make it look."

"I know."

"I parked where . . . where they told me to. Out back, in the alley. Piece of junk like mine, I'm not worried about anyone stealing it."

"That's the only kind of car to drive in this town," I agreed.

S ands wasn't exaggerating about his car being a piece of junk. A mid-Eighties Oldsmobile coupe, in a dull-blue color the factory once had a fancy name for. He meandered through Chinatown until he got to Canal, then turned left and drove all the way down to the river. He took the West Side Highway uptown until the fork, then stayed on Eleventh Avenue to Forty-ninth, where he took a left, heading toward the Hudson.

I watched as Sands' Oldsmobile stopped in front of a five-story gray brick building. He stayed in place for a long thirty seconds before he took off.

"It is a pretty nice house, mahn," Clarence said, the next afternoon. He was still wearing his cover—an off-the-rack tan suit—and holding a red leatherette-covered Bible. "The people, I think, they have mostly been there a long time."

"You didn't have any trouble getting in?" I asked.

"No, mahn. None at all. There is no intercom, just buttons for each apartment. I pressed until I got buzzed in."

"They just buzzed you through? Didn't come down and check you out through the glass or anything?"

"No. At least, not the one that answered, she did not. An old lady, but very sharp, I tell you."

"Sharp, but not suspicious?"

"I think maybe she was lonely, mahn. She was a Jewish lady. I could tell that from the what-do-you-call-it on her door."

"A mezuzah," I said.

"Yes. The little stone thing, carved. But she listened to me talk about the glory of Christ. Even asked me some questions. *Good* questions, mahn. Made me think. And I had some tea with her."

"She just let you right in her apartment, too?"

"That she did not do. She looked at me through the peephole first. Then, even when she opened the door, she kept the chain on until she was satisfied."

"Did she ask for any ID?"

"No, mahn. She seemed like one of those old people who has been alive for so long they trust themselves more than any piece of paper, you understand?"

"Yeah."

"After I left, I just went through the building. She was on the third floor, so I worked my way up first. There is no elevator. The apartment is on the top floor, the corner one."

"You're sure?"

"That yellow tape is all across the front, mahn. Wrapped up like a Christmas package."

"That's the door for sure," the Prof said. "Damn thing's probably not even locked. From what Clarence says, it's not the kind of place where the cops would be worried about anyone looting."

"I could go back," Clarence said. "Visit that old lady again. She invited me to come back. I would not mind doing that."

"She already got a good look at you," I said, not liking it.

"Nighttime's not always the right time," the Prof said, overruling my objection, "and my son, he's the one."

The ancient Chevy Vega station wagon had sheet metal where the side and back windows originally resided, converting it into a mini–panel truck. It was refrigerator-white, with Chinese characters painted on the side.

I parked it across the street and up the block from our target. Max and I watched from the front seat as Clarence strolled past, red Bible under his arm.

We checked for pedestrians, then climbed out. I was wearing a suit and carrying a clipboard. Max toted a large brown paper bag full of smaller white cartons and a delivery slip for the address of the target building, written in a hand so cramped that it would have been easy to mistake the number. There was a phone number on the printed delivery slip. If anyone called, Mama was ready to answer. In Cantonese.

Max crossed the street. I stayed where I was. The Prof slipped out the back of the van, dressed in Contemporary Homeless style, a canvas bag of leaflets for a downtown topless bar over his shoulder.

If anyone was watching, this is what they would have seen: A neatly dressed young black missionary was just about to enter the apartment building when he noticed an Asian deliveryman coming up the steps. The young black man courteously held the door for the deliveryman before going inside. The deliveryman, in turn, held the door open to a nondescript man holding a clipboard, who followed right behind him. The nondescript man must not have closed the door properly, because a short man with a sack of leaflets walked right in a few seconds later. Happens all the time.

Inside, we split up and went to work.

Yellow crime-scene tape crisscrossed the door to 5-C. The Prof held up one finger, meaning, "Me first."

He played with the lock as I stood alert for any of the people on the floor suddenly coming out of their apartments. Max was on the stairway; nobody was going to surprise us from that direction.

The Prof let out a tiny snort of contempt as the lock gave way. He reached through the tape and turned the knob with a gloved hand. The door swung open. I took out a small pair of surgical scissors, and carefully slit the tape at the point where the door met the jamb, cutting only enough to let us slip through.

The Prof clear-taped the yellow strands back into place, then gently closed the door behind us. I pointed toward the back, showing him the area I intended to cover. The little man nodded, and went off in another direction.

The place was empty. Not just of people, of *signs* of people. Not a stick of furniture anywhere. Old-fashioned paper shades were pulled down in every room.

The refrigerator was empty. And warm. I stepped into the bathroom. The single tiny window was coated in light-blocking silver paint, starting to wear away in pieces. No shower curtain.

I opened the medicine cabinet, swept the interior with my pencil flash. A few stubby hurricane candles, a box of wooden matches, a disposable razor in a plastic sheath, two bars of soap, wrapped. An unopened tube of Xylocaine, a small jar of Vaseline, a fresh packet of Sudafed, and a dark-brown plastic bottle with a white screw-on cap. I opened the bottle. Empty.

As I was turning away, my eye caught something in the place where the grouting between the sink and the tile was wearing away. A little pointed . . . something.

I took a dental pick out of my kit, and gently worked it loose. Turned out to be a triangular pill, the color of old ivory, invisible in that slot unless your eye was at exactly the right angle. I pocketed it.

When I got back to the front entryway, the Prof was waiting.

He shook his head, using the index fingers and thumbs of both hands to form a giant goose-egg. Zero.

I cracked the door, checked outside. The Prof stepped out. He pulled the door shut until the snap-lock clicked. Then I held the crime-scene tape back in place while he did a more permanent job of reattaching it, using a drop of epoxy between the slightly over-lapping ends. When I stepped back, it looked as if it had never been touched. And we knew, when the cops re-entered, they would just tear it down without a second glance.

We followed Max down the stairs. He stepped through the front door first, still carrying his delivery, shaking his head in disgust at being given the wrong address. The Prof and I left together.

"Gonna bail by rail, Schoolboy," he said, moving off.

When I stopped for a light, Max jumped out and dumped the food delivery in a wire-mesh trash can. The pigeons were on the job before the light changed.

"He never lived there," I said that night.

"*Nobody* lived there," the Prof agreed. "Not for a long time. But the place was clean."

"The techs . . ."

"Not the police, youngblood. They sweep, but they don't sweep *up,* see where I'm going?"

"Yeah. It was vacant, but it hadn't been empty for long."

Max made a gesture of a man shoveling coal into a furnace. Then the universal sign for "money." He raised his eyebrows in a question.

"The super holding back a vacancy?" I said. "Sure, could be."

"The power was off, right?" the Prof said.

"Uh-huh. That's why the candles, I figure."

"Didn't seem like a squat, though," the little man said. "Not even a bedroll, or some old newspapers . . ."

"He wasn't living there," I said. "But he knew about it. Had a key, probably. Maybe he *had* kept stuff there—change of clothes, whatever—and the cops hauled it away with them. No way to tell.

The razor and the soap . . . but no towels, so maybe that *is* what happened.

"But that place didn't connect with him, that's for sure. Only way anyone would know he was there would be if they followed him."

"*And* had a key, mahn," Clarence reminded me. "*Two* keys, even, one for downstairs, the other for the apartment itself."

"Maybe he wasn't the only one," the Prof said. "It's not like someone just walked in by accident and popped him."

"He was prepared to stay there for more than a couple of hours at a time," I said. "Maybe even overnight."

"Because of the candles?"

"Because of these," I said, showing them the single pill I had removed from the off-the-books apartment.

"You know what that's for, son?" the Prof asked.

"It's a double-oh seven, Prof. Dilantin. For epileptics." I spasmed my upper body, to sign it out for Max.

"That's him? He's got that?" the Prof said.

"Easy enough to check," I said. "It's one medication they let you take in the joint."

"Wish we knew what the mangy motherfucker was doing in that place," the Prof said.

"There's two people who know for sure," I told them. "And I think it's time to try the other one."

"The sister?" Clarence asked.

"She was there. She's the one who called it in. I'm still waiting for the package on her to come in. But as soon as it does . . ."

"You want a lot," Pepper said.

"It's not for me," I reminded her.

"I don't mean the *work*," she said. "Keeping it all from . . . her. That's not so easy."

"I already told you why."

"I know," she sighed. "All right. This one shouldn't be too hard to run down. I'll call you."

The man behind the free-form bird's-eye-maple desk was nice-looking, well put together, made great money—the kind of guy you'd want your daughter to marry. "You really should be asking a neurologist," he said.

"Doc," I said, "when Mr. Davidson made the appointment for me to consult you, I'm sure he made it clear that I'm not looking for testimony. I don't need the 'reasonable degree of medical certainty' thing here. Just tell me, could it have gone down the way I laid out?"

"If the . . . if the person had a seizure disorder—and, yes, Dilantin *would* be the drug of choice in most such cases—and he was subjected to a sudden shock, he certainly could have an . . . episode. We had a woman experience something quite similar here, a couple of years ago. The stimulus was nothing more than a nurse suddenly turning on an examination light."

"And it would look like a coma?"

"It would *be* a coma," he said, "depending on how you define the term. Certainly, the . . . person could lapse into an unconscious state. And remain there for some period of time before recovery."

"Spontaneous recovery?"

"If you mean unassisted, yes," he said, carefully. "But if he was a . . . gunshot victim, there would be a variety of stabilizers applied, starting with the EMTs in the ambulance."

"Doc, could the person look dead?"

"Superficially, perhaps. But any trained medical—"

"Sorry," I said, "I'm not expressing myself well. What I mean is, this person gets shot, okay? He gets a seizure, and just falls out. Would it look like he dropped dead?"

"A seizure is an all-body experience," he said. "But there would be a pulse. And signs of breathing. It would depend on how closely anyone looked."

The Thai looked like a bantamweight boxer—slim, with big shoulders and a tiny waist. He wore a white silk T-shirt tucked into a tightly fitted pair of broad-waisted, pleated black satin pants that billowed at the knees and narrowed to a severe peg at the cuffs. His shoes were black mirrors, and he sported gold at the neck, wrist, and fingers. His hair was thick at the back, cropped close on the sides, and spiked in front, held in place with industrial-strength gel.

"This Jao," Mama said to me. "Burke," she said to the Thai.

I started to bow when I saw his outstretched hand. We shook. His grip was firm, palm very soft.

"You understand, we're doing this with *permission,* right?" the Thai said. The only accent in his voice was TV gangster. "So we have to show respect."

"I'm always respectful," I said.

"Bringing *him,*" the Thai said, twisting his neck in Max's direction, "that's maybe not so respectful."

"Max always go with Burke," Mama reassured him.

The Thai opened his mouth, then snapped it shut without saying a word. His teeth were perfect enough to make an orthodontist go back to drilling for money.

"I don't know you," the Thai said. "But I know your name. Lots of people know your name. I heard you were dead."

"That was my brother," I said.

"Yeah. Well, maybe it runs in the family. You know what I mean, right? No funny stuff."

"All I want to do is talk to the girl," I told him. "And the whole conversation is going through you, so what's the risk?"

"The risk is to *me,* if the people who gave *permission* get the idea it's really them you're interested in."

"If I was, I wouldn't need a translator," I said.

"**H**ad you ever seen him before the night it happened, Wawn?" I asked.

"How I see him?" the tiny girl said. She had long, straight midnight hair, and a doll's blank face. Wearing a pale-yellow shorty robe, indifferent to the fact that she was nude beneath it. She couldn't have weighed a hundred pounds.

"A customer, maybe?" I asked.

The girl turned, said something in rapid-fire Thai to Jao. Whatever he told her seemed to reassure her.

"Not look customer face," she said. "And man, man who . . . find me, wear mask." She covered her own face to demonstrate.

"Yes," I said, being very still within myself, so I could get this done. "But there are other things."

I reached out my hand to her, palm down. She tilted her head in a question, but didn't speak. After a couple of seconds, she took my hand in both of hers.

"See my hand?" I said.

"Sure. See okay."

"Hands look different, just like faces."

"Not have heart," she said, touching the tiny tattoo on my right hand.

"Maybe a scar?" I said, touching one of my mine with my left forefinger. Keeping the excitement off my face—she had just told me that the rapist hadn't worn gloves.

She shook her head "no."

"Where it happened, in your house . . ."

Another exchange between the girl and the bantamweight Thai.

"Not in house," she said.

Not lying. Good. I already knew, from the police reports, that the rape had gone down in an alley behind the Roosevelt Avenue whorehouse where the girl had worked at the time.

"Can you tell me what happened?" I asked.

Another long exchange in Thai. When it was over, she pointed at the translator, indicating she had already explained everything to him.

"She was leaving work," the Thai told me. "A little after four in the morning. The guy jumped her in the alley. He had a knife. A switchblade, it must have been—she said it scared her when it snapped out. He told her if she made a sound he'd cut her throat.

"Wawn didn't fight him. She just went limp. He turned her so she was facing the wall. He was in the middle of it when somebody yelled. Wawn thinks it was this drunk who's always hanging around the alley at night. An old man, with white hair and a long coat, is all she remembers. The guy who was on her, he took off."

"You're telling me *she* called the cops?"

"No, no. When the drunk, or whoever it was, started yelling, someone must have called 911. The cops showed up so quick, they must have been right around the block. She didn't have a chance to get herself together."

"They took her to a hospital?"

"No hospital," the girl said. Probably same as she told the cops that night.

"She dummied up, right?" I asked the Thai. "Said she didn't speak English, didn't see anything, just some drunk pawing her in the alley, no big deal—wanted to get out of there before anyone started asking green-card questions?"

"Right," he said.

"Did he hurt you, Wawn?" I asked her.

"No. Not even get . . . in me. I don't fight him."

"You know my job is to . . . make him pay for doing these things to women?"

"Good job," she said, emotionless.

"I just want to ask you one more question, Wawn. Did he take anything from you?"

"Take?"

"A piece of jewelry, maybe? Something out of your purse? Something you were wearing?"

"No," the hollow girl said. "Not take nothing."

"You were cool," the Thai acknowledged on the drive back. "Maybe you're not so much like your brother after all."

"How's that?"

"What I heard about him was, you show him a girl who's been hooking since she was twelve, somebody's going to get fucked up."

"It's just business," I said. "People do things for money, right?"

"You mean what *I* got paid? That isn't what made it happen. I told you, man. *Permission.* That old woman's got a lot of clout with my bosses."

"Uh-huh."

"Her restaurant looks like a ptomaine pit, though."

"Tell all your friends," I said.

"The Thai girl was in the first group," Clarence said, looking up from the computer screen. "So was the stripper, the one who lived out in Middle Village."

"They fit on a number of cross-correlates," Terry said. "And the time line works, too."

"I'm not sure what you're saying," I said.

"A prostitute and a stripper. Both in some kind of sex business. He could have been watching them for a long time, to get a sense of their movements. The prostitute, as near as I can tell from the data, she was the very first one. At least, the first one in this pattern."

"He was still feeling his way," I said. "Trying it on for size. Maybe he figured hookers wouldn't be as likely to resist."

"That is stupid, mahn," Clarence said, indignantly. "Just because a woman—"

"It only has to make sense to *him,*" I said. "Remember?"

"That is true," the West Indian said, acknowledging the first rule of freakdom—no matter what they say in the papers, there's no such thing as a "senseless" crime.

"If the Thai girl was first, he had some support for the theory, too," I reminded them. "She *didn't* resist. And—you've got all the clips scanned in, T.—did it even make the papers?"

Terry worked his own keyboard a few strokes, said, "No. Not a word."

"Okay, now the girl who lived in Ozone Park. She gets off work; he follows her. Probably did it a few times. Knows she doesn't have a garage, but there's a driveway off to the side of her building where she parks. On the night he picks, he gets there ahead of her, lies in wait. She gets out of her car, he jumps her.

"Only *this* girl, soon as he shows her a blade and tells her to turn around, she starts screaming. Had a set of lungs on her like an opera singer, too. And that part of town isn't Kitty Genovese territory: 911 logged seven calls in under a minute.

"The victim, the report shows her as 'angry.' She *wanted* the fucking maggot. But she didn't have anything to really tell the cops. It was dark; he had the mask on. Gloves, by then, too."

"And she didn't report anything taken," Terry said.

"And that one, she *would* have, I think, mahn."

"Yeah," I summed up. "And that was the last one he tried outdoors, is that right?"

"Right," they said, as one.

"**M**r. Ubell, my name is Baker. Scott Baker. I'm a private investigator, working for—"

"I already talked to the cops," the super said. He was one of those guys whose age you could miss by a couple of decades in either direction. He stood straight-spined in the doorway of the basement apartment the realty company provided as part of his salary.

"Yes, sir, I understand that. But, like I said—"

"The cops said if anyone ever came around I didn't have to talk to them."

"Cops always say things like that," I said. "They only look out for themselves. They didn't tell you that you *couldn't* talk to anyone else, isn't that true? Anytime there's money to be made, you know the cops, they're not going to tell *you* about it."

"Nobody said anything about money." He didn't invite me in, but he didn't slam the door, either.

"*I'm* saying something about money," I told him. "A lot of money. For a few minutes of your time."

"What are you," he said, tilting up his chin, "writing a book or something?"

"No, sir," I said, handing him a business card. "I'm trying to prevent an innocent woman from going to prison. And it's worth some real money to her lawyer to help me do my job. If you'll just give me a couple of minutes, I'll show you exactly what I mean."

"Come on," he said, stepping aside.

The apartment was solidly furnished. Heavy wood everywhere, period pieces. Even the kitchen table was wood, with a white oilcloth cover. That's where we sat.

"I hope you ain't allergic," the man said, firing up a Marlboro.

"Not me," I said. I took out a pack of Kools, lit one from a small box of wooden matches, and leaned it against the saucer he used as an ashtray.

"You said a couple of minutes," the man said. "And that you were going to show me something."

"Absolutely right," I agreed. I reached in my side pocket, took out a thick roll of bills, and held it in my lap, in my right hand. With my left, I extracted a fifty and put it on the table, saying, "The building you handle on Forty-ninth, the tenant in 5-C died back in March."

I put another fifty down, next to the first. "Her name was Kravitz. Almost ninety years old. Been there forever, way before you took over."

Another fifty. "The landlord's been trying to co-op the building for a few years now. But he's never been able to get enough of the tenants to go along. The Kravitz apartment, that could be the swing vote, depending on who ends up renting the place."

Another fifty. I reached over, tipped my cigarette ash off, but didn't take a drag. The super didn't notice. His eyes were riveted to the tabletop as if his Get into Heaven hand of seven-card stud was being dealt out. "So the landlord doesn't care if the place stays vacant long enough for him to find the *right* tenant. If he put it on the market, it'd be snapped up in an hour. But if there's work that has to be done on the place first, to get it in rentable condition, well . . ."

Another fifty. "So a man comes to you, with a perfectly reasonable proposition. He wants to use the place. Just for a little bit. Not *rent* it, or anything like that. He isn't going to *live* there, just come by once in a while, clear his head, meditate. He's not going to move in any furniture, not going to get mail, not going to have a phone installed. Hell, he doesn't even need the electricity turned back on. Not a soul would ever know he's there."

Another fifty. "All he needs is a couple of keys. One for downstairs, one for 5-C. If anyone *should* see him around, well, he's just one of the helpers you hired to do some of the work in that apartment. No risk, no problem. Nobody's getting hurt."

Another fifty. "Naturally, this is the guy who turns around and gets himself shot. So the cops show up with a lot of questions. Maybe you told them how it was. Maybe you told them you got no idea how he got a key. Doesn't matter. Not to me, not to anyone."

Another fifty. I ground out my cigarette, as he lit another from the butt of his first. "Now, I figure you're a man who knows how to keep his mouth shut. And you're also a man who doesn't miss much. A man who can keep count. What are we up to, anyway?"

"Eight," he said, voice somewhere between greedy and scared.

"I'll bet you're right," I told him, putting another fifty into the pot. "Today's jackpot is five hundred. Want to go for it?"

"For what?" he asked, eyes on the tabletop.

"Did you ever deal with anyone else except him?"

He shook his head "no."

"Ever see anyone but him go into the place?"

Another negative shake.

"The cops showed you his picture when they asked you all their questions?"

This time, the shake of his head was an affirmative.

"And that was the same guy?"

Another nodding "yes."

"Okay, Mr. Ubell," I said, putting down the final fifty. "Here's the question: what day did he make the deal?"

"Tuesday, June tenth," he said, promptly.

"He got the keys right then, or he had to come back?"

"Right then."

"You ever see him again?"

"No."

"How long was the deal supposed to be good for?"

"Two weeks," he said. "No more. Even if I had to change the locks."

"Congratulations, sir," I said, getting to my feet, leaving the money on the table. "You're today's winner."

"**H**e was shot Friday the thirteenth," I said to Wolfe. "Which means he'd only had that deal going with the apartment on Forty-ninth for a few days."

We were sitting on a bench in Forest Park, a big piece of greenery that borders a few different communities in Queens. It was just turning dark—too late for the kids who still watched after-school specials, and too early for the kids who knew they were all lies.

"And you sure he wasn't planning to actually live there?" she asked, thoughtfully.

"The techs may have taken some stuff away with them," I said, "but you know how they work. They take samples, not suites of furniture."

"He could have had camping equipment," Wolfe said.

"You mean like a sleeping bag and stuff?"

"Yes. You can carry enough stuff in a sea bag to be comfortable for a long time."

"That's right," I said. "I remember. You were a Sea Scout when you were a kid."

"Uh-huh," she said, absently, shading her eyes with the edge of her hand, as if she were scanning the horizon. "Someday, we're going to get a little sailboat and go out on the Sound, aren't we, boy?" she said, patting the Rottweiler.

The beast snorted—he'd heard that story before.

"It's an old building," I told her. "Solid brick, thick walls. And even if a neighbor heard footsteps, or a toilet flush, they would just think it was people working on the apartment. That was the story the super circulated—the place needed rehab before he could rent it again. So Wychek *could* have been camping out, like you say, but I don't buy it. He only bought access to the place for a couple of weeks, anyway."

"If you believe the super."

"I do believe him," I said. "He's a guy who likes his money, but he's not a risk-taker. A couple of weeks, no big deal, he could explain it away if he had to. More than that . . ."

"You think he gave a statement?"

"I'm *sure* he did. I don't know if he told them the whole story or not, but I'm betting he did. Why not? NYPD, they're not going to go running to the IRS, especially if they think the witness is cooperating all the way."

Wolfe took a long, deep drag off her cigarette. The white wings in her hair stood out against the night. "They would have asked him about me, too," she said. "Shown him some pictures."

Is she telling me that she . . . ? I rotated my neck, breaking the adhesions loose, buying time.

"And they would have drawn a dead blank," she went on, "even if they tried everyone in that building—I've never been there in my life." She took another hit of her cigarette. "But that doesn't help all that much," she said, shifting to a more clinical tone. "As far as we know, nobody noticed the sister going in there to meet him, either."

"Or the shooter."

"Or the shooter," she agreed. "That's a lot of traffic to miss."

"Not really," I said. "Not for that place. I was in and out, no problem. Never got so much as a strange look. And I had people with me, too. There's only five units per floor, and I don't get the impression that anyone who lives there's all that sociable."

"The sister wasn't the shooter," Wolfe said, sure of herself. "She was the one that called it in. I know people do that," she said, holding up a hand as if I was going to say something, "but that's an 'Ohmygod, what have I done?' thing. In the heat of the moment. Or a fugue state, then they snap out of it, realize what happened while they were out. If the sister was the shooter, she would have said so, told her own story before he could tell his. Otherwise, all she had to do was walk away. He was in no position to call for help."

"There's a wild card," I said. "Something I found."

"What?" she said, shifting position on the bench to face me squarely.

"Dilantin," I said.

"So he was an— Oh!"

"Yeah. Getting shot *hurts*," I said. "Hydrostatic shock . . . blood in the wound channel. Enough of that, you pass out. Or die. But there's also *neural* shock. Like getting punched or kicked, only from the inside. That can KO you, too.

"You can shoot someone real up-close-and-personal with a twenty-five, and they won't necessarily die from it. Ask Amy Fisher. But this guy, he wasn't hit anywhere good. Sure, the thigh could do it, if you tore the femoral artery. But he had lots of time to bleed to death, if that's what he was going to do."

"I know you're an expert," Wolfe said, nothing in her voice but distance.

"Listen to me for a minute," I said. "I think what happened was that he had a seizure behind being shot. The light's terrible there, no electricity. So the shooter probably thought he got the job done and took off. And the sister came later. Maybe even a lot later."

"It's still attempt murder," Wolfe said, a career prosecutor on automatic pilot.

"Yeah," I said. "For the shooter, not for you."

"What's your point?"

"You didn't shoot him," I said. "But he *was* shot. And before he lapses into this bullshit 'coma' the DA was screaming about, he, supposedly, names you as the shooter."

"Yes . . . ?"

"We've been assuming, up to now, that he did it on purpose."

"What?"

"Named you. That he did it to get even. Because he hates you for being the only one to put him away. But what if he was all scrambled when he came out of the fog? A grand-mal seizure, that's a brainwave malfunction, right? He had you on his mind, no question about that—that letter he sent you proves it. So, when he opened his mouth, your name popped out."

"That was a while ago," Wolfe said, thoughtfully. "So it's not the greatest defense, since he's had plenty of time to get his mind straight since then."

"If he ever takes the stand."

"You better not be saying what I—"

"No, nothing like that," I said. "I'm thinking maybe he's already come clean."

"Admitted it wasn't me who—?"

"I'm thinking it was more than that," I said. "To get the kind of protection he's getting, he had to have told them a better story than the DA's been telling in court."

"All right," Wolfe said, after a two-cigarette silence. "I can't make sense out of it. What are you trying to say?"

"There's no such thing as a three-shot accident," I told her. "Wychek wasn't in the wrong place at the wrong time, like a drive-by, or a mugging that went wrong. This wasn't any case of mistaken identity, or where an armed burglar gets surprised in the middle of doing an apartment and panics. This was a hit."

"Fair enough. Especially since you say he never really lived there. But so what?"

"Whoever shot him knew where to find him," I said. "And they didn't do it by investigation—that setup was totally off the books. So whoever tried to take him out, they had Wychek in the crosshairs way before the thirteenth."

"Burke, I know you're going somewhere with this. . . ."

"I think he knew the shooter," I said. "And he's got his own reasons for not naming him."

"So why name *me?*" Wolfe challenged. "Maybe he gets to throw at me for a couple of rounds, but he has to know I'm going to come back at him."

"Anybody who's ever dealt with you would know that," I agreed. "But you're talking courtroom stuff. That wouldn't seem real to him at the time. And even if it did, it wouldn't be an immediate threat. The *real* comeback Wychek's got to be worried about is the shooter making another pass."

"So how does—?"

"He names you when he comes out of the coma because he's not thinking straight. He knows what he *can't* say, but he's still foggy, so . . ."

"But you're saying you think Wychek's recanted, right?"

"I'm not saying it, but I think it's possible."

"Anything's possible," Wolfe said. She didn't sound impatient, just . . . disappointed.

I leaned toward her, dropped my voice, even though there wasn't anyone within eyesight, and Bruiser was too calm for lurkers to be near. "Wychek wants police protection. Not even a twenty-four/seven guard's going to make him happy—he wants to be held at some undisclosed location. You think they're going to do that because he tells them *you're* gunning for him?"

"No," Wolfe said, thoughtfully. "I've got my enemies in the DA's Office, but none of them would buy a story like that."

"They're buying *something*," I said. "Because he's still under wraps. And that means only one thing. . . ."

Wolfe fired up another cigarette, but didn't step into the pause.

"He's got something they want," I said. "Some information that's important enough for them to keep him covered. And the only way they can do that, without tipping their hand, is to keep this bullshit 'case' alive. Otherwise, the real shooter would know he's on the spot."

"You're saying Wychek *admitted* that he lied? About me, I mean. Why would he admit—?"

"Because he has to establish credibility," I said. "The cops know when he was shot—the time period, anyway. As far as Wychek knows, they did their own checking. On you, I mean. If they know where you were when the whole thing went down, had you bracketed, they *already* know you didn't do it. Wychek, he'd figure that out. If he comes clean on his own, they're more likely to believe whatever *else* he has to say. He's in that hospital bed, doing the math. He couldn't take the risk of staying with the lie."

"He's a liar in his bone marrow," Wolfe said, almost spitting the words. "And an inventive one, too. Look at that 'delusional consent' thing he was going to run with. Lying's what he does."

"Sure. But he's not compulsive about it. For Wychek, lying's a tool; he knows when to use it, and when not to. He's got something he says he wants to trade for protection, you know what the cops would do, first thing?"

"Polygraph," Wolfe said, quietly.

"Bingo. So it would be the smart play for him to come clean, at least about you being the shooter. If they debrief him, and he shows deception on *any* of the questions, they're going to kick him to the curb."

"The only people who play like that are the feds."

"Right. And we both know *they'd* never leave a bogus charge hanging over someone so they could camouflage an ongoing investigation."

Wolfe snapped her cigarette into a puddle, hitting it dead center.

"What could someone like Wychek possibly have?" she said.

"He just got out of prison. He may have stumbled across something juicy in there," I told her. *Like, Who's Who in the Brotherhood,* I thought to myself, still wondering about that protection contract.

"Maybe . . . ?" she said, dubiously.

"It could be anything," I said. "A freak like Wychek, who knows what he might have crossed paths with."

"So all we have to do is wait them out," Wolfe said. "Sooner or later, they'll drop the charges against me. There's no need to keep investigating."

"You got *that* much faith in the system?" I said. "We have to keep going, even if it's only for a safety play."

I turned my head, as if I was scanning the area, on the off-chance the truth would show on my face. *Just fucking admit it,* I thought to myself. *You need this case to stay open. You want to be the one. You want to rescue her.*

"I guess it makes sense . . ." she said. "Until Davidson gets it knocked out, anyway. This one, it's never going to go to trial."

"That's the truth," I said.

"**S**ure, there's a way to do it," Terry said. "But I don't have the skills. Not to where I'd be real confident. You're not talking about computers—not the kind of thing I do with them, anyway—you're talking about advanced Web stuff."

"Why could you not learn, mahn?" Clarence asked. "A few weeks ago, I knew nothing about any of this."

"Oh, you picked it up like a natural," Terry assured him. "But I was right there with you, every step of the way. Like you did with me, teaching me to shoot . . ."

The kid interrupted himself to flick his eyes over to me. I nodded him a promise to keep those lessons to myself.

"If you made a mistake, I could show you where you went wrong," Terry went on. "What Burke's talking about, we'd be on our own."

"What if I got you someone?" I asked.

"To teach me to—?"

"To set it up. If you learned from watching, cool. But even if you didn't, all you'd have to do would be the maintenance, once it was in place."

"We could both watch?" Clarence asked, eagerly.

"Yeah," I said. "I already told her there would be two of you."

"You still working on that book?" I asked Hauser. He had been putting together an in-depth investigation into a case where a woman who ran a day-care center with her husband had been convicted of killing three of the children, in separate incidents. Originally, the deaths were marked down to SIDS. But the pattern was too strong to ignore, and, eventually, they made the case with the autopsies. It was the prosecution's theory that the woman had Munchausen by proxy—she killed the babies so that she would be the object of heartfelt sympathy from the shocked town. Hauser had a theory of his own.

"Getting closer," Hauser said, grimly. "It's a *big* manuscript. A hundred and fifty thousand words. I know I've got to cut some of it, but even my editor can't see what could go. It's *already* lean. There's just so many facts. . . ."

Hauser loved and treasured and collected facts like some people do stamps. And he was just as reluctant to part with any of his prizes.

"When do you think it will come out?" I asked him.

"Hell, I don't know. Not for another year and a half, minimum."

"They don't run your picture with your column in the paper, right?"

"No," he said, suspicion clouding his voice.

"You got a Web site?"

"Not a real one," he said. "Just a home-page kind of thing. A bibliography, a few clips, links to stuff I've had published in various places . . . When the book is ready to launch, I'll get a professional to put one together for me. I've already bought a domain name. Why do you ask?"

"So your picture's not on the site, either?"

"No, why should it— Oh!" he said. "Get real!"

"It would only be for a—"

"Forget it," Hauser said.

"After you hear me out," I promised. I've known Hauser for years—not hearing the whole story of *anything* would kill him.

I gave his silence a three-count, then went into my pitch. "You'd get *everything*," I told him, when I was finished. "I can't promise what, exactly, but you *know* there's a story in all this, somewhere."

"I'm not so sure," he said.

"Look, there's nothing to give you away. You said it yourself—nothing you wrote about Wolfe's case came out under your own name. And it could mean the difference for her," I told him, playing my trump. "All the difference."

"Ah," Hauser sighed.

"And all you have to do is not go near your Web site for a couple, few weeks. You told me you're taking the whole family on vacation, anyway. So how hard would that be?"

"Not hard at all," he admitted. "I haven't updated the damn thing in a year."

"So it gets hijacked," I said. "And you never know."

"But my e-mail address is on the—"

"That gets hijacked, too," I said, repeating what I'd been told. "Everything *not* from this one person, it gets forwarded right on to you, unopened, to any other address you say. So, from where you sit, there never was anything wrong with the site. And if you get a certain e-mail at your work address, you can just forward it on to me, see?"

"Did you ever think about *not* being a criminal of some kind?" he asked.

"God, she's beautiful," Terry said.

"Oh, for true, mahn," Clarence echoed. "That woman is a goddess."

"Kim had quite an impact on you guys, huh?" I said.

"I meant her *work*," Terry said.

"I did also," Clarence claimed.

"Right. That's why you asked her if she was married. Twice."

"So she is both," Clarence said. "One does not mean she cannot be the other."

"Wait till you see, Burke," Terry said. "We're ready to go, anytime you want. The hardest thing was talking Kim out of fixing his site when she added your picture."

"It's not working right?"

"Well, it comes up when you dial the URL. But it's all miscoded. The navigation sucks. And the frames are—"

"I got it," I cut him off.

"What's next, mahn?"

"I go in," I said.

"Laura W. Reinhardt," I read aloud from the paper in front of me. "Born 1968, to Laura Smyth and Brian Wychek, of Richmond Hill, New York. Graduated high school in '86, right on schedule. Kept right on through to a B.A. in economics and an M.B.A., awarded 1992.

"I'm guessing she met her husband in college," I said. "Shows she got married in 1990, the year she graduated. To one Matthias Reinhardt. Didn't last long: they were divorced in '93."

"When the card turned green, he split the scene?" the Prof said.

"Could be," I told them. "The divorce was a no-fault, based on a separation agreement. And there's a lot of foreign college students who don't want to go back home."

"Well, she didn't exactly drop out of school to have babies," Michelle said. "It doesn't sound like she missed a day."

"How old is the man who is lying about your . . . about Ms. Wolfe?" Clarence asked.

"He's . . . thirty-nine," I said. "Born in '64. So she's younger."

"Little sister," Michelle said, thoughtfully.

"Little Sister sure took a different road than her brother," I told them. "She's got a good job with Rautroix International, a multinational financial-services firm."

"Wasn't that one of the places that was in the—?"

"Yeah, it was," I said to Michelle. "They relocated to midtown after the World Trade Center was leveled. I guess she wasn't at work when it happened. Or else she got out in time."

"But she lives in Queens?" Michelle asked.

"They all do. Or did, anyway. The parents stayed in Richmond Hill until the father retired in, let me see . . . '97."

"The same year Wychek was convicted," Clarence said, consulting his laptop screen.

Everybody stopped talking. "It is a simple search program," he said, embarrassment and pride tangling in his voice. "We have the data, so we can sort by matches in date and time. You just type in the trigger phrase, and—"

"Oh pul-leeze," Michelle cut him off. "Talk English. You sound like the Mole."

"It is Terry who is teaching me," the West Indian said.

"He's *such* a genius," Michelle said, reversing herself quicker than a bribed judge.

"Where did they go when they retired?" I asked Clarence, before Michelle got into a higher gear.

"Not them, mahn. Just him. The wife, it says here she died in 1990. The same year the daughter married."

"Died of what?" I asked.

"Just says 'natural causes,'" Clarence said. "There is no death certificate or anything in the data bank."

"The daughter, Laura, she lives in Maspeth, in a condo. Has a three-bedroom, two-bath in a converted factory building. Supposed to be very high-end, state-of-the-art," I told them.

"How much does one of those go for?" the Prof asked.

"Says here she paid three seventy-five for it. And that was back in '97, a long time ago."

"It's not pennies," Michelle said. "But she couldn't *touch* that much space for that kind of money in Manhattan."

"Or in parts of Brooklyn, either," I agreed. "But, for what she put down on the total, she could have swung a place in the City."

"She bought it for cash money?" the Prof said, leaning forward, interested now.

"No. But it says here she owns two other units in the same

building," I told them. "Bought all three at the same time. Hers is on the top floor; the other two are smaller, both on the second floor."

"Adjoining?" Michelle wanted to know.

"Yep."

"Smart girl," Michelle said. "She rents them out for now, probably covers her own mortgage that way. And if she finds the right buyer, she can always take down the wall between them, make a *big* place out of it."

"How much?" the Prof asked.

"Total purchase price was nine fifty," I said. "Probably made herself a nice package deal with the people who did the conversion. There's one mortgage on the whole thing, all three units. And that's for . . . seven. So she put up around a quarter-mil in cash, Prof."

"They make that kind of coin where she works?"

"I . . . think so," I said, shrugging my shoulders to show I wasn't certain. "I don't think a six-figure salary and an annual bonus is out of the question. If she saved her money . . ."

"She wasn't working there long enough," Michelle said. "She started *after* she graduated, so sometime late in '92. And not even five years later, she has that kind of money on hand? Maybe her mother left her something?"

I looked over at Clarence. He tapped keys with confidence. Paused. "There was no will," he finally said. "Everything was in the names of both of them. The parents, I mean. The house, the bank accounts, everything."

"Life insurance?" Michelle asked.

"There was . . . yes," Clarence said. "Fifty thousand. But the husband was the beneficiary."

"Maybe borrow money," Mama spoke for the first time.

"A mortgage *is* borrowing—"

"Sure, sure," Mama cut Clarence off. "Borrow down payment. Plenty people do this. Not tell bank."

"That's right," I said. "Banks don't like it when you have to borrow the down. They always have to be first in line."

"Her father," Michelle guessed. "He tapped his pension, maybe?"

"Clarence?" I said.

A couple of minutes passed. But no matter how many key combinations Clarence tapped, he kept shaking his head. "There is nothing in here like that, mahn," he announced apologetically, as disappointed as a played lover.

"Michelle could be right," I said. "Nothing in all this paper screams big bucks. She drives a nice car—an Audi TT ragtop—and her credit cards show she spends pretty decent, but nothing outrageous. Woman's probably just smart with money. She should be; that's her business."

Mama pointed to the stack of paper in front of me. "Big pile," she said, "but not so much." She wasn't talking about money.

"Yeah," I agreed. "Lots of windows. But no doors."

There was nothing I liked about the neighborhood. Even in broad daylight, I could feel the waves of hostility wash against the Plymouth's flanks before I turned off the ignition. Years ago, a black kid had been beaten to death not far from where I was parked, by some self-appointed protectors of the community.

Despite my skin shade, I was still guilty of that black kid's crime—I wasn't from around there.

Even before my face got changed, I had never looked my age. When I was a kid, I was always the one to buy the wine. There have been slashes of white in my hair since I've been nineteen. But somewhere along the road, the process went into reverse. I don't mean I could pass for a man in his twenties anymore. But I can do forty easy enough, and my odometer clicked past that one a long time ago.

So I had dressed in a red windbreaker—reversible to white—zipped over a plain white T-shirt, a pair of jeans, and lace-up black boots. The car was part of my outfit. I was a working guy, spent my weekends restoring the Roadrunner maybe. Nothing special. Nothing threatening.

I had a phone number, but that was a last resort. The number was in another person's name, and unlisted on top of that. Security precautions, for a woman who had been raped in her own home and, for whatever reason, had stayed there afterwards. I didn't want to set off a "How did you get this number?" panic.

I knew the woman worked the evening shift at a local restaurant, and guessed she might be home in the daytime.

She wasn't home. Or wasn't answering the doorbell.

There were four of them waiting, lounging against the Plymouth like it was their clubhouse wall. Young men, looked mid-to-late twenties. Three of them had longish, neat haircuts, black running shoes, different-colored warm-up outfits. Two sported gold around their necks, one wore wraparound blue sunglasses. All three had pagers clipped to their waistbands.

The fourth one came extra-large, a fat guy whose hard bulk probably made him look older than he was. He was wearing a short-sleeved black shirt outside his pants, cream-colored slacks with cuffs, and black slip-ons. A heavy gold watch hung at the end of a forearm so incongruously thin that it looked like someone had mismatched the parts. His other forearm was normal. I mentally shrugged my shoulders—too many possibilities.

As I approached, I ran through the options in my mind. It's always tricky. Come on meek and they might be content with a little bullying and the kind of physical stuff that wouldn't send you to the ER. Come on *too* meek and they might get excited enough to do some real damage.

Or you could get off first. Hurt one of them quick, buy yourself enough room to get gone. That's a desperation play, especially in daylight, where they can get a good look at you, at what you're driving. Because, even if it works, it's not over.

Sometimes, money pays the tolls. But flashing it can also make people greedy. And suspicious.

I wished I had gone with a good suit, and a nice upscale rental car, too.

I wish a lot of things.

"You looking for someone?" one of the gold-chain guys asked, when I got close enough.

"No," I said, not reaching for my keys.

"You just like going into buildings, ringing the bells?" Sunglasses said.

"I like doing a lot of things," I said. "One of them is minding my own business."

The gold-chain guy who hadn't spoken pushed himself away from his lounging position and took a step toward me. The fat guy made some sound I couldn't decode, and the gold-chain guy stopped in his tracks.

"Angie *is* our business," the fat guy said. He pointed to the building I'd just left. "You just went up to her place, rang her bell," he said, pulling a cell phone out of his pocket to tell me he was interfering by invitation.

"My apologies," I said. "I don't just mind my own business, I never talk about anyone else's."

"But now that you know . . ." the fat guy said, stepping closer to me, his eyes on my hands.

"Now that I know . . . what? That you men are looking out for her? I'm glad you are."

"Is that right?" the fat man said. "Maybe you know some special reason why we should be doing that?"

"I might," I said. "But I don't talk about people if they're not in the room."

"Don't talk about her," he said, barely moving his lips. "Talk about you."

"I can't do that without talking about her."

"How come?"

"Let's say I told you I was a doctor. You'd want to know, What's wrong with Angie, a doctor has to come and see her? Am I right?"

"You're not a doctor," Sunglasses said.

"I'll go halfway with you," the fat man said, moving his shoulders to show me he spoke for them all.

I nodded, as if overwhelmed by his logic. "I'm a private investigator," I said.

"You don't look like no—" one of the gold-chain boys said.

I made a "That's the point, right?" face at the fat man, who chopped the gold chain with a glance.

"You carry?" he asked.

"I'm licensed to," I said. "But I usually don't bother. My job isn't going after people, it's helping them."

"And you're here to help Angie, is that what you're saying?"

"That's as much as I'm *going* to say, out here in the street," I told him.

"You supposed to be, like, undercover, dressed like you are?" Sunglasses said.

"Somebody sees me walking over to Angie's building, I look like—what?" I said to him. "Nothing, right? But I show up in a suit, carry a briefcase, that's the kind of thing people pay attention to. And you know how they are, with the mouth, all the time. I figure Angie doesn't need that kind of aggravation."

"That's why you drive this shitbox?" Sunglasses said. "Keep up your image?"

"No," I said, seeing the opening. "The car's a fakeout. Part of the job."

"Fakeout?" one of the gold-chain guys said.

"Want me to show you?" I asked them.

"**M**other*fucker!*" Sunglasses yelled.

He was in the Plymouth's backseat, directly behind the fat man, the gold-chain boys to his left, watching the picket fence of cars out his right window. The Plymouth blasted through the left lane of the Belt Parkway at a buck and a quarter, closing on traffic ahead like an incoming antitank round until I backed off the gas and gave the brakes a chance to do their stuff.

"Holy—" one of the gold chains said, as I took the off-ramp at double the limit, deliberately letting the rear end step out a little, just for the drama.

By the time we were back on city streets, the Plymouth was sounding as docile as a taxicab.

"Do him," the fat man said, pointing at a jacked-up yellow Camaro with tomato-can-sized dual exhausts. It was in the right lane a block ahead of us.

"You do the talking," I told him.

I pulled behind the Camaro. Trailed him for three lights, until I saw an opening, and slid in alongside. I hit the Roadrunner's "meep-meep" horn. The Camaro's driver looked over at us.

"Fifty bucks says that thing can't run," the fat man said.

"What've you got?" the Camaro man asked.

"Ah, never mind," the fat man said, disgusted.

The Camaro revved his engine sharply, clearing out the induction. I feathered the Plymouth's throttle against the brake. Most stick-shift cars can leave on me, but unless they're packing nitrous, I can usually drive around them between lights.

This one wasn't even that close. By the time the Camaro got done spinning his rear tires, I was gone. The backseat echoed to the sound of high-fives.

"You could make real money with this," the fat man said.

"It's a sleeve ace, all right," I told him. "But it's for bigger games."

"Angie's always worried he'll come back," the fat man said on the return run. His soft tone was a counterpoint to Magic Judy Henske's "Betty and Dupree" torching through the Plymouth's tinny speakers. "But where's she going to go? She's a neighborhood girl, all her life. People look out for her, here."

"I can see that," I said.

"When Angie called, that's what I thought, at first—that the motherfucker really came back," he said. "She was whispering—looking at you through the peephole. I got my hopes up. But then she says, no, it—you—wasn't him."

"But she never saw—?"

"Not when it happened," the fat man said. "Not then. But she went to court. Over in Queens, when they finally got him. She wore a scarf and a veil and everything, looked like she was an old lady. He never would have recognized her."

"She had a lot of heart, to go there," I said.

"Ah, Frankie was with her all the time," Sunglasses said.

Angie was a frail, parchment-skinned young woman with long black hair that looked too thick and heavy for her delicate face.

"I'm afraid," she said. "I'm afraid all the time. Ever since it happened. I wasn't always like this. I used to go out. To work. And to have fun, even. I loved to dance. . . ."

"Did you know someone shot him?" I asked.

"No," she said, glancing at the fat man. "Frankie never said. . . ."

"I didn't want to . . . I didn't even want to say his fucking name in front of—"

"Frankie!"

"Sorry," he said, looking at the floor.

"He was shot several times," I told her. "But he didn't die from it."

"Too bad," she said, more sad than angry.

"It is," I agreed. "Do you remember the woman who prosecuted him over in Queens? The DA?"

"Do I remember her? I pray for her every Wednesday and every Sunday of my life. I say a special prayer, that God always keep her safe."

"Wychek said *she* was the shooter," I told her.

"The DA? Eva Wolfe? *Her?*"

"Yes."

"Could *I* help her?" Angie asked, eyes alive for the first time since I'd entered the apartment. "Is there anything I could do?"

"There might be," I said, cautiously. "But I would have to ask you some questions."

"I don't care," she said, chin up defiantly. She stood up, walked over to the couch where the fat man was sitting, and sat down next to him. "Right, Frankie?"

"Right, princess," the fat man said, reaching for her hand.

What the freak had taken was a rosary.

"My aunt Jean gave it to me, when I made my first Holy Communion," the woman said. "I always kept it in a little wood box. My treasure box, I used to call it."

"You didn't see him take it?"

"No. After he . . . I . . . I think I fainted. He was gone. I was still . . . tied up. If it hadn't been for . . ."

"When Angie didn't answer the door, I took it down," Frankie said, no emotion in his voice. "I called for an ambulance, and they sent the cops, too."

"How did he get into the building?" I asked. "This neighborhood . . ."

"He just walked in," Angie said. "I mean, I *let* him in. It was January, after New Year's. It was snowing real bad. He was wearing a ski mask and gloves and a big coat and boots. He was stomping his feet and clapping his hands, like from the cold. He said he came to see Mrs. Trotti; she was his aunt, he came all the way from Jersey.

"Mrs. Trotti, she *had* to be home, but she wasn't answering her bell. I even pushed it myself. It didn't work. So I let him in, so he could go up and knock on her door himself. That's when he took out the razor. . . ."

That white postcard," I told Frankie later. We were sitting in the front seat of the Plymouth, alone this time. "He sent them to all the victims who still live at the same address where they were first attacked."

"You think that means he's going to—?"

"I don't know what it means," I said. "Not for sure. I know, as soon as he got out, he sent a letter to the DA who prosecuted him. Kind of a 'fuck you' note."

"You know where he is?" the fat man asked, like he was asking if the Mets were playing at home that weekend.

"No. So long as the charges are hanging over Wolfe, the cops are keeping him under wraps."

"I never even knew he got out," Frankie said, bitterly.

"You can't do her any good in jail," I told him.

He didn't say anything, just stared straight ahead.

"She's much better now, isn't she?" I asked.

"That's . . . How did you know?"

"I know about things like . . . things like what happened to her," I said. "She needs you with her, not doing time."

"He did . . . that to Angie, he deserves to die," Frankie said. "You're not arguing, right?"

"Not me," I said. "But, for some things, a wedding gets it done better than a funeral would."

"**W**ho knows what a reporter dresses like?" Michelle bitched, rummaging through the row of metal lockers I use as closets.

"Honey . . ."

"Yes, yes, I know. You didn't *ask* me. But you know what they say—first impressions?"

"Right," I said, surrendering to the inevitable.

"If you were younger, we could probably go with casual, but . . ."

"I get it."

"You do *not* get it, you thug," she mock-snarled. "We are looking for a *look,* and I'm not sure you have anything here that will—"

"Michelle," I said, "you're not going shopping."

"Oh, grow up! We certainly can't have you wearing brand-new togs. This isn't a date. Now, let me see. . . ." She continued, an unstoppable force, going through every piece of clothing I owned. "You don't even own a single sports jacket. Ridiculous. You know, a nice suede jacket is something every man should have in his wardrobe. You can wear it with anything, and you look *dressed.*"

"I don't—"

"A suede sports jacket," she said, in a tone of finality. "But not some boxy American cut, and not three-button, either. A cotton shirt. Blue. Oxford cloth, button-down collar, but *no* tie. Gray slacks, a *good* pair of black shoes . . ."

"Michelle . . ."

"Oh, just *stop* it, Burke. A suit would be too much. Especially those gangster things you have."

"Hey, those are *lawyer* suits," I protested.

Michelle put her hands on her hips and stared me down.

"No silk shirts, either," she said, satisfied she was in control. "Or those hideous pullovers. You can wear the jacket I am going to get you every time you see her, like a trademark. She'll love it."

"I don't know if she'll even agree to meet with me," I said. "Why don't we wait until I—?"

"No," is all my little sister said.

"**M**s. Reinhardt, my name is J. P. Hauser. Thank you for taking my call."

"You told the receptionist this was a 'family matter,'" she said. Her voice was measured, precise . . . just this side of wary.

"I understand you have an important position," I said. "I assumed I wouldn't be able to reach you without giving some sort of reason. I didn't want to lie, but I didn't want to give out any information to a third party. So I—"

"What is it you want?" She didn't sound frightened, or even nervous, just impatient.

"I want to talk to you about your brother," I said.

"Are you with the—?"

"I'm an investigative journalist, Ms. Reinhardt."

"You mean you're a reporter."

"I *am* a reporter," I said, "but I'm not calling you in that capacity. My goal isn't some article, or a column. I'm writing a book. And I was hoping we could—"

"A book? About my brother?"

"A book about how America's criminal-justice system has gone off the rails," I said. "A book about how innocent men are being sent to prison, even executed, every day, for crimes they never committed. About how, every time an innocent man is imprisoned for crimes, the real criminal remains at large."

"And you think my brother . . . ?"

"Your brother's case would be the perfect centerpiece to the book, Ms. Reinhardt. Plenty of people have been sent to prison by overzealous prosecutors, but how many have been *shot* by them?"

"Ah. So you're covering the trial, is that it?"

"No. I mean, certainly, I'll be at the trial, but that isn't the point of my book. It wouldn't surprise me at all if the same 'system' that wrongfully convicted your brother in the first place now finds a way to acquit the person who tried to kill him. I see your brother as a personification of everything that's wrong with the way we 'fight crime' in America."

"So why call me, Mr. . . ."

"Hauser."

"Hauser. Isn't it my brother you really need to speak to?"

"Not really," I said. "I don't mean I wouldn't welcome the opportunity, but what I'm really looking for are those within what I call the 'concentric circles of impact' from a wrongful conviction. My thesis is that it isn't just *one* life that can be ruined, it's all the lives *surrounding* it."

"I'm a very private person, Mr. Hauser."

"I respect that, Ms. Reinhardt. All I'm asking is maybe an hour of your time, *entirely* off the record. The truth is, I haven't made my decision yet."

"I don't understand."

"Well, I am absolutely committed to the book. In fact, I've signed a contract for it, and accepted the advance. I was working on it, in my off-hours, a year before your brother's case came to light—the one where he was shot, I mean. I thought it would lend some real . . . drama to the material. Put a human face on the problem. But there are other, equally outrageous miscarriages of justice all around the country. To be brutally honest, I have a . . . point of view. Or, I should say, a point to make. I have to be certain my lead actor, if you will, is right for the role."

"Mr. Hauser . . ."

"I apologize," I said quickly. "I've been so caught up in this project for so long that I seem to assume other people I talk to understand exactly what I'm doing. Let me be very clear, all right? I don't want the . . . centerpiece of my book to be a person with a . . . negative background. I have several *documented* cases of innocent people sent to prison, but in some of those the individual's life prior to conviction wasn't exactly . . . Well, they weren't what you would call model citizens. I researched your brother's case, and it seems, before his wrongful conviction, he led an exemplary life. *That's* really what I want to talk to you about."

"I wouldn't want my name to be—"

"Ms. Reinhardt, I said off the record, and that's what I meant. I can't give you—I'm sure you understand—any form of 'approval' over what I write, but I can promise you that your name, or any information about you, will not be in the book, period. Fair enough?"

"I . . . don't know," she said, calmly. "Is there a number where I can reach you?"

"Of course," I said. And gave her Hauser's private line at the newspaper. "I also carry a cell phone with me at all times. Let me give you that number, too. . . ."

"**W**hy should she talk with you, mahn?" Clarence asked.

We were sitting around my green-felt-topped poker table, playing five-card draw. Table stakes, for wooden matches.

"Damage control," I said.

"Schoolboy means she might show just to see what *he* know," the Prof amplified.

"You didn't tell her you knew anything about her?" Terry asked. "Like where she lives?"

"That's the next round," I told him. "It's already chambered, but we don't pull the trigger unless she nixes the meet. Calling her at home would spook her—the number's unlisted—and so would a surprise visit. She doesn't even know that I know she was the one who made the 911 call . . . not for sure, anyway."

"We have the next screen done, mahn," Clarence said. "You know, the one you asked for?"

"The victims who changed addresses after the rapes?"

"Yes. That was *most* of them," the West Indian said. "In fact, five of them left the city altogether."

"'City'?" I asked.

"Burke's talking native tongue, son," the Prof explained to Clarence. "When you born here, 'the City,' that's Manhattan, okay? But you, you talking New York City, right? They got themselves *all* the way out of town, not just over to Brooklyn or someplace?"

"That is right," Clarence said. "In fact . . . give us a minute, mahn."

He and Terry got up and went back into the part of my place that they had turned into their personal HQ.

"He's picking up stuff from Terry like he was born to it," I said.

"Yeah, bro. True clue. Only . . . you might want to have a little talk with the kid about what's *he's* picking up. Lot of heat on that two-way street."

"You mean Clarence has been teaching him to—?" I asked, shading that I'd already been tipped.

"Oh yeah," the little man affirmed. "Kid's not going to be no Wyatt Earp, maybe, but he can handle a piece pretty good already."

"Don't even," I told him. "If Michelle gets wind of that, she's going to—"

"What'd I just *say*, okay?"

"Burke!" Terry said, busting into the room.

"Terry, I want to—"

"Wait. Just a minute. Clarence had this idea, for another field. It only took a couple of minutes to run it."

"And . . . ?"

"And the ones who moved, we thought it might be split—like, maybe the ones who weren't *born* here, they'd be the ones to go back home. But that didn't work. I mean, two of them were students, just here to go to college, and *they* went back home . . . to where their parents lived. But there's no pattern to any of the others. Some of the women who came here, like for jobs or whatever, they just moved to different addresses. And a couple who were born here, they just up and left. Like starting over."

"Fifty to one, none of them got a white postcard," I said. "You got a list of the ones who stayed around here?"

"Sure," Clarence said. "But these records are not fresh, mahn. They could have *kept* moving."

"Yeah, I know," I said, reaching for my cellular.

"**W**hat do you think, Mama?" I asked. It was the following afternoon, still light outside, but in my booth too dark to read a newspaper. I'd been talking nonstop, from the first cup of soup through the crackle-skinned duck, running it down from the beginning. Mama hadn't said a word, just making the occasional sound to let me know she was listening. Like always.

"Must be money," she finally said. "Money someplace."

"Money for us?" I asked, getting to it.

"Girl have money, yes?" she demanded.

"Wychek's sister?"

"Yes, sister."

"Well, like you said before, Mama, it may not be cash money. Just on paper. A woman who does what she does—in her business, I mean—she probably knows how to leverage. It could all be a house of cards, no way to pull cash out of it."

"You think police girl not shoot him, right?"

"I know she didn't."

Mama watched me with an assayer's eyes for a long moment. "Not make sense," she finally agreed. "And you think they *know,* yes?"

"They almost have to, by this time."

"But keep . . . fake because he have something they want?"

"Right."

"So?"

"I don't—"

"So *money,*" Mama said, in a tone of finality. "Maybe not cash money, but *worth* money."

"That's what I think, too."

"No matter," Mama said.

"What?" I said, shocked at the blasphemy.

"You not looking for money," she said, accusingly. "You do all this for police girl."

"Wolfe's done plenty for—"

"Sure sure," she said, done.

"Shhe called." Hauser's voice, on one of my cell phones.

"How long ago?"

"Fifteen minutes," he said. "She was pretty slick about it, too. Didn't ring the direct line; just called the switchboard and asked for me."

"You're sure it was—?"

"She asked to speak to me . . . to J. P. Hauser. I told her, He's out in the field, but we have his pager if it's an emergency. Or she could just leave her number and . . . That's when she hung up."

"Sounds right," I said. "I guess we'll know pretty soon."

"Just be sure you—" Hauser started to say. The ringing of another of my cell phones cut him off.

"**H**auser," I answered.

"It's Laura Reinhardt, Mr. Hauser."

"Thanks for getting back to me," I said. "Does this mean we can talk?"

"We can *meet*," she said—not hard, but in control. "And I can listen a little more."

"Fair enough. Just pick a time and a place."

"Do investigative reporters have expense accounts?" she said, the barest hint of teasing in her tone.

"Well, as I told you, this isn't a job for the paper. But expenses *are* part of my book contract, so . . . ?"

"So—do you know Tramello's? It's in Richmond Hill, Queens?"

"I can find it," I said.

"Eight o'clock, then," she said, firmly. "There'll be a reservation. In my name."

Tramello's turned out to be just off Hillside Avenue, in the shadow of the Long Island Railroad trestle. I gave it a quick pass at seven-thirty, a slower one a few minutes later. All I could tell about the place was that it wasn't any new addition to the neighborhood.

I found a parking spot near the public library and strolled over, checking my watch. At five minutes to eight, I walked into a joint that looked like it had been lifted from a Scorsese movie. The man at the front desk was wearing a mortician's suit, thinning black hair plastered to his scalp, like the greeter's grin to his face.

"I'm meeting Ms. Reinhardt," I said, politely. "I believe we have a reservation?"

"Your party is already here, sir," he said. "Let me show you to your table."

He was moving off before I could thank him, threading his way through a large, dark room that was maybe a third full. He turned to his right and stepped aside to usher me into a much smaller space—four tables, lots of room between them.

The woman sitting alone at the corner table was wearing a business suit the color of dried blood. Her blouse was a white, frilly-front affair, defying closer examination. She stood up as I approached, extended her hand.

"Mr. Hauser," she said.

"Ms. Reinhardt. Thank you for taking the time to—"

"Oh, I had to eat anyway," she said, making a brushing gesture with her left hand as she sat down, smoothing her skirt.

She was a small, slender woman, with auburn hair worn in some short, stylish cut that Michelle would have a name for. Dark-blue eyes, highlighted with more mascara than I would have expected. Her lipstick was the same shade as her jacket. No rings on her fingers, but the Patek Philippe watch on her right wrist—a small, black-faced rectangle on a gold bracelet—had double rows of diamonds running along its length.

"Not what you expected?" she said, giving me a tiny smile.

"This place?" I said, looking around at the heavy dark-purple crushed-velvet drapes that blocked all the windows.

"I've been coming here since I was a little girl," she said, ignoring my question. "The food is a little on the heavy side, but it's as fresh as anything you could find in Little Italy."

"You're part Italian?"

"Just in my soul," she said, chuckling softly. "I'd rather shop in Milan than Warsaw."

"I didn't mean to pry," I said. "Although I guess that sounds ridiculous, coming from a reporter. I meant—"

"Oh, I understand," she said. "Maybe we should—"

A waiter materialized, standing more behind me than between us.

"Do you know what you want?" she asked.

"Chicken Marsala," I told the waiter.

She ordered a house salad, pasta primavera, and a glass of wine.

"I hope you don't mind," she said, taking a silver cigarette case out of her purse.

"That would make me a gross hypocrite," I told her, reaching for my own pack.

She handed me a heavy gold Dunhill lighter, and I fired up both our smokes.

Neither of us said anything until she had smoked hers almost down to the filter.

"Your Web site isn't very impressive," she said, smiling, as she ground out her cigarette.

"How did you . . . ? Oh, *that* thing. Yeah, I'm kind of a technophobe. Old-school all the way. No laptop, no PDA—I even take notes the old-fashioned way, with a pen. But everyone kept telling me I had to have a Web site, with a book coming out and all, so I just followed the instructions. I guess I should have hired a professional to do it right, but it seems like, I don't know, a waste."

"It had good information, though," she said. "Your credits, stuff like that."

"I . . . guess," I said, unconvinced. "But there's not much point in a résumé when you're not looking for a job."

"At least your photograph did you justice."

"Hey!" I said, half grinning at her. "I said I was a journalist, not a movie star."

"I—"

The waiter appearing with our food cut off her response. As if by mutual agreement, we stayed silent until he was done placing everything to his satisfaction.

"Good," I said, taking a bite.

"It is, isn't it? My favorite is the bracciole, but every time I have it, I have to go out and buy bigger skirts."

"It can't be that bad."

"Bad? It's *wonderful*. But I know me. My personality, I mean. When I like something, I'm always at risk for overindulgence. And I don't have the time to go to the gym three times a week like I'm supposed to."

"You look . . . I'm sorry, I . . . I realize this isn't a date. It's just that . . ."

"What?"

"You look like you spend a *lot* of time in the gym."

"What I spend a lot of time doing is sitting down," she said, twisting her mouth into a mock pout. "And even female executives are prone to secretarial spread."

"I didn't mean to . . ."

"Oh, *relax,*" she said. "Don't you like flirting?"

"I'm no good at it," I confessed.

"Maybe you should take lessons."

"I never . . . Ah, I get it."

"No, you . . . Oh, never mind. I don't think small talk is your forte, Mr. Hauser."

"Could it be J.P.?"

"J.P. it is. Does it stand for anything? The initials?"

"Jonas Paul. But nobody ever called me that."

"Not even your mother?"

"Only when she was mad at me."

"That's the only time I ever heard my full name, too," she said, delicately working on her salad.

I had a little more of the chicken, sipped the ginger ale I'd asked the waiter for when he'd come back to replenish the bread basket.

Accordion music started up in the large room. I turned toward the source of the noise, spotted a short, fat man in a dark-blue tux, strolling from table to table.

"Don't worry," she said, "he never comes back in here."

"Whew!" I said, miming great relief.

We ate in silence for another couple of minutes, stealing glances at each other, then looking away.

"Why my brother?" she said, suddenly.

"Well, like I told you on the phone, you can't write a book about a concept. It has to be . . . personified in some way. You need a character the reader can identify with. Otherwise, all the research gets dismissed as academic."

"Academic? I would think that would be a credential."

"Maybe for a professor," I said. "Not for a journalist."

"Meaning, it wouldn't sell as many copies?"

"Not even close," I conceded.

The waiter cleared away the remnants of our meal, asked us if we wanted dessert. Laura Reinhardt raised her eyebrows at me. "I could go for a little *tórta,*" I said.

She held up two fingers.

"Now, *that* may have been going too far," she said, patting her lips with a white napkin when she was done. She leaned back in her chair, seemed to think better of it, and bent toward me. I lit another cigarette for her.

"Tell me about the book," she said.

"You've been reading about the death-penalty cases—the ones where they find out, years later, that a man sentenced to death was innocent all along?"

"I've seen things on TV, that's all."

"It's a national scandal," I said, locking her eyes with my sincerity. "In Illinois, the last governor canceled every single pending execution before he left office. He said he just couldn't be sure that people on death row are really guilty. In one case, this guy was accused of raping and murdering a little girl. Turned out it wasn't him."

"How would they—?"

"Sometimes, it's DNA," I told her. "Sometimes, believe it or not, the actual criminal confesses—usually when they've caught him on a whole bunch of other things. Sometimes, it's as simple as an alibi they never checked out. But it always comes down to the same thing, which is what my book's about."

"Innocence?"

"No. I mean, innocence is a *part* of it, but that's not the theme, not the . . . drive-force. I'm trying to go deeper. These things aren't due to incompetence. Well, *some* of them are, sure. But the dark underbelly to all this is the kind of people who become prosecutors. I'm not talking about corruption, either—although *that* happens, too—I'm talking about people who have lost their way."

"Prosecutors?"

"Prosecutors. Some of them lose sight of the difference between fighting *crime* and fighting *criminals*."

"I don't see the difference myself," she said. "If you fight criminals, you *do* fight crime, isn't that true?"

"In *that* order, yes," I agreed. "But not when it's reversed."

"How could it be—?"

"A child is murdered. A woman is raped. A building is torched, and a fireman dies when the roof collapses. A . . . You know the type of crime I'm talking about. Public outrage. Lots of media attention. Demands for results. The pressure on prosecutors is tremendous. And, sometimes, they can be so hyper-focused on the *crime* that they ignore the *criminal*. It's almost like, if they can put *someone* in prison, the crime is 'solved.' It just . . . consumes them. Like going snow-blind.

"And it's our—the public's—fault, too. How do we judge prosecutors? On their conviction rates, right? So, if a DA has any sort of political ambitions, he'd *better* clear his cases. That's where plea bargaining came from, originally. It *is* a bargain. The criminal gets a much lighter sentence, and the prosecutor doesn't take a chance on losing a trial."

"But why would an innocent person agree to a plea bargain?"

"They *don't*," I said, lighting another cigarette. I left it in the ashtray next to the candle-in-Chianti-bottle that had been burning since before I sat down. "And that's where the gate to hell opens. That's when the pressure builds to get a result. *Any* result. That's when an innocent man goes to prison."

"A man like—?"

"John Anson Wychek. You understand what they did to him, don't you? I don't mean the wrongful conviction," I said, holding up my hand to stop her from speaking, "I mean the *rest* of it."

"I know it ruined his—"

"Ms. Reinhardt . . ."

"Laura."

"Laura, the fact that you couldn't be closer to the situation and even *you* don't understand the scope of the tragedy, well, that *proves* why my book has to be written. Look, your brother was convicted of a *single* crime, right?"

"Yes. They said he—"

"In fact," I interrupted, "he was convicted of more than a *dozen.*"

"What? How can you—?"

"Laura, these cases don't have to be *solved.* They just have to be *cleared.* Do you understand the difference?"

"I guess I don't."

"When your brother was convicted of that one crime, the police 'cleared' a whole bunch of *other* crimes, naming him as the perpetrator. I don't mean they *charged* him with the crimes. I don't mean he was ever *tried* for them. But, as far as the police are concerned, those crimes are closed cases now.

"They *never* could have proved those cases against your brother. He was innocent, and I think they must have known that. So they never brought him to trial. But with that one single conviction they announce that *all* the crimes—all the *similar* crimes that were committed throughout the entire metropolitan area!—are solved. And John Anson Wychek, well, he's the guilty man."

"They never said—"

"They don't have to say anything to *you.* All that counts is the press. And for the press, it's an instant no-story. They can't print that your brother is guilty—he'd sue them for millions. But they can't pressure the DA to 'solve' the cases, either. See how it happens?"

"My God," she said, eyes widening.

"Yes," I said. "I know just what you're thinking. Somewhere in this city, maybe somewhere close by, a vicious serial rapist is walking around loose. *That's* the hidden penalty society pays every time we stand by and allow an obsessed prosecutor to railroad an innocent man."

"And you think John's story could change all that?"

"For what I want, I think he's perfect," I said, pure truth beaming out of me, like I was radioactive with it.

The check came inside a small leather folder. The waiter dropped it off and vanished. I opened it up. Much less than I'd expected. I put a fifty inside the folder, closed it back up.

"Wouldn't credit cards make a better record for your accountant?" she asked.

"The only accountant who'll ever see this bill is the publisher's. And they're not going to care."

"You're not one of those guys who pays cash for everything, are you?"

"Me? No. I use credit cards when I have to, I guess. Probably more of that old-fashioned thing. I'm a long way from paying bills over the Internet."

"Because you're worried about the security?"

"The security?"

"You know," she said, raising her eyebrows just a touch. "Identity theft, stuff like that."

"Oh. Well, you can't work where I do without hearing about it. But . . . no. I guess I just don't see what's so great about doing it any new way."

"Sometimes, to make things better, you have to try new ways," she said.

The waiter came back, picked up the leather folder, and walked off without a word.

"What's the next step?" Laura Reinhardt asked me.

"That depends on you," I said.

"But you're going ahead, doing a story on my brother, even if I don't . . . cooperate, I guess is the word I was looking for."

"I . . . I can't say that. Not for sure. My contract is for a book on the consequences of false—or, I should say, 'wrongful'—imprisonment. I thought your brother would be the ideal way to present the material, but he's not the only candidate. Let's face it, if he *was*, I wouldn't have much of a book."

"I don't under—"

"If this kind of thing was an isolated incident, it makes a good *news* story, but it's not a book," I told her. "What I'm talking about is a phenomenon. An epidemic. There's a lot of reasons for wanting your brother to be the centerpiece. I admit, it would be easier for me, with everything based right here in the city, but there are others who would fit the bill."

The waiter came back with the leather folder. I opened it. Found a ten-dollar bill, a single, and some change.

"You're a gambler, huh?" I said to him.

"OTB's right down the street," he said, flashing a grin.

I extracted the single, closed up the folder, and handed it back to him.

"Thank you, sir," he said, nodding as if a deeply held belief had just been confirmed.

"**C**an I give you a lift anywhere?" I asked, as we stepped onto the sidewalk.

"I have my own car," she said. "But I'd appreciate you walking me over to it. This neighborhood has changed a lot since I was a little girl."

"My pleasure."

She walked with a compact, efficient stride, matching my normal pace easily, despite the difference in our heights.

"Did you and your brother eat at that same place when you were kids?"

"No. It wasn't really for family outings. I mean, it *is,* but I only went there with my father. Like for special treats, just the two of us. There was a Jahn's close by, too. I always had a sundae I used to think they made just for me—pistachio ice cream with butterscotch topping."

"You ate that *voluntarily?*"

"I'm a lot more adventurous than I look," she said, with a little giggle. "I liked eating something the boys were afraid of."

"Just *hearing* about it scares me," I admitted.

"That's mine," she said, stopping midblock. She reached in her purse and took out a set of keys. A chirping sound identified her silver Audi convertible as clearly as if she had pointed her finger.

"Very nice," I said. "You don't see many of those in the City."

"The TT?"

"Convertibles. Costs a fortune to garage them. And if you don't . . ."

"That's true," she said. "But where I live, indoor parking's part of the deal."

"I've heard about places like that."

"You don't look as if you're starving," she said, fingering my new suede jacket.

"I'm not," I said. "But this coat's not part of my wardrobe; it pretty much *is* my wardrobe."

"So I can't interest you in some of our more . . . adventurous investing prospects?" she said, smiling.

"Maybe after my book hits the charts."

She crossed the street, opened the door to her convertible.

"I had a very nice time . . . J.P.," she said, almost formally.

"I did, too. I wish . . ."

"What?"

"Never mind. I . . . I don't want to . . . Look, Laura, I know you've got a lot to think about. About what I told you, I mean. Or people to talk it over with, or whatever. But can I ask you just one thing?"

"What would that be?"

"Will you call me, either way? I mean, if the answer's 'no,' even then?"

"If you want, sure. But couldn't we just say, if you don't hear back from me by—?"

"I would much rather you called," I told her. "And I promise you, if the answer's 'no,' I won't try to talk you out of it."

She climbed into her car, got behind the wheel, looked up at me. "I'll call you," she said. "Count on it."

"All right, Schoolboy. You got a look, but did you set the hook?"

"Tried like hell, Prof. But I can't know unless I feel a tug on the line."

"Yeah," he said, unconvinced. "Your girl, she's holding the case ace, right?"

"Wolfe? If I'm right about Wychek already recanting, sure. But we can't know if—"

"And we got the boss hoss for a shyster, too, right?" the Prof pressed.

"Davidson's as good as there is," I agreed.

"But you still got my boy and the T-man working those computers like they trying to find the cure for cancer," the little man said. "And you, you got no doubt, but you still out and about."

"Am I missing something here?" I said.

"Not you, bro. It's me that don't see."

"Why I'm still working?"

"Don't play dumb, son. Every one of us know what you got in this. And when it looked dicey, dealing us in, that was fine. But now . . . ?"

"What, Prof?"

"Tell me there's some green in the scene," the little man pleaded. "Tell me you a man with a plan. A scheme beats a dream, every time."

"It's not a—"

"Don't have to be no sure score, honeyboy. But there's a longshot that we got money on *somewhere* in all this, true as blue?"

"True as blue," I promised.

He wants to meet you, again." Pepper's voice, over my cellular.

"Did he say why?"

"Another file, is all he said."

"Couldn't he just leave it with—?"

"I got the impression he couldn't even *copy* it."

"Tell him—"

"I did," she cut me off. "Tomorrow night, Yonkers Raceway. In the outdoor grandstand at the top of the stretch. It's a Thursday; he'll find you easy enough, he said."

I moved the first two fingers of each hand across the tabletop, miming a trotting horse. Not a pacer, a trotter—Max knew the difference. Then I turned an imaginary steering wheel, spread my hands to ask a question I already knew the answer to.

"You know how I like it, honey," Michelle insisted.

"Word for word," I acknowledged. Then I started again, from the beginning.

Michelle made a moue of annoyance when I told her I didn't recall whether Laura Reinhardt had worn any perfume, never mind what it might have smelled like. But mostly she stayed patient, her long red fingernails resting on the tablecloth.

"Maybe it's just her . . . habit," Michelle said, when I was finished. "There's no way to tell unless we could talk to someone else she met for the first time."

"What habit?"

"Playing."

"Just what she said about flirting?"

"No, stupid. Talking about her . . . When a woman mentions a body part, she either wants reassurance about it, or she wants you to pay attention to it."

"I don't—"

"Yes, I know," she cut me off. "Look, I'm not talking about *asking*. That's more . . . intimate. You don't ask a man if he thinks a certain dress makes you look fat unless you have something going with him."

"She didn't ask me—"

"She didn't *ask* you anything, sweetheart. She *told* you all about 'secretarial spread,' though, didn't she?"

"I . . . Yeah, she mentioned it, anyway."

"But you couldn't *see* what she was talking about, right?"

"Not with her sitting—"

"Exactly. Now, sometimes, if something *bothers* a woman, they can't keep themselves from picking at it. The way magazines are today, I'm surprised *more* young girls don't starve themselves to death or run around getting plastic surgery. So—a woman says to you, 'I know I have a big nose,' you're supposed to say, 'What?,' as if it never occurred to you. But she tells you she has a big butt, what are you supposed to say then?"

"I don't know."

"For once, that was just as well," she said, grinning. "There *is* no right answer to that one, not in the situation you were in. You can't deny it, because you haven't *seen* it. And you can't say you *like* big butts, because this wasn't supposed to be a date."

"So what you said about habit . . . ?"

"Either it's something that really bothers her, and she can't keep herself from referring to it—there're women who are compulsive like that, God knows—or it's her way of getting sex into your mind."

"She didn't do any of the . . . other stuff."

"Like bump her hip into you by accident when you're walking together? Or licking her lips after she has some ice cream?"

"I . . . I'm not sure," I said, trying to remember. "But she . . . It was more than that. More than *not* that, I mean."

"Well, the way you left it, the next move is all hers, anyway."

"What are you saying?"

"That *she* can't tell, either."

"Huh?"

"Burke, sometimes you are the thickest-skulled . . . Look, baby, let's say the girl *was* interested in you. Not in this book you're supposedly writing, or in doing something for her brother, or whatever. Just in you, okay? So she shows you a couple of little things, sees what you do. But you, *being* you, don't do anything.

"Now *she's* confused. Maybe you missed her signals. Maybe you weren't interested. Or maybe you were interested as all hell, but you're trying to be a professional—the book and all—and you didn't want to blow it. See?"

"I can't read her, honey. All I can tell you is, she's not from down here."

"'Down here' is not an address, baby," she reminded me.

I moved my head. Not so much a nod as a bow, to the truth, letting my little sister's core sadness reach out to hold hands with my hate, like the first time we met. "So you're saying, even if she blows off the book, I could maybe—?"

"What could you possibly lose?" Michelle said. "You know what the Prof always says: When you're looking to score, a window works as good as a door . . . ?"

"And a nun lies as good as a whore," I finished for her.

"Y ou got an e-mail!" Terry, on the phone.

"Me?"

"Hauser. It came to the e-mail address on his site, and bounced right over to us. Just like the Dragon Lady said."

"Read it to me."

"It just says, 'I knew I shouldn't have had that torta.' The word 'knew' is in italics, well, not really italics—but if you put asterisks around a word it means—"

"Just read the whole thing to me, kid, okay? Then you can fill in whatever I don't understand."

"Right. Okay, it says, 'I knew I shouldn't have had that torta. It's back to the gym now for sure. I enjoyed our conversation, and I would like to have another. And to hear more about your project. Call me.'"

"Was it signed?"

"Yes. Just the letter 'L.'"

"Okay, can we just—?"

"Wait," he said. "Let me tell you what else, remember? Okay, first of all, after the word 'torta,' there's the Internet symbol for a smile."

"Like one of those happy-face things?"

"No. It's just keystrokes, like from a regular typewriter. You take a—"

"Never mind, kid. Sorry to have interrupted you. What else?"

"After she says 'for sure,' there's an exclamation point. And where she says she enjoyed your . . . conversation, there are three periods between the two words, like a pause."

"Like you just did?"

"Egg-*zact*-lee!" he said. Dealing with my slow learning curve, the kid had learned to take his happiness where he found it . . . just like his mother. "The only other thing is, the letter 'L' that she signed it with? That was in lowercase, with no period after it."

"Does that mean something?"

"Well, it could . . ." he said, doubtfully. "But there's no way to tell. Some people use that lowercase 'l' to stand for 'love,' some people use a lowercase initial to be modest, or even to be . . . submissive, I think. But with e-mail, you can never really tell, because people write it and send it off so fast, they never check what they type. So sometimes you think something means something, and all it means it that whoever wrote the e-mail was sloppy."

"Not this one," I said.

"Huh?"

"Whatever she is, she's not sloppy."

"Oh. Well, you want to answer it?"

"Couldn't I just call her? That way, she'd know I got her message."

"You could, sure. But the message just came in, and it's almost midnight."

"I see what you mean. Anyway, I'm not supposed to have her home phone number—it's not listed."

"The e-mail came from her home account," Terry said. "So we have that now, too."

"What good does that do us?"

"I don't know, not for sure. But the Dragon Lady says she might be able to tell us some things from the headers and the IP number—"

"Terry . . ."

"Sorry! I just got . . . Anyway, sure, you can answer her. But if you do it now, she'll know you're awake, and she might want to IM.

You can't do that from your computer—the one we left there—not without me there. She'd know pretty quick you weren't used to doing it."

"Doing it? I don't even know what it *is*."

"See?"

"Yeah. Hey, wait a minute, T. Would she have any way of knowing when her mail was received?"

"Not unless you have the same . . . Ah, never mind, the short answer is no."

"Okay, let me think for a second. I have to go meet someone tomorrow night, so it can't be then. For her, I mean. How about this? We send her a message around three in the morning . . . like I couldn't sleep, so I turned on the computer and found her e-mail."

"That's easy. All I have to do is queue it to . . . Never mind," the kid said, cutting himself off again. His learning curve was a lot flatter than mine.

"All right, how about this, then: 'Me, too. All counts, except the gym. I'm meeting a source tonight, but I'll call you at work, okay?'"

"That's cool," Terry said. "You've got the e-mail rhythm down just right."

"Beginner's luck."

"How do you want to sign it?"

"Uh, how about 'J.P.'?"

"Caps, with periods—like initials?"

"Perfect. Thanks, T."

"Hey, this is *fun*. And it'll give Clarence another excuse to talk to the Dragon Lady, too."

It was just going on eleven the next morning when I dialed her number.

"Hi!" she said, when they put me through. "Boy, you keep late hours."

"More like erratic ones," I told her, setting the stage.

"I was planning to call you if I didn't hear from you," she said. "I realized, as soon as I sent the e-mail, that you might not check it for days. Some people don't."

"That's me," I admitted. "Only it's weeks, not days. I don't get a lot of e-mail at that address; mostly, it just comes to work."

"I'm surprised, with that sexy picture of you on the site," she said, teasing.

"Don't remind me," I groaned. "That was the publisher's idea. They said there has to be a photo on the book jacket, anyway, so it would be better if . . ."

"I think it's cute," she said.

"You and my mother," I said. "That's about it."

"Mothers are like that, aren't they?"

"I guess they all are," I said, thinking that was the biggest lie that had ever come out of my lifelong liar's mouth.

"'Meeting a source.' That sounds so mysterious. But I guess, when you think about it, that's what I am, too, right? A source."

"I hope not."

"What do you mean?" she said, softly.

"It's . . . kind of complicated," I said. "I'd rather tell you in person."

"All right. Not tonight, I know. Tomorrow?"

"Just name the—"

"Can you pick me up after work? I know the traffic is hellish at that hour, but it would be a real treat not to have to ride that miserable subway. Especially this time of the year. *Double*-especially on a Friday night."

"No problem. Is there a place to park around there?"

"You won't need one. Just be out front—you have the address, yes?—at seven."

"Oh. Sure. I thought you meant we'd eat someplace close to where you worked, and then I'd drive you home."

"Would you prefer that?"

"To what?"

"To what I have in mind."

"No."

"How do you know?"

"Journalist's instincts," I told her.

Sands hadn't mentioned a specific time to Pepper, and Max wanted to get there early enough to plot out the first race, anyway. I scored a prime parking spot around back, right near the entrance closest to the grandstands.

We bought a program and found seats about midway up and over to the left side, facing forward. The grandstand was more than three-quarters empty. Over an hour to post time—all the tote board showed was the morning line.

I started working on the program, Max watching avidly. I'd taught him to handicap years ago, and he understood all the arcane symbols I used to make notes. But what he was really checking was to see if my scientific method squared with his mystical one. Between gin rummy and casino over the past twenty years, Max was into me for a good quarter-mil. He wasn't any better at picking horses, but his faith was too pure for him to be deterred by mere experience.

There was nothing I liked in the first. A sorry collection of pacers going for a twenty-five-hundred-dollar purse. You could claim any of them for four grand, and the only sure thing was that there wouldn't be any takers.

But there was one that drew my eye in the second—a shipper from the Midwest that looked good on paper. I noticed she was a front-runner, with a nice clean stride. No breaks on her program, unusual for a trotter. She always seemed to tie up a bit in the last quarter and get shuffled back, unless the pace was leisurely enough for her to hold on at the end. She was coming out of Sportsman's Park—a five-eighths-mile track, favoring closers—but Yonkers is a quarter-mile, with a very short run to home.

The mare I liked was in a twenty-K claimer. A couple of the other horses had pretty decent last outs, so I expected her to go off at a nice price. I wasn't crazy about the post she'd drawn, but, with her early speed, I thought she could grab the rail from the five-hole before the first turn.

I put a big question mark at the top of the first race, then drew a box around the one I liked in the second.

Max made a circling gesture.

I nodded agreement. We'd wheel the Daily Double, putting the five horse in the second race against all the entries in the first. If my horse won the second, we'd have the Double. But even then, it didn't mean we'd show a profit. The Daily Double wheel was eight bets. At a deuce per, we'd have to win *and* get a payoff of more than sixteen bucks to come out ahead.

You might think, what kind of Double *wouldn't* pay off more than that? But if the crowd liked one of the horses in the first race well enough to send him off real cheap, the chalk-players might be spinning *their* wheels, too. So we could win and still end up short.

Max knew all this. He held up his hand, for "Wait!" I nodded agreement—we'd see if the money got distributed nice and even on that first race before we made our play.

Max took the program from me and started working on that first race, paying special attention to each horse's mother's name.

I spotted Sands a few seconds before he saw me. He had a giant paper cup in one hand; I was pretty sure it wasn't popcorn.

I stood up, like I was stretching. Sands walked past us, then sat down at an angle, so he could watch us without turning his head.

I strolled over, sat down next to him.

"Who do you like in the first?" I said.

"I see you brought a friend," he answered.

"He'll stay where he is, if you want."

"Is he who I think he is?"

"Yeah."

"I *heard* about him for years. Friends of yours, stories get so wild about them, people never seem to know if they're real or not."

"Your call," I said.

"Some of your friends, people don't even know if they're *dead* or not," Sands said, dropping his voice.

"People don't know a lot of things," I said. "But it never seems to stop them from talking about them."

"Nobody's doing a lot of talking about her now."

I knew he meant Wolfe. "Meaning they *do* know something?" I said.

"You're too cute for me," Sands said. "I get enough of that on the job. The way things are today, the smart guys are wearing their vests on backwards. Why don't you go back to your friend? I'll let the place fill up a bit before I stop by."

Max and I each bet a sawbuck on his pick in the first. Or, I should say, we bet twenty bucks together—if we didn't go partners, it wasn't any fun for either of us. Max came back from the window with a ten-dollar wheel on the Double, too, meaning we had a hundred invested, total.

By the time they called the pacers for the first race, it was dark enough for the track lights to come on. Max's horse, Dino's Diamond, was a ten-year-old gelding who had been racing since he was a kid. He slipped in behind the gate like a journeyman boxer climbing through the ropes. Another tank town, another nickel-and-dime purse—getting paid to be the opponent.

The pace car made its circuit, then pulled in the gate. None of the horses seemed to want the lead—they hit the first turn in a clump. On the backstretch, Max's horse fitted himself sixth along the rail. "Saving ground," the track announcer called, but it looked more like phoning it in to me.

The horses came around the second turn Indian-file, Max's pick still where he started. Two horses came off the rail, one drafting behind the other as they challenged the leader. Max's horse closed up the gap they left. When the two challengers stayed parked out past the three-quarter pole, the file passed them by, moving them out of contention. At the top of the stretch, the leader was tiring, but none of the others seemed to have the will to make a move.

I felt a sudden stab of pain in my forearm. Max, using his rebar forefinger to tell me what my eyes had just picked up—the lead horse, exhausted, was drifting wide . . . and Dino's Diamond was charging the inside lane like a downhill freight.

It was photo-close, but Max's horse got a nose in front at the wire. Max stood up and bowed to the valiant warrior who had found his way home one more time. His flat Mongol face was split in a broad grin.

I spent the next few minutes acknowledging the celestial perfection of Max's handicapping methods, admitting that we should have wheeled his pick instead of mine—sharing in my brother's joy.

Dino's Diamond paid $35.20, making us major winners, no matter what happened in the Double. Max would brag on this one forever, starting with Mama.

It was one of those times; anyone I'd have to explain it to, I wouldn't want to.

They had just called the trotters for the second race when Sands sat down next to me.

"There's three more," he said, without preamble.

"Three more not in the—?"

"Yeah."

"Why not?"

"No complaining witnesses."

"Then how would you know they were cases at all, never mind his?"

"One of them, he was almost caught in the act. But the vic denied it ever happened."

"A hooker who—?"

"No. Stop asking questions. I can't hang around here. Just listen. It was on the Lower East Side. A neighbor hears sounds of a struggle. Glass breaking, a scream. She calls it in; she's too scared to go out and see what's happening herself, so she turns off all the lights in her apartment, peeks out the window. And there's the perp, going down the fire escape. She doesn't get enough for an ID, but it's our man, no question, right down to the ski mask and the gloves. In fucking July.

"By the time that one went down, everyone knows there's a serial rapist making the rounds, so the uniforms don't bother to knock. The door goes right in. And there's the vic, still tied up, blood coming out of her. Nails on one hand all broken. She must have put up a hell of a fight. Place is ransacked, too.

"But the woman, she says nothing happened. She was playing with the ropes—'experimenting,' is what it says in the report—then she fell down and hurt herself. Utter, total bullshit. But she doesn't budge an inch.

"The uniforms don't know what to do. Fuck, neither would I—whoever heard of something like this? I mean, sure, people playing sex games, they get carried away, someone gets hurt . . . so they don't tell the truth about how it happened. Anyone who works ER around here is going to see a few of those every year. But this one, with the witness and all, it was for real, all the way.

"So they call in the detectives. Nothing. They even try a social worker. Blank. Zero. Nada."

"Christ."

"The second one, she gets found by her aunt. Comes to pick her up in the morning for church, can you believe it? We get a statement. Same pattern, right down to the mouthpiece.

"Then, a week or so later, out of the blue, the vic calls up, says she doesn't want to 'press charges.' Like it was some bitch-slap incident or something.

"Okay, so the plainclothes guys go to see *her*, too. A total washout. She's not talking. Not saying it didn't happen, just saying she's not going to cooperate."

"So they figured she probably knew the perp?" I said.

"That *is* what they figured. And we were going to put surveillance on her. If she was covering for the guy, or, better yet, blackmailing him, we could end up with a solid ID."

"What happened?"

"She moved. To fucking Cedar Rapids, Iowa. Lock, stock, and barrel. They tried to get a wiretap going, but the judge laughed at them, said they were a mile short of probable cause. And what was the crime, anyway?"

"Maybe she just wanted out of New York," I said. "Some people do that, put a lot of distance between themselves and . . . whatever happened to them."

"I don't know," Sands said.

"You said three."

"Yeah. The first one, who denied anything happened? She turned up, later. Dead."

"You think it was Wychek?"

"He was already locked up by then," Sands said. "For the one Wolfe nailed him on. Besides, something else was going on."

"What do you mean?"

"She was tortured," Sands said, voice flat and hard, a shield against his feelings, like the booze. "Somebody worked her over with a stun gun. Or electricity. Had those burn marks all over her . . . in the worst spots."

"In her own apartment?"

"Nobody knows where it was done. Where they *found* her was in a building that was getting rehabbed over in Williamsburg. One of the workers spotted her, hanging, when he opened up in the morning. It was in the papers."

"She was hung?"

"Not to kill her. They did *that* with a bullet. Two of them, one in each eye."

"A message."

"Yeah. Maybe it was for the third one."

"Huh?"

"Her best friend. Roommate. Wasn't home when the rape—the one she said never happened—went down. That one—the third one— just plain disappeared. The detectives looked for her as soon as the original vic wouldn't cooperate. On the books, she's a missing person."

"Missing and presumed."

"Yeah."

"So the homicide case is still open, too?"

"Yeah."

"You got names and—?"

"I see you already got a pen," he said, nodding toward the program.

Max nudged my shoulder, bringing me back from wherever I'd gone. I looked up at the board. The third race was two minutes to post.

Max pointed to the info I'd jotted down, held up three fingers, made a questioning gesture.

"I don't know," I told him. I drew a stick figure of a man, surrounded by a ring of swastikas. "But it looks like Wychek's friends may have started taking care of him earlier than we thought."

Max hadn't left my side, so I knew he hadn't gotten a bet down since the second race. I turned to that page in the program, made a "What happened?" gesture.

He held up the ticket. All the answer I needed. If my horse hadn't gotten home first, he would have torn it up.

I found a place in the program with some white space showing, handed it to Max. He diagrammed the race for me in increments, drawing it as clear as a video.

My mare had left hard, cranked off a good first quarter, put some real distance on the field without a challenge, and maintained strong fractions until her second time past the clubhouse turn. Then they *all* came at her, slingshotting around at the top of the stretch. She was fading fast, but still game, staggering home a half-length ahead of the nearest horse. Paid $8.80 to win, anchoring our four-hundred-and-change Double, a personal record.

Max held up his hand, fingers spread, to emphasize that we didn't just have it, we had it five times!

Neither of us wanted to stay around after that. The minute they get ahead, suckers say they're "playing with the track's money." That's why they're called suckers.

"Anything new?"

"Stone-fucking-*wall*," Davidson said. "Cocksuckers must think they're playing with an amateur."

"I spoke to Wolfe; she doesn't seem worried."

"I wouldn't play poker with her, I was you."

"Yeah, I know. So you're saying . . . ?"

"I'm saying that *somebody's* cooking up *something*. I don't give an obese rodent's rump what that is, so long as it isn't my client on the burner."

"I'm still with it," I promised.

"You maybe got something?"

"Maybe. A *long* maybe."

"Want to tell me?"

"I'm your investigator," I said, "not your client."

"No, no, *no*," Michelle said, hands on hips. "You can*not* wear that same jacket."

"But you said it would be like a—"

"Never mind what I said. This is different."

"How?"

"Stop being such a dolt, Burke! We already went over this. That girl wants something. And if I'm right, we have to go for it."

"I don't see why I can't wear the—"

"She's a money-girl, right?"

"I . . . No, I don't think so. Everything we have about her background says middle-class."

"Give me strength," Michelle muttered. "Sweetheart," she said, her voice a mockery of patience, "I don't mean a *from*-money girl, like a trust-funder. I mean she *works* with money. That's her *thing*."

"So?"

"So I'm guessing she wants to see you know how to make some. Or you already have."

"Maybe she just wants to go slumming."

"That could be," Michelle admitted. "But any woman who's willing to buy a man a cell phone and let him use her credit card can get all the downmarket action she wants. We play it like it's something else," she said, firmly.

"What do I have to buy *this* goddamned time?"

"You don't have to buy anything," she said, triumphantly. "Remember that beautiful Bally jacket I got you when we were working that movie scam?"

"How could I forget? It cost—"

"Well, maybe *now* you see the value of the classics," she said. "You wear *that* number over a nice shirt with a plain tie. . . ."

"A tie now?"

"She said *dinner*, am I right?"

"Yeah. But she said 'dinner' that first time, and *you* said—"

"Oh, *do* shut up," she said, closing the subject.

That night, I motored up Third Avenue, taking my time—as if I had any choice, at that hour. Still, I was in place twenty minutes before I was to meet Laura. The Plymouth isn't the kind of car any cop lets sit at the curb, so I circled the block, budgeting ten minutes for each pass.

I wasn't far off. At 6:55, she was already standing at the curb, wearing a fuchsia dress. As I pulled over, I could see her shoes matched it.

"I hope I didn't keep you waiting," I said, out the window.

"Oh!" she said, as if startled. But she trotted around to the passenger door and let herself in.

"You look—" I said, deliberately cutting myself off, like I'd said too much.

"What?" she said, flashing a smile. Her lipstick was only minutes old.

"I was going to say 'great,' I guess. But I didn't want you to think I was—"

"What? Being polite?"

"No, no. Being . . . unprofessional."

"Hmmmm . . ." she said.

"Where to?" I asked.

"The Midtown Tunnel," she said. "I'll guide you once we get out."

"Yes, ma'am," I said, touching two fingers to my forehead.

"This is quite an . . . unusual car," she said, as we waited in line at the tunnel entrance.

"It's one of my hobbies," I said. "I restore muscle cars from the Fifties and Sixties. This is an original Plymouth Roadrunner."

"Roadrunner, like in the cartoon?"

I "meep-meeped" the horn for her. She clapped in delight.

"Oh, that's *exactly* it. Are these . . . cars valuable?"

"Well, it's not a Bugatti or a Duesenberg," I said. "This one was mass-produced, and not exactly to the highest standards. But clean survivors are pretty rare now. When I get it all done, it should be worth, oh, thirty-five thousand."

"And how much will all that cost you?" she said, looking over the raggedy dashboard out to the gray-primered hood.

"Depends on how much of the work I do myself," I said. "Like, see this steering wheel? It's an original Tuff model," I bragged. "Pretty hard to find."

I tapped the thick-rimmed, smaller-than-stock wheel, with its center horn button and three brushed-aluminum "holed" spokes. It wasn't exactly a bolt-in—the turn-signal lever had to be shortened, so I wouldn't risk snagging my left leg when I got out—but the look was still semi-original.

"Were they fast?" she asked, rolling up her window as we entered the tunnel. "When they were new, I mean."

"The Hemi Roadrunner was one of the legitimate kings of the street, back in its glory days," I said, not mentioning that the reincarnation I was driving wasn't a Hemi. Or that the hogged-out wedge motor in mine would have *inhaled* anything that was prowling the boulevards back then.

"Didn't they come with air conditioning?" she said, reaching in her pocketbook for a tissue.

"Not the serious ones," I told her. "Those were stripped to the bone."

"That doesn't sound very pleasant."

"Different people, different pleasures," I said.

"Did you want a car just like this when you were a kid?" she asked, as we exited the tunnel and got in line for the toll booths.

"I wanted a lot of things when I was a kid," I said, wishing I could pull back the ice in my voice as soon as I spoke.

"Oh! I didn't mean to . . . I've just noticed that some of the men I know, they collect all kinds of things they wanted when they were young. One of the guys I work with, he's got every baseball card ever made, I bet."

"Well, I *say* it's my hobby, but this is the only car I have," I said, chuckling to muffle what she had triggered with her innocent question. "And I've had it a long time, like a project that never gets completed."

"Are you going to make it perfect?"

"Perfect?"

"Like, what's the word I'm looking for . . . *concours*? I have clients who fix up old cars so they're exactly like they were brand-new. Then they have shows for them."

"No," I laughed. "I'm going to make it perfect, all right. But perfect for me, not for anyone else. Besides, I don't see a piece of Detroit iron like this making the grade in that company."

We took an E-ZPass lane, letting the scanner read the box I had fastened to the windshield instead of having to pay the toll in cash. Very efficient system. Speeds the traffic flow. And keeps very good records. I have "spares" I can use when I want to go certain places to do certain things, but tonight wasn't anything I cared if the government knew about.

"The LIE's a pain at this hour," she said. "But it's still the fastest . . ."

"I'm in no hurry," I said.

"It must be frustrating."

"What?"

"Having such a fast car, and not being able to *go* fast."

"Not all the time, no. But that's okay. Sometimes, knowing you *can* do something is pretty much as good as doing it."

"That's how *I* feel," she said. "About my work. But that's a mistake I can't make too often."

"I don't understand," I said.

"In my job, being very good at something, even being *brilliant* at it, doesn't count. Only results do. If you allow yourself to just, I don't know, *luxuriate* in your abilities, like a bubble bath with soft music and candles, you can forget that the world—*my* world, anyway—isn't about strategy, it's about success."

"I thought those were the same thing."

"No," she said, turning in her seat so her whole body was facing me, despite the seatbelt. "Strategy is what I *love*. The game of it. But if I come up with a perfect strategy to, say, put a deal together, and I don't *make* the deal, my bonus is going to be light that year."

"I think I know what you mean." I goosed the throttle to switch lanes ahead of an overfilled minivan. "Kind of like my book, isn't it?" I said.

"Strategy?"

"Not exactly. I mean, I already sold it. The book, that is. I'm talking about my *idea* for it. I know it's perfect. But if I can't bring it off, the book will still happen, but it won't be as good as if—"

"That's *one* idea," she said. "I was talking more about . . . models."

"Models?"

"Ways of doing things. Ones you develop over time, testing and retesting . . ."

"Like a system for picking winners at the racetrack?"

"A little more sophisticated than that, I hope," she said, chuckling. "And a little more successful, too. None of those 'systems' really work, do they?"

"I never heard of one that did," I told her, pure truth.

"Here we go," she said. "You know the Maurice Avenue switch-off?"

"Sure," I said. "I once worked as a cab driver. To get perspective for a piece I was doing."

"Okay, now just follow it around until we get to Sixty-first."

"That's Maspeth, right?"

"Yes, it is. Not many people from the City know that."

"That's one of the things about having a car," I said. "You go places where the subway doesn't."

"I have a car, too, remember? Turn . . . there! Yes. Now just go along until I tell you to turn again."

"You like that Audi?" I asked her.

"Oh, yes," she said. "Whoever did the interior-design work on it was a genius."

"Is it pretty quick?"

"It has a turbocharger," she said, almost smugly. "I got a ticket when I went upstate for a ski weekend once. The officer said he clocked me at a hundred and ten. But he only wrote me up for eighty-five."

"If it had been me, he would have written me up for a hundred twenty."

"Because your car is so fast, you mean?"

"No. Because I'm about the polar opposite of a pretty girl."

"That's cynical," she said, grinning to show me she didn't really think so.

I followed her directions for a few minutes, watching the densely packed little houses give way to flatland.

"There!" she said.

"Where? That's not a restaurant. It looks like—"

"An old factory?" she said, pleased with herself. "That's what it was, once. Now it's condos. And one of them is mine."

"Okay, I get it. You want to change out of your work clothes before we—?"

"I do want to change," she said. "But I also want to cook. Okay?"

"Beautiful," I said.

"**W**hat did this place use to make?" I asked her, following her directions to drive around to the back.

"Some kind of containers, I think. Metal. As I understand, the conversion to plastic would have been too expensive. And the work wasn't there anymore, anyway."

"This is pretty neat," I said, looking at a vertical steel-barred fence with an inset gate.

"Use this," she said, handing me a credit-card-sized piece of plastic.

I inserted the card in the slot, and the gate swung open. We were facing a four-story building that looked like poured concrete, painted the color of cigarette smoke. Laura reached in her purse, pulled out a remote garage-door opener. She pressed the button; a triple-wide steel door rolled up soundlessly as the gate closed behind us.

Inside, there were individual spaces for parking, enough for thirty or so cars.

"Use number seven," she said. "It's mine."

I backed the Plymouth in carefully—the car in stall number six was her silver Audi.

"That's slick," I said. "You own the space on the other side of it, too?"

"Actually, I do. But I don't just own the parking spaces; they come with the units upstairs. So I have six slots; you get two with each apartment."

"You own *three* apartments?" I asked, cutting the ignition with the car in gear so the engine wouldn't diesel on me—big-block Mopars will do that sometimes.

"Me and the bank," she said, flashing a quick grin.

We got out, me extra-carefully, so that the Plymouth's door wouldn't ding her Audi.

"You don't have to worry," she said, standing by the front fender. "There's a *lot* of space between the slots. This used to be the loading bay for the factory. Even with two slots per unit, we have a ton of space left over. See that?" she said, pointing to a chain-linked enclosure to my right.

"Yeah."

"That's for storage. Every unit-holder gets a certain amount of space in there, too. You supply your own lock."

"Damn! Something like that in Manhattan would set you back a—"

"If you think this is a bargain, wait till you see upstairs," she said.

"There's an elevator," she said. "But I always walk. Sometimes, it's the only exercise I get all day. Do you mind?"

Without waiting for an answer, she unlocked the stairway door and started up ahead of me. Halfway up the first flight, I realized Michelle had read Laura Reinhardt better secondhand than I had in person; if she was suffering from secretarial spread, I couldn't see a hint of it.

Her unit was on the top floor. Two locks, deadbolt and door-knob. She stepped inside, flicked on a light, said, "Well?"

The apartment opened directly into a broad expanse of hard-wood floor, bleached so deeply it was almost white. The side wall was exposed brick, beautifully repointed. At the end of the room was a corner-to-corner set of pale-pink drapes. She hit a switch and the drapes parted, revealing a floor-to-ceiling glass wall.

"Jesus!" I said.

I wasn't acting. The wall opposite the exposed brick was a complex arrangement of brass piping, holding what looked like teak shelves. Hardcover books with somber jackets alternated with framed photographs and an assortment of small objects I couldn't make out from where I was standing. Modernistic furniture was scattered about as if at random, but it looked so . . . tailored that I figured it for a professional's touch.

"Come on," she said, "I'll give you the quick tour."

I followed her into a kitchen that I knew the average yuppie would commit several felonies for. A stainless-steel refrigerator-freezer lorded it over a granite-block island and a black porcelain double sink. The cabinets looked like they had been fashioned from the same teak as the bookshelves. The stove didn't appear to have any burners on it. A chrome table sat off to one side, with eight matching chairs. An eat-in kitchen, big enough to hold Thanksgiving dinner.

Before I could ask about that, she was on the move again.

"My office," she said, pointing to a spacious room with a window facing the same direction as the one in the living room. It looked like high-tech heaven, mostly in carbon-fiber black. A flat-screen computer monitor; a multi-line phone with both wired and cordless handsets; one of those fax-photocopier-scanner things. Under a desk with a black marble top, a large paper-shredder—my money was on cross-cut.

"There's more," she said, pulling me by the hand.

We passed a blue-tiled bathroom, a bedroom—"It's really a guest room," she said—and then came to a room dominated by a big-screen TV and a single white leather recliner. "If I were a man, I'd probably claim this was a den," she chuckled.

The master bedroom was a good three hundred square feet, with plenty of room for the queen-sized bed with a Mondrian-pattern headboard, and a garage-sized closet. The attached bath had a two-person Jacuzzi, and it didn't cramp the area. One wall was a triptych of mirrors.

"How big do you think the whole thing is?" she asked, walking back toward the living room.

"Twenty-five hundred?" I guessed.

"Closer to *thirty*-five," she said. "See what I mean about a bargain?"

"I guess that depends on what you paid. But I can't imagine anything *like* this going for less than—"

"Right around four hundred," she said.

"About the going rate for a decent two-bedroom on the Upper West Side."

"You wish," she said. "For that kind of money, you're buying a rehab project."

"Well, *this* one sure didn't come the way it is now."

"Oh, that's true," she said, perching confidently on one of the modern chairs. "But I didn't have to do *structural* stuff. It wasn't really all that expensive. And it's a good investment."

"That I can believe," I said, sitting down myself.

"I'm going to go change," she said, getting to her feet. "Take a look around, you'll see what I mean."

I listened to her heels click on the hardwood floors. Couldn't pick up the sound of a door closing anywhere, but that didn't tell me anything—the walls were thick, and the bedroom was a couple of sound-muffling turns away.

She's gone from arm's-length to "make yourself at home" pretty damn quick, I thought. But there were too many possibilities, dice tumbling in my head.

I stood up, made a slow circuit of the living room. In one corner, I found a white pillar so smoothly mounted it looked as if it had grown from the floor. On its base, a black-glazed pot sat in a tray of gray pebbles, still gleaming from its last watering.

Inside the pot was a bonsai tree. Magnificently sculptured, thick-trunked, with a complex branch formation . . . but no fruit, and only the occasional leaf. Dangling from the branches were dozens of tiny glass bottles: some clear, the others in shades of green, blue, red, and brown. Each bottle had markings of some kind—pieces of labels, smears of paint, logos, brand names.

I'd seen bottle trees before. In a lush back courtyard of a pala-tial mansion in New Orleans, and a dirt patch that passed for the front yard of a shotgun shack in Mississippi. But a miniature one? In the middle of a New York living room?

I fanned my hand rapidly in front of the branches, listening hard. The tinkle of the glass was so faint I couldn't be sure I actually heard it.

"Like my tree?"

She was standing behind me, not quite close enough to touch. Wearing a tangerine kimono that came to mid-thigh. Her feet were bare, and her dark hair glistened, as if she had just showered.

"It's . . . exquisite," I said.

"I'll bet I've been working on it longer than you have on that car of yours," she said.

"Working on it? You mean, keeping it—?"

"No. I *made* it. I bought the bonsai, but you have to prune them to get the exact shape you want. It's constant work. The bottles . . . I took a course in glass blowing, and I figured out how to do the rest."

"How did you get them all marked?"

"It's just a form of miniature," she said. "Painting, I mean."

"Another course you took?"

"Actually, it's something I was always good at it. In school, sometimes I'd draw whole pictures no bigger than my fingernail. With a Rapidograph. For some projects, the most important thing is to use the right tool."

"Did you want to be an artist? Wait, scratch that. You *are* an artist. I meant, did you want to make it a career?"

"Oh, never," she said. "It was always just for me. From the beginning. Once I make something, with my own hands, I can never let go of it. I've always been that way. That's the hardest part of what I do. I make deals, I put together packages, I devise strategies . . . but I can't keep them. I have to let go of them. Otherwise, they're worthless."

"I never thought of it like that," I said. "I guess because I'm no artist. I know some people write books just to be writing them. Because they *need* to, I guess. For me, *that* would be the waste. If nobody ever gets to read it . . ."

"Ah," she said. "Your book."

"I was just—"

"You like me, don't you? Pardon my bluntness, it's just the way I am. The way I have to be, in my business."

"Yeah. I do like you."

"So this is . . . confusing for you, yes? You want information from me. For your book. And, like you said, it's not professional to, I don't know what, get involved with a . . . Oh, that's right, you said I wouldn't be a source. Whatever you said I was, it wouldn't be . . ."

I took a step toward her, put my hands on her shoulders. I'm not sure how the kimono came off.

She was slim from the waist up, with small round breasts set far apart, but her hips were heavy enough to be from a different woman. Her thighs touched at their midpoint, and her calves were rounded, without a trace of definition, tapering radically to small ankles and feet.

"You don't smell like cigarettes," she said, her face in my neck. "I wish I knew how you did that. No matter how many showers I take, or what perfume I use, I always—"

I parted her thighs. She was more moist than wet, tight when I entered.

The bed was too soft. I stuffed a pillow under her bottom, reached down, and lifted her legs to my shoulders.

"I hope you don't think—" she said, then cut herself off as she let go, shuddering deep enough to make me come along with her.

I do that sometimes," she said, later. She was lying on her stomach, propped up on her elbows, smoking. "Talk too much. When I'm nervous. It only happens in . . . social situations, I guess you'd call them. When I'm at work, I guard my words like they were my life savings."

"Everybody has pressure-release valves," I said. "They're in different places for different people."

"Where's yours?" she said.

I put my thumb at the top of her buttocks, ran it gently all the way down the cleft until I was back in her sweet spot. "Right there," I said.

"That's a good place."

"It's not a place," I said. "It's a person."

"I thought they all looked alike in the dark," she said, teasingly.

"Looking isn't what does it for me," I said, moving my thumb inside her.

She rolled away from me, then tentatively put one leg over. "Do you mind?"

For an answer, I shifted my weight, so she was straddling me.

She made a little noise in her throat.

"Sit up," I told her.

She did it. "Oh!" she said, bouncing a little.

"You're not going to take a shower, are you?" she said, much later.

"I can use the bathroom in the other—"

"No, I didn't mean that. I just . . . I just like how you smell. Like you smell *now*. You can take one before you go, okay?"

"Sure," I said.

"Cooking is *not* one of my hobbies," she said, later, standing in her ultra-kitchen. "And I never took a course."

"You still want to go out? There's a diner on Queens Boulevard that never closes. It's not the Four Seasons, but it's got a fifty-page menu—got to have *something* you'd like."

"You wouldn't mind?"

"I already feel like a guy who expected a Happy Meal and got filet mignon," I said.

"Uh-huh," she said, smiling. "And you already figured out we're not going to get any talking done here, right?"

'll drive," she said, electronically unlocking her car as we walked toward the stalls.

"Is there anything under here?" I asked, pointing at the concrete floor.

"Oh, there's a basement of some kind. For the . . . power plant, I think they called it. The boiler, things like that. The utility people go down there to read the meters—they're separate for each unit—and the phones lines are all down there, too."

"I figured they had to be somewhere," I said. "And running power lines up the side of a building like this wouldn't be too stylish."

"Not at all," she agreed, climbing behind the wheel. She turned the key and flicked the lever into reverse without waiting for the engine to settle down—there was a distinct clunk as the transmission engaged.

She drove out of the garage, piloting the car with more familiarity than skill.

"Queens Boulevard, you said, right? I think I know the one you mean. On the south side?"

"Yep."

"We're not urban pioneers, you know," she said.

"I don't know what you—"

"Where I live. It's not like it's a depressed neighborhood. It's solid, middle-class. A good, stable population. Low crime rate. Our building may be upscale for the area *now*, but that won't be forever. It's not like those people rehabbing brownstones across a Hundred and Tenth Street, in Manhattan."

"And you're not displacing anyone, converting a factory," I said.

"That's *right*. The people around us, they were thrilled when they heard what was going on. Instead of an abandoned building where kids can get into trouble, or that the homeless could turn into a squat, they get something that actually improves their property values. Adds to the tax base, too."

Why are you telling me this? I thought, but just nodded as if I gave a damn.

She drove the Audi like an amateur, going too fast between lights so that she ended up stopping for all of them. Or maybe she mostly used the car for those upstate trips she had talked about, wasn't used to city driving.

"There it is," I said, "just up ahead."

She made the left, swung into the parking lot. It was relatively empty—well past dinner, and too early for the night owls.

We walked inside, followed a young woman in a pale green dress toward the back.

"Would you prefer a booth or a table?"

"A booth, please," I said. "As private as possible."

"You can take that one there," she said, pointing. "But this place can fill up just like that," snapping her fingers.

"I know it can," I said, slipping her a ten. "And if we end up surrounded, I know it won't be your fault."

Laura ordered a Greek salad and a glass of red wine. I made do with a plate of chopped liver, potato salad, and coleslaw, French fries on the side. Not Delancey Street quality, but decent enough. And I was hungry.

"What good would it do him?" she said, out of the blue.

"Your brother?"

"Yes. I did a little . . . well, 'research' would be too strong a word. Just a little looking around in the . . . genre, I guess you'd call it. The books I found, they're either about how an innocent man was finally freed, or they're an attempt to *get* him freed. Don't you think that's accurate?"

"Pretty much," I conceded.

"Well, except for the people still in prison—I mean, anyone could see what good a book would do *them*—the other ones, the people who were the . . . stars, I guess you'd call them, didn't they get money, too?"

"I guess in some cases they did. Like when you see their names as 'co-writers,' you can probably bet on it. Some, maybe not—they might have just wanted to get their stories told."

"But they never have control, do they?"

"I don't know what you mean."

"Well, I read about one man, Jeffrey MacDonald, I think his name was. He was accused of murdering his wife and children. Didn't he . . . cooperate with a journalist? And it backfired on him?"

"MacDonald played his own hand," I said. "And, anyway, there's no similarity. Your brother's already free. And he's not charged with any crimes. The book you're talking about, it was the investigation of a crime. My book is an investigation of the system."

"But you said yourself, John is the centerpiece."

"I said I'd *like* him to be."

"All right, you'd *like* him to be. But it comes down to the same question."

"What's in it for him?"

"Yes," she said. "I don't mean to sound so cold-blooded. This doesn't have—doesn't *have* to have—anything to do with you and me. But I have to view all deals the same way. The interests of the parties."

"If it doesn't have anything to do with you and me, maybe we should just split it up," I said.

"What do you mean?" she said, spots of color in her cheeks.

"You're not your brother's . . . agent, I guess is the word I'm looking for. Let's put them all face-up, okay?

"One, I would rather have simply approached your brother, made my pitch, and either started working with him, incorporating him into my project, or moved on. Quick and easy, yes or no.

"But, in his current situation, he's not only less accessible—I don't have a clue where he even is, never mind how to reach him—he's more attractive. Because of the whole prosecutor-on-trial angle.

"Two, I . . . like you. I guess that's obvious. I don't want one thing to screw up the other. I don't want to put you in a position of making choices you shouldn't have to make."

"You mean . . . ? I don't know *what* you mean."

"I want to meet your brother," I said. "Talk to him. And leave you out of it. And, regardless of how *that* works out, I want to keep seeing you."

"Oh."

I didn't say anything, just went back to my food. At least the Dr. Brown's cream soda was the same as you could buy on Second Avenue.

"You wouldn't still want my . . . recollections?" she asked. "The family history, things like that?"

"Sure I would," I said. "The truth is, your brother's story—the *factual* part of his story—pretty much tells itself. There's court documents—indictments, trial transcripts, appeals—all over the place. I *was* looking for more. Deep background. What I told you was one hundred percent true. The impact on the family is a microcosm of the impact on all society.

"It wasn't until we . . . it wasn't until I realized I had feelings for you that I decided I didn't want to risk one thing for the other."

"We went to bed," she said, scanning my face. "I don't know a lot about men, but I know enough to know that doesn't take a lot of 'feelings' on their part."

"I didn't expect it to happen," I said. "Any of it. Sure, you're a gorgeous girl, and I'm not pretending I wouldn't want to get next to you even if I had never spent ten minutes talking to you. You don't know a lot about men; I don't know a lot about women. But I know some things. I know you're not the kind of girl who makes love to a man unless you've got feelings of your own."

"You know that . . . how?"

"I couldn't tell you if you gave me a shot of truth serum," I said. "But that doesn't mean I'm not right. It's just something I . . . sense, maybe. I don't know."

She toyed with her salad, not looking up.

"Tell me I'm wrong, and that'll do it," I said.

"What do you mean?"

"Tell me you don't have feelings for me, and we'll drop the whole thing."

"You're confusing me."

"Look at me, Laura. You don't have to be a map reader to know I've been around for a while. I'm not too old to play, but I'm too old not to play for keeps. If you just like sex, and figured I might be fun, I hope I didn't disappoint you. But it would sure disappoint *me*."

"And if I said that . . . that I was just horny?"

"No hard feelings," I said. "You're a big girl, you get to make your own decisions."

"You'd still want to do the book? With my brother, I mean?"

"Sure."

"Just . . . what, then?"

"Just nothing. I thought, if I told you I could just meet your brother, leave you out of it, maybe you and I, we could try being together, see how it worked."

She pushed her plate away from her, said, "You can't meet my brother. I don't even know where he is. I hear from him, once in a while. But they're keeping him safe. Until the trial, anyway."

"I understand."

"I wish you could smoke here," she said.

"I can fix that," I said, catching the attention of our waitress with a check-signing gesture.

She made a sound of pleasure, exhaling a stream of smoke into the warm, soft night, leaning against the side of her Audi in the parking lot.

"I like to know where everything is before I do anything," she said. "Going to bed with you—*taking* you to bed—that's not me, you're right. But I did it before I thought about it. And now you're *making* me think about it."

"I don't know money talk," I said. "But isn't there some terminology you guys use for long-term investments?"

"Lots of them. Why?"

"That's what I'm looking for."

"With your book?"

"Stop dancing around, Laura. You don't need to do that. I'm not pressuring you. That's why I said what I did, to take the pressure *off.*"

"I . . . checked you out," she said, quietly, looking down.

"And?"

"And . . . are you married?"

"Divorced," I said.

"Do you have children?"

How deep did she look? I knew Hauser kept his private life rigidly segregated from his work, but, still . . .

I gambled. "No," I told her. "I had a vasectomy, in fact."

"You don't like kids?"

"I don't *dis*like them. Just never wanted any."

"Me neither," she said. "I wouldn't have invited you to my house if I didn't know you were a legitimate person. Some of those books, the ones I read after we first talked, they were just . . . terrifying. Like . . . I don't know, pornography."

I shifted my body slightly, so my chest was against her shoulder.

"I don't mean that I think there's anything wrong with . . . sex," she said, hastily. "That isn't what I meant by pornography. Those books—are they *all* about sex murderers or rapists?"

"I guess they could seem like that, especially if you were looking at the paperback originals. The real pros, though, they're journalists, and crime happens to be the topic of a particular book. Look at Jack Olsen. He was the dean of so-called true-crime writing, and he wrote about sex killers, sure. But he also wrote about Gypsy con games. And about an innocent man spending most of his life in prison."

"Oh. Is that where you—?"

"I think so," I said, as if I was considering the idea for the first time. "I met Jack Olsen once," I told her. "He was a great truth-seeker. Any reporter would want to follow in his footsteps."

She turned to face me. "So what happens now?"

"You make some decisions," I said. "In order of importance: Do you want to give me a chance with you? Do you want to talk to me about the impact the wrongful imprisonment of a loved one has on a family? Do you want to ask your brother if he'd be interested in doing an interview?"

"But I—"

"You don't have to decide *any* of it tonight, Laura," I said, holding her eyes in the reflected glow of the diner's windows.

It was almost one in the morning when we pulled into her garage. She killed the engine. Turned to look at me. "I want you to come back up with me," she said.

"Because you decided . . . ?"

"On *all* of it, yes."

She leaned over, kissed me under my bad eye.

"Okay?" she said.

"You have a lot of scars," she whispered, later.

"I've had a lot of surgery," I said. "Different things."

"Where did the doctor who did this one get his license, in a school for the blind?" she said, licking the chopped-off top of my right ear.

"Sometimes, it's not neatness that counts."

"What, then?"

"Speed."

"Oh. Were you wounded?"

"Yeah."

"In Vietnam?"

"No. Africa."

"Africa? You were a . . . like a mercenary?"

"No," I said. "I was there covering a story."

"What story?" she asked.

So I told her a story. About the genocidal slaughter in Rwanda, the rape of the Congo, the "blood diamonds" of Sierra Leone, and how they got that name.

Everything I told her was true, except for the part about me being there. I filled in the blanks—right down to how it feels to get malaria—from my Biafra days. But I didn't say a word about *those* experiences. J. P. Hauser wouldn't have been old enough to have them.

"You've really led a life," she said.

"Not me, personally," I told her. "Reporters aren't supposed to lead lives, they're supposed to lead people *to* lives . . . other people's lives. I didn't have to be in Africa. The story wasn't me, it was those people who *did* have to be there, see?"

"Yes. But, still, it must be exciting. There's a woman I watch on CNN all the time. It seems, every time something major happens, anywhere in the world, she's there. You can't tell me that's not . . . I don't know, glamorous."

"I don't have the face for TV," I said.

"No, you don't," she agreed. "But at least you could be in the profession you wanted."

"Are you saying you couldn't?"

"You know why there's such a shortage of nurses and teachers now?" she said.

"No," I admitted. "I guess I haven't thought about it."

"It's because, years ago, those were about the only real opportunities for an educated woman. Maybe there were others, like being a social worker, but all in the 'helping' professions. When things started to change, started to open up, a lot of women took other roads."

"And you're one of the them, right?"

"Yes. I didn't get an M.B.A. to teach home economics. It wasn't just the money—although that was a factor—it's the . . . freedom, I guess."

"I thought money was tightly regulated. I mean, with the SEC and all. . . ."

"You're talking about interest rates, and things like that," she said. "It doesn't matter if the government regulates money, so long as it doesn't regulate *making* money. But that's not what I'm talking about. What I'm saying is, if you get good enough at putting together deals, you get to call the shots. Be your own boss. I don't mean self-employed; I mean a *real* boss. With people under you.

"There's women who manage major mutual funds now, head up corporations, all kinds of opportunities. But what *I* want isn't anything like that."

"What do you want?"

"I want to put things together," she said. "Not working for anyone, working for *me*. I want to sit back and analyze situations. Then I'd approach all the different parties with a proposal to solve their problems—by using what they already have but don't understand."

"Like what? What could they have and not understand, for example?"

"Capabilities in concert," she said, licking the words like they were rich cream. "Sometimes, assets and liabilities of one company fit those of another one—like a jigsaw puzzle. And if you look at them from an objective distance, you can see how, if they did things together, they could both benefit."

"You mean, like a merger?"

"Like that, but not *exactly* that," she said. "Mergers are usually about controlling markets. Or a company looking to expand. I want to specialize in rescue operations. Like leveraged buyouts and third-party ventures from unrealized asset pools and—"

"You know you've already lost me, don't you?" I said.

"I guess," she giggled. "Don't mind me. I get so . . . enthusiastic sometimes. I don't show that side of me at work. They *expect* women to be more emotional than men. Women in my profession, they have to come across as . . . well, not *cold,* exactly. Objective, I guess. That's the right word."

"That's why you dress the way you do? For work, I mean."

"What's wrong with the way I dress?"

"Wrong? Nothing. It's very, uh, tasteful. I just meant, you couldn't walk in there in a micro-skirt and fishnet stockings and spike heels, right?"

"I don't *guess*," she said, chuckling. "Why? Do you like those kind of outfits?"

"On some girls."

"What kind of girls?"

"Girls who can bring it off."

"And you think I could?"

"Guaranteed."

"You're an angel," she said. "But I know my flaws. It's part of . . . objectivity. Looking at things as they really are. My legs aren't thin enough to show off."

"You're nuts," I told her. "They're . . . flashy."

"Stop it!"

"I especially like these," I said, running the back of my fingernails down her thighs.

"I'm *fat* there," she said, reaching over to light another cigarette.

"That's a class thing."

"What?"

"It's not . . . objective," I said, using her language. "Middle-class men have a different image of what a good-looking woman is than working-class men have. And girls pick up on that, real early. Maybe even from their parents."

"You really think that social class determines what's physically attractive?" she asked, sounding truly interested.

"Not a doubt in my mind," I told her. "I've been all over, and it never seems to fail. Marketing plays a role, too. Women who were all the rage decades ago would be dismissed as overweight today."

"Like who?"

"Marilyn Monroe, Bettie Page, Barbara Eden . . ."

"You're quite the connoisseur, are you?"

"Just an observant reporter."

"Uh-huh. And what social class do *you* come from?"

"My family didn't have much money when I was small," I told her, weaving the lie. "My dad had to work like an animal. But later he became pretty successful. Good enough to get us a nice home, send me to college. So I guess I ended up middle-class," I said, then switched to the truth, "but my roots, my earliest experiences and conditioning, that's what set my standards."

"And you like what you see?"

"I'd like it even better if . . ." I said, turning her over onto her stomach.

"I told you I was no cook," she said the next morning, offering me a choice of half a dozen different cold cereals, none of which I'd ever heard of. "There's plenty of juice, though."

"We could go out," I offered.

"If you're not starving, could we do that later?"

"Sure."

"What do you want to know?" she said suddenly.

"About . . . ?"

"For your book."

"Oh. All right, just sit there, I'll get my notebook."

My cell phone made its sound.

"Excuse me," I said. "This could be important."

I pulled the phone loose, opened it up, said, "Hauser."

"We've got her." Pepper's voice.

"Really? Can you be more specific?"

"Not alone, huh, chief?"

"Not even close."

"The missing woman."

"The friend of the—?"

"No. The one who went to Iowa."

"Okay. When you say 'got' . . . ?"

"Address, current employment, license number . . . Nobody's approached her. Yet. But we figured we'd go along with you on this one."

"Why is that?"

"Mick's from around there," she said. "He might be able to help you with the directions."

"Okay," I said, not believing a word.

"When can we book it for?"

"I can't do anything until Monday," I told her.

"Call me tomorrow," Pepper told me. And hung up.

"Lucky that didn't ring last night," Laura said, as I returned to the table in the kitchen with my notebook.

"Oh, I turned it off," I lied. "I didn't want anything to . . . disturb us. I turned it back on while you were in the shower, earlier."

"That was sweet of you."

I ducked my head, busied myself with lining up a trio of felt-tipped pens.

"Was John a typical big brother?" I asked when I looked up.

"What do you mean, typical?"

"Well, did he resent you tagging along when he went places, stuff like that?"

"I never went anyplace with him."

"Yes, I guess that makes sense. Too much difference in your ages. Well, what about—?"

"How far apart do you think we were?" she said, tilting up her chin.

"Well, I know your brother's age, from the court records. He was born in 1964, so he'd be almost forty now. You're, what, thirty? Ten years, between kids, that's a million miles."

"I'm only four years younger than him," she said. "I'm going to be thirty-six."

I made a noise in my throat.

"What?" she said, quickly.

"I . . . just thought you were a lot younger. I only made it thirty, when I guessed, because I thought you might be insulted if I thought you were too young to have the kind of job you do. Oh, hell, I don't know. I'm not exactly an expert at dealing with women."

"You seemed to know your way around last night," she said, smiling.

"You're confusing skill with motivation," I said.

She blushed prettily. Opened her mouth, then snapped it shut, as if biting off whatever she was going to say.

"All right," I said, "let's try it another way. Was John very protective of you?"

"Like how?"

"I don't know. Like giving your boyfriends the third degree when they came to the house."

"No," she said. "He was never protective."

"You weren't close?"

"Not at all."

"Each had your own lives, huh?"

"Yes. We even went to different schools."

"Parochial school?" I guessed.

"I did. He didn't," she said.

Her answers were getting shorter, more clipped. I shifted gears, asked, "How did your family react when he was first arrested?"

"My mother had been dead for years," she said. "So she never knew about any of it. And my father had already retired, moved to the Sun Belt. I don't know if my brother told him what was going on at the time. Maybe he didn't—my father's got a bad heart."

"So that left you."

"Not really," she said. "I was just starting to make headway in my job, trying to put enough money together to risk a few little moves of my own. Working eighteen-hour days, sometimes. I was frazzled, a real wreck. And, to be truthful, I never took it seriously."

"Him being charged with rape?" I asked, allowing just a trace of disbelief into my voice.

"I thought it was some kind of mistake," she said. "I was so sure I'd get a call from him saying they realized they had the wrong man."

"Did you go to the trial?"

"I was supposed to," she said. "I even arranged for some time off. But I got the dates wrong. By the time I showed up, the jury was already out."

"You were in the courtroom when they came in with the verdict?"

"Yes. It was . . . it was about what you'd expect. A shock."

"Did they let you speak to him before they took him away?"

"I was too stunned to even move," she said. "It was like, I closed my eyes, and when I opened them, he was gone."

"Did you visit him in prison?"

"No. John wrote and asked me not to. He said the visiting conditions were disgusting. The guards were very abusive to women. He didn't want me there. Besides, he expected to be released any day."

"He never lost faith?"

"Never once. But, with John, it isn't 'faith,' exactly. It's more like . . . certainty."

"You really don't know much about the case itself, then?" I asked, walking the tightrope.

"Well, I know John didn't do what he was accused of. What more is there?" she asked, blue eyes on mine.

"The . . . impact thing, remember? Are you saying that your brother's faith—his certainty—that he'd be vindicated made the whole thing less hard on you? And maybe on your father?"

"I'm sure that's true," she said. "Although I never thought about it until right now. Is that common?"

"In a way, it is," I lied. "For other families I've interviewed, it was always the belief that someday the truth would come out that kept them going. I guess the difference is, sometimes the families had an awful lot more faith than the person who had been convicted."

"But they would be the only ones who *really* knew, isn't that true?"

"I guess that *is* true," I acknowledged. "In some of the cases, the evidence was so shaky, or there was such outright corruption, or there was a journalist already on the job, beating the drums so hard, that the public got to share the sense of innocence before the courts ratified it. But in your brother's case, that wasn't so. Until he was actually set free, I couldn't find one line of coverage of the case after the trial was over."

"And when he got shot . . ."

"Exactly. Truth is, Laura, if that hadn't happened, I never would have heard of your brother's case at all."

"I'm not surprised," she said. "It wasn't that big a deal."

"I'm sure it was to you."

"I know how this must sound, but when I told you my brother and I were never close, that's an understatement. When I heard about it, my first thought was how . . . humiliated I was at the idea of anyone connecting me to him. We don't have the same name. . . . You think that's disgusting, don't you?"

"I think it's human," I told her. "After all, for all you knew . . ."

"Who knows what anyone's capable of?" she said.

"Exactly."

"This doesn't do a lot for your book, does it, J.?" Her expression shifted, too quick to read. "Can I call you that? J.? 'J.P.' sounds like you should be a banker or something."

"Sure," I said.

"Does anyone do it? Call you that?"

"Never in my life," I said.

"I never liked my name," she said, wistfully. "When I was a little girl, I always wanted to change it."

"To what?"

"Oh, all kinds of different things. 'Laura' always sounded so old-fashioned to me. I wanted a *fabulous* name."

"Like Hildegarde?"

"Stop it!" she laughed. "You know what I mean. I went to school with girls named Kerri, and Pandora, and Astrid, and . . . names like those."

"So why didn't you?"

"What do you mean?"

"I did some research into this, for a story I was working on. All you have to do, to change your name, is file a petition in court."

"Just like that?"

"Just like that. You have to file a notice in the papers—in case you're trying to duck a bunch of debts and get some new credit— but it's no big deal."

"I could never do that now," she said. "In my business, a name is very important. Not *what* the name is, what it represents. Like a brand. 'Laura Reinhardt' isn't what to call me, it's what I do. Understand?"

"Sure."

"So I guess I'm stuck with Laura the Librarian."

"That's not how I see you. Although I bet you'd look real cute in glasses."

"I *have* glasses," she said. "I never really use them—I wear contacts—but I have them. I always thought I looked dorky in them."

"Let me see."

"I . . . All right, wait here."

I thought I heard the bottle tree tinkle as she swept out of the kitchen, but I couldn't swear to it.

She was back in a minute, wearing a pair of plain round glasses with rust-colored frames.

"All you need is your hair in a bun," I said.

"I *knew* it."

"It's your own fault," I said. "You picked out the glasses, right?"

"Sure."

"But you didn't pick them out the same way you picked out your dresses. Or your jewelry. Or your apartment, even."

"I see what you mean. . . ."

"They've got thousands of different frames. You could get some that would show off your eyes. Like putting something especially beautiful under glass."

"Oh God, that's so . . .," She started sniffling.

Thanks, Little Sis, I said to myself, holding Laura Reinhardt against me.

"I should go home," I said, later.

"Am I making you—?"

"I just feel grungy in these same clothes," I told her. "I need to change."

"Want me to come with you?"

Fucking moron, you didn't see that one coming? I thought. "I'd like to have you *stay* with me," I said. "But not until I . . . do some stuff to my place."

"You mean, like, rehab?"

"No. I mean, like, *clean*."

She giggled. Then said, "You probably think I'm the world's best housekeeper, looking around this place."

"It does look immaculate."

"It should. I'm hardly ever here. I have a girl come in twice a week, and I'll bet all she does is watch TV."

"You don't let her touch your bottle tree, do you?"

"Never! I blow the dust off it with my own breath."

"I'm not surprised."

"When I put something together myself—even a deal, which is not really a thing you can *touch*—I get very protective of it. I don't want anyone handling it but me."

"I understand."

"You're the same way about your car, I bet."

"I guess I am, now that you make me think about it," I confessed, lying. The truth was, the Plymouth had been built as a multi-user appliance—power steering and an automatic transmission made it possible for anyone to drive the beast, if they didn't get too crazy with the gas pedal. "How about this? I go and get some fresh clothes, and come back in time for dinner?"

"Do you want to go to—?"

"Let me surprise you," I said.

A block away from Laura's, I thumbed my cellular into life.

"Gardens."

"It's me, Mama. Can you get everyone over there?"

"Now, yes?"

"Yes."

"Basement?"

"No."

"Okay."

Max was the only one there when I walked in. He was in my booth, trying to play a game of solitaire. Mama was seated across from him, tapping the table sharply every time she detected what she considered a major error in progress.

"Have soup at big table," Mama said, confirming everyone was on their way. I never would have asked her. In my family, some things you know inside yourself. Other things—like "basement" meaning "weapons"—you learn.

The Prof strolled in the door just as the soup came up from the back. He snatched a cup from the tray and put it on the table in front of him as he sat down.

"I'm in," he said, as if the cup were a poker chip.

"Where's Clarence?" I asked.

"He's with Terry, over at your place, cooking on those computers."

"But that's just around the—"

"You want the Mole on the set, letting him drive ain't the bet, bro. They have to go and haul him over."

"Fair enough," I said, just as Michelle swept into the joint.

"This had better be important," she said.

She didn't bother to wait for anyone to pull out a chair for her—Clarence is the only one who ever does. And I didn't bother to assure her the meet was important—she was just being herself.

"So? What's up, pup?" the Prof asked.

"Let's wait until everyone's here," I said. "I don't want to tell it twice."

"Righteous," he said, lighting a smoke.

"You *did* get to be with that girl?" Michelle demanded.

"Yeah," I said.

"And you *are* going to talk about that?"

"Yes, Michelle."

"Not in front of my son, you're not," she said, in a tone of utter finality.

"Honey, he's old enough to—"

"Don't you say a word!" she warned me.

"Terry's been teaching Clarence some *boss* stuff," the Prof slipped in. "Boy's talking about going to school, for real."

"I'm sure," Michelle said, not mollified. "And I'm glad, Prof," she added, quickly. "But if you think I'm going to have Terry sit here and listen to the gory details of—"

"There won't be any details, honey," I promised.

"How can I know if my . . . expertise is needed without specifics?" she said, exasperated.

"I can tell you *that* part right now," I said. "Before they get here. Fair enough?"

"Sold," she said.

"It was a Seimens," I told the Mole, almost an hour later. "One of those jobs that work as a regular phone and as a cordless, too. The main one is in the kitchen. She's got three of those pod-things in different rooms. You just lift the cordless unit out of them and talk. It's a two-line job. Probably uses the second one for the fax. Or maybe the Internet."

The Mole shook his head. "That is a difficult one to plant a device in," he said. "You don't have the . . . knowledge. It would be better at the junction. In the basement."

"You see security cams?" the Prof asked.

"Not in the garage. I don't know where they'd go to; I didn't see a monitor in her apartment."

"Just a voice system, like they got in regular apartment buildings?"

"I guess so," I said. "I haven't gone in the front door."

"But you're going back this evening, yes?" Michelle said. "So then we'll know if—"

"No," I told her, holding up the plastic card Laura had given to me. "She gave me hers, for the garage. Said she wouldn't be using her car all day, so . . ."

The Mole took the card from my hand, studied it for a few seconds. He nodded, asked: "It doesn't have to *look* the same?"

"As long as it works," I told him.

"You can test it later," the Mole said, pocketing the card.

"I don't see a play *except* the phone," I said. "We don't have the personnel to shadow her—"

"Not in *that* neighborhood, for sure," the Prof said, sourly.

"—but the house phone's not enough," I told them. "What if he contacts her on her cell? Or even at work? Hell, what if he drops her a goddamned postcard?"

"What makes you so sure they're going to meet at all?" Michelle asked.

"They met once," I said. "Or planned to meet, anyway. If the story we got is true, the sister shows up, he's already down from the shots. Whatever he wanted to tell her, he couldn't—or wouldn't—do it on the phone. And he didn't just want to meet her in a public place. He went to a lot of trouble to set the whole thing up."

"You think he wanted to give her something, mahn?" Clarence asked.

"If he had it with him, whoever shot him got it," I said. "But Wychek's still running scared. *Big* scared. He's got—*still* got—something good enough to convince the cops to keep him on ice. But, whatever it is, it has to be something . . . physical. Not just info he could carry around in his head. Otherwise, he would have already cut the deal he wanted. And there'd be no need to keep the charges running against Wolfe."

"Maybe he's still trying to work that one out," the Prof said. "How he can turn loose of what he's got, and still keep himself protected?"

"Even if that was so, why keep the charges alive?"

"They don't want to tip off whoever shot him? That he's ratting them out?"

"No," I said. "Doesn't work for me. Wychek's dirt. If all he could do for the cops is dime out the guy who shot him, what's *that* worth? Not the DA's Office cooperating in a bogus charge against Wolfe. Too much potential downside for them, especially with all the press attention."

"He's got something," I went on, filling in the blanks with

guesses. "And either he needs the sister to get it for him, or he needs her signature on a safe-deposit box, or . . . something like that. Whatever he has, he's had it for a long time. Since before he went into the joint."

"Because . . . ?" Michelle said.

"Because he was protected in there. Off a contract. Somebody paid real money for that. And for the fancy appellate lawyer, too."

"So why'd he wait?" the Prof demanded.

"He . . . *Damn,* Prof! It isn't just that he waited so long to hire Greuchel. He never even made bail on the charge Wolfe dropped him on. And he wouldn't have needed PC at Rikers if the Brotherhood was protecting him there. So, whatever he found out, it must have happened *while* he was at Rikers."

"Yeah?" the Prof snorted. "You think someone in there sent him a kite, made him see the light?"

Nobody said anything. Whatever they were thinking, I don't know. Me, I was wondering if Wychek had ever asked his sister for bail money.

Suddenly, Max tapped a knuckle against the tabletop, drawing all our eyes. The Mongol looked up at the ceiling, dropped his gaze to eye level, let his eyes wander around aimlessly. He glanced at the floor. Picked some imaginary object up, gave it a quick, examining look, shrugged, and put it in his pocket.

Max got to his feet. Walked over to one of those promotional calendars, mostly a large poster, with a little pad of months you can tear off one at a time on the bottom. The one on Mama's wall featured a Chinese woman, elegantly dressed, having a cocktail. The writing on the poster was all in Chinese, and the calendar pad was for 1961.

Max turned the pages of the calendar, indicating the passage of time. Then he snapped his fingers, made an "I've got it!" face, and reached into his pocket. He brought out the imaginary object in one hand, and used the fingers of the other to turn it, as if examining it from all sides.

He nodded a "Yes!," then went over to Mama's cash register and patted it, like it was a good dog.

I stood up, bowed deeply. "You nailed it, brother," I said, making a gesture to match the words. "He got it *before* he went down, but he didn't figure out it was *worth* anything until later."

"Adds up," the Prof said.

"Very logical," the Mole agreed.

"And I think I know *where* he got it now," I said. "So I'm going to Iowa."

I walked out to the back alley with Clarence and Terry, the Mole stumbling in our wake. I pulled Clarence aside, asked him a quick question, got the answer I expected.

Back inside, I sat down in my booth. I felt . . . depleted. Like I'd fought ten rounds, to a decision that wasn't going to go my way.

Mama came over and sat across from me. "All for police girl?" Mama said, accusingly.

"There's money in this," I said, stubbornly.

I closed my eyes, felt Michelle slide in next to me, ready to defend her big brother. Mama had known about Wolfe for years. "Police girl" said it all. Our family is outlaws; we don't believe in mixed marriages.

"If Burke says there's money, there's money," Michelle said, loyally.

"Maybe. But not *for* money," Mama replied.

"So?" Michelle challenged her.

"So no . . . focus," Mama said, pointing at Max to emphasize what she meant. For all his skills, the *ki* radiating from Max the Silent was all about focus. Without it, he'd just be another tough guy.

"I'm feeling my way," I admitted. "But Wychek's got *something*. Even Max says so."

"Something for police, maybe."

"Wolfe's not on their side anymore," Michelle said. "She went into her own business a long time ago."

"Still police girl here," Mama said, patting her chest. Case fucking closed.

It was just past seven that same night when I test-slipped the Mole's clone card into the slot for Laura's garage, my other hand on the genuine one Laura had given me, just in case.

The gate went up.

I walked up the back stairs, carrying the stainless-steel cylinder by its handle.

I rapped lightly on the door to her apartment. The door opened immediately. I hadn't heard the sound of a deadbolt retracting, and the chain wasn't in place.

"Hi!" she said, giving me a quick kiss as I crossed the threshold.

She was wearing another kimono—white, with gold and black dragon embroidery.

"I didn't know where we were going, so I didn't want to get dressed until . . ." she said, blushing a little.

"You're perfect," I said, holding up the gleaming cylinder.

"Oh my God, this is the *best* Chinese food I ever had in my life," she said, about forty-five minutes later.

I had opened the complex series of interlocking pots, each with its own dish inside. A few quick blasts with the microwave, and we had a five-course dinner that money, literally, couldn't buy.

"I told you it would be a surprise," I said.

"Where did you *get* it? I'm going to order from them for the rest of my life."

"Oh, it's not from a restaurant," I said. "I know this old Chinese woman who makes special meals to order. She used to serve them in her house—"

"Oh, I *heard* about those kind of setups. You don't get a menu or anything, and you have to book, like, *months* in advance, right?"

"Exactly. Only she's not up to having people in her home anymore. She's like a hundred years old," I said, involuntarily tensing my neck muscles against a psychic slap from Mama. "I called her, gave her a few hours' notice—that was what took so long—and she said she'd do it."

"Wow. She really put herself out. It must have cost a—"

"Money wouldn't make her do anything, not at her age. I told her it was very special, very important to me."

"I . . . I wish I knew how to do things like that."

"I guess I don't, either. I never did it before. I was just thinking . . . about you, about going out to eat, how things . . . happened. Then I remembered this old lady, and . . ."

"Did you use to eat there a lot?"

"A lot? I ate there *once*. About, let me see, six, seven years ago? I was doing a profile on a big Chinese businessman. A puff piece, really, but I can't support myself doing nothing but investigative stuff. He was the one who took me there."

"Did you mention it in your article?"

"I wasn't going to. It isn't that kind of place, you could see that. But it wouldn't have mattered. The piece got spiked, and I had to settle for the kill fee."

"What's a kill fee?"

"Say a magazine commissions a piece for five thousand. Then, after they see it, they decide not to go with it. If there's a decent contract, they have to pay the writer some percentage of the fee, agreed on in front."

"Why would they do that? Commission an article and then not use it?"

"There's a hundred reasons." I shrugged. "They decide they need the space for something else that month. Or the subject isn't hot anymore. Or maybe they just don't like the job you did on it."

"But if they did that, you could just turn around and sell it to someone else?"

"If you can, sure. It doesn't happen often. Every magazine is a different market, even when they're competing with each other. What's good for one isn't always good for another."

"Y̶ou don't have to do that," I said, later.

"You weren't planning to return all the cookware without washing it?" she said, incredulous.

"No. I just meant, I could take it home, throw it in the dishwasher myself."

"I don't know about that," she said, dubiously. "I mean, not everything can go in the dishwasher. It's easy enough to wash them by hand; I'll be done in a few minutes."

"Okay. Thanks."

"Do you want to go out somewhere. Or just . . . ?"

"How about we go for a drive?"

"To . . . where? Oh. I guess that's the point, right?"

"Sure is."

"I̶s this still Queens?"

"Yep. That's Flushing Bay we're looking at. You can't see it from here, but La Guardia's over to the left. The Bronx is on the other side of the water."

"I was born, what, maybe forty-five minutes from here? And I never even knew it existed."

"It's a nice little community," I said. "You got everything from working stiffs to big-time gangsters, with house prices to match."

"With those other cars around, it's like a drive-in movie, almost."

"People come here for the same reason they go to drive-ins, true enough."

"Did you know that in Singapore young couples go to drive-ins because the culture frowns on public displays of affection?"

"I didn't have a clue. You know a lot about Singapore?"

"I'm hardly an expert. But everyone in the money game knows *something* about Singapore."

"Have you ever been there?"

"No. You?"

"Yeah, I was there, once."

"What's it like?"

"Very clean, very efficient. And very scary."

"Scary?"

"I can't explain it, exactly. Felt like everybody was so . . . anxious. Like something could descend on them any minute."

"Were you there for a story?"

"No. I was on my way to Australia. But something happened with the connecting flight, and I ended up having to lay over."

"I wonder why people would be so anxious there. It's supposed to have a very low crime rate."

"Maybe it was a misimpression," I said. "I was only there for a short while. I wouldn't ever write what I told you."

"Why not?"

"I'm old-school," I told her, trying to be Hauser in my mind. "I don't like this 'personal journalism' stuff. Never did. What I told you, that was my own feelings, not facts. Private, not public."

"That's what this place feels like," she said, snapping her cigarette out the open window and sliding in close to me.

Twenty minutes later, she moved back toward her side of the front seat. Rolled down her window, lit a cigarette.

"I never did that before," she said.

"In a car?"

"Not just . . . in a car. Never."

"Oh. I . . ."

"You don't know *what* to say, do you, J.?" she said, a slight edge around the softness of her voice. "If you say you never would have known, it sounds like you're calling me a liar. And if you say it was obvious I'd never done it before, you're saying I'm not very . . . good at it, right?"

"*None* of that's right, Laura. Not one word of any of it. Some people, they do things perfect the first time they try. Others, they could do it a thousand times and still . . . not do it very well."

"I only meant—"

"But what's *really* not right about what you said was the other part. It would never cross my mind that you were lying."

"I thought reporters were supposed to be cynics," she said, expelling smoke in a harsh jet.

"Cynicism is for adolescent poseurs. A person who's been around the block a few times learns better."

"What's better?"

"Better is knowing some people are liars. I don't mean they just told a lie, I mean they're liars; that's what they do. Better is knowing that even essentially truthful people lie sometimes, for different reasons. Better is knowing how to tell the difference."

"You know when people are lying?"

"Not always," I said, reaching over and taking her hand. "But I know when they're not."

We were both quiet for a while. Then she said, "I never asked you. Do you have any brothers or sisters?"

"I have a sister."

"Older or younger?"

"She's my baby sister."

"Is that why you asked me, before, if John was protective? Because you were?"

"No. I was just trying to get a picture of the whole family dynamic."

"But you *were,* weren't you?"

"Protective? Sure."

"You think that's normal, don't you?"

"I'm a reporter, not a judge."

"J., I'm just asking you an honest question. Can't I get an honest answer?"

"Ask me your question," I said, watching her eyes.

"If someone tried to hurt your sister, what would you do?"

I saw pieces of Michelle's childhood, playing on the inside of my eyelids like a movie on a screen. The kind of movie freaks sell for a lot of money. Felt the familiar suffusion of hate for *all* of them—from her bio-parents, who used her like a toy, to the agencies that treated a transgendered child like a circus freak, to the predatory johns who took little pieces of her in exchange for survival money, to . . . *Oh, honeygirl, I wish I had been there,* I said to myself. Again.

I waited a beat, still on her eyes.

"Kill them," I said.

"**D**o you have something to pick up?" Laura asked me, as I wheeled the Plymouth into the gigantic parking lot for the Pathmark supermarket in Whitestone. At just after two in the morning, the lot was almost empty.

"Nope," I said, pulling over to the side. I put the lever into park, opened the door, and got out. I walked around to her side of the car, opened her door.

"You're leaving the engine run—"

"Just come on," I said, taking her hand and pulling her around the back of the car. "Get in," I told her.

"You want me to—?"

I was already on my way back around to the passenger side. We both closed our doors at the same time.

"This isn't like your Audi," I said, as she wiggled around, trying to find the best driving position. "The gas pedal isn't hypersensitive, but if you step on it hard we'll launch like a rocket. The brakes are a little stiff when you first touch them; they take a little pressure. But if you floor them, we're going to *stop*. I mean, right *now,* like someone dropped an anchor into the road behind us."

"You're making me nervous."

"Oh, great," I said. "The first time I ever let anyone drive my baby and you tell me *you're* nervous."

"J.," she giggled. "Stop it."

"Your Audi's a front-driver. This one's not. If you get on the gas too hard in a corner, the rear end's going to want to come around."

"You make it sound like a ticking bomb."

"It's nothing of the kind," I said. "Only reason I'm saying all this is that it's a great contrast to what you're used to driving. Take it slow, get used to it, and it'll practically drive itself. You'll see."

"I . . ."

"Come on, Laura. I'll bet you'll be perfect at it, the first time."

She gave me a look I couldn't read. Then she put her left foot on the brake and pulled the lever down into drive.

I nodded approval. Laura took her foot off the brake, and the Plymouth started to creep forward. She delicately feathered the gas and we picked up speed.

"There's nobody around," I told her. "Give it a little gas."

"This isn't so bad," she said. "I could just . . . *Oh!*" she gasped, as the Plymouth shifted stance and shot forward.

I had expected her to deck the brakes, but she just backed off the gas, got it under control instantly.

"It *is* fast," she said.

I made her try the brakes a few times, to get used to the pedal.

"I can feel the power," she said. "Like a huge dog, on a leash."

"Let's give it some running room," I said, pointing toward the highway.

"**W**hat a *wonderful* car this is, J. It was so nice of you to let me drive it."

"My pleasure."

"I was . . . wondering."

"What?"

"Well, how come you . . . The outside of the car is so . . ."

"Grungy?"

"At *least*. But it runs so beautifully. Is it the money?"

"If you mean, did I put my money into the engine and the transmission and the suspension and then kind of run out of cash, the answer is 'yes.' But it's been this way for a long while now, and I think I may actually like it better."

"Better? Why?"

"It's kind of . . . special-sweet to have something very fine, something that most people wouldn't even recognize. They'd have to *drive* my car to know what it was."

"And you're not going to let them?" she said, smiling in the night.

"Why should I?" I answered. "I'm building her for me. Not for my ego."

"What does that mean, for you, not your ego?"

"It means she's perfect for me. Just for me. I don't care if anyone else thinks I'm driving a rust-bucket; I know I've got a jewel."

"Is that the way you are—?"

"About everything," I assured her. "Everything in my life. Right down the line."

O'Hare was in its usual state of high cholesterol, but the three of us had plenty of time to catch our connector to Cedar Rapids. On the way out, Pepper had ended up seated next to an elderly lady; Mick and I were side by side. By the end of the trip, the old woman wanted to take Pepper home with her. Mick and I hadn't exchanged a single word.

All they had left at the car-rental agency was an Infiniti SUV. Mick kept calling it a stupid cow every time he had to take a curve.

He found the address easily: a smallish wood-frame house on a side street. Pepper turned around in the front seat so she could face me.

"You want us to go in with you, chief?"

"I think it might help if *you* did," I said. "But if Mick's going to pull his—"

"I'm in the fucking room," he said.

"Mick!" Pepper said, punching him on the arm hard enough to floor most middleweights. "Come *on*!"

"The paper says she's from around here," Mick said. "She came home. If anyone here scares her, it's not going to be *me*."

"Let's go," I said.

"**M**iss Eberstadt? My name is Michael Range. This is my assistant, Margaret Madison. And her husband, Bill. We apologize for coming by without notice, but I thought it would be better if you got to look us over before we asked you anything. People can give a real false impression over the phone."

"I . . . What do you—?"

That's when Mick took over. "We all work for a lawyer, ma'am," he said. "Mr. H. G. Davidson, from New York City. I don't mean *I'm* from there; I guess you can tell," he went on, a warm, friendly smile on his transformed face. "I'm a paralegal, Mr. Range is an investigator, and Margaret here is an administrative assistant. Anyway, there's a case back there that concerns you, a little bit, and we were sent out here. Well, I guess the truth is, the boss sent Mr. Range out, and we came along for the ride. I wanted to take Margaret home to see my folks, anyway."

"What does this have to do with—?"

"Could we come inside for a little bit, ma'am?" Mick asked, in a voice I never would have recognized. "Unless this town has changed a lot since I was last home, I wouldn't want to be talking about stuff like this out on the front step."

"I . . . All right," the target said.

Pepper and I watched in respectful silence as Mick danced with Eileen Eberstadt for almost an hour. We listened to her explain that her initial report had "all been a big mistake, like going to New York in the first place," and how she "had nothing against anyone."

Mick countered gently, explaining that Wolfe, the only one who had ever prosecuted Wychek, was now being charged with shooting him, and any help she might be able to provide would be greatly . . .

But the woman held firm, until I stood up and walked over to where she was sitting.

"Everything costs," I said, softly. "And everybody pays. The only question is when, and how much. There's a lot of people behind Ms. Wolfe. Serious people. Very committed. You've got your reasons for lying—don't waste my time," I said, when she opened her mouth to speak—"and nobody cares about them. We're not cops, and we're not the bad guys, either. We're not on anyone's side except Ms. Wolfe's. But we have a job to do, and now you're it."

"I'm not going to—"

"Just tell me what he took," I said, even more softly. "Just tell me that one thing, and we're gone."

I tossed "forever" into her long silence.

"A skirt," she said, looking down. "A little red pleated skirt. It was the bottom half of my cheerleader's outfit. From high school."

"I got a call," Davidson said.

I didn't say anything, just watched the smoke from his cigar turn blue in the band of sun that came in the top of his office window.

"Toby Ringer, you remember him?"

"That's a long way back," I said.

"Sure. From when he was an ADA in the same office that's prosecuting Wolfe now. Toby's gone up in the world since then. Moved over to the feds. He was the boss of Narco there for a while, then he kind of dropped out of the public eye. But he's the same man."

"Meaning . . . ?"

"Meaning, you know how it works in our business. A man's no better than his word. And Toby's has always been gold."

"Okay," I said, neutral.

"So, anyway, Toby gives me a call, says we haven't had lunch in a long time. How about Peter Luger's, his treat?"

"Did he pat you down when you showed up?"

"Asked me to give my word that I wasn't wired."

"This was about Wolfe, right?"

"I'm getting to it," Davidson said.

I went quiet again.

"Toby said it would be in my client's interest *not* to push for dis-covery right now. He said, if we could be a little patient, he was absolutely confident—that's the exact phrase he used—that the case would just go away.

"I told him we weren't interested in a case going away. That happens, the case can always come back. He said he meant go away for good. Disa-fucking-*peer*.

"I told him he knows the game as well as I do. I can't just sit on motions, or I end up waiving my right to them. He went over the time lines with me, said another few weeks and it would all be over."

"So he's just trying to save you time and aggravation?"

"I asked him the same thing. He fenced for a while. Finally, after he could see he wasn't getting over, he told me Wychek's going in the Grand Jury soon."

"How is that supposed to—?"

"He's not going in as a victim, he's going in as a witness," Davidson said. "His appearance has nothing to do with Wolfe, or her case."

"So?"

"So, by way of preamble, first they're going to immunize him. Full boat—use *and* transactional. Then he's going to tell the Grand Jury that he made it all up about it being Wolfe who shot him. When the DA's Office gets 'notified' of that, they then intro-duce a transcript of *his* statement during a presentation of *her* case. And No True Bill it."

"Sure."

"It sounds fishy to me, too," Davidson said, tilting his chair back. "If we're a target, we're entitled to Grand Jury notice, and we haven't gotten any. But it *could* work the way Toby says. A *fed-eral* grand jury—investigating who knows?—brings Wychek in. He makes a statement under oath. Suppose he *does* say that he lied about Wolfe? The feds have to turn that statement over to the DA in Manhattan. And then they'd *have* to drop the case. If the statement ever came to light, they'd be cooked. Not just legally, politically."

"What's in it for us, to wait?"

"That's where Toby stopped being blunt. But I got the distinct impression that Wychek is telling the DA's Office one story and the feds another. And that they're not sharing."

"He's in federal custody?"

"He's not in *anyone's* custody," Davidson said.

"You mean he's still in the hospital?"

"Nope. That's why I'm inclined to go along with Toby. He said the DA's Office is giving Wychek an allowance, maintaining him as a protected witness. But Wychek knows, long-term, it's got to be the feds, if he wants the total package—new ID, maybe even a new face, some serious maintenance money, you know."

"So Wychek goes in the Grand Jury—the federal one—and then he gets gone?"

"What Toby says."

"Toby say where Wychek's staying?"

"I never asked him," Davidson said.

"**Y**ou had a successful trip?" Laura asked.

"In my business—actually, I'll bet it's a lot like your business—you don't always know right away. You make an investment, then you wait to see if it pans out."

"That sounds a lot more like gambling than investment."

"Isn't that what investment is, gambling?"

"At some end of the continuum, it is."

"What do you mean?"

"A person who buys shares of stock—or of a mutual fund, or any similar instrument—*is* gambling. Their idea of 'research' is maybe fifteen minutes on the Internet . . . and that's for those who even go that far. For most investors, it's more like religion than it is science. They trust; they have faith; they believe. They believe in a broker, or a mutual-fund manager, or in something they heard on a TV program. Everybody in the business knows this is true, but nobody knows why."

"If people didn't *want* to believe, they wouldn't," I said. "I don't care if it's a televangelist or a stockbroker; it's easier for people to say 'I trust you' than to find out the truth for themselves."

"You make it sound like they're all suckers."

"And volunteers for the job," I agreed.

"I'm not in any of that."

"What do you mean?"

"I don't sell stocks or bonds. I don't even analyze them. What I do is, I put deals together. There's big sharks and little sharks, sure. But all the players are sharks, do you see what I mean? There aren't any fish."

"Then where do the little sharks get their food?"

"Y ou haven't asked about him at all," she half whispered, her mouth against my ear. "Have you changed your mind?"

We were lying on her bed in the dark. Me on my back, she on her stomach. It was the first time we'd had sex that she hadn't lit a cigarette afterwards.

"Changed my mind?"

"About your book."

"No," I said, my tone suggesting that would be absurd. "I've made the commitment. I took the advance. And spent most of it, too. Your brother's case didn't give me the idea for the book—it was something I came across during my research."

"But you said he'd be perfect."

"He might very well be. But I can't believe he's the only one. There were two things that drew me to him—"

"What?"

"—and neither was the underlying fact pattern," I went on, ignoring her interruption. "One, I have to be honest, was nothing but convenience. He was—at least, I *thought* he was—right here, and available for in-depth interviews. Everything about his case is right here, too: the court records, the local newspapers, the judge who sat on his case, maybe even some of the jurors. The second thing, of course, was him getting shot."

"Couldn't you—?"

"But, the more I think about it, I'm not so sure."

"Not so sure about what?"

"Whether the hook is really such a good one after all. At first, I thought it was perfect. If you're writing a book about overzealous prosecutors, what's better than one who tries to kill a man they convicted, after the courts set him free?

"But, in looking at these cases, you don't see that . . . personal element at all. You see the criminal-justice system jumping the rails. You see cops concerned with their crime-clearance rate, just like you see prosecutors obsessed with their conviction rates. Working together. But that kind of mind-set is just as likely to tip the scales the other way."

"I don't understand," she said, moving away from me and sitting up.

"A prosecutor who wants a perfect conviction rate can give some plea bargains that are *real* bargains. I've seen cases where a defendant confesses to a couple dozen different crimes, and only gets sentenced for one of them."

"But that person would still be guilty, wouldn't he?"

"Maybe, maybe not."

"Why would they ever—?"

"Did you ever read about the Boston Strangler case?"

"I *heard* of it. But it was a long time ago, wasn't it?"

"The Sixties. A serial killer was at large. The public was panicked. The media—and this is the key to the whole dynamic—was demanding action. Everyone was on the spot. They already had this guy—Albert DeSalvo was his name—on a whole ton of sex crimes. Different MO—not a homicide in the bunch—but more than enough to give him a life sentence.

"So now they've got DeSalvo in a prison where they evaluate defendants to see if they're competent to stand trial. Out of the blue, he makes a deal to confess to all the strangling cases."

"Plead guilty?"

"It was a little trickier than that. He 'clears up' the cases, gives the police information about the crimes, stuff like that. But the deal is, since there's no *other* evidence he was the Strangler—no fingerprints, no blood, no body fluids, no witnesses, *nothing*—the confession can't be used. So DeSalvo gets the same life sentence he would have gotten anyway, and everyone's happy."

"I still don't see what's so horrible. I mean, what he *did,* of course. But he still went to prison for life."

"What if he wasn't the Strangler?"

"What? Then why would he—?"

"I don't know," I said. "I wasn't there. But a lot of people, today, think he was lying about those crimes. Especially relatives of the victims. There's a whole new investigation going on now."

"It doesn't make any sense," she said, her tone just below angry.

"He was going down for the count anyway. And he wasn't going to do an extra day for the Strangler's crimes. Maybe he got some money . . . from a book deal or whatever. Maybe he just wanted to be famous—the cops get confessions like that all the time."

"Did the crimes stop after he was arrested?" she asked. I caught the faintest whiff of triumph in her voice—the cold-blooded researcher, confronting the "believer" with the hard facts.

"They did," I said. "But if he got the information—about the crimes—from someone else, *that* person could have been locked up, too. With DeSalvo. Maybe in the nuthouse."

"What does *he* say?"

"DeSalvo?"

"Yes. Well, what does *he* say about it, now that all that time has passed?"

"He's not saying anything," I told her. "A few years after he went to prison, he was stabbed to death."

"Oh my God. Who did it?"

"Nobody knows," I said. "Or, at least, nobody was ever charged with it."

Laura bent over to light a pair of candles on an end table. "Can you see me?" she asked over her shoulder.

"Perfectly. But I'd rather have a closer look."

"You will. But, first, could you close your eyes? Just for a minute?"

"Sure," I said, dropping my eyelids, but leaving a slit open at the bottom. I learned how to do that when I was a kid—the trick is to keep your eyelids from fluttering.

Laura dropped to her knees, pulled out the lowest drawer in a dark wood bureau. She rooted around for a few seconds. When she stood up, she held something clasped in her hands.

She came over to the bed, climbed on next to me, and knelt, keeping her back very straight.

"What do you do when you're afraid of something?" she said, very softly.

"What do people do, or what do *I* do, personally?"

"You."

"It depends on what it is that I'm afraid of."

"Tell me."

"If it's something I can avoid, I do that. If it's something I can't, I try to overcome it."

"How?"

"How? I don't know. It depends on what it is."

"Give me an example?"

Oh, I could do that, I thought. *I could give you enough "examples" to haunt your dreams for the rest of your life.*

But I'm a Child of the Secret. We don't talk to outsiders. Except when we lie. Because They taught us well. We know we're never safe.

And just because you're one of Us doesn't mean you can't also be one of Them.

"Public speaking," I said. "I was scared to death to get up in front of—"

"That's not fear," she cut me off, sharply. "That's a . . . phobia. Didn't you ever—?"

"A bully," I said. "How's that?"

"That's very good," she said. Kneeling, with her hands clasped.

"When I was a kid," I said, feeling the dot of truth inside my story expand the margins of the lie, "I was scared all the time. Of this one guy. He took stuff from me. Just because he was bigger. Just because he *could* do it. And he hurt me, too."

"Did you tell your parents?"

"It wasn't the kind of thing I could tell my parents about," I said. More truth, wrapped in a mourner's cloak.

"What did you do?"

"I tried to stay away from this other guy," I said. "But he made it impossible." *Yeah,* I thought, *"impossible," when you're a little kid, and the other guy is the teenage son of the degenerate freaks who have custody of your orphaned body.*

"What happened, finally?"

"I hit him with a baseball bat," I lied.

"Oh! Did you hurt him badly?"

"Bad enough so he never bothered me again," I said. The baseball bat was true enough. I didn't tell Laura how I had followed it with a can of gasoline, and a match. By the time I was done, every human living in that house of demons was, too.

"Good! I *hate* bullies, don't you?"

"Ever since I was old enough to know what they are," I said, switching to pure, undiluted truth.

"See what I've got?"

I opened my eyes. She was holding up a pair of handcuffs.

"Being . . . restrained has always terrified me. I . . . I keep these as kind of a test. Usually, I'm afraid to even look at them."

"You were handcuffed once?"

"Oh, no," she said, way too much certainty in her voice. "Nothing like that. I've always been this way. When I was a little girl, and they played cowboys and Indians, I would never let anyone tie me up."

"Some things, it's good to be afraid of. Just common sense."

"Maybe that's why I went into my line of work. There's a *lot* of risk—one day, you're getting a huge bonus; the next, you're out of a job—but there aren't any . . . restraints."

"Maybe you just like the risks. I've known people like that."

"Maybe I do," she said. "Do you know how these work?"

"See how much faith I have in you?" she purred. "With my hands behind my back like this, you could do . . . anything."

"If you trust me, you know I won't."

"I know you would never do anything to hurt me," she said. I wondered if she realized how much she sounded like one of the no-research investors she had been sneering at.

"I wouldn't, Laura," I said, guiding her shoulders down.

"I could still ask him," she said. It was much later; the candles were burned out.

"Okay."

"You don't sound very enthusiastic, J."

"I guess I'm . . . not, actually. I thought *he* was the one who would have been enthusiastic. Most people *want* to tell their stories, especially if they believe it's going to make them look good."

"But you haven't lost interest completely?"

"No, of course not. But I can't put the whole project on hold waiting for—"

"Oh, I understand," she said, squirming in close to me.

"It's not that big a risk," Wolfe said. "If Toby's . . . prediction doesn't come true, it's not like the DA has a *better* case against me. Besides, I trust him."

"Toby?"

"Yes. Who else?"

"Not me, I understand."

"What does *that* mean?"

"It means you think my arteries are hardening—the ones to my brain. Your pal, Molly? No way *he* made copies of all the files he had in his storage unit. And no way you *didn't*. You never trusted anyone in administration when you worked there. Probably got copies of every single piece of paper that ever went through your hands, somewhere."

"It's Molly who doesn't trust you," she said, not denying anything. "He said he was willing to take the chance of you shopping him, but he wasn't going to give you the chance to do it to me."

"Very protective of you, is he?"

"You have a problem with that?"

"No," I said. "None of my business."

"This whole thing is none of your business now," Wolfe said, quietly. "It's done. Maybe not wrapped up with a red ribbon and tied with a bow, but it's done. I appreciate what you did, but . . . but I want you to stop now. Just stop."

I got to my feet. "I'm sorry," I said. "I thought I was helping."

"Come on, Burke. Be yourself."

"You got it," I promised.

The next day, I kept my promise. I sat down with my family, and we made our plans.

If you think a "perfect crime" is some kind of rare event, you probably think all sociopaths are handsome, intelligent, and charming, too. Truth is, thousands of perfect crimes take place every day. Nobody ever gets arrested for them, much less convicted.

And if you think it takes a criminal genius to commit the perfect crime in America, you don't know anything about incest.

"There's other players, remember," I warned my family. "Whoever shot him has to know by now that they didn't get the job done."

"He's a piece of dry wood, Schoolboy," the Prof said. "Lying on the ground, waiting for the forest fire to catch up to him. Why don't we let the flame take the blame?"

"Nobody needs him dead now," I said. "Nobody on our side, anyway. Wolfe doesn't think she'll even go to trial. Neither does Davidson. If whoever wanted him finds him before we do, there's no loss, sure. But we can't *make* that happen. Even if we could stake him out, how would we get the shooter to show up? Besides, it's not about him anymore. It's about the money."

"You think there's cash in his stash?"

"I don't know, Prof. But there's cash *somewhere*. Heavy cash. This whole thing reeks of it."

"You mean, because he had protection when he was Inside?" Michelle said. "His little sister's got money . . . and she was the one coming to see him the time he got shot."

"The sister has some money," I conceded. "And it doesn't take a fortune to buy protection Inside. But Silver said the order came from the top, and there's no way she'd even know how to make a contact like that."

"He has not called," the Mole said.

"What? You mean you—?"

"The card opened the garage," he said, shrugging. "The basement has all the lines. We already had her numbers. It's a simple relay unit—we record the calls at our end."

"I didn't know you were even going to . . ."

"I was in a Con Ed van," the Mole said. "In and out in under fifteen minutes."

"You leave any paint behind?" the Prof asked.

The Mole ignored him.

"He could use a lot of other ways to get in touch," I said. "Or maybe he hasn't reached out for her at all. I've spent a lot of time with her. Consecutive hours. She didn't get *any* calls. So either her phones were turned off—and that doesn't seem likely—or he's not coming through that way."

"Maybe he only has her work number, or her e-mail address," Michelle said. "If I was his sister, Satan forbid, I wouldn't want him to know where *I* lived."

"Could be. I don't know. And she never said."

"So how would we be able to have a strategy, mahn?" Clarence asked. "Either he calls her at home—and he has not done that—or she convinces him to give you that 'interview.'"

"We're holding garbage," I agreed. "But we already anted heavy, so it's worth staying to see the last card."

The tenants in the Lower East Side building were so old, I got called "boychick" more than once. Four of them stopped their canasta game long enough to tell me that the two girls who had lived in the second-floor apartment had been very nice, but kind of standoffish.

"You would think, coming from such a big family, that Hannah would have been a little more friendly," an elderly lady with heavily rouged cheeks and an elaborate hairdo told me.

"She had a big family?"

"Well, either her or Jane—that was the roommate—*must* have. I never saw so many boys. Brothers or cousins. I could tell by the way they were acting, all together."

"And they came after the . . . after it happened, too?"

"Oh yes," another lady said. "But not right away, a few days later. Maybe they were from out of town."

"Who can tell anymore?" a third lady said.

"Did Hannah and Jane leave with them?" I asked.

"Who pays attention, a time like that?" the rouged-cheeked lady said.

"And who should be surprised, her moving out, after such a thing?" a different lady said.

"You saw Hannah move out?" I asked.

"Hannah? Hannah never moved out, young man. She was *murdered*. Didn't you know that? It was in the papers. Horrible! That's when *Jane* moved out."

"Like the Devil was chasing her," the rouged-cheeked lady said. "In the middle of the night. Manny, the super, he said she hardly took any of her clothes, she was in such a hurry. Who could blame her? To have such a thing happen to your own roommate. It would be . . . I don't have the words for it."

As I exited the apartment building, I had to step back to avoid a pair of skinheads strutting down the sidewalk. As they passed, I saw they had bar-code tattoos on the back of their necks. Couldn't tell if they were identical.

I drove over to the building in Williamsburg where Hannah had been found hanging. The rehab was long since completed, and I calculated my chances of getting inside about as good as a counterman at Taco Bell buying a condo off his tip money.

Walking away, I felt a tremor in my wake. Just a slight pattern-shift in my visuals, maybe. Afterimages that didn't match up with my expectations.

That was enough to send me Queens-bound on the subway instead of driving back to Manhattan. I changed trains three times, careful not to box myself, working my way back to Canal Street. When I got to the network of back alleys that leads to Mama's, I found a place to wait.

And that's what I did, for over an hour.

Nothing.

Spiders have it easy. When they need a web, they make their own threads. I had to work with the ones they gave me.

Something about those bar-code tattoos . . .

I knew a stripper who had a tiny bar code tattooed on one cheek of her bottom. "It's a trick," she said, smiling at the double meaning. "Supposed to mean my ass is merchandise, see? But if anyone gets close enough to *read* it, they're mine."

I opened one of my notebooks, found what I had drawn from my memory after I'd left Silver.

V71.01

What had he told Silver? "A message, written in the code of Nietzsche."

I'd seen the "Whatever doesn't kill you makes you stronger"

tattoos in prison. Sometimes with swastikas where the quote marks would go. Not exactly a secret code.

So?

In the room I use for sleeping, I took a polished piece of steel with a hole drilled at the top out of one of the standing lockers. In the middle of the steel, I used a Sharpie to draw a red dot. Then I hung it on a nail on the wall. When I settled into position, the red dot was exactly at eye level.

I focused on the red dot until I went into it.

When I came back, the room was dark. A sliver of moonlight glinted on the steel. I couldn't see the dot.

"He's guilty," I said.

"That view ain't new, son."

"I'm not talking about the evidence, Prof."

"Then how you know, bro?"

"He said it."

"Confessed?"

"No, sis," I said to Michelle. "I've never spoken to him. But in prison, Silver saw this on his forearm. . . ." I drew it on a paper napkin, showed it to everyone.

Max shook his head.

Mama shrugged the same message.

"What is it, then, mahn?" Clarence asked, for all of them.

I took out the two pages I had Xeroxed. "This is from the *DSM-IV.* The manual the shrinks use to put labels on people. Listen."

They all turned toward me.

"V71.01 is a code number. All the disorders have one. Like schizophrenics or pyromaniacs or whatever. That 'V' prefix is kind of a catchall. They say it's for 'other conditions that may be a focus of clinical attention.' I remembered it, finally, because it goes in front of malingering."

"What is that, mahn?"

"Bottom line, it's when you fake being sick to get out of something, Clarence."

"Like when you plead insanity?"

"Like when you *fake* insanity."

"How do you know all this stuff, mahn?"

"Schoolboy was the shrink's clerk, Inside," the Prof said, proudly. "One of the cushiest jobs in the entire joint. Once Burke got that deal working, we made bank in the tank, son. Bank in the tank."

"From meds?" Michelle asked.

"No, honey," the Prof told her. "From *reports*. That's where you tap the vein. You know what it's worth to a man going before the Parole Board to have a few little changes made to his jacket? Or a guy trying to get into a work-release program? Or—?"

"I get it," Michelle said, grinning.

"Let me read it to you," I said, clearing my throat. " 'V71.01. Adult Antisocial Behavior. This category can be used when the focus of clinical attention is adult antisocial behavior that is *not* due to a mental disorder, for example, Conduct Disorder, Antisocial Personality Disorder, or an Impulse-Control Disorder. Examples include the behavior of some professional thieves, racketeers, or dealers in illegal substances.' "

"What does that—?"

"Means us," the Prof cut Michelle's question off. "Our kind of people."

"That filthy little maggot isn't—"

"No," I said. "He's not us. He's not even *like* us. That code isn't some diagnosis a psychiatrist put on him—that's what he's saying about him*self*. What he's telling the world. He didn't do the . . . things he did because he was nuts; he did them because he wanted to.

"That Nietzsche thing he told Silver? He did those rapes, hurt those women, took those trophies because he *could*. In his mind, he's not some sicko; he's a superman. And the tattoo is his little private joke."

I handed the photocopied sheets of paper to Max.

"Where he find that book?" Mama asked, pointing at the pages I was holding.

"What I think is, he had a *lot* of therapy, probably when he was very young," I said. "I'm guessing here; the sister didn't say anything about it. But a freak like him doesn't spring into full bloom overnight.

"First, he experiments. I'll bet he hurt a lot of small animals, set some fires. . . . And when he finds out what certain things do for him, how they make his blood get hot with power . . . he escalates. Until he gets caught.

"His family had money. Not enough money to quash a major felony, but enough to get him sent for 'treatment' instead of the juvie joints when he was a kid."

"So tattoo is big insult?" Mama said.

"Yeah, exactly," I agreed. "A joke nobody's supposed to get but him. I don't know when he got the idea for it, but it's his way of sneering at the whole idea of him being a sick man. He's the *opposite*. In his mind, he's a god."

Max picked up a pair of chopsticks, held them together in his two fists. He twisted his hands, and the chopsticks splintered like matchsticks.

"Y ou do have a backup plan?"

"What do you mean?"

"Well, you wanted to interview him. But if you can't . . ."

"I already told you. I was working on the book way before this whole business with him came to light. His case wasn't even part of the proposal."

"Yes, but . . ."

"But what, Laura? What difference does it make now?"

"I guess I'm just . . . insecure."

"About what?"

"About . . . us. In my world, people are *always* plotting. You have no idea of all the *crimes* people in business commit every day. Like it was nothing. Or there's a set of special rules for them. Remember when Bush made that whole speech about 'corporate ethics' last year? What a fraud. You think stuff like Enron or WorldCom is an aberration? It's only the tip. Business is a religion. Probably the only one practiced all over the world."

"What does that have to do with—?"

"If you want to succeed, you have to plan *very* long-term," she went on, talking over me. "Tools and research. Research and tools," she said softly, stroking the rock of her faith for comfort. "You have to be *very* patient. There's no forgiveness in my world. You only get one chance."

"Laura . . ."

"You and I met because you wanted something. *That* part is real, I know. What happened, with us, I mean, I don't know how real *that* is. And now that you're not going to get to meet my—"

"I'm still here," I said.

"Yes."

"There's never any more than that."

"Yes there is," she said, fiercely. "There's . . . promises."

"I never made any—"

"That's exactly it," she said, taking the handcuffs out from under her pillow.

"Oh no," she said softly, as she climaxed. "Oh no. Oh no. Oh no!"

In the silence after she let go, I thought I heard the bottle tree whisper. But I couldn't be sure.

"Sorry, chief. She doesn't want you." Pepper caught herself, quickly added, "Working the case, I mean. There *is* no case, far as we're concerned. You understand, right?"

"Sure, but—"

"It's done," she said, gently. "Let it go."

I don't know who the hell you are, or what you're talking about, pal. But I can tell you this: don't ever fucking call me again. Understand?"

Molly, at the other end of a phone call. The dead end.

Well, sure, it's still theoretically open," Davidson said. "But I've got my deal in place with Toby, and my client and I are both certain the result will be as agreed."

"What about the other rapes he did?"

"You know the statute of limitations on a felony as well as I do," he said. "Better, I'm sure, given your . . . profession. He could call a press conference, confess to everything, and walk away giggling."

"He's already done that," I said.

"What do you want from me, Burke? Some bullshit about bad karma? We both know how it is. Real life isn't on *Oprah*. What goes around sometimes *doesn't* come around. Chalk it up."

We already had this conversation."

"I found some new—"

"No," Wolfe said, drawing the line all the way down to the exit wound. "You found something new that proves what we already know, so what? We *already* know Wychek did those rapes. We *already* know I didn't shoot him. With what Toby Ringer told Davidson—and *I* trust him, even if you don't—we're never going to have to prove either one."

She tapped a cigarette out of her pack. Didn't offer me one. Snapped her lighter into life before I could move.

"And if Toby's gone in the tank, *double* so what?" she said, not looking at me. "If they force us anywhere near a trial, we'll prove *both*. Steamroll those punks in the DA's Office like fresh asphalt in August."

I just sat there, silent.

"I'm not going to prison, Burke. It's over. *Everything's* over."

She blew a harsh jet of smoke into the night air. "I appreciate all you did," she said, looking away. "But there's no more for you now."

"**D**idn't *that* prove anything to you?" Laura said. She was lying on her stomach, both hands around the big tube of KY she had taken from under the pillow. Before the handcuffs.

"Is that why you did it?"

"Maybe."

"To prove what, exactly?"

"That I would do things for you. Things I wouldn't do for anyone else."

"I think you know," I said.

"Know what?"

"You know I'd never hurt you. What you said, a while ago, about trust? If you didn't trust me, you wouldn't use those—"

"I trust you *now*," she said, softly. "That first time, I couldn't know. Not for sure. It was a risk. A chance. I was frightened. But it was time, and I knew it."

"Time?"

"I always know when it's time to do something, to make the move," she said. "That's my gift. That's what I do. So that's me."

"**I**'m going to be gone for a couple of weeks or so," I said, much later that night. Setting the stage for my fadeout.

"Really? To where?"

"Out to the coast. There's a couple of interviews I need to do for the book. And my so-called agent claims he's got a couple of meetings set up, with a production company that specializes in TV pilots."

"You don't sound very excited about it."

"I'm not. I've had those kind of meetings before. But since I have to be out there anyway . . ."

"You're here now," she said, tongue flicking against my chest.

When are you leaving, exactly?" she asked, looking up from a bowl of grains and nuts she was breakfasting on. The sun slanted against the far wall of the kitchen, but it didn't reach where we were sitting.

"I don't have a flight yet. Next couple of days or so. I have to pack, make arrangements for coverage at the paper. . . . A trip like this, you never know how it's going to play out. If I come up with something dynamite, I may just—"

"Did you ever hear of StandaBlok Machine Tools?" she said, stopping me in mid-sentence.

"No. Is it one of your—"

"It was a small operation, not so very far from here. You know the area around Liberty Avenue? Anyway, it's out of business now. The building they used would be just perfect for a conversion like this one. The only thing is the neighborhood."

"Sooner or later, there's no neighborhood in New York that won't be worth money," I said, reciting the conventional wisdom.

"That's what I think, too. But for now it's just an abandoned building. After vandals broke all the windows, it got boarded up and padlocked. *Tight.* Nobody goes there now."

"All right," I said, just to fill the empty space between us.

"The day after tomorrow, I have to go there. Alone. At midnight."

"What for?"

"To meet my brother," she said. "Do you want to come?"

"**W**hat she told me was, Wychek called her at work Monday afternoon. He asked her for a safe place where they could meet. Said he wanted *her* to choose it, after what happened last time.

"That building she told me about? She's got the key. The way she was talking, I figure she already owns it. Or a piece of it, anyway. Some development deal.

"All Wychek's got to do is make sure he's not followed. If he told her the truth—that nobody knows where he is now— shouldn't be any problem for him."

"And she wants to just bring you along?" Michelle asked. "Like a little surprise?"

"No. What she wants is just for me to stand by, close. Once she meets him, she's going to pitch the idea of him doing the interview with me. For the book. If he says 'okay,' she'll call and wave me in."

"No chance you make that dance, son."

"That's true, Prof. But she can't know that."

"Why does she do it, then, mahn?"

"She's gotten more and more . . . I don't know the word for it. She keeps trying to 'prove' something to me. Like if I thought she was for real I'd . . . be with her, I guess."

"So you think all this cloak-and-dagger is so she can say, 'I tried, honey'?" Michelle.

"You tell me."

"Well, she *is* a woman. And having a freak in your family doesn't make *you* one," my little sister said. "We all know that song. By heart."

"**G**uy down here, boss."

"Seen him before?"

"Yeah. The lumberjack."

"Let him pass, Gateman."

"I'm in."

"In what, Mick?" I asked.

"What you're doing," he said, his glance covering all of us, seated around the poker table.

"It's over," I told him. "Like Wolfe said."

"I don't think so."

"You looking to join for the coin?" the Prof asked suspiciously.

"There's only one thing I care about in all this," Mick said, eyes just for me. "Same as you."

Nobody said anything, waiting.

"And I don't trust the fucking feds," Mick said. "Same as you."

Thursday, 3:22 a.m. The building was two stories of solid brick, standing squat and square, as if daring anyone to ask it to move.

By the time we finished offloading, the Prof had seduced the lock.

We left him just inside the door, cradling his scattergun. I led the way up the stairs, a five-cell flash in one hand, a short-barreled .357 Magnum in the other. Clarence was just behind me, to my right. As soon as we cleared the area, Max and Mick brought up the gear.

Except for a thin film of interior dust, the place was immaculately clean, as if a former tenant had swept up before moving on.

We set up camp on the top floor. Clarence started to unpack methodically. Max and Mick went around making sure we had more than one way out. I took care of setting up observation posts, carefully using a box cutter to make eye-slits in the blackout curtains we hung behind the boarded windows.

"No people, no food, and it's nice and warm out," the Prof muttered, looking around. "So the miserable little motherfuckers got business elsewhere." The Prof hated rats.

By daybreak, we were ready to start sleeping in shifts.

"I say he gets here first," the Prof whispered to me.

"Michelle put the padlock back in place behind us," I said. "And only the sister has the key."

"What time's the meet?"

"Midnight."

"I got a century to a dime the cocksucker gets here by eleven-thirty, minimum."

I was still considering the offer when Max slapped a ten-dollar bill on top of one of the duffel bags.

"Pssst!"

"You got him?"

"Got *somebody,* mahn. This scope makes everything green, but it's a man, walking."

"Alone?"

"Yes," Clarence said. "Closing now."

The Prof snatched Max's ten and his hundred off the top of the duffel bag in one lightning move. Then he and the Mongol took off downstairs. Mick was already there, waiting.

Thirteen minutes later.

"You're not feds," Wychek said, despite my dark-blue suit, white shirt, and wine-colored tie. If being stripped, handcuffed to a pipe, and surrounded by the men who had choked him into unconsciousness and carried him up the stairs frightened him, it didn't show on his face.

"Good guess," I said.

"And you're not with . . ."

"With who, John?" I said, pleasantly, not a trace of urgency in my voice.

"Oh no," he said, lips twisting in a stalker's smile.

"When did you last take your medication, John?"

"Just before I— What difference does that make?"

"You know why I asked," I said, very softly.

"I don't—"

"Ssshhh," I said, soothingly. "We're already here. You know what that means."

"If anything happens to me—"

"Nothing's going to happen to you, John. But we wouldn't be here if we didn't know who else was coming."

"She doesn't have it," he said, smoothly. "She doesn't even know where it is."

"One of those is a lie, John. Maybe, *maybe* it was true that first time, on Forty-ninth. But it's not true now. Not tonight. So, the way we see it, all we have to do is wait. Soon as she shows up, we won't need you anymore."

"The feds know where I am. If anything—"

"You said that already, John. That's why we took your clothes. To make sure you didn't have any way to stay in touch."

Wychek watched me blank-faced, same as he had watched dozens of social workers and therapists and cops and prison guards for a lot of years. His other face only came out under a ski mask.

He hadn't been carrying a cell phone. No tape recorder, no body mike.

But he had his straight razor. And a roll of duct tape.

I walked around in a little circle, as if I was making up my mind. Finally, said, "You want to know what this is about, John? What it's really about?"

"Yeah. Because if you think—"

"It's about money," I said, moving closer to him. "And you're going to—"

Clarence stepped into the room, chopped off my speech with a hand gesture. I followed him out of the room, over to where he had an observation slot.

A silver Audi TT convertible pulled up to the front of the building. Its headlights went out. Just as Laura Reinhardt opened her door, I caught a flicker of movement at the edge of the lot.

I gestured to Max and the Prof, pointing two fingers down, forked. They took off.

"Big SUV," Clarence said, watching through the scope. "Coming on."

"I'll cover you from up here," I said, and went back to where we had Wychek trussed up.

"This is so you don't hear or see what's going on," I said, a doctor explaining a medical procedure to a nervous patient. "Just breathe through your nose," I told him, very softly.

"Do *not* panic," I cautioned him, just before I fitted a set of sound-canceling earphones in place. "We're all going to be busy for a few minutes. You have yourself a seizure now, it's your last."

I slapped a couple of turns of duct tape around his mouth, then dropped the black hood over his head, with another quick turn of the tape to hold the earphones in place.

I heard the downstairs door open.

A flashlight blazed downstairs for a half-second. Then it went out.

The SUV was a moving brick, black against the gray night. It came to a shadowed stop about fifty yards from the building. The front doors opened, and a man climbed out of each side. No light went on inside the truck.

"Can you see anyone still inside?" I asked Clarence.

"It looks empty, mahn. But someone could be on the floor."

"All right. She should be out of the way by now. Go on downstairs. Remember, if there has to be any—"

"I know," he said, threading the tube silencer into his nine-millimeter.

I lost sight of the two men just as they entered the building. I moved over to the top of the stairs. Looked down. Shadows inside shadows.

The front door opened. Closed.

A *blast!* of sudden light.

"Freeze, motherfuckers!" the Prof barked.

I heard a harsh grunt. Then the *puffft!* of a silenced handgun.

T he broad strolls in. Max takes her from behind, same as he did the freak. She goes right out, never saw a thing. We wait for the two guys following her. As soon as they come in, I light them up, give them the word. One raises his hands, the other goes for his steel. Clarence cut loose, and—"

"Where's the sister now?"

"Sleeping," the Prof said. "I gave her the hypo the Mole put together. One shot, he said she'll be out for a few hours. Wake up with a bad headache. Be all fuzzy, too, like coming out of a bad dream. That's why he needed you to tell him how much she weighs, get the dose perfect."

"We've got two men," I said. "One in the room next door, one upstairs. No way to know if the guys in the SUV had backup—"

"Not in their truck, they didn't," Mick said, telling us he had gone out to make sure.

"—but they both had cells. Don't know if they're supposed to call in, how much time we've got. . . ."

"Got to pick one and run, son."

"Yeah, Prof. I know."

"Which one?"

"Wychek knows where. But the guys who came in after Laura, they know why, I think."

"We came for the green," the Prof said, settling it.

T he man was in his late forties, tall and rangy, with leathery skin. In the soft light from the candle, his eyes were colorless.

"I'm not with them," he said, in that calm, deliberate voice people use when they're trying to keep an unstable person calm. "I'm a professional. Freelance, just like you, am I right? No reason for anyone to get wild, now. Just tell me what I have to do to walk out of here, and it's done."

"We want the money," I told him.

"Sure. Give me the book, and you can name your price."

"Just like that?"

"Just like that. It would have *been* just like that if that fucking Yusef didn't have to play with his toys."

"That's what took Wychek out the first time?"

"Yeah. Could I have a cigarette?"

The Prof fired one up, held it to the man's lips. He inhaled gratefully. "Thanks. I'm the same as you, okay? A professional. I get hired, do a job, get paid. Only they don't trust outsiders, so they sent that degenerate psycho along with me."

"Yusef?"

"Right."

"He came with you tonight? He's the one—?"

"Yeah. Like I said, he's one of them. You had the drop on us, cold. Stupid asshole must have figured he was going straight to Mecca," the tall man said, deliberately distancing himself from the dead body at the foot of the stairs. "After what he pulled the first time, I couldn't believe they'd ever send him again."

"The first time? You mean with the girl in that apartment on the Lower East Side?"

"Right. Fucking sicko. They told me he hooked her up to a car battery. He kept jolting her, but she kept telling the same story."

"And later they found out it was the truth."

"Not from her. Or from the other one, either. Fucking scumbag morons don't know from interrogation. All they know is torture. It wasn't until Wychek contacted *them* that they knew for sure."

"He took the book from her apartment? After he raped her?"

"Right. When she found it was gone, she panicked. I don't blame her, seeing what happened."

"She couldn't tell them anything but the truth."

"Right. But they didn't know it *was* the truth until Wychek started holding them up for money. That was when he was in the joint. By then, it was way too late for her. Fucking half-wits outsmarted themselves. They figured, even if they got busted themselves, nobody'd ever think to look for the book in some white girl's apartment."

"She was the girlfriend of one of the—?"

"If you mean, was she fucking one of them, yeah, I guess. But that wasn't why they let her hold the book. She was one of them. One of those rich little 'revolutionaries,' you know what I mean? Like shopping isn't enough of a thrill for them anymore, so they need to go liberate the downtrodden masses."

The contempt in his voice invited me to join him, but I didn't say anything, waiting for him to fill the silence. Maybe me holding Wychek's straight razor helped.

"At first, the little weasel didn't want that much," the mercenary said. "I handled everything for them. I was the bridge man to get him that protection contract."

"From the Brotherhood."

"Right. You know what happened next. Fucking Wychek steps it up. He wants a lawyer. Okay. Still within budget. And by then they knew he hadn't turned the book over to anyone. So they figured, Wychek gets out, they can deal with him."

"He gets out, all right. Only what he wants is a *lot* of money. Now, these sand nig—" He pulled himself up short, segued into— "assholes, they *got* the money," without missing a beat. "They got all *kinds* of money. But instead of just paying him, they decide to get cute.

"Yusef's got this little pistol. A twenty-five. Custom job. Between the suppressor and the reduced-powder hand-loads, it *looked* bad enough, but it wouldn't kill a fucking cockroach. Yusef promises them, no electricity this time. He'll use fear. Figures, he puts a couple of rounds into Wychek, it won't kill him, but it'll scare the shit out of him, make him give up the book.

"And that's what Yusef does. He pops Wychek a couple of times. Then he puts the piece right between Wychek's eyes, tells him 'Last chance,' and . . ."

"Wychek goes out."

"Yeah. Fucking Arab assholes. Yusef swore Wychek didn't have the book on him. Stupid amateur. He was too busy searching the body to check and see if Wychek was even still breathing."

The tall man took another hit off the cigarette the Prof was holding for him. "After that, they're in a panic," he said. "In case Wychek's got backup—you know, someone he left it with. But the book never surfaces, so they start to breathe easy.

"All of a sudden, there's that story in the papers. That Wychek didn't die. And they got this woman charged with shooting him. But Wychek's supposed to be in a coma, and they're not worried about him talking. Then, a couple of weeks later—bang!—they get *another* call. Wychek himself. He's out of the coma. And he *still* wants to sell them the book. But now, behind what happened, he wants the money in front."

I didn't say anything, watching the play of candlelight on the razor's edge underline the reality of his situation.

"They figure, *pay* him, okay?" the tall man said. "But they also figure he makes copies, right?"

"I would."

"Sure. Look, *you* got the book now. And *you're* not some sick-fuck amateur, like him. I could get them to go a flat million, for real. All cash. Or gold, if you want it that way. Any drop you say."

"Then I'm in the same place he is," I said. "On the spot. And I don't even know who'd be looking for me."

"If you'd ever looked in the book, you'd know, man. Those camel-jockeys put it *all* in there. Names, addresses, phone numbers, codes . . . the whole thing. Most of them are still in place. Once they realized Wychek wasn't going to do anything but hold them up for money, they got cocky. They're sitting ducks, man. One call, you could take them all down," he said. "They *have* to pay."

The tall man was reciting his credentials. A mercenary to his core, keeping it real. One man-for-hire to another. Whatever was in the book he was talking about, his own name wouldn't be. In the sociopath's moral compass, true north is always in his mirror.

"We understand each other, right?" the tall man said. "I'm the same as you."

I looked over to the Prof. He shook his head.

"**W**e're a lot smarter than the Arabs were," I told Wychek. "If we wanted, we could keep you alive a *long* time. Long enough for you to tell us whatever we need."

I deliberately stepped back a couple of paces, to lower the threat-level.

"But I got a better deal for you," I said. "Fifty-fifty. That's fair. Come on. You should have hired people like us in the first place. You know what happens if you go anywhere near those psychos yourself. This way, we collect the money for you, split it down the middle. What do you say?"

"How do I know I can trust you?" he asked, eyebrows raised above his reptile eyes.

"You can trust us to hurt you *bad,* if you make us go that way. Go the right way and you walk, with half of the score. Call it a commission."

He didn't say anything.

"We don't have much time," Mick said to me, tapping his wristwatch.

"Right," I said, catching his rhythm. "We're up against the clock now," I told Wychek. "So the way it works is this: no answer from you is a 'no' answer, understand?"

I started counting inside my head. I was up to seven when he let out a long, thin breath. "My sister's bringing it," he said. "It was in a safe-deposit box. Only has her name on it. Her married name; not mine. I told her to go and clean out the box.

"She's bringing me my . . . other stuff in a suitcase. But the little book, you'd never find it," he said, twisting his lips into something like a smile.

"Just tell us—"

"I ordered her to carry it in her cunt," Wychek said. "In a Ziploc. She knows how to do it. As soon as she gets here, just bring her to me and I'll—"

I drove Laura Reinhardt's Audi back to her place. My cloned card opened the gate. I put her over my shoulder in a fireman's carry and took the stairs. Moving slowly, the .357 in one hand.

When she woke up, she would find herself in her own bed. Alone.

I looked down at her. Feeling . . . I wasn't sure what.

"I never meant to hurt you, Laura," I whispered, gently adjusting the blanket, touching her body for the last time.

The book had been where Wychek had promised. Boasted. "You were just another casualty," I said. "That's the way it is down here. The way it has to be. I'm sorry."

I kissed her beneath one drug-closed eye. And went out the way I'd come in.

The newspapers said three bodies had been discovered inside a Ford Explorer in the swampland near JFK Airport. All three were charred beyond recognition. The Mole's package would have been enough on its own; but when the fire hit the gas tank, the whole vehicle had just about vaporized. The police said it was an obvious gangland hit, a "message" of some kind. The Queens DA promised that those responsible would get the maximum sentence.

Wolfe probably never even saw the papers. She had been somewhere off the Maine coast for the past few days. On a little sailboat, with Pepper and Bruiser.

Pepper had made all the arrangements. Used Wolfe's credit card to rent the sailboat. And the car that they drove up in. And the motel where they stayed.

Pepper's a real friendly girl. Wolfe's mostly standoffish. But lots of people saw them. Pepper had some of them take their pictures, the three of them together, for souvenirs of their vacation.

Whenever the coroner's office got around to doing the autopsy, all they would have to work with was bones. But if they looked close enough, they would find three .25-caliber slugs rattling around in whatever was left of Wychek's skull.

"You know what was in what you gave us?" the man asked. I knew him only as Pryce, and I hadn't seen him in years. Not since the last-minute abortion of a plot to blow up Federal Plaza by a "leaderless cell" out of the White Night underground.

We had planted my brother Hercules in that cell. For him, it was that or go back Inside, forever.

They had ringed the downtown building that housed everything they hated—from the IRS to the FBI—with trucks stuffed full of enough explosives to level the ground down to zero. The drivers thought the plan was for them to set the timers and run, but the boss—hiding in the van outside the blast zone—held the real detonator. He was still holding it when a close-up blast from a girl he thought was a hooker shattered his neurons.

The pure-white sheep were still in their trucks when Pryce's crew went into action. A surgical strike. Only one was left at the end. And when he was clued into what the *real* plan had been, he sang a canary aria that thinned the rest of their herd, big-time.

Hercules walked away. I don't know where he is now. But I know where he's not.

The last time I saw Pryce, he was holding out his hand for me to shake. "I'm gone," he said quietly. "None of the numbers you have for me will be any good after today. And I won't have this face much longer, either."

I took his hand, wondering if the webbed fingers would disappear, too. Watched the muscle jump under his eye. I'd know that one again.

"I'm gone, too," I had promised him.

If my new face threw him, it didn't show on *his* new face. The fingers of his hands were still webbed. The muscle still jumped under his eye. I wondered what he still saw in me.

"I couldn't make any sense out of it," I lied. "Just enough to know you'd be interested."

"It was all pre-Nine/Eleven stuff," he said. "There were a hell of a lot more people involved than anyone ever imagined. We've been making arrests like there was no tomorrow. True-believers and freelancers, they're all going down."

"It's hard to think of—"

"What, Americans working for them? You know the kind of money they're throwing around? The little princes learned from what happened to the Shah. They eat peacock tongues off gold plates while the rest of their country dies of malnutrition. All the secret police in the world won't keep them safe from their own people. They know they can't stay on their thrones unless they provide a shunt for all the pressure building up, a bleed-valve for all the anger and hate."

Pryce shifted posture, as if his spine hurt, but his pale eyes stayed chemical-cold. "You think those people wiring up their own children and sending them into crowded markets in Israel are revolutionaries? Wake up. They're fucking flesh-peddlers, selling their kids for the bounty. It's the most lucrative form of child labor ever invented. You know what the bounty is up to now? Fifty grand. Fifty thousand dollars, for people who don't know what an indoor toilet is. For people whose *other* kids are going to grow up to be cannon fodder, anyway. The car-bombers, the one-way pilots, the . . . For *all* of them, who's putting up the money? Not the terrorists themselves, my friend. The little princes who finance them."

I didn't say anything. What could I?

"It's been more than two years since the World Trade Center," Pryce said, softly. "I guess the scumbags thought they were safe in their little sleeper-cells. They knew, if we'd had that book, we would have rounded them up a long time ago. So, therefore, we *didn't* have it, see?"

"Yeah," I said, nodding. "And the case against Wolfe—"

"It's gone," he assured me. "And it's never coming back. One of the bodies in that truck they found out in Queens? It was Wychek."

"Really?"

"Really," he said, no expression on his new face. "That book, it was what he was holding over . . . the agency. That's why they gave him—"

"I don't care."

"But if you got the book from . . . ?"

"I didn't get the book from him," I said. "And that's the truth."

"Why did you just hand it over?" Pryce asked me, his eyes everyplace but on mine. "You had to have some idea of what it could be worth. You're a merc yourself. How come you didn't try to make some kind of a deal? When you reached out for me, I thought that was what you were angling for."

"It's not true, what they say," I told him. "You know, that everyone's got a price. I know people like that. I was raised with them. I'll never be a citizen. But I'll never be them, either."

"**M**ayday!" Hauser, on the phone.

I met him an hour later, in the park across the street from the Appellate Division courthouse.

"I was in Atlanta, on assignment," he said. "Just got back. Turns out, a while back, a woman came to my house in Westchester. It was about four in the afternoon, right after school. My wife was at her Wednesday tennis lesson. One of the kids answered the door. Long story short, when she left, she knew damn well that you're not me."

"She saw a photo of you?"

"More than that," he said, ruefully. "I've got great kids. They're proud of their father. So, when a woman shows up and says Daddy's getting an award . . ."

"*When* was this?"

"I don't know *exactly* when, but it was a while back, only I just now found out about it," Hauser said, impatiently. "Kids, they forget things. . . ."

Images of Laura Reinhardt flooded my mind. They turned slowly, like a roulette wheel near the end of its spin. I watched as she built her "business model" as meticulously as she had her bottle tree.

With her own hands. Unrestrained.

"Some kids do," I told Hauser.

Then I hung up. On all of it.

ONLY CHILD

It's been years since Burke has been home, years since he's seen his "family" and worked in the underbelly of New York City. When he is contacted by a mob boss to investigate the murder of his illegitimate daughter Vonni, Burke takes the job and begins searching for a brutal killer. Posing as a casting director looking for tomorrow's stars, Burke reaches out to the high school students who knew Vonni and who may know the identity of the killer. Before long he unearths a perverse enterprise—a young director pursuing a brutal new type of cinema verité.

Crime Fiction/1-4000-3098-6

BLUE BELLE

Burke is an outlaw who makes his living preying on the most vicious bottom-feeders, those who thrive on the suffering of children. In *Blue Belle*, Burke is given a purse full of dirty money to find the infamous Ghost Van that is cutting a lethal swath among New York's teenage prostitutes. He gets help from a stripper named Belle, whose moves on the runway are outclassed only by her moves in a getaway car. But not even Burke is prepared for the evil that is behind the Ghost Van or for the sheer menace of its guardian, a cadaverous karate expert who enjoys killing so much that he has named himself after death.

Crime Fiction/0-679-76168-3

DOWN IN THE ZERO

In *Down in the Zero*, Burke investigates an epidemic of apparent suicides among the teenagers of a wealthy Connecticut suburb. There he discovers a sinister connection between the anguish of the young and the activities of an elite sadomasochistic underground, for whom pain and its accompanying rituals are a source of pleasure—and power. In an age in which guilty secrets are obsolete and murder isn't even worth a news headline, Vachss has given us a new kind of hero: a man inured to every evil except the kind that preys on children.

Crime Fiction/0-679-76066-0

BLOSSOM

In this savagely convincing novel, an old cell mate has summoned Burke to a fading Indiana mill town, where a young boy is charged with a crime he didn't commit and a twisted serial sniper has turned a local lovers' lane into a killing field. Intent on finding the real sniper and exonerating the wrongfully accused, Burke acquires an unlikely ally—a brilliant, beautiful woman named Blossom, who has her own reasons for finding the murderer, as well as her own idea of vengeance.

Crime Fiction/0-679-77261-8

FLOOD

Burke's newest client is a woman named Flood, who has the face of an angel, the body of a stripper, and the skills of a professional executioner. She wants Burke to find a monster for her—so she can kill him with her bare hands. Vachss' renegade private eye follows a child's murderer through the catacombs of New York, where every alley is blind and the penthouses are as dangerous as the basements. Fearfully knowing, crackling with narrative tension, and written in prose as forceful as a hollow-point slug, *Flood* is Burke at his deadliest.

Crime Fiction/0-679-78129-3

ALSO AVAILABLE
Born Bad, 0-679-75336-2
Choice of Evil, 0-375-70662-3
Dead and Gone, 0-375-72526-1
Everybody Pays, 0-375-70743-3
False Allegations, 0-679-77293-6
Footsteps of the Hawk, 0-679-76663-4
The Getaway Man, 1-4000-3119-2
Hard Candy, 0-679-76169-1
Pain Management, 0-375-72647-0
Sacrifice, 0-679-76410-0
Safe House, 0-375-70074-9
Shella, 0-679-75681-7
Strega, 0-679-76409-7

VINTAGE CRIME/BLACK LIZARD
Available at your local bookstore, or call toll-free to order:
1-800-793-2665 (credit cards only).